ALL THE BETTER PART OF ME

Molly Ringle

central
avenue
publishing

2019

Published by Central Avenue Publishing, an imprint of Central Avenue Marketing Ltd.
www.centralavenuepublishing.com

ALL THE BETTER PART OF ME

Trade Paperback: 978-1-77168-167-4
Epub: 978-1-77168-168-1
Mobi: 978-1-77168-169-8

Published in Canada
Printed in United States of America

1. FICTION / LGBT - Bisexual   2. FICTION / Romance / LGBT / General

1 3 5 7 9 10 8 6 4 2

PRAISE FOR MOLLY RINGLE

"Ringle navigates her twisty revelations and dramatic conclusion with just enough weight to avoid mawkishness, and her characters earn their happy ending. Readers looking for introspective romances with winding plots will enjoy this heartfelt novel."

— *Publishers Weekly*

"*All the Better Part of Me* is a standout novel in so many ways—breezy and sensitive as it touches the heart."

— Steve Kluger, author of *Almost Like Being in Love*

"A lovely combination of breezy plot, page-turning prose, and very, very likable characters. This one will definitely please old fans, and I suspect create many new fans too."

— Brent Hartinger, author of *Geography Club* and *The Otto Digmore Difference*

"A tender and poignant romance, a gorgeous hero, and the perfect balance of humour and realism."

— Jamie Deacon, Author of *Caught Inside*

"*The Goblins of Bellwater* has some of the eerie sensuality of Christina Rossetti's poem, and the setting is wonderfully conjured. Anyone who likes their fantasy sexy, fast-paced and contemporary will love it."

— Kate Forsyth, Author of *Bitter Greens*

"*The Goblins of Bellwater* is a journey to a world that feels both familiar and freaky—a wonderful place to get lost."

— *Foreword Reviews*

"Ringle . . . has created a vivid and enjoyable . . . romp through the world of magical beings."

— *Shelf Awareness (The Goblins of Bellwater)*

"Ringle employs familiar fairy tale tropes but turns them on their heads to deliver something wholly unexpected and fresh."

— *Publishers Weekly (The Goblins of Bellwater)*

Dedicated to the Millennials and Generation Z,
the sweet, brave love children of us kids of the '80s.

O! how thy worth with manners may I sing,
When thou art all the better part of me?
What can mine own praise to mine own self bring?
And what is't but mine own when I praise thee?
Even for this, let us divided live,
And our dear love lose name of single one,
That by this separation I may give
That due to thee which thou deserv'st alone.
O absence! what a torment wouldst thou prove,
Were it not thy sour leisure gave sweet leave,
To entertain the time with thoughts of love,
Which time and thoughts so sweetly doth deceive,
And that thou teachest how to make one twain,
By praising him here who doth hence remain.

Sonnet XXXIX
William Shakespeare

CHAPTER 1: NOCTURNAL ME

THE WOMAN IN THE RED JACKET WAS STARING AT ME.

Possibly, she'd been staring at me for several minutes, but it had taken me awhile to notice because I'd been busy, inwardly scowling while composing imaginary sarcastic emails to my parents. A dumb thing to waste energy on. Acting like an emo rebel might be forgivable in a sixteen-year-old, but was approaching pathetic in a twenty-five-year-old living on his own in another country.

Maybe I was outwardly scowling too, which could explain why the woman was staring at me. I relaxed my facial muscles, sent her a neutral smile, and turned to pull a pint for a man who had breezed up to the bar.

Summary of the day's emails that had incited this mindset:

Granddad and Grandmom say they haven't seen a picture of you in a while. I'm not sure we have any recent good ones. Do you? Maybe something where you're dressed nicely for a stage part, if they've given you any respectable costumes lately. And do you have any in which you aren't wearing makeup? That would go over better.

Mom

I always wear makeup onstage, Mom. It's required. So are non-respectable costumes sometimes.

Sinter

I understand, but are there any photos where the makeup isn't quite so obvious? Also where your hair is cut normally.
Mom

Then no. No there are not.
Sinter

In truth, I could have sent my latest professional headshot, in which I wore a plain black T-shirt, my face was clean of makeup, and my hair was tame, though still dyed black and almost shoulder length. But Mom had pissed me off and I didn't want to cooperate, and anyway, what the hell did my grandparents need photos of me for when they didn't like what I was doing with my life or how I looked? Just checking to see if I'd improved lately?

Deep breath.

What I should do, I realized, was forward the exchange to my best friend, Andy. He'd find it hilarious. Just imagining his laughter made me smile, and my shoulders eased a little. But contacting him would have to wait till after my shift.

I served drinks to the growing dinner crowd, picked up abandoned foam-smeared pint glasses and clinked them into the washtub, then navigated back to check on the woman in the red jacket and her blonde companion, parked at the end of the bar.

Red Jacket still stared at me, though not flirtatiously—no batting eyelashes or coy smiles. On the plus side, no hostility or derision either, which you sometimes got when you were a dude with dyed hair and eyeliner. Instead, she seemed to be contemplating me with fascination. Always another option with my look.

She appeared to be in her late twenties, with thick-rimmed glasses, light-brown skin, and dark hair cut in a messy bob. The red jacket was either leather or faux leather, and oversized like people used to wear in the '80s. Appealingly geeky. Cute. I would be content with "not hostile" from her.

I tapped my fingers on the bar in front of them. "Another round?"

The blonde woman, likely in her thirties, was halfway through her martini and shook her head with a smile.

"Not yet, thanks," Red Jacket said, lifting her partially full cider glass. Then, before I could step away, she raised her voice to counter the Arctic Monkeys song playing over the speakers. "I love your shirt."

I glanced down to refresh my memory on what I was wearing: a vintage Echo and the Bunnymen T-shirt I'd owned since high school. "Thanks."

She sat up and pulled open the sides of her jacket to display a Siouxsie and the Banshees T-shirt.

I grinned. "Right on."

"Are you a new-wave fan?" she asked.

She and the other woman locked their gazes onto me as if truly invested in my answer.

"Yeah, I am," I said. Wasn't everyone? Well, not my parents, but everyone who appreciated legendary, charismatic, trendsetting art.

They glanced at each other in satisfaction. The blonde woman said, "The eyeliner, too. Tipped us off." As if realizing it could sound scornful, she turned to me and added, "I love it, by the way."

"I don't suppose you're an actor?" Red Jacket asked me.

"I am, as a matter of fact." Score one for this woman, who evidently knew, unlike my parents and grandparents, that actors and makeup went hand in hand.

Then again, it was a safe bet that anyone working at a pub in London's West End was also an actor. Or aspired to be.

She exchanged another look with her friend. "It's fate. We spend the whole day sorting through headshots with no luck, then come here for a drink, and look what we find."

The blonde woman conceded with a tilt of her martini glass toward Red Jacket.

At the mention of headshots, I snapped to attention. Before I could ask what they were casting for, the dark-haired woman asked me, "And you're American?"

"Yes. Sorry." I always apologized for that in the UK, just to be safe.

"No no, that's perfect! The part's American. The character, I mean. Oh dear, I'm making no sense." She folded her fingers around her cider glass and let her shoulders droop with a laugh.

"It's okay. Um, the part?"

At that moment, her friend jumped, plucked a phone out of her coat pocket, and read the message that had buzzed her. "Ah. There they are." She slid off her bar stool. "Sorry. Must go meet my nanny and child. See you tomorrow, Fiona." With a smile at me she added, "You as well, perhaps." She walked out.

My boss emerged from the kitchen to help serve the burgeoning Friday-evening crowd. He frowned at me. I really ought to stop chatting and take some drink orders. But the woman had mentioned a character, a part, and acting was my *real* job. So I placated my boss with a lifted index finger to signal *Just a sec*, and turned back to the woman—Fiona, was that her name?

"Sorry, the part?" I asked. I settled my elbows on the sticky bar, leaning in to hear her better. I caught a hint of scent from her that reminded me of candle smoke and luxury cosmetics.

"I'm a writer and director for TV films. Chelsea's my writing partner." She flipped her thumb backward after the woman who had just left. "We've finished a script and begun casting for it. Then we came in here and happened to see you . . . " She raised her palms as if to sketch the whole of me. "It's amazing. Bunnymen shirt and everything. I don't suppose you'd audition? Say you will. I'm begging you."

"Sure, yeah." You always said yes at this phase. Actor commandment. *Yes, I can and will do anything.* "Um, what's the part, the film?"

"It's set in London in the early 1980s, post-punk, new-romantic era. Most would say 'new wave.' It's a star-crossed lover setup, between this posh totty who's slumming it, sneaking off to the clubs, and this poor American musician who's outstaying his visa and trying to join a band. He's who you'd read for."

I couldn't sing or play instruments, at least not with any real skill, but they'd find that out in due time if it was relevant. Alone in my room in my teen years, I had logged hundreds of hours lip-synching in the mirror, so I could fake it, in any case. I would *love* to fake it, if we were honest. "Yeah, that sounds great. When are auditions?"

"We're running screen tests this week. When are you free? Are you acting in something?"

"I'm in a stage show, fringe theater. But it ends this weekend, so I can schedule a screen test whenever."

Give me a movie role. Please. Don't make me work in food service my whole life to pay the rent.

She beamed and whipped out her phone to open the schedule. We fixed a screen test for the next afternoon. She gave me her business card—*Fiona Saanvi Wyndham*—and using the number on it, I texted her my name and the agent representing me in London.

"Got it," she said. "Sinter Blackwell—is that your name? I mean, with actors sometimes—"

"It's my real name. Well, my name's Joel, but no one except my parents calls me that. I go by my middle name."

The absolute last thing my parents would have done was pick a goth-sounding middle name for their kid, but they had inadvertently done so by choosing the surname of a prolific pioneer ancestor of ours. "Sinter" had always put me in mind of "cinder" or "disintegrate" or some sort of industrial solder, so I had insisted on being called that from middle school onward.

"I'm so not a 'Joel,'" I told Fiona, as if that explained everything.

"Fair enough." She splayed both hands in front of her, still holding her phone. "Also, I'm required to tell you ahead of time, there's some going topless in this film. As rock performers do. So if you feel up to it, we might have you strip off your shirt for the screen test."

"Right, no problem." I'd been shirtless onstage before. I was not what anyone would call ripped. I was more what they'd call slim and alarmingly pale. But possibly that would suit a rock musician role.

She clasped her phone between her hands. "Excellent. Then we're all set. I'll chat with your agent as soon as possible. Tonight, if he'll answer his phone after hours."

We shook hands, and she sailed out of the pub.

I jogged toward my harassed boss. "Sorry." I held up the card. "She's a director. I have an audition."

"Congratulations." He slapped a coaster on the bar. "Serve some bloody drinks, would you?"

After my shift ended, I ate dinner in the form of a toasted sandwich from the kitchen and set out for the theater a few streets away to prepare for the night's performance.

As I walked, my breath clouding in the autumn air, I checked messages on my phone.

Fiona: So good to meet you! Got your cv from your agent so that's all settled. Looking forward to seeing you tomorrow

Sinter: Excellent. This all sounds really cool, thanks so much

Fiona: Is this your first time in the UK btw?

Sinter: No it's my fourth, all work abroad stints, but this is my first time getting acting work, so I'm liking it the best

Fiona: Four trips, wow you must love it here

Sinter: I really do. I keep hoping the UK will adopt me, ha

Fiona: Perhaps we will do :) We'll talk soon!

Sinter: Great, cheers

Three of my four work-abroad trips, including this latest, had taken place not long after a breakup with a girlfriend. I had a habit of fleeing to the UK for comfort at such times. England had been my dream destination and go-to spot ever since my first year of college, when I had made the stunning realization that Shakespeare, Dickens, the Brontës, the Beatles, the Cure, the many '90s Britpop groups of my childhood, Sir Ian McKellen, and Dame Maggie Smith all came from the same place and that it therefore *had* to be superior to America.

I navigated to a different messaging app, one I used for keeping in touch with people back in the States, like my best friend Andy, since international texting was expensive. I'd forgotten to complain to him about my parents' latest instance of passive-aggression, but I decided to drop that. Much more fun to tell him I was about to get my first-ever movie screen test instead.

Then I stopped outside the theater's stage door, frowning at my phone. He had sent me a message about an hour earlier, which I had missed in the evening's madness.

Andy: Well shit
Sinter: Argh sorry just saw this. What's up?

I hauled open the backstage door and entered. Warm air replaced the outdoor chill, and I breathed in the smell of cut lumber, powdery cosmetics, electronics, and hairspray. My fellow actors milled around in various stages of undress and makeup. Some waved in greeting. I waved back and made my way to the clothing rack where my costume hung.

Andy: Relationship drama. Sigh. Super busy work morning but I'll fill you in at lunch
Sinter: Yeah let me know, hope everything's ok

Vaguely worried on his behalf, while at the same time excited at the prospect of the screen test, I put my phone away and started stripping off my clothes to put on my costume, elbow to elbow with the other actors. Just another evening in theater.

CHAPTER 2: PICTURES OF YOU

ANDRÉS ORTIZ AND I HAD LIVED TWO BLOCKS AWAY FROM EACH OTHER IN OUR SUBURB NEAR PORTLAND, Oregon, and had been best friends since sixth grade. I still considered him that, though I hadn't seen him much in person over the past seven years. We kept in touch online and met up in real life when we happened to be in the same city.

Andy had studied computer science at Stanford while I earned my theater arts degree at the University of Oregon, and he was living in Seattle with his boyfriend, Mitchell. They'd been together about a year, and I'd only met Mitchell on a few brief occasions. He was older than us by four or five years and struck me as sort of reserved and fussy, but if Andy liked him, I gave him the stamp of approval.

Now they were suffering "relationship drama"? What did that mean?

During the long lull between getting into costume and my first appearance onstage, I lounged beside the back door and messaged him again. It would be lunch hour in Seattle, since it was half past eight in the evening in London.

Sinter: I just scheduled a screen test for tomorrow. Crazy. So what's up?

He answered within two minutes.

Andy: Oh that sounds cool, screen test for what?
Sinter: Movie set in the 80s. We'll see how it goes

Andy: Right on, sounds perfect for you

Sinter: So what's this relationship drama?

Andy: Yeah well . . . seems I'm single now

Alarm flared to life inside my chest.

Sinter: What???

Andy: Mitchell's moving out as we speak. He'll be gone by the time I get back

Sinter: Dude. And you're just letting me talk about movies?

Andy: Heh, well I knew I'd fill you in eventually

Sinter: What happened?

Andy: It's . . . blah. Can I call? Too much to type

Sinter: Sure, I have 20 mins before I have to be on

I slipped out the door into the alley so my conversation wouldn't earn *Be quiet* scowls from our stage manager. Cold evening air flowed around me, curry-scented from nearby restaurants. Traffic hummed at the ends of the block. A light buzzed above the door, illuminating a span of pavement and wall. I made sure the wedge of wood was where it should be, propping open the door a crack, then started pacing back and forth in front of it.

My phone rang half a minute later. I picked up. "Hey."

"Hey." He sighed. "So okay, here's the quick version."

My mouth pulled into a nostalgic smile at the sound of his voice, tired but familiar, awash in West Coast American vowels. "Hit me with it."

"Things hadn't been great between us for a while. But I'd thought they were getting better." He sounded jagged, broken, the way people tended to after a breakup. It had been a long time since I'd heard that tone from him, probably not since some instance of college-era heartbreak, and it swelled the knot of sympathy in my chest. "I mean, we'd leased the apartment together, right? That was a commitment, sort of."

"For sure."

"But apparently, I was wrong. Because there's this coworker of his— older, like forty—who Mitchell's been in love with for a long time but thought he couldn't be with, because they work together, and because of relationship-baggage issues, and I don't even know what all. This just came out the other night. It was complete news to me. Anyway. Now they're together."

My costume boot heels clicked on the pavement as I paced. "Wait, so he left *you*? For someone else?"

"Oh yes. I got dumped good and proper."

"What the fuck? Just out of nowhere?"

"Pretty much. He's moving in with *Jeff*, and that's that. And you know, our apartment is expensive. It's on Capitol Hill. It has a view. We could just about afford it when we split the rent, but now? I have to find a new roommate. I can't live there alone. Not forever, anyway."

"What an asshole. God."

"Well . . . " Andy sighed. "He did pay his share for the next month, to give me time. Which is something, at least."

"Still. He didn't deserve you."

"I don't know. I must have failed somehow. I . . . wasn't enough."

"No. That's not true. It was all his deal, man."

"But if it was all him, then I was so deluded, thinking he wanted to be with me." He sounded miserable. "How did I get that deluded?"

I suffered from emotional contagion, catching people's moods, which was useful as an actor but hurt like a hundred paper cuts at moments like this. Andy was the person I cared about most in the world these days, given I was single too, which made the pain even sharper. I had friends in London, but no one here—in fact, no one anywhere— had ever known me as well as he did. I adjusted the phone against my sweaty ear and attempted an ironic tone. "You're talking to the king of delusions, so I'm not sure I should try to answer that."

"Ha. Fair enough. So you said you had to be 'on' soon? Like on-stage?"

"Yeah, in a bit."

"Wait, are you wearing some sort of costume right now?"

"I am dressed as the ghost of a medieval prince." It was a weird play. Even after rehearsing and performing it for weeks, I still didn't under-stand what it all meant, and neither did any of the reviewers.

"You're . . . okay." A dash of interest shored up his voice. "Then you know what, I'm switching to video."

"God," I complained, but when the video-call request pinged in, I tapped the button to allow it. You had to humor your recently dumped friends.

His face filled the screen. His skin looked a little more sallow than usual, and he had dark smudges below his eyes, though the shadow of his glasses could have been contributing to that. His brown hair glinted in the sunlight, short but edging into "needing a haircut" territory. He was evidently outside his work building, getting some midday sun, which was as much a rarity in late October in Seattle as it was in London. A green fleece coat was zipped up to his neck. I only had a second to register the marks of exhaustion in his features before he transformed, breaking into a grin and squinting at me in wonder.

"Oh my *God*," he said. "Is that actually you?"

"Yep." I held the phone at arm's length to let the camera take in the costume.

"You look like you're covered in powdered sugar."

"This is spray paint." I flicked the shoulder of my quilted jacket. "On my skin, it's powder."

"Is that a cape?"

I lifted the edge of the cape, draped over one shoulder. "Uh-huh."

"And is your hair in a *ribbon*?"

"Yeah, I'm a prince, duh."

"What did they do to your face? It's freaking me out."

I brought the phone in closer to display the white-and-brown blend of special-effects makeup. "Supposed to help me look ghostly under the stage lights. Do I look dead?"

"Yes. It's creepy." He grimaced. "Send me a selfie when you've washed all that off. I need to make sure you still look like you."

"If you insist."

He twisted his mouth. "I miss you. Why aren't we on the same continent?"

"We will be. Someday. I mean, I probably can't stay here forever."

"And I'd love to come visit, but apparently I have to save all my money for *double the fucking rent*."

I heard the whispered shuffle of a scene change from backstage and glanced in. "Oops. Got to go. We'll talk soon."

"Thanks for humoring me. And listening to me whine."

"After all the times you've listened to *me* whine, I think I owe you."

———

After the show, I caught my train and hopped off at the Mile End stop. The stairwell in my building smelled perpetually of fried chicken from the ground-floor shop, along with worse scents I didn't want to contemplate. Holding my breath, I took the steps two at a time and locked myself into my studio flat.

I stayed up until two a.m. researching screen tests. Since its inception in high school, my acting career so far had been entirely in the theater, unless you counted roles in friends' movies recorded on iPhones, so I needed to learn what I was getting into.

The main tips I took away from the internet were to get a feel for whether I had rapport with the director, and to remember that film was about intimacy and nuance, and therefore I should tone down the projecting and gesticulating I might bring to a stage audition.

I also googled Fiona Saanvi Wyndham. She was twenty-nine years old, had been born and educated in London, and so far had writing, casting, and/or assistant-director credits on four films made for the Hart Channel on satellite TV.

Clicking through, I also learned Fiona's mum, Leela Sharma, worked in HR for the BBC, and Fiona's dad, Alec Wyndham, was the chairman of Islands Broadcasting, the company that owned Hart Channel and several others.

I glanced around my pocket-size flat with its crusty carpet worn bare in spots, its crack in the kitchen wall from which cockroaches sometimes emerged, and its thin window glass that did basically nothing to mask the Mile End traffic noise. She wanted *me* for this part? She wouldn't, not once she realized what a nobody I was.

I shut my laptop. No point stressing out. Without a script to study, I couldn't do anything further except get some sleep.

Remembering my promise to Andy, I snapped a selfie after showering and drying off: wet hair, bare shoulders, and face making a Grumpy Cat expression. I sent it to him and put on sweats for bed.

He answered in a few minutes.

Andy: Wow shirtless even. Aren't I lucky
Sinter: It's not everyone who gets my sexiest pics
Andy: Haha much obliged. Thank you
Sinter: I'm about to go to bed. You doing ok?
Andy: I guess. As ok as I could hope

Which surely wasn't very. The first few days after getting dumped sucked worse than anything. I remembered the pain too well from the time the gorgeous, bewitching Jo at U of O had thrown me over for another guy. And it was only six months since my relationship had ended with my latest girlfriend, Vicki—a mutual decision, but it had still depressed me for a couple of weeks. It was easy to feel like an unlovable failure at those times. *I wasn't enough*, as Andy had said. *How did I get that deluded?*

Sprawling on my bed, I chewed the inside of my lip and finally responded.

Sinter: Message me as much as you like. Whine all you want. I'm cool with it

Sinter: And if there's anything you want from London let me know. I'll send it

Andy: Really, you'd ship over Tom Hiddleston? That's sweet

Sinter: Haha

Andy: Nah your selfies are the most important thing I could want from London right now. Thanks man

I smiled, every bit as charmed as when a woman complimented me. Weird.

Sinter: Cheers mate. As they say here

Andy: Cheers. Goodnight

Sinter: Goodnight

I set the phone to "do not disturb," switched off the lamp, and lay back. The never-ending street traffic whooshed like the ocean and sent white and red lights careening across my ceiling.

Something disturbed me about all this. Not just that he'd been grievously hurt and I wanted to punch any bastard who did that to my best friend. I was also disturbed because I felt a little bit relieved. Victorious. Like, *Good, now that Mitchell's out of the way, I get top spot in Andy's affec-*

tions again. I didn't want to be petty like that.

But best friends sometimes did harbor a touch of jealousy concerning their "mate." That must have been all it was. After all, I wasn't gay.

Yeah.

But.

CHAPTER 3: IT'S A SIN

ANDY CAME OUT TO ME WHEN WE WERE FIF-
TEEN. ONE ORDINARY WEEKNIGHT AFTER DINNER, WHILE I
was trying to sneak in some TV-watching during my homework, he
texted me.

Andy: What if I told you I was gay?

I dropped all interest in Netflix and stared, astounded, at my phone.
He was messing with me . . . right?

Sinter: April fools?

Might as well check that possibility. Even though it was October.

Andy: No. I honestly am

In that case, I sucked as a best friend, because the possibility had
never occurred to me.

I could guess what my parents would say. My whole life, they'd been
dragging me to their church, where people threw around words like "unnatural" and "deviant," and the older I got, the more I simmered in fury
at it. This was the Portland area in the twenty-first century, for fuck's
sake. Even in our high school, people were mostly cool about LGBTQ
issues—though sure, they did make "you're so gay" jokes at the same time.

Understandable that Andy hadn't felt like leaping out of the closet yet.
But he at least knew I disagreed with my parents. Didn't he?
That was probably a good place to start.

Sinter: Well that's ok with me. I'm not like my parents or the people at
their church
Andy: Thank you. Good to know
Sinter: Have you told anyone else?
Andy: No you're the first. I just didn't want to lie to you anymore

My heart was racing, though I hadn't moved from my desk chair.
Why was I freaking out? *Was* I freaking out? What was this?
I tried to sound calmer in text, at least.

Sinter: It's cool with me, seriously
Andy: I can see how you'd be weirded out though

I bit the side of my lip hard enough to hurt. This *was* weird. It felt
like talking to some entirely new and different Andy. Ordinarily in our
texts, we ridiculed teachers or classmates, bitched about our parents, or
made ass jokes. This was all . . . adult, or something. As to my being
weirded out: was I? Did it bother me that he thought about guys? Had
he thought about *me*?

Sinter: Ha well luckily I'm too ugly for you
Andy: No you aren't. But you're into girls and that's ok

While I pondered what *that* meant, he added another line.

Andy: Though now would be a good time to tell me if you feel the same
I guess

Sinter: I do like girls . . . I'm sympathetic but . . . idk?

Andy: No that's cool. Guess it'd be too awesome a coincidence if you were gay too, heh

Sinter: Shit why did I never know this?

Andy: Because I was trying my best to hide it? :)

Sinter: Ha well good job

Andy: Hasn't been easy. Has kind of sucked actually

Sinter: I bet

Now it would suck for him even more, because I still liked girls. I bit my lip more savagely.

Andy: Arrrrgh. Look I don't want this to screw everything up. That's the last thing I want

Sinter: No it won't

Andy: Just still be my friend. And since no one else knows yet, if you could not tell anyone? And like delete these messages, heh

Sinter: Totally, yeah. But wouldn't your parents be ok with it?

His parents were Catholic, but they affixed Democrat-candidate bumper stickers to their cars, which suggested they were more liberal than my parents. Or such was my fuzzy understanding of anyone else's politics at the time.

Andy: Idk, probably but I really don't want them to know yet

Sinter: Ok no problem. I won't say anything

Andy: Thanks. Guess that's all. We have Hughes' test tomorrow, better study

We had a US government test the next day, but did he think I was going to be able to concentrate now?

Sinter: Ok then . . . ?

Andy: Really it's fine, just promise me things won't be weird with us

Sinter: No weirder than my usual :)

Andy: Ha, good enough. Thanks man, see you

I read over our texts about a hundred times, then deleted them in case my parents or anyone else got hold of my phone. Then I went back to staring alternately at Netflix and my government textbook without absorbing much from either. All the while, I pulled at the roots of my short ash-blond hair until it stood up like a tumbleweed.

The next morning, when Andy and I encountered each other at the locker we shared, we froze and exchanged a moment of charged eye contact. A nervous grin seized control of my face. He snorted softly and shook his head. We stashed our backpacks in the locker and went to take our government test. All day, he was quieter than usual, but picked up conversations readily when I introduced them, so I supposed he was just worried I might act weird, and was relieved when I didn't.

Meanwhile, I mulled over the possibility—the likelihood, even—that he'd been checking out other guys, including me, the way I checked out girls. I waited for that notion to creep me out, but it never quite did. I mean, he was still Andy. There he sat beside me as ever, taking notes like the rest of us, eating lunch like the rest of us, detesting or admiring certain teachers like the rest of us. He surely had crushes too (like the rest of us); the only real adjustment I had to make was the kind of person he daydreamed about.

By the end of the school day, I'd fully reached the place where I was ready to tease him about it.

"So which guys at our school are cute?" I asked while we hung out at my house after school with *South Park* playing on my computer screen. The house was silent beyond the walls of my room. I was an only child, we had no pets, and my parents were still at work. Andy and I were sitting on my bed, two feet of space between us.

He splayed his hand across his face. "Here we go."

"Come on, no one's around. Who's got the hottest ass or whatever?"

"You were doing so well with the not being weird, too."

I settled my elbows on my knees, facing the screen. "I'm just curious. I'm fine with it, I swear."

Andy fell onto his back on my bed and blinked at the ceiling. "But how fine with it would you really be? Like, me kissing a guy. You'd be okay with that?"

"I think so. Why? Planning to suck someone's face in the halls?"

He smirked. "I wish."

"Have you ever kissed a guy?"

"Not yet. Unfortunately."

"So who? Who do you want to make out with?"

"Oh my God," he mumbled. "You're so dense."

"Why am I dense? What does that mean?"

He draped his arms across his eyes and spoke with careful slowness. "I've only told one person. I've asked him if he's gay too. He isn't, which is what I figured. So."

My face grew hot; it must have been turning redder than a cherry. "Oh."

"Yeah."

"Shit. Sorry. You're right; I'm dense."

"I'm actually kind of glad you never noticed."

I stared at *South Park* for a minute. Andy lay still. Eventually, he dropped his arms beside his head instead and gazed at my bedroom wall.

"But I *am* okay with it," I insisted.

"Great. Good."

"I wish I could . . . " I failed to find the right word and shrugged.

"Reciprocate?"

"I guess."

"Me too. But thanks anyway."

A bleak sadness shaped his eyes and gave a downturn to his mouth. He had a full lower lip, much like the mouth of a girl I liked. I'd never noticed that before.

I thought about the hateful things my parents and their church said. I thought about how I detested them for it. I thought about Andy, who clicked with me better than anyone else ever had and who'd been suffering without my having a clue, and whom I could absolutely kiss if that's what he wanted.

The allure of rebellious behavior always danced somewhere within reach, tempting me to do things my parents would hate. I usually resisted its call, because why invite trouble, but that day . . .

I turned and pounced on top of Andy—not actually touching him, but with my hands and knees on either side of his body and my face hovering above his.

"Okay," I said. "One-time offer."

A grin broke across his face, and he squinted at me. "*What* are you doing?"

"I'll kiss you, just this once. If you want."

He snorted. "Right. Sure."

"I will. People do that. They kiss their friends. It happens."

"Dude, no. I didn't mean . . . look, I don't want pity or whatever." But he wasn't shoving me off or wriggling away. He stayed put, beneath me, on my bed.

"It's not pity." My arms, locked straight, were getting tired, so I sank onto my elbows. Our chests touched. "It's generosity."

He laughed, then studied me. Flecks in his green eyes matched the golden tan of his skin. He had tiny, dark freckles across the bridge of his nose. I hadn't noticed any of that before either. He was breathing fast; I felt his ribs expand against mine with each inhalation.

The weirdest thing about it, honestly, was that this position was kind of turning me on. I was still a virgin, but I knew what being turned on felt like and that it could happen in unexpected situations, so I didn't let it bother me. I just made sure not to let my groin touch him.

"Are you sure?" he said.

"Why not?"

Enough conversation. I leaned down and kissed him.

Party games and dares were the only times I'd kissed anyone so far, and only girls. Same with him, as far as I knew. I thus belatedly realized, as I pressed my lips to my best friend's, that this was my first *real* kiss, and likely his too.

It started out clumsy, an awkward squishing together. We hardly moved, and his lips felt dry against mine. Then I tilted my face to improve the angle, a breath slipped from his mouth and warmed our lips, and he started kissing me back. My eyes closed. His hand slid onto my back, and—

"*Joel Sinter Blackwell!*"

"What in the—"

My mom. My dad. Oh dear God, my parents had walked in.

I whipped up and sprang to my feet—yeah, that move didn't look guilty or anything. Andy sat up, clutching the edge of the mattress, mouth shut tight and eyes wide.

No one said anything for a few seconds. My parents were both dressed for work in gray suits, Mom with her tastefully curled blonde do and pink lipstick, Dad with his receding, silver-streaked hair, crisply shaven jaw, and furious blue eyes.

"It was nothing," I said through a larynx that felt like it was being squeezed shut. "We were just goofing around."

They didn't answer, only stared at me from my doorway. They moved so silently sometimes it was creepy. I hadn't even heard them enter the house, and our TV show hadn't been turned up *that* loud.

Andy got off the bed. "It's late. I should go."

"Yeah. Okay. See you tomorrow." I tried to sound normal, like everything was cool.

He grabbed his backpack from the floor, slung it onto his shoulder, and hesitated in front of my parents, who still blocked the door.

Ordinarily, my parents liked Andy well enough. He was short and slim and non-threatening, and Mom had remarked in the past that she appreciated his polite manners.

That day, her gaze raked over him in disgust, then she stepped aside to let him pass.

He shot out. I heard his footsteps patter down the stairs. A moment later, the front door opened and shut, echoing in the silence.

"Seriously, it was nothing." I couldn't think what else to say. I hadn't figured out yet what it *was*, other than me trying to do my gay best friend a favor, and I couldn't say *that*. Even with my mind in complete panic mode, I knew I couldn't reveal Andy had come out to me. I had to take the fall for this one. So if I could just convince them we were only . . . um, wrestling or something . . .

"I think you better sit down." Dad's tone was glacial.

I sat down.

My parents hadn't hit me since some vaguely recalled instances of being spanked when I was a little kid, but for a frightening moment, I really thought they were going to.

They didn't. Instead, they slapped me with words for the next two hours—*immoral, harmful, dangerous, unnatural, sick*. And I slapped back—I'd had enough, and it all came out, all the things I despised about their beliefs. *Yes, I kissed him, but this was the first time. Yes, it actually was; fine, don't believe me then, but it was, and no, I'm not gay, but there isn't anything wrong with it, by the way. And no, it wasn't his idea so don't you dare call his parents, just punish me, I mean, I guess you get to do that, but in actual truth, I did not do anything wrong. I don't care what you believe . . .*

Everything said by the three of us would fill an entire book, a repetitive and seriously unpleasant book.

By the end of it, my cheeks stung with angry tears, I'd been grounded, they'd taken my phone away for the month (thank God I had deleted those texts from Andy), and I had run out of words and just nodded to indicate I was never, ever going to do anything like that again.

And it was almost four years, in fact, before I kissed another guy.

CHAPTER 4: (EVERY DAY IS) HALLOWEEN

I attended the screen test. They had me take off my shirt for the camera and hold a glittery blue electric guitar. They let me put my shirt back on. I read through scenes from *New Romantic* ("Working title, ignore that," Fiona said), first alone and then with Ariel Salisbury, the actor signed on to play Jackie, the posh girl. I vaguely recognized Ariel from a British TV show, though I couldn't remember which one. She looked like an underwear model (in fact, I was pretty sure she'd been that too), smelled like cigarettes and vanilla perfume, and had greeted me with, "Hi. God, I'm so hungover."

All the same, by the end of the screen test, I craved this role with every fiber of my being.

My agent called the next day while I was in the cereal aisle in Tesco. I fumbled the buzzing phone out of the pocket of my motorcycle jacket. "Hi, this is Sinter."

"Sinter, it's Jerry." He sounded excited. "So listen, Fiona Wyndham just called. How would you like the part of Taylor? Because they loved you in the screen test and she's really hoping you'll say yes."

Giddy delight swarmed through me, the feeling another actor had once called "the casting dazzles." It was a rare feeling, only experienced when you got the news of winning the part, so I let myself enjoy it, grinning at boxes of Weetabix. "Yes. Of course. Wow, this is great."

"Fantastic! I'm thrilled, honestly. This part is quite a catch. Can you meet me at the studio today so we can get the paperwork in order?"

"Yeah, I'm free this afternoon. Maybe around one?"

"Perfect. I'll let them know. See you then. Cheers."

"Cheers." I hung up, beamed at cereal until an old lady gave me an alarmed look on her way past, then finished my shopping and pelted back to my flat.

———

After my punishment for kissing Andy expired and I was free to do what I liked again after school (within limits), I found I had little taste anymore for hanging out at my house. It had become a prison to me during that month, owned by a pair of wardens hopelessly behind the times. (I'd never say my parents were *evil*. They weren't. They were just about salvageable, in fact. But they were also out of touch with nearly everything I enjoyed in the world.)

I'd been fanatical about TV shows, movies, and music ever since I was a little kid. Enthralled by some show or performance on TV, I studied details, imitated lines, and did my terrible best to sing until my parents requested I shut up. I hadn't chosen theater or music as electives so far, but whenever I was required to perform as part of a class project, my educational ennui vanished and I lit up like a floodlight. Sitting in the high-school auditorium to watch my classmates in concerts or plays during assemblies also enchanted me, and not just because I got to miss part of math class for it.

I liked the auditorium itself: how it could be made into anything, bright or dark, cheerful or spooky, no matter the season or time of day. It had comfy cloth-covered seats that folded down like in a cinema. When you got close to the stage, it smelled like paint, wood, cosmetics, old dusty fabrics, and the resins and oils the orchestra students used on their instruments.

But not until I became officially sick of my own house did I slow to a stop in the school halls one day to read a flyer on blue paper, pinned to a bulletin board.

Auditions for MURDER AT WILDWOOD
3:00 Thursday
Auditorium
Cast and crew needed. All welcome!

Beside me, Andy stopped too.

"I might go," I said.

"To try out?"

"I don't know. I'll see what they need."

"Do you think they'd want people to work the light boards?" he asked. "I've always wanted to go up there."

"Come ask 'em."

We showed up and got assigned our requested jobs: Andy with the sound-and-lighting crew, me building sets and assisting the stage manager during productions. The play was a murder mystery, not particularly well-written or memorable. But I fell in love with the whole experience.

The way the lights looked, spilling onto the stage while the rest of the house was in darkness. The glow-tape arrows and soft blue bulbs illuminating the backstage area during performances so actors and crew wouldn't crash into stuff. The palpable thrill of excitement running through us all before the curtain rose on opening night. The vulnerability and courage of the actors, those people in my classes whom I'd never paid any attention to before, who got to wear outlandish clothes and makeup, and yell and sob and kiss in front of a live audience.

I had to try it. I auditioned for the next play.

It was *Romeo and Juliet*, so my first audition ever, through which I sweated and trembled, involved mouthfuls of Shakespearean English, practically a foreign language from a fifteen-year-old's perspective. But I'd read through the play beforehand, grasped the gist of things, and managed my "canst thous" coherently enough. Besides, theater always needed more guys, so if you were male and showed up and could read any lines at all, you'd probably get a part.

I was cast as Mercutio. Even my parents were impressed. They could appreciate Shakespeare. That is, while they didn't like his "crass jokes" or his frequent theme of cross-dressing, they liked his poetry and his classic-lit pedigree. They attended one of the performances, dutifully watched me get killed by a sword, and told me it was nice I'd found some extra-curricular activities.

It wasn't long before they started to see the downside.

For the play, our drama teacher wanted us Montagues to have black hair, to contrast with the blonder Capulets, so she handed out boxes of dye to those of us with light coloring. With the help of Andy and the girl playing Lady Montague, I dyed my hair in a makeup-room sink after rehearsal one day without telling my parents I was going to do it.

They blew a gasket when I came home. They threatened to force me to visit a hairdresser and get it put back to its natural color, because imagine the disgrace of showing up in public—in *church*—like that. When I challenged them to show me where in the Bible it said God cared what color our hair was, they spluttered and eventually shut up, then said fine, I could stay home from church and read their assigned Bible passages every Sunday from now on instead. I said fine, works for me. I hadn't attended since.

If that was the outcome, then yeah, I was going to goth it up *forever*.

But I wasn't just doing it to get out of church. I honestly became fascinated with how different it made me look to wear cosmetics or costumes or a wild hairdo, especially when I added a new posture or voice on top of those, how it all turned me into a new person, someone deeper and more mysterious than just another suburban kid.

My first attempts at doing my own makeup took place backstage at school, using the theater's drawers of cosmetics. While I sneezed from an overdose of face powder and poked myself in the eye with the eyeliner pencil ("Ow, fuck fuck fuck, ow"), Andy doubled over with laughter and told me, "You look . . . like . . . a panda!" But once I learned how to wield makeup appropriately, he nodded in approval and declared that the emo style suited me.

I started wearing black more often, got my ears and eyebrow and lip pierced (more conniptions from my parents), attended class with eyeliner on. Popular kids occasionally called me a weirdo or a freak, but that was to be expected. Theater or stoner kids, on the other hand, sometimes told me I looked like Gerard Way—nice of them, but let's be honest, Gerard was cuter than me.

I turned my bedroom into a batcave of band posters, dark curtains, and the occasional skull. I think by then my distraught parents were seeking advice from their pastor. Andy, meanwhile, calmly remarked, "I like how you've found a way to use Halloween decorations year-round."

Andy never auditioned for a play, but he stayed on the tech crew for the remainder of high school, keeping me company through several productions. He and two other techies ended up founding the school's Anime Club, and frequently got into passionate, you're-dead-to-me debates over fandom. (One evening we had to pause dress rehearsal because they were arguing too loudly in the light booth about whether Joel or Mike was the better host of *Mystery Science Theater 3000.*)

In college, I signed on as a theater arts major. Loneliness swamped me the first time I walked into that auditorium, a new place with no faces I recognized, no Andy hanging offstage with the techies. But I stuck with it because there was nothing else I wanted to do, and soon I made friends there and began enjoying it again. My parents were perplexed by my choice of major, and irritated when I compounded the folly with a minor in English. They never came to my plays anymore, though my acting had vastly improved since my rookie turn as Mercutio. It was too far to drive from our Portland suburb down to Eugene, they claimed.

In my sophomore year, they told me they'd still pay my tuition, but not my lodging and food. Those would be up to me. And, they added, I ought to consider a field of study I could actually find work in, such as finance or business. Being bankers, they'd long had funds prepared for my future, but the college fund was being rapidly depleted by rising tuition costs, and the other was untouchable until I was thirty ("For buying a house," they said). They hadn't grown up rich; their money had accumulated through investment over time. They bought dependable cars and clothes, never luxury goods. And they had insisted I work for my money from as far back as I was able to hold a job. Given the last thing I wanted to do was borrow money from them, I acknowledged they probably had a good point about the career prospects.

Still. I stuck with theater and English. I took side jobs and scraped together the money for rent and food. I graduated cum laude. After graduating, I sought out acting work relentlessly, and because I showed up on time, gave each role my best, and didn't act like a diva, people hired me. And why *would* I act like a diva? I loved theater. It was worth enduring miniscule paychecks, my parents' dismay, nerve-wracking auditions, exhausting nights-and-weekends working hours, and the devastating times someone else got cast for a part I wanted.

When I was acting I got to be an array of different people, an ever-changing spectrum of roles, and audiences applauded me for it.

Which, most days, was far better than being just me.

CHAPTER 5: BEST FRIEND

TO CELEBRATE THE CONTRACT SIGNING, JERRY AND I SHARED CHAMPAGNE WITH FIONA AT A ROOFTOP BAR, huddling near the patio heaters in the October chill. After saying good-bye with hugs all around, I staggered alone into a park and sat on a bench. The realization that I was actually going to do this had slammed into me. A TV movie. With a sex scene.

I got the script out of my backpack and found the notorious page. Beginning with *He pulls up her shirt* and *She shoves down his jeans*, it moved on to *Gasp, clutch, shudder; finish the job*, followed by hauling clothes back into place and some tense postcoital conversation. No easy fade-to-black or anything.

I laid my knuckles on my cheek, feeling the burn of the blush.

But, okay. I could handle this.

Like any normal person, I started by sending a message to my best friend.

Sinter: Umm so I got the part. Thus I'll be doing a sex scene with Ariel Salisbury for a TV movie. There's a nudity clause in my contract. Holy crap, help

I'd always figured I would have to perform a scene like this eventually, but suddenly there we were, and it wasn't a theater production, where all the viewers were at least twenty feet away from me, no, but a camera tak-ing close-up footage that people could replay over and over, and capture in screenshots and GIFs and put all over the internet, and, and . . .

I calmed down by watching people in the park, all leading their own lives, which helped put my internal freakout in perspective. One pair of kids amused me in particular: a boy and girl, both about ten years old, were flinging a Frisbee back and forth. It kept flying off course and smacking into trees or making pedestrians dodge out of its way, and the kids were busting their guts laughing.

Andy and I had been the two worst players on our middle-school Ultimate Frisbee team. It was how we'd met, one of the first things we'd bonded over. Something good had come out of that awkward phase of my life, so surely something good would come from this one too.

It was only eight a.m. in Seattle. Andy was probably just getting to work. I rose from the bench and headed for the nearest tube station.

On the way, he answered at last.

Andy: Wow, congrats! Sex scene and everything, haha

I lingered by the top of the tube stairs to reply, off to the side to keep out of everyone's way.

Sinter: My parents will be so proud
Andy: Lol! What's in this nudity clause anyway?
Sinter: It actually says it WON'T show anything below the waist. All filmed in shadow. But still "simulated sex acts"
Andy: Whoa take it easy there, it's too early in the morning for porn
Sinter: Haha
Andy: Well I am going to brag all over the place that my bff is a movie star
Andy: That'll show mitchell
Sinter: Sure, milk it for what it's worth
Sinter: You can even tell him you're fucking me if it helps ;)

In high school we hadn't dared make such jokes, but we eased into it during our college years. After all, even straight friends made those remarks with each other.

Still, a frisson of . . . something . . . went through me as I sent off the message. Nerves? My brand of weird, possessive jealousy? Fear of annoying him?

Luckily, he answered in a light enough manner.

Andy: Ha! That would be more believable if we were on the same continent

Sinter: I'd come visit you on my private jet every few days of course

Sinter: Being a movie star and all

Andy: Of course

Sinter: I wish

Andy: Me too

Andy: Uh, about the jet and the visits. Not . . . well never mind ;)

I smiled, glancing at the pigeons clustering around my shoes in search of crumbs. A wiggle of my foot sent them away in a clatter of wings.

Sinter: Then I'll ask the studio if I can have a jet :)

Andy: So hang on, is this the 80s new wave movie?

Sinter: Yep. Can't wait to see wardrobe and makeup

Andy: For real. You've got to send so many selfies. I mean if you're going to look like this I need to see it

Below his message a photo popped in: Adam Ant on the *Prince Charming* album cover, red stripes across his cheek, tiny heart painted above one of his asymmetrical eyebrows, frosted lipstick, dark glossy fingernails, hair plastered up on one side, and gaudy faux-military coat with metallic gold cuff-ruffles. A laugh snorted out of my nose. Adam's look there was way beyond even my most Goth/emo days.

> Sinter: Niiiiice. Are you high on caffeine by any chance?
> Andy: Yes, yes I am. Couldn't sleep last night. I am on so much espresso, you have no idea
> Sinter: Haha, well that's what Seattle's for
> Andy: Seriously though, thank you for cheering me up. This is ridiculous and therefore exactly what I need
> Sinter: You're welcome
> Andy: Better get to work. Take care, Flock Of Seagulls
> Sinter: Later man. And please switch to decaf

I shouldered my backpack and descended to the Tube, my brain full of Adam Ant's wardrobe, sex scenes with me in them, my parents watching said sex scenes, and whether my flirtatious texts to Andy could be attributed to genuine attraction on my part.

A question cropping up in my mind strangely often lately.

———

I'm not gay. When I said that, I wasn't lying to my parents, or to anyone else who happened to ask for the rest of high school. It was far less complicated to like girls. I'd been attracted to lots of girls. So clearly, I wasn't gay. The possibility that I could be something else—say, bisexual—didn't seem to occur to anyone. Not even to Andy, or at least, he never asked. It didn't even occur to *me.*

If I'd been attracted to him during that one kiss, well, I couldn't quite process it, considering the kiss had been derailed so spectacularly with my parents walking in on us. The memory felt more like trauma than desire.

The day after the kiss, at our locker, Andy asked if I got in a lot of trouble. I said yes, but my parents didn't know he was gay and weren't going to call his parents. He thanked me quietly, his gaze cast down. For a while it astounded me that they hadn't told his folks. But gradually, I understood why: they didn't want other people to know. They wanted to hush up the whole thing, hide the shame. It made me despise them more than ever, but Andy and I weren't exactly eager to broadcast it either, so I let it be.

Andy and I rarely talked about sexuality for the rest of high school, and didn't talk at all about having kissed each other, but we were cool. We remained best friends. I told myself that any fondness I felt for him was simply a result of our long-standing friendship. I wasn't gay, couldn't be.

Although . . . okay, bi-curious, maybe. I hadn't ever said that out loud either, only inside my head when finding myself over-fascinated with, say, two guys kissing in a movie.

Someday I might say it out loud. I might also someday be brave enough to try more than one kiss with another guy.

But I didn't have to figure any of that out yet. As for flirting in messages with Andy, it was okay if I got some secret pleasure from that. He took comfort in it too, at a time when he was hurting. I was just being a good friend. Maybe it didn't even have anything to do with sexuality.

———

Andy: God almighty I'm pathetic

I found his message when I woke up the next morning. It had arrived at 3:08 a.m. London time, yesterday evening in Seattle. I rolled out of bed and answered.

Sinter: Sorry, just woke up. Why are you pathetic?

Of course, now it was 1:30 a.m. his time, and *he'd* be asleep. So I went about my day: shower, breakfast, then out to resign from my pub job since the movie was going to be a full-time gig. My boss complained at me, congratulated me, and told me to get out.

While I sat at my kitchen table, munching crisps and reading my *New Romantic* script, Andy responded at last.

> Andy: Right well, my caffeine wore off by the end of the day and I kind of crashed. I snapped at two different coworkers over really minor shit. I never do that
> Sinter: Ah everyone's had days like that
> Andy: I did manage not to cry at work at least
> Sinter: Ha, that's good
> Andy: Yeah except instead it was crying on the commute home, in traffic

I winced. Pushing the crisps aside, I cradled the phone in both hands. His message conjured up a memory of the day in college when I wore sunglasses throughout a literature class because my girlfriend, Jo, had dumped me a matter of hours earlier, and my eyes were swollen from crying. "You're not stoned, are you?" my professor had teased at the end of class. "No, of *course* not," I had said, in a playful tone that implied I actually was, because I would've rather had people think I smoked pot (which I almost never did) than admit to being emotional over a breakup.

I also remembered that I hadn't told anyone the truth about that incident except Andy, in an emo-fest of text messages. He'd been sympathetic and outraged. (*Dude, you totally deserve better. She's a heartless excuse for a human being.*)

I slid my thumbs in to answer.

> Sinter: Ugh I've had those days too. They completely suck. I'm sorry
> Andy: See, pathetic.

Sinter: So your commute . . . you don't take the bus I hope?

Andy: Lol! No, I drive. But thank you for making me laugh

Sinter: No problem but are you really ok?

Andy: Yeah it's all right. See, then I got home and looked up new wave fashions and pictured you in them

Andy: Which is inherently funny, so, here's today's

He sent over the photo: Duran Duran at some point in the early '80s, all in leather trousers and poet shirts, with fluffy teased hair and scarves around their waists.

Sinter: I could live with these outfits. Except leather trousers are not the slightest bit comfy. I've tried

Andy: You know, they look funny but also kinda hot. Which is part of why I'm willing to look such things up

Sinter: So I should keep wearing eyeliner you're saying? :)

Andy: Hell yeah ;)

Harmless. Flirtatious texts were completely harmless.

CHAPTER 6: A LITTLE RESPECT

"HUH, WELL, *YOU'RE* NOT BRADLEY MACCROS-
SAN." THE DEADPAN REMARK CAME FROM THE LONG-HAIRED
man dropping into the chair next to mine. It was the day of the table read,
where the whole cast gathered to read the script aloud, start to finish.

Bradley MacCrossan was an actor around my age whom I, along
with the rest of the world, had admired in his starring role on a BBC
sci-fi series. He was not there, nor did I expect him to be. He was, I pre-
sumed, off filming bigger things elsewhere.

"Uh, no," I said. "I'm Sinter."

The bloke tilted back his chair and offered me a hand. "Sebastian."

We shook hands. "Right. Good to meet you."

I had looked up the rest of the cast online, enough to recognize most
of them as they came in. Sebastian Trevisani was the lead singer of the
Swinburnes, and had been cast as the lead guitarist of the band Taylor
ended up joining. The Swinburnes, along with other bands, would be
contributing '80s covers and original tunes for the film soundtrack.

Sebastian looked a bit like a young Iggy Pop: long face, doleful eyes,
wide mouth. His denim jacket bristled with silver studs and safety pins,
and his thumbnails were painted black. Next to him I looked almost
nerdy in my plain dark-blue hoodie. At the screen test, Fiona had been
enthused to find I had various piercing holes (many of them healed over,
but the ones in my earlobes still functioned), so I had scrounged up a
pair of tiny silver loop earrings and stuck them in, but they were my only
punk style points that day.

"I love your album," I added. The Swinburnes had one album out, new this year. I had listened to it this week. Indie pop with an '80s influence, I would have said—the kind of thing I tended to like, and theirs was no exception.

"Mm. Cheers." Sebastian surveyed the cast and crew, still milling around and talking. "We've had to put off the next album in order to work on this. But it's worth it for Fiona."

"For sure. So were you expecting Bradley MacCrossan, or . . . ?" I was still lost about that opening remark.

"Oh, no one told you?" He kept his gaze on Fiona. Ariel had arrived, once again looking like the most bored person in all of London, and Fiona was sending interns scurrying to make coffee for her. "They almost had him for your role. The scheduling didn't work out, though. He wasn't able to commit. Everyone was pretty pissed off."

Hoo boy.

"Ah, no, I hadn't heard. That would've been huge, getting him."

"But, you know, Fiona *loves* you in the part. She says you're perfect. She pushed for casting you, got her father and everyone on board. So, she's happy."

Ahhh shit.

"Always good when the director's happy, I guess." I dropped my gaze to the script in front of me.

Every time you're cast for a role, someone will be unhappy about it, because they wanted that part or had hoped to see someone else in it. I'd dealt with that jealousy in theater all the time, had felt it myself. It made sense that films would be no different. Still, British TV politics? Wow, was I ever out of my league.

"She's quite amazing, you know," Sebastian said, still watching Fiona.

"Definitely. You know her from before?"

"We served as the background band in another of her films. We've hung out. Became friends."

"Awesome, that's great."

"Awesome." He mimicked my Yank pronunciation and smirked. "You come with the right accent, at least."

I spread my hand across the cover of the script. "Actually, Taylor's from New York, so it'd be more like, 'Awesome, that's great.'" This time I slanted my vowels into a generic New York City accent.

Sebastian glanced at me with guarded interest, but said, "I don't hear the difference."

I shrugged, affecting casualness. "I'll work on it."

The others at the table kept chatting. Hardly anyone looked at me. How many of them wished Bradley MacCrossan were sitting in my seat instead? Probably almost all, and it wasn't like I could blame them. My spine sagged, slouching me down into my seat.

The last chair got filled by a thin young man. "Is Bradley MacCrossan here yet? Oh . . . " He made the last word a falling note of disappointment as he looked around the table, then broke out a cheeky grin. Everyone chuckled.

I smiled too, though I sank my nails into my thigh under the table. Fiona, across from me, glanced at me in commiseration, but her smile soon shifted into a steely *I've got this* look. She raised her voice to quiet the room. "Okay, everyone! I'm so excited to have us all here at last. I'm especially excited to have you meet Sinter, who fell into my lap from the heavens at the very moment we needed him. We're so lucky, because I know he's destined for great things, and you're going to love working with him."

Bless the woman. However, those were big accolades to live up to. I flapped a wave at the group and mumbled thanks.

She poured praise on Ariel, Sebastian, the rest of the Swinburnes, and the other cast and crew. When we had all been properly feted, we began the read-through.

I wasn't at my best at first, New York accent sliding all over the place.

But the others were stilted too, as expected at any first rehearsal. By the midpoint we hit something of a stride, and by the end were all throwing some real emotion into our lines.

Afterward, a few cast members came to talk to me, friendlier now. I got a "Bye bye, good read" from Ariel before she left, and an aloof "See you on set, then" from Sebastian on his way out.

Fiona waited for me, arms wrapped around a thick pile of documents. "There, you've completely won them over. I knew you would."

"Thanks to you."

She made a derisive "psh" sound. "It's simply that I'm stubborn, and when I've got my teeth into something, I don't easily let go. My mum and dad call it my bulldog tendency." She tipped her chin down and smiled up at me. With her small frame and soft, messy hair, she looked more like a kitten than a bulldog. Still, kittens did have claws and teeth.

"I like that. So . . . " I curled my script in my hands. "Almost got Bradley MacCrossan, huh?"

She reached out and closed her hand around my forearm. "We were in talks, it didn't work out, and honestly, you're so much better a fit for Taylor. Don't let people bother you. It's the gossip for now, but they'll have forgotten in another few days."

"It's all right; I just hadn't heard."

She wrapped her arm back around the stack of papers and looked me in the eye. "I want you for this part, and I want the rest of them to love you in it, and I'm the bulldog, so that's what's going to happen."

I chuckled and let the script uncurl. "Cool. Well, thanks."

"Give us a hug." Around her stack of documents, we hugged, then she let go. "Now off to hairdressing with you."

CHAPTER 7: PROBLEM CHILD

Sinter: You do not have to send me a new wave photo today because check this out

I sent Andy the selfie of my new hair: trimmed up to mid-neck length with shorter pieces layered in, black dye renewed to inky darkness, and four streaks bleached and dyed a Kool-Aid orange.

Andy: Duuuude. So cool!
Sinter: They did nice work. But I smell like hair dye now, like really strong. Like flowers and wet dog
Andy: Lol. Sexy
Sinter: Yeah hoping that fades. So how are things?
Andy: Better with my coworkers. Still no word from mitchell and I haven't tried contacting him. Sad, bitter. You may have to send me some black eyeliner
Sinter: I can recommend some cheap brands :)
Sinter: Well it's been what, a week? May be ok to send him a "how's it going?" or something. If you think it'd help

My phone began buzzing with an incoming call. A video call, in fact. From my mom. I grimaced—this wasn't my parents' style—and tapped the green icon to accept it.

"Hi, Mom."

Her face appeared on the screen, frowning down into the camera.

She had a suit on, and ceiling lights gleamed above her. "Joel? Hello?" She clicked her tongue in annoyance. "I must have tapped the wrong button."

They'd both gotten iPhones recently. To paraphrase Douglas Adams, this had widely been regarded (at least by me) as a bad move.

I heard my dad's voice offscreen. He sounded uninterested. "Yes, it's too easy to do that with these."

"Okay, should I hang up?" I said.

Mom squinted at me. "What happened to your hair?"

"It's for a part. A role I just got."

"Playing what?"

"A guy in the '80s. You know, back when you guys were my age." I couldn't resist.

"Well, we didn't look like that."

"Nope, you didn't." They'd looked like less-glamorous versions of Charles and Diana, to judge from photos. Despite having lived through the entire 1980s, they didn't own a single new-wave album, or any rock albums at all besides some early Beatles. When David Bowie died, I'd had to explain to them who he was, which nearly made me give up on them forever.

"Are you at work?" I asked. They worked at the same bank.

"Yes, on lunch break."

The phone tilted and Dad's face loomed into view, examining me through his half-moon reading glasses.

"Hi, Dad."

No smile, just scrutiny. "Joel. Is this role in London as well?"

"Yep. So I meant to tell you guys; I'll be staying longer. At least a couple more months."

A notification of a new message from Andy scrolled in at the top of the screen, then vanished. I tightened my mouth, impatient to get back to that conversation.

"Is that legal?" Dad said. "Working there that long, as an American?"

"Yeah, it's legal, the studio takes care of my visa."

Mom leaned into the screen so it became half of each of their faces at a wildly diagonal camera angle. I tilted my head to make sense of it. "Studio?" she said. "I thought you worked at a theater."

"Usually, but this time it's a film, for a satellite TV channel. A big corporation." I felt like the words "big corporation" might win them over. Why I cared about winning them over, I'd never quite understood.

"Royal Shakespeare Company hasn't taken you on yet, huh?" Dad said.

The remark irritated me but also hooked me deeper into the conversation. They took at least *some* interest in what I did. If I acted at the RSC or the Globe, they would be proud. Nonsensical fringe theater or new-wave movies, not so much.

"Not yet," I said. "Still hoping."

"They show those on PBS sometimes," Mom said. "That would be neat."

Some Oregon kids had the type of embarrassing parents who still said "groovy." I had the type of embarrassing parents who still said "neat."

"It *would* be neat," I agreed.

"When are you coming back?" she asked.

"I'm not sure. Filming's supposed to last ten weeks but could go longer. I'll let you know."

"London is incredibly expensive," Dad said. "You'll want to find something more stable than these acting jobs that only last a couple of months."

"That's how acting works, and I'm aware jobs aren't easy to find and the city's expensive. I live with that fact every day."

"Well, this is why we keep telling you—" Mom said.

"Hey, I have some texts coming in," I interrupted. "I've got to go."

"Let us know when you—" she began.

"I will. Bye, guys." I stabbed the red hang-up button. The screen darkened.

I expelled a breath, indulged in an eye-roll, then returned to the window with Andy.

Andy: Considering it. I might end up yelling at him though

Sinter: Sorry, my parents just accidental-facetime-called me. God.

Andy: Haha! That's hilarious

Sinter: They're hopeless. Right, with mitchell I'd say just email then? Like to check in, nothing intense

Andy: Seems fair. Whew, stressing out thinking about it though

Sinter: Only if you want

Andy: Did your folks like your hair btw?

Sinter: As it happens they did not

Andy: Huh, no accounting for taste

———

Painted up with sticky layers of makeup and hairspray, I stood among a crowd of extras in a fancy house. An assistant camera operator clapped a slate in front of the lens. Fiona called, "Action!" And we were off.

Hardly any rehearsing. My hair had gotten dyed the day before. Now we were filming a movie. Holy shit.

The day's scene was from near the end of the film. The order in which they filmed movies was insane, or so it seemed to me, coming from the stage, where you usually started at the beginning and proceeded through to the end. Movies had to take into consideration which locations were available on which days and grab those time slots. So there we were in the ballroom of a mansion in Knightsbridge, which we were using as the house of Jackie the posh girl, because the mansion's owners were only going to let us in for this particular day.

I, as Taylor, was crashing a party in order to beg Jackie to run away with me. The extras had been gloriously costumed in 1981-style ball gowns and tuxes, everyone sporting fluffy hairdos and excessive blush. I stood out as the poor rebel who didn't belong: ragged suit jacket (sleeves rolled up), skinny tie, vintage Levis, combat boots, silver dagger earring in just one ear, heavy eyeliner, and a hairdo that would have fit in perfectly in a Duran Duran group shot.

I'd already sent Andy a selfie. He'd sent back:

Andy: Lol yes!!!
Andy: Seriously you look awesome

We ran several takes of the scene, from my drawing Jackie aside, to her shrinking away in fear, to my getting thrown out of the house by her irate father and threatened with police action. I sustained bruises from getting slammed past doorways and tossed onto the ground, though I tried to roll with each tumble to avoid injury.

Fiona helped me up personally after the third crash onto the ground. While the crew adjusted set pieces and lights, she dusted me off. "Any more violent than this, and we'd get you a stunt double."

"Nah, I like doing it." I rubbed my throbbing elbow, trying for a cocky smile.

"You're being such a good sport, I can't thank you enough. Sure you're okay for once more?"

"Yeah, I'm good."

"You are." She touched my face lightly with her fingertips so as not to mess up the makeup. "You're excellent. All right, everyone, back in. Places!"

———

"That house we filmed in yesterday, it gave me the creeps," Fiona said. It was dinnertime the next day, and the two of us had secured a corner table in the studio's break room. "Too much like my dad's. And my mum's, actually."

"Ah, right. Your folks, they're . . . "

"Absurdly wealthy and obnoxious, yes."

We both grinned. She dipped a slice of naan into bright red sauce. Catering was going Indian that night. "This is good," she commented. "But my grandmother makes it better."

"You're lucky. Everything my grandparents cook involves either potatoes or Jell-O."

She laughed and tore a new slice of naan in half. After another bite, she said, "I lived with my grandparents a short time while my parents were getting divorced. I was thirteen."

"Jeez. That must have been hard." I dug into the tikka masala.

"Yeah. I would've stayed with my sister, but she'd just started university. Feels as if I saw lawyers more than I saw my parents for a few months there. Asking questions, settling things, working out what would become of us all."

"God, that sucks."

"Ended up basic joint custody. Half the month with Mummy, half with Daddy. And they both stayed in London, so it wasn't as disruptive as it might've been." She took a drink of ice water. "How about your parents? Still together?"

I nodded. "But that mostly means they gang up on me."

"They're a bit stuffy, then? Not a fan of your goth look?"

"They're bankers, and kind of religious, and everything I did was wrong once I became a teenager. The usual."

"Sounds like me. Two big houses to split my time between, and all I wanted to do was make art films, listen to bands in dodgy clubs, hang out with starving musicians and actors."

"You're doing great at all that." I smiled when the remark made her laugh. "But they've got to be proud by now? Your dad being a producer, and your mom—she does studio work too, right?"

"HR at the BBC. But no, I wouldn't say they're proud. My films are too eccentric for them. Not 'commercial' enough. They keep saying things like, 'If you're going to do these historical films, why not write us the next *Downton Abbey* instead?'"

"I'm sure you could."

"But I don't *want* to. These odd little stories are what I want to film."

"Then there you go. You're doing what you love. Screw 'em if they don't like it."

She scooped up a cube of paneer cheese. "But it's strange, isn't it? Even when your parents are a pain in the arse, you can't just disregard them. They still mean a lot to you. Their opinion still matters, still hurts. It's evolutionary or something."

"Wow. I've always felt like that, but didn't figure anyone else got it. I thought I was just a sucker for punishment."

"You're not. Everyone's that way. Some people just hide it better."

While we pondered those sober truths, my phone buzzed on the tabletop. I glanced at it in time to see Andy's name pop up in a message notification.

"Anything you need to get?" she asked.

"Not right this minute. My best friend back home. He's, uh, going through a breakup, and I'm entertaining him by telling him about the film and stuff."

"That's sweet of you. How long were they together? He and the girl."

"Almost a year, I think. But it was a guy, not a girl."

"Oh, indeed?" She gazed at the rest of the cast, mingling at other tables. "I wanted to write this screenplay as a gay love story, you know. Taylor falling for some upper-class bloke instead of a girl. But Chelsea and the others, while sympathetic, convinced me it would have a much wider audience as a girl-boy story."

"Maybe you can write the boy-boy one next."

"Would you audition for that, though?"

"Of course. I can Brokeback things up as good as the next man."

She laughed, then sat back with a sigh. "Oh, you're too perfect. It's normal for writers to adore their characters, I suppose. But usually the actors turn out rather different from the characters, whereas you . . . you're very like what I pictured. Even willing to go along with my original vision of him." Her glance roamed down my torso.

I was still in wardrobe and makeup—a torn T-shirt, spiked hair, a chain from a hardware store as a necklace, and a lagoon's worth of eyeshadow. After shoveling all this tikka masala into my mouth, my face was going to need a touch-up, but still, I must have looked especially Taylor-ish at the moment.

Her gaze was so suffused with admiration that I hardly knew what to feel. Flattery seemed reasonable, even if it came with a whisper of discomfort over the knowledge that I couldn't live up to an imaginary ideal.

"You're forgetting the part where I totally can't play guitar," I said.

"Contentedly overlooking it, let's say." She tapped her shoe against mine.

CHAPTER 8: BIZARRE LOVE TRIANGLE

Sinter: Hey guess what I got to do today

Andy: What?

Sinter: Snog a model on camera

Andy: Haha, how was it?

Sinter: It was ok. Kissing for film or theater involves so much makeup it's kind of like chowing down on a lipstick

Andy: Lol. Yum. But Ariel looks like a Victoria's Secret model. This isn't hot at all?

Sinter: Not my type. She's all right but she smells like cigarettes and feels like silicone, and you aren't going to tell anyone I said all this btw

Andy: Said what? :D Yeah I guess you do tend more toward the geeky cute type. Or at least naturally pretty, not silicone

Geeky cute. That would be you, mate.

Those thoughts had popped up a lot lately. A little unnerving. Also weirdly fun.

Sinter: Btw, did you ever email Mitchell?

Andy: Yeah. He answered yesterday and was . . . such a dickwad

Andy: Like, "it was always so awkward with each other's families, and we were both emotionally unavailable, so this was for the best, don't you agree"

Andy: Just . . . wtf? I was not the emotionally unavailable one thank you

Sinter: Seriously. What a jackhole. Why would it be awkward with your family? They're completely nice

Andy: It wasn't. He's delusional. So I basically said, "if that's how you saw things, then we really weren't on the same page. Goodbye"

Sinter: Good. Did he answer?

Andy: No but I don't expect him to. Think that's that. I'm still pissed off, but doing better

Andy: No more crying in the car anyway :)

Sinter: Good riddance then

Andy: Amen

Sinter: Oh btw, Fiona said it could've been a guy I was making out with. That was how she wanted to write the script

Andy: Whaaaaat? This movie could've been 20 times better you're saying?

Sinter: Evidently. Would have added some variety to my life

Andy: You ever want that kind of variety, let me know, I can hook you up

Sinter: Lol, I will keep that in mind

———

I could have said it to him right then: *Actually, I'm bi-curious.* Why didn't I? What made that so challenging?

Maybe because Andy was a fully out gay man, rainbow stickers on his car and the whole deal, whereas I was just . . . curious. It seemed almost disrespectful for me to throw him a remark like that. Also I didn't want to go claiming something as an identity that I might never back up with action.

Did I *want* to back it up with action?

I thought about the scene we'd filmed that day, making out with Ariel for the camera, and imagined swapping Andy in instead. How would that feel?

We had already said goodnight in our messaging app. I had another early morning on set the next day. I should be going to bed instead of staying up and pondering stuff like this. Nonetheless, I thumbed in "guys kissing" on the browser on my phone and scrolled through the images it brought up.

Looked about the same as a man and a woman kissing, really. I'd feel some stubble maybe. He might taste different? Likely no lipstick (unless he was made up for acting), which would be on the "pro" side of the pro/con list. Gazing at one pair of dudes snogging after another, I let my mind drift back to our kiss at age fifteen.

What if my parents hadn't come home till much later? Maybe we'd have kept kissing, started using tongues. I might have lain down all the way onto him, felt his body against mine. We could have figured out how to grind against each other, please each other, the way neither of us had actually done with other people until college. It might have become something we had indulged in regularly after school, our little secret, the teenage experimentation we should have had.

When I realized I was completely turned on by thinking all this, I set my phone aside, closed my eyes, stretched out on my bed, and imagined it some more.

Should I not think of my best friend like this? Was this creepy? Well, no—he had liked me in high school, or at least had strongly hinted at it, so chances were he had already cast me in this mental scenario long ago.

Which was also a turn-on. So I went ahead and pictured it.

And liked it.

A lot.

———

Of course, there was also that time I had kissed Daniel.

I was nineteen. It was my first trip to London, the summer after my freshman year of college. Daniel, my dorm roommate, had come with me. He was from London, and willing to show me around.

I had hit the jackpot when it came to roommates. Random chance had put us together, and when I approached that dorm the first time, I feared he'd be any number of horrifying things: a serial killer in training, a haughty, rich snob, a jock determined to shove my head in a toilet, a top-40 fan. But instead I got Daniel. Daniel with his London accent, his floppy dark hair, his cologne that made him smell edible, his wandering around shirtless after showers, his tolerating me and treating me as a friend and confiding in me about girls he liked. What was I supposed to do with a gift like that?

We'd both been through recent breakups by the time of our summer trip. I was mostly over Clare, my first girlfriend, but Daniel was still in a deep funk over the latest woman he was besotted with. I let him ramble about it over beers in a pub one night.

We stumbled back to our rented flat in Camden. As we stepped in, he thanked me for liking him even though he was so pathetic.

I slung an arm around him. "I love you for your weaknesses."

He smirked.

Then, before I realized what I was doing, I hooked my other arm around him and kissed him on the mouth, same way I used to kiss Clare.

I think we were both shocked, but it also cracked us up: we started laughing a second later. Then we stopped, and I just sort of stared at him in fear and confusion and desire.

He smiled a little and punched my arm. "Bloody lunatic."

I faked a smile too, and shuffled to the kitchen to get a drink of water. "I probably won't remember this tomorrow," I said. "Don't remind me. Okay?" Amnesia: wise policy.

He stood where I'd left him, by the front door. "Okay," he echoed after a few seconds.

He kept to his word. We'd never spoken of it, though we remained friends. He was even in London, had recently moved back with his girlfriend, Julie, after finishing university in the US. He probably chalked up the experience to my being drunk, if he ever thought of it anymore.

I never told anyone about it, not even Andy. In my own head, my defense—aside from being drunk—was that Daniel's Britishness had attracted me. Like, I wasn't gay or bi, just deeply Anglophilic. It wasn't Daniel I was snogging that night; it was the *United Kingdom*.

But now . . .

How deep in denial could you get, Blackwell?

———

By the time another couple of weeks had passed, I'd become certain I was caught in two different attractions. Flirtations? What to call them?

One was with Fiona, who championed me, supported me in my vulnerable acting moments, and gazed at me with the happy intensity of a fangirl with her favorite celebrity. I was the character she'd created and loved. A crush was understandable on her part. I found her attractive and appreciated her kindness, so I flirted back, with eye contact and smiles and conversations between scenes.

I'd known temporary bonds like this before, working on stage shows. I always spent big chunks of time and emotion with the people involved, and often formed mini-relationships, "showmances," which usually dissolved when the production ended.

So my director wanted me a little, and I basked in it a little. Nothing unusual there.

But the attraction to Andy? That was more unprecedented.

And yet not. Hadn't I kissed him when we were fifteen, remained his closest friend all this time, stayed in touch despite thousands of miles of distance? Hadn't I thought, *Good, now I'm his favorite again,* when he and Mitchell broke up? It was like this feeling had been waiting in the wings since adolescence and was finally leaping out onstage.

Why now, though? I came up with no particular reason except that this was the first time we were both single in years—I'd had girlfriends, he'd had boyfriends, we'd had crushes and other distractions. But now we were both available, and in our familiar online conversations, something had clicked for me. Maybe I felt sorry for him because he was hurting, and I was confusing sympathy with attraction. But if so, that only proved I was capable of *romantic* feelings for other guys, not just physical ones.

In other words, *yes, you're bi, Sinter, so drop the denial already and roll with it.*

Roll with it how, though? These feelings still didn't have to mean anything, nor did I have to take any action. It was only an interesting new development. One I kept obsessively analyzing. Besides, I couldn't do anything about it yet. The guy I currently wanted was, for one thing, in heavy rebound mode, and, for another, five thousand miles away. Meanwhile, I had a job to attend to, one that kept me busy five to six days a week for eight to twelve hours a day.

So I attended to that. Which meant giving, inadvertently, more attention to my temporary work girlfriend.

One afternoon during a filming break, I sprawled in a folding chair on the studio set, my head tipped back and all four limbs hanging limp around me. I was sweaty and almost shaking with exhaustion.

I'd felt like this before. In my determination to make enough money to be independent of my parents, I'd started working side jobs in my second year of college. Between work, studying, and theater, I barely had time to get enough sleep. I felt achy and unfocused all the time. When one day a head rush swept over me as I walked down the street, strong enough that I lost my balance and fell on my ass, I got seriously scared. I went to the student health center, thinking I must have some fatal brain disease. After a few tests, the doctor told me I had a mild anxiety disorder—common among students, she added—which could be helped by meditation and deep breathing. "I think you're all right, just tired," she said. "Try to rest more."

I hadn't succeeded at fitting meditation into my life yet, but I did at least remember to take deep breaths at these times. Besides, I could attribute half my exhaustion to the fact that I was getting over the cold that most of the cast and crew had caught.

We filmed anyway, a miserable experience when you have a sore throat and fatigue. We shot the film's opening scenes during one of those nights, outside in a dressed-up parking lot in the bitter cold. It had looked like such fun in the script, Taylor running from the authorities to avoid getting caught for overstaying his visa. Turned out, sprinting along frozen pavement when you felt like crap was not the least bit fun. I nearly threw up from the exertion, and bruised my knees and skinned my hands by slipping on icy spots.

This week, we were running music-performance scenes, which was proving almost as taxing. It took immense energy to bounce around on-stage with a guitar, even when you were only pretending to play it. I also had to mouth lyrics, looking pumped up and intense, plus get into a brawl, flinging myself into the crowd to swing fists at a guy putting moves on Jackie. And I had to do it all over and over again, full-time.

Fiona had tasked Sebastian with teaching me to move like a proper rock star, and he took sadistic pleasure in the assignment, telling me he'd *never* let me in his band if I held a guitar like *that*, and *what* did I think I was doing knocking against his elbow when we shared the mic? Though I seethed, I listened and learned, and improved my moves until we'd reached the point where he said, "That'll do, I suppose."

I lay draped over the chair, feeling the room sway as if we were on a ship. I hoped my equilibrium would return before the next take, so I wouldn't stumble into Sebastian and have to run the scene again.

I kept my eyes shut, even as someone's fingers began arranging my hair. Our hair and wardrobe people were always doing that, stepping up between takes to fix whatever got messed up.

But it wasn't the voice of the hairdresser that spoke. It was Fiona's. "You're working so hard." She said it softly, for my ears only. "I want you to know I know that, and I value it."

I opened my eyes and let my head roll to the side to regard her. "Not as hard as you're working."

She continued styling my hair. "I keep long hours, but when it comes to physicality, you're leagues ahead of me, or the rest of us." Her voice was roughened; she had the cold too.

"I don't know. The caterers. The runners."

She left my hair alone and set her hand on my shoulder. "Stop deflecting praise. I know it's hard, everything you're being put through. But it'll be worth it, you'll see."

Her hand slid down my dangling arm. When it reached my fingers, I grasped it, still gazing at her. "Thanks," I said, though my self-doubt really wanted to deflect praise some more.

"Would you like a longer break?"

I shook my head. "I got this."

She lifted my hand, kissed my knuckles, and jumped up to return to her spot.

Her vote of confidence did the trick. I pulled off a good take, and we got through the day.

After I'd washed off my glittery makeup for the evening, I stepped out of the dressing room to find Fiona in the corridor. She was tapping at her tablet, but looked up and smiled when I emerged.

"A few changes for tomorrow. I've just sent them to you. Now your call time is later. You can sleep in a little."

"Sweet. Thank you."

We sauntered closer to each other.

Fiona closed her hand around one of the lapels of my leather jacket. "Thank you again for your endurance."

"It's my job. I like it."

"Goodnight then." She tugged my jacket, lifting her face, and I leaned down in compliance, expecting a cheek kiss. She kissed me on the lips instead. I had just enough presence of mind to move my mouth in response.

She let go, and I drifted up to stand straight again. "Yeah." I smiled. "Goodnight."

With a pretty flush in her face, she ran a hand through her unbound hair, then waved and strode away down the hall.

I walked the opposite direction, toward the front entrance, my mind abuzz. When Sebastian popped out from another dressing room and fell in step beside me, it startled me so much I nearly yelled.

"Whoa," I said. "Didn't see you."

"I hope you realize what you've got there." He sounded chillier than usual, and nodded in the direction I'd come from.

Crap. Had he been lurking, spying that kiss by peeking around the doorway?

I coughed, my cold reasserting itself. I used the moment to collect my scrambled thoughts. "I don't think I *have* anything. I do appreciate her. A lot."

"I'd say she rather more than 'appreciates' you." Sebastian pushed open the door to the lobby and held it for me, but it seemed less like courtesy and more like an opportunity to skewer me with his gaze as I passed. "If you're an arsehole to her, you'll have me to answer to."

I clicked my back teeth shut and crossed the lobby at his side. "I absolutely don't plan to be. But, warning taken."

"Good." We paused at the front door, confronted by rain pouring onto the streets. "God, it's pissing down. Well, see you tomorrow." He strolled out, turning up his overcoat collar.

———

Andy: Do you think it meant anything?

Sinter: I'm not sure. I mean, people kiss in theater a lot. I assume film is the same. But then Sebastian said that, so . . . ??

Andy: Well do you want there to be anything with her?

Sinter: Not in a serious way I don't think

Sinter: I am kind of enjoying the flirtation I guess. Which probably makes me a douche. Ugh

Andy: Nah everyone enjoys flirtation sometimes. We get to do that, as humans

Sinter: I guess. Anyway I really think she's just . . . projecting. Seeing me as this character. It happens

Andy: Complicated lives you actors lead :)

Sinter: Yeah. Or not. I'm thinking it's not serious, never mind. Anyway what's new in Seattle?

Andy: Well I will finally have a roommate, though probably just for a month or so

Sinter: Oh yeah?

Andy: Yeah, Peyton, knew him in college. He's looking for work in Seattle and his own place. So he'll stay here till he finds those

Sinter: That's good, splitting the rent and all

I held my fingers back from typing the nosy question that nagged at me: was this Peyton gay? Bi maybe? Andy didn't talk like he was interested in him, but what right did I have to ask that when I wasn't telling anyone, Andy included, that I was bi?

I ought to tell him. If an opportunity came up to slip it smoothly into the conversation, I swore to myself I would.

———

My mom emailed in early December.

Joel,

Do you have Christmas plans? Will you be coming home? Your father and I have been invited to Cousin Grace's in California, but we will decline if you plan to be here. Or you could perhaps come to California too.

Let us know soon please. None of us wants to put off airline reservations

too long this time of year.
  Mom

I winced, reading it with groggy eyes in the dark pre-sunrise hours before work. My crumpet popped up from the toaster, and I set the phone down to pluck out the two halves and spread them with Nutella, trying to imagine if there was any possible reason I'd want to fly all the way to the West Coast for Christmas, then back again a couple of days later. We did get a bit of time off from filming then, so I *could* swing it, but why bother? Unless . . .

I grabbed my phone and messaged Andy.

Sinter: Hey random question. Think you'll be in Oregon for Christmas?

Since I was up early, he was still awake before bed over there, and he responded soon.

Andy: Nah probably staying here. My folks were talking about coming up
to see me and Emma. Why? You going home??

Emma was his sister, older than him by two years, and the sibling he was closest to. She lived in the Seattle area too.

Sinter: Blah I don't know, doubt it. Mom was asking today. The only pos-
sible reason I'd want to is if you were in town, heh
Andy: Aw well thank you
Andy: You could just come to Seattle and not tell them, ha

It was kind of astonishing, the speed at which my brain filled itself with madcap travel scenarios, complete with kisses under mistletoe in front of a window showcasing the Space Needle. However . . .

Sinter: Tempting, but ugh, guess I shouldn't

Sinter: I only get a few days off around then, and I'd be exhausted, the travel . . . etc.

Andy: Yeah the airports are horrible that time of year. I'd avoid it if possible

Andy: So when are you done filming?

Sinter: Probably by first week of January. So hey, travel's not near so crazy after that ;)

Andy: Then come! Are you going to stay in the UK after this?

Sinter: Well that is a good question. Agent has a BBC drama he's trying to get me onto, but otherwise I've been too busy to look. If that falls through . . . I don't know, work visa is a headache to maintain. And expensive. Coming home is easier in some ways

Andy: Hmmm is it wrong to hope you don't get that part? ;)

Sinter: I can forgive it. Would be awesome to see you :)

Andy: Hope so, one way or another! Hopefully peyton will have his own place by January and you could stay here

Sinter: How's that going btw? Living with him

Andy: Not bad, he's pretty chill. Although kind of a slacker. I keep having to remind him to lay off the video games and do his job hunt

Sinter: "Daaaaad stop nagging me"

Andy: Lol, I know, when did I become such a grownup?

Sinter: Speaking of, I've got to get to work

Andy: Yes back to your grownup life of putting on makeup and snogging models

Sinter: They make me get up at SIX AM for this stuff, man, don't disrespect

CHAPTER 9: BOYS DON'T CRY

THE DAY AFTER FIONA KISSED ME, I NUDGED HER PLAYFULLY WHEN WE WERE WATCHING THE DAILIES, TO show I was up for physical friendliness. Over the next week, she let her hands linger when positioning me for scenes, and spent more time fussing personally with my hair and wardrobe. And a few times that week, she found the opportunity to kiss me on the lips again.

Never in front of anyone else, which suggested she was being discreet and not showing favoritism. Still, it didn't feel like passion. The kisses were more "fond," I would say, stemming from adoration of Taylor. And given no one else on set was all that fond of me, I appreciated it.

Sebastian disliked me *because* Fiona liked me. The supporting cast and producers, Fiona's dad included, treated me like I was a bit thick in the head when it came to how British TV worked, being American and all. Maybe they were right to a degree, but it was rubbing off some of the shine when it came to my delight about living in Britain. Ariel, with whom I spent the most time on-screen, didn't particularly seem to care about anyone or anything. Her neutrality was actually something of a comfort.

Finally we reached the day of the sex scene.

The day before, I had nervously taken Fiona aside to ask how it would go.

"Closed set," she assured me. "Only the essential crew. The scene's about four minutes in total, but only about thirty seconds of that is the actual act. Most of it's lead-in action and the conversation afterward."

"All basically in shadow," I checked.

"Yes. Low light. Quite low."

Still, I awoke early on the morning of the shoot and spent awhile looking at my naked self from various angles in the bathroom mirror, critiquing the skin that film-watchers weren't even going to see in any detail.

Yeah, only the twelve or so "essential" crew members would.

Chelsea, instead of the usual wardrobe assistant, brought me the costume this time. Holding up a tiny flesh-colored pair of underwear, she told me with reddened cheeks, "This in place of the usual pants, please." (I'd learned the awkward way, long ago, that "pants" was UK English for underwear.) "You'll still be in shadow. It's just to help everything look convincing in those few glimpses the cameras might pick up."

Oh hell.

I took the pants and mustered up a smile. "Okey dokey."

Before leaving, she gave my shoulder a stilted tap, as if to bolster me. "You'll do fine."

I sank into the chair in my dressing room and messaged Andy.

Sinter: They just handed me nude toned underwear for the scene today.
I . . . I can't even

I knew the message would make him laugh when he woke up and read it, and sending it to him gave me enough backbone to strip down, put the freaky thing on, get into the rest of my costume, and move along to makeup. I felt tightly strapped-down under my jeans, and hoped maybe the constriction would contain any untimely erections. It was seriously unlikely *that* would happen—I didn't desire Ariel at all, and everything I'd heard about sex scenes indicated they were anything but sexy. Still, you never knew when your body might decide to be contrary.

Chelsea arrived and summoned me. I popped the snog-preparatory peppermint gum into my mouth and walked onto the closed set, my stomach tying itself into knots.

———

Andy: Was it horrible? Traumatizing?

Sinter: More just . . . weird and embarrassing and exhausting

Andy: "So, here's how *I* climax . . . does this look normal to the rest of you?"

Sinter: Ha! Yes. That. Not to mention all the "grab the breasts harder please" type of directions

Andy: Oh gawd. Was it weird for Fiona too, directing that?

Sinter: Definitely, she was almost as nervous as me. Meanwhile Ariel was like, "Sure, whatevs, I'll strip and fake orgasms. No big"

Andy: Haha! Was she good at it?

Sinter: Strangely yes. Freaking surreal day

Andy: That is an honestly rough day at work. Poor guy

Sinter: True but it is kinda funny. I do see that. :) Just, wow. I thought it couldn't be harder than the times I've had to cry for a part, but it really was

Andy: Yeah crying on command, how do you do that? Chop onions?

Sinter: Ha, well eye drops are one possibility, but most of us try the "think of something sad" method

Andy: Oh, like a pet dying, or your favorite cheesy movie scene or whatever

Sinter: Yeah I have a few go-to scenarios

Tell him? Not tell him?

Impulse made the decision for me. I started typing.

Sinter: One is actually . . . heh ok this is stupid . . .

Andy: Oh now you have to tell me :)

Sinter: The day you left for college. You probably don't even remember
Andy: Omg. Dude. Now I'M tearing up. That day sucked!! Wow good one

I caught my bottom lip in my teeth, pleased beyond reasonable limits. He remembered. I had moved him.

Sinter: Well there you go. You're one of my trade secrets
Andy: A high honor it is too

———

On a mild morning in September, I had walked to Andy's house to help him pack up his green Volvo. He was about to leave for California for his freshman year. I'd be heading to the University of Oregon the next week, in Eugene, a much shorter drive south.

I was utterly freaking out, but I wouldn't let anyone see it. I kept the panic locked down, telling myself this transition was no big deal, a good thing even. College was bound to be better than high school.

Except the part I'd avoided thinking about until that day: the part where I had to be five hundred miles away from my best friend.

His two sisters, his parents, and I carried boxes out for him. His other sibling, his older brother, lived in the Bay Area and would be meeting him at Stanford to help him move in.

Though I was in full emo gear that day—spiky black hair, eyeliner, earrings, studded belt, wallet chain, band T-shirt with holes in it—his family welcomed me and treated me like one of their own. They'd long since grown accustomed to my look, even when my own parents still hadn't.

Andy gave them each an emotional but jubilant hug in farewell, and I climbed into the car with him. He had offered to drop me at my house on the way out of town.

"I could've walked," I told him with a chuckle as we rolled off down the street. I only lived two blocks away, after all.

The breeze blew into our open windows, smelling of suburban lawns.

"Yeah, well." His voice sounded rusty, and it finally occurred to me that he wanted to say goodbye to me alone, without an audience.

Something in my chest had clenched up into a knot by the time he stopped on my street. He parked the Volvo a few houses down, next to a stand of trees that blocked the view of my parents' house.

"Here, I'll . . . " He turned off the car and got out.

I climbed out too.

He came around to the sidewalk and we stood under the trees in the dappled, gold-and-green morning sunlight. He stared downward a moment, then lifted his face. Tears shone in his eyes. He didn't speak.

The knot in my chest rushed into my throat. I was in agony, though I couldn't have articulated why. I was scared; the future was huge and uncertain; I'd be alone; I was worried about him . . . ?

Andy forced out a chuckle and glanced aside. "Shit."

I swallowed to regain my voice. I could not cry. My eyeliner was super heavy, and it'd smear everywhere. "We'll be okay," I insisted. "Me in Eugene with the freaks, you in the Bay Area . . . "

"With the queers." He managed a smile. We had gone over it a few times this summer, our respectively safe choices for universities. Somehow it felt like zero comfort.

"You'll do awesome," I went on. "And we'll text all the time, so it won't even feel that different."

He nodded, though muscles twitched in his cheeks, tugging down on his lips. "Well." He stepped up and hugged me.

We had never hugged before, at least not that I could remember, and definitely not like this. In recent years, only fellow theater people had hugged me this tight. My parents hadn't; no one else had. But Andy and I stuck together like magnets from knees to necks, and it was clearly ridiculous that we weren't in the habit of hugging, when our shapes matched up so well, and when I cared more about him than I cared about all those theater people.

All of them put together, in fact.

He sniffled against my shoulder, and it was absolutely everything I could do to not cry. I couldn't, I wouldn't.

"Maybe it'll be awesome," he said, his voice choked. "But it isn't going to be the same without you."

Hot tears filled my eyes. I stared at the treetops to keep them from spilling. "No, it won't be the same," I mumbled.

We let go. He scrubbed his hand across his reddened eyes, slipped his sunglasses on, and gave me a wobbly smile. "Talk soon, Blackwell."

"Drive safe. Text me when you get there."

"You too."

He got in the Volvo and drove slowly away, lifting one hand out the window to wave to me before turning the corner.

My parents were home. I couldn't face them right then, or anyone. But I couldn't stand around either, so I got into my old silver Honda, started it, and began to drive. I just needed some time cruising around the neighborhood to calm down, then I'd be all right.

Then new-wave music gave me its little shove over the edge. The CD currently spinning in my car's stereo was a collection of B-sides by the Cure, a graduation present from my drama teacher. She liked giving her students mixtapes on CD, curated to fit their individual tastes in music. The track "To the Sky" came on—sweet, mellow, pretty, and one of the most melancholy songs I'd ever heard. Robert Smith sang his opening line about being all alone, his voice heartbroken in his trademark way.

I sniffled sharply and turned the wheel to park in the empty lot of a restaurant. I pulled the parking brake, covered my face with my hands, and started crying, gulping down the air, hardly even sure what my problem was except that I *couldn't stand this.*

After a couple of minutes, I settled down. I was just stressed, I told myself. We'd get through this. At least I'd be out of my parents' house, which had to be an improvement.

But it didn't feel like one. I felt utterly damaged, broken in some manner that would surely take years to repair, and I didn't understand why. I started up my car and drove home, my eyeliner a smudged-up disaster.

CHAPTER 10: MODERN LOVE

FIONA MIGHT HAVE BEEN THE WOMAN I CUR-
RENTLY DESIRED MOST, BUT ANDY WAS THE *PERSON* I CUR-
rently desired most. Accepting bisexuality as my orientation meant having realizations like that.

I knew it because while I checked out Fiona's bum sometimes in a certain pair of flattering black trousers, I didn't look up porn videos of straight people and picture the two of us in them. Yet I kept looking up guy/guy videos and mentally casting Andy and myself. I knew it by the graphic acts he and I performed in my dreams. I knew it because while I admired Fiona, liked talking with her, enjoyed her occasional kisses and hugs, and even would fancy having sex with her, I didn't feel the distracting desire to ask her out. And shouldn't I have felt that, if I truly wanted to be with her?

My text conversations with Andy, in contrast, were often my favorite part of the day lately, and my priorities had shifted to the point where I'd started researching the theater scene in Seattle, in case my BBC drama prospect fell through. The idea of living near him had become as appealing as living in the UK and filming an '80s new-wave movie. How could *anything* match that for me?

Then came this exchange in mid-December:

Andy: We get a guest this weekend. Peyton's little brother Jackson
Sinter: Oh yeah?
Andy: He's in college at UCLA, off for winter break and coming to visit

Peyton

Sinter: Cool, going to show him around town?

Andy: Yep. Peyton's not gay but Jackson is, so he's into the idea of checking out Capitol Hill

Cue the wave of uneasy jealousy, rolling over me and slowing me down in my pre-dawn walk to the Tube for work. Other commuters slipped around me, wrapped in winter coats, their elbows brushing mine in a faintly huffy way.

Sinter: Ah nice. Just for the weekend?

Andy: Yeah he and Peyton are both going home afterward for xmas

Sinter: And they live in . . .

Andy: California, somewhere in the OC, I forget the town

Good. A long way from Seattle, and he didn't even remember which town. That comforted me.

Sinter: Should be fun

Andy: Maybe I'll even meet some proper rebound dude if I get dragged to a party

I hated how cold and dark it was in London this time of year. Hated the reckless taxi drivers careening by. Hated the passive-aggressive commuters crowding the Tube.

Then he added:

Andy: I mean it's about time. Think I'd feel a lot better if I got laid, heh

Though I gritted my teeth, I at least knew how to answer honestly.

Sinter: Yeah so would I actually

Sinter: Well I've got to catch my train, keep me posted

Andy: Yep, goodnight! Or good morning for you :)

I continued on to the studio, thoroughly grumpy.

If I were in Seattle I could go out with them, and over drinks could tell him I was bi and would love some experimentation. Then, if he was up for it, it would be me in his bed this weekend instead of whichever random guy struck his fancy.

Argh. I was lusting after my best friend, and he had no idea. I didn't even want a proper relationship with him—or at least, I couldn't wrap my head around that. I just really, deeply, badly wanted to *try* being with him, be his "rebound dude" or whatever label he wanted to slap on it.

Would he even still want me after all these years? Could I dare propose that, next time we were in the same city?

I had to stop thinking like this. There was nothing I could do. He got to have sex with people if he wanted. *I* got to have sex with people if I wanted. Maybe it was me who needed to get laid, if I was getting this wound up about things I had no right to.

Not even Chelsea's adorable two-year-old daughter, Mina, on set with her for the day, could cheer me up. But she did make me smile when she tottered up wearing a purple sequined vest and a neon-green feather boa. She took hold of my leg to steady herself.

I crouched by her. "Someone's been having fun in wardrobe."

"I should say so," Fiona remarked, smiling from her chair nearby.

"I have a snake." Mina held up the end of the green boa.

"That's terrifying," I said. "It's so dangerous, wearing it like that."

She giggled and flapped it.

"She likes you." Fiona rested her temple on her knuckles as she watched us.

"She likes everyone." I tried to pinch the end of the feather boa while the kid squealed and flipped it out of my reach.

"Mm," Fiona agreed, sounding wistful.

Maybe I was messing with her mind by being nice to little kids? Some people could get sentimental when their crush did stuff like that. I remembered feeling all sweetly sappy when one of my girlfriends held a baby and made googly eyes at them. But swaying Fiona wasn't my intention, and I wasn't up to sussing out her intentions either. I was still way too peeved about Andy's plan to invite a gay college boy into his apartment and get laid one way or another.

Focusing on the present, I told Mina, "You're lucky, getting to hang out on film sets. You have a cool mum."

"I have a snake," she corrected, and flailed the feather boa.

"Yes," I agreed.

———

Andy: Agh Sinter what have I done?

The message came Sunday evening while I stood in the kitchen at Daniel and Julie's flat, eating appetizers and chatting. Daniel was the college roommate I had once kissed, not that this was how I introduced him to others. I had visited him and his girlfriend, Julie, when I arrived in London this year, but hadn't seen them since the film started. They had invited me over to have dinner and tell them about it.

Reading Andy's message, I felt a punch of anxiety in the belly. Even though it was totally rude of me, I murmured, "Sorry, hang on," wandered into the living room to their lit-up Christmas tree, and tapped a message back.

Sinter: I don't know, what have you done?

Andy: I hooked up with Jackson. My roommate's 19 yr old brother. Agh.

The crackers in my stomach fused into a stone ball. But he sounded like he regretted it, so . . .

> Sinter: Oh. Gosh. It wasn't good?
> Andy: It was ok. But I immediately thought afterward, "This was a mistake."

In that case, as good as I could hope for. Maybe. I glanced guiltily back at the kitchen, toward Julie's and Daniel's voices. Then I kept typing.

> Sinter: Well that's ok. Rebound hookups get to be like that
> Andy: I guess, but gah. 19!
> Sinter: That's still legal. Uh when you say hooked up, what does that mean?
> Andy: Are you asking "anal or no"?
> Sinter: Ha not necessarily, just trying to understand how serious an offense this was ;)

"Everything all right?"

Daniel's voice, close up, made me jump.

He grinned and handed me a clear, bubbly drink.

"Yeah, it's fine. Cheers." I took the glass and gulped some down. Gin and tonic, light on the gin, as I had requested. "Just Andy. He's . . . getting back to me about something."

He and Julie had met Andy years earlier, when Andy came to visit me at U of O for a weekend.

"Ah, brilliant, how's he doing?"

My phone buzzed and I looked at it.

> Andy: Well answer is no anal, just handjobs. Heh

I pressed my lips together and breathed carefully for a couple of seconds. "He's good," I told Daniel, my voice on the high side.

"Daniel?" Julie called. "Where are the tongs?"

"Be right back," he told me, and sauntered to the kitchen.

Sinter: Haha . . . ok, got it

Andy: Sorry for the mental image ;)

Sinter: That's ok, I'm down with it

Andy: Thank goodness. But ugh I've never felt so old and slimy.

Sinter: You're 25. That isn't old to a 19 year old

Andy: Old. And slimy. Slimy like a slug. Like seaweed.

Sinter: Are you done with your metaphors

Andy: I think these are similes

Though he'd been a computer science major, he'd also been, like me, an English minor. It made him remarkably hot at moments such as this.

Sinter: Right, you're right

Andy: And no. There are many slimy things and I'm like them all. Slimy like mayo

Sinter: Gross

Andy: Exactly, I am gross

Sinter: Ha no, mayo is gross

Andy: Slimy like a dog's tongue.

Sinter: Seriously stop. Does Peyton know?

Andy: About Jackson and me? Yes. He doesn't care. Just teased us a little. Anyway they both took off today for the holidays

Sinter: But they're coming back after?

Andy: Only Peyton. Jackson's got school in California. And Peyton's moving into his new place the first of January, so I'll be back to my double rent

His apartment would be available for an extra person. He'd had a rebound hookup but regretted it. My path was clear . . . except for a few major logistical items like coming out to him, testing the waters on any mutual interest, deciding whether to stay in the UK or move to Seattle (which depended on whether I could score that BBC role, about which my agent still hadn't heard), and in what order to do all of the above.

And before that, I had to finish filming a movie, and really, right then, all I should be doing was focusing on my friendly hosts.

Sinter: Well I'm at Daniel and Julie's for dinner, but can we talk more later?

Andy: Sure no problem, sorry. Just wanted to share my terrible moment of shame, not much else to say

Sinter: Not really so terrible :)

And there was plenty more to be said before I, for one, would sleep easily.

———

The door to Daniel and Julie's building had barely closed behind me before I got onto a social-media site I ordinarily used very little, located Andy's page, and found exactly what I dreaded I'd find: a photo tagging him from the night before, at some party. Andy, Peyton, Jackson, and two other guys were squished in together for the camera.

Andy looked amazing. He had a healthy twinkle in his eyes, wore glasses with thin brown frames that flattered his face, and was extending his drink with a smirk in an excellent imitation of Leonardo DiCaprio as Gatsby. He'd gotten a haircut since our video call; it was up to cube-worker respectability, with modest hipster sideburns. I savored him for a few seconds, from swept-back hair to the spot where the open top button of his shirt revealed the hollow at the base of his throat, which would be an excellent spot for my tongue to go.

Then I stabilized myself with a breath and examined the dude tagged "Jackson" beside him.

He looked like someone from a boy band. Not the sexy, charismatic one from a boy band either, but the one with a dumb grin and a goatee and hair that stuck straight up. Oh, he was cute and all, but nothing special.

Of course, I'd never met him and was basing this judgment on one photo and a truckload of jealousy.

Daniel and Julie's street was quieter than Mile End by a good margin, and my sigh echoed audibly as I leaned against the wall of their building.

There. Look at it. Real life: those two guys hooked up last night. Regret today on the part of the much smarter one with the green eyes and the adorable smile. No call at all for jealousy on my part. If I was going to talk to Andy about it any further, it had to be as his friend, not as some closeted stress case.

After staring moodily at the photo awhile longer, I decided I could manage that. I got into the message app and resumed our conversation of three hours earlier without preamble.

Sinter: Do you think Jackson thought it was a mistake too?

I headed for the Tube station. Andy answered as I crossed the first street.

Andy: I don't know, he seemed affectionate, "let's stay in touch" and stuff.
But I doubt he's in love with me or anything, heh
Sinter: Guess the distance will be a bit of a barrier

Said the guy five thousand miles away.

Andy: It'll work as an excuse. Anyway, it was a one night stand, yay, whatever

Sinter: I've had those. Can't judge

Andy: I know, that's nice about you :)

He knew these things about me. Knew not only about Clare, Jo, and Vicki, my three girlfriends from age eighteen through earlier this year, but also about the six or seven other women of the short-term variety, some terms as short as one night. College was like that. Theater was like that. According to Andy, gay life in your twenties in a big city was like that. Hell, most people's twenties were probably like that.

I breathed easier, inhaling the traffic-and-stone-scented air as I trotted down the steps to the Tube station.

Then, of course, he had to hit me with another message.

Andy: Anyway I guess it means I'm dating again, so that's good. With luck can meet someone better for me

Sinter: Yeah for sure, hope so

Not jealous at all, no, I was *so not jealous*.

CHAPTER 11: A QUESTION OF LUST

IN MID-DECEMBER, WE SHOT MY LAST SCENE (RANDOMLY, A CONVERSATION FROM THE MIDDLE OF THE movie). Fiona announced with poignant joy, "That's a wrap for Sinter Blackwell."

And people who had been wishing I was Bradley MacCrossan all this time hugged me and applauded. Even Sebastian gave me a half-friendly clap on the shoulder.

I wasn't truly done with the film yet—I had to come back into the studio for a day the following week to do re-recording, in which I would speak my lines over again to give the engineers better-quality audio options to work with. But I was finished with the on-screen acting portion, and that left me sad.

Which confused me, considering I'd spent all week giving only minimal mental attention to the film, instead brooding over Andy, and my future as a bisexual.

I was still ruminating over this mix of problems Thursday evening when the whole cast and crew gathered at Ariel's flat for a holiday party.

Everything she owned seemed to be made of glass, titanium, or gray cushions. White twinkle lights adorned all the windows and potted trees, and ice sculptures stood at the ends of the catering tables. The flat was packed with cast and crew as well as Ariel's friends from the modeling industry. I stood in a sea of nineteen-year-old women with straightened blonde hair and sparkly cocktail dresses, most of whom were being chatted up by band members and electricians. When Ariel introduced me as her fast-rising American costar, one of the models cozied up to me, and had been leaning closer and closer while we talked about her upbringing in a tiny Irish town.

It was making me claustrophobic. I was relieved for the excuse to turn toward the stage when Sebastian took the mic and announced he was dedicating this next song to our cameraman Mick, who tolerated technical difficulties, freezing weather, and diva actor temperaments without breaking a sweat. The Swinburnes dove into a cover of Toni Basil's "Mickey," dialing the cheesiness up to eleven. Halfway through, Sebastian hopped offstage, still singing, to shimmy up to Mick. We were all grinning, but Fiona was laughing so hard, she was wiping away tears. Sebastian kissed her on the cheek and tickled her ribs before swinging back to the stage.

After the song, I escaped the crowd and climbed a staircase to the indoor balcony, where I sipped my third bottle of beer and gazed down on the party. Fiona strolled up a minute later, carrying a green-tinted drink. "Quite the place, isn't it?"

"I've never been to a party with ice sculptures before. I thought those were a myth."

She rested her elbows beside me on the railing. "Ariel is many things, but low-key is not one of them."

Fiona looked the hottest I'd ever seen her, which wasn't helping my conflicted hormones. She wore a black leather miniskirt with tights, fur-topped boots, and a clingy red sweater that scooped low enough to show some cleavage.

When I realized my gaze was lingering there, I snapped it back to her face. Her smile twinkled with mischief, and she eased closer, settling her weight on one leg so her hip bumped against mine and stayed there.

This time it didn't cause me any claustrophobia.

"You're getting a lot of attention from the young models." She looked down at Ariel's guests.

"If only I wanted a nineteen-year-old."

Like some people. Bitter? Not me.

"You're fast approaching the phase where you could have anything you want. Use your powers wisely."

"Doubt I'm there yet." I sipped my beer, reflecting on breasts. On flat male chests. On kissing people. On the kind of intimacy I hadn't experienced in many, many months and was aching for.

Her arm nestled against mine. "What do you want, then?" She spoke it like a friend, with a suggestive, lazy warmth.

If I were into the casual hookup, which I wasn't (even my one-night stands were with women I'd known and liked awhile), I wagered I could get lucky with the Irish model or probably other people there. But in the absence of Andy, who was really inconveniently far away and didn't know I was pining for him, I'd pick Fiona.

I might yet stay longer in London, if I got that BBC part. I could still visit Andy, but plane tickets were expensive, and maybe it made more sense to form lasting attachments in the UK.

Besides, Andy got to go out and drink and get off with someone he found attractive. Half the people at this party were going to do the same. Why shouldn't I?

I turned to look at her. We appraised one another close up.

It took only a tilt of my face. She answered the silent invitation and met my lips.

Two seconds in, it became clear this was hotter by many degrees than our previous "fond" kisses. When her lips parted, I flicked my tongue against their inner edges, tasting mint—evidently crème de menthe was the green drink—and she sighed, almost a moan, and thunked her glass down on the railing. We pulled out of sight of the rest of the party. I left my beer bottle on the edge of a planter and wrapped my arms around her. She pushed me up against a wall; I grabbed her rear with both hands, feeling plump flesh through warm leather.

"This is so unprofessional of me," she panted against my mouth.

"It's a party, who cares?"

She kissed me harder, our tongues wrapping around one another.

"God, I've just really wanted to," she said. "You're so . . . delicious . . . "

"Is this . . . " I skated one hand around to enfold her breast. "All right?"

"Yes, of course, yes." She was pressing close, had to be able to feel how aroused I was (which hadn't been a problem even for a moment in the scenes with Ariel, but this was a different story), and must have liked it from the way she writhed against me.

Voices reverberated closer: people climbing one of the staircases.

"Come on." Fiona pulled me into a nearby room and shut the door. I hit a light switch, and a bright row of bulbs came on.

It was some sort of immense walk-in closet, or so I assumed by the long lines of hanging clothes, the array of mirrors, and the unbelievable numbers of shoes on shelves. There was even a loveseat, for the benefit, I supposed, of whoever was helping (or watching) Ariel get dressed. Fiona and I shot each other bemused grins.

She turned the lock on the door handle, then drew me to the loveseat, pushed me onto it, and straddled me.

All thoughts of unprofessionalism, efficiency of door locks, or really anything else, flew out of my mind. We started kissing again. Her hand slid down between my legs. I shoved up her sweater and groaned at the heat of her breasts filling my palms. I tucked my hands inside the cups of her bra to feel her nipples harden. Yep, it would seem I was still attracted to women too.

"I have condoms," she said in my ear.

"Okay," I said, the only logical answer at the moment. I even felt comforted because there, see, we were being responsible about it.

Strangeness had already crept into the scenario, what with the bright lights and the legions of Ariel's expensive clothes. It no longer felt quite as sexy as it had on the balcony. Still, I was a little bit drunk and a lot mixed-up, and she was right there and willing, tugging down her tights and unfastening my jeans.

She found the condom in her bag, I got it on, then we shifted around so she was on her back in the limited space of the loveseat, and . . . and then we were having sex. In Ariel's gigantic closet.

Fiona had seen me perform a sex scene (repeatedly, no less), and now, in having actual sex with me, I had to assume she was comparing the two experiences. I would be, in her place. It riddled me with self-doubt, because I didn't particularly want her to end up disappointed by either of the performances.

Still, having started, I saw it through. It would surely be insulting to stop, and besides, judging from how readily my body went along with this surprise encounter, I was in need of something like this.

Gasp. Shudder. Finish the job. As the script said. Though I was first, at least she didn't seem to mind, and followed soon after.

But . . .

As we untangled, creaked our limbs back into place, and fastened up our clothes, all "Wow" and "Ha" and "That was unexpected," my mind echoed Andy's sentiment after getting with Jackson: *This was a mistake.*

And it was his voice that said in my head, mournfully, *Oh, Sinter, what have you done?*

Fiona stood to tug her skirt and tights back where they should be, then smoothed herself down. "Sorted." She reached out to me.

Still sitting on the loveseat, I set my hands in hers and looked up at her.

She studied me a moment, then touched my cheek, and I remembered to smile.

"Suppose we should slip out," she said.

We unlocked the door, peeked out, and escaped.

The band—a different group this time, not the Swinburnes—was

playing a cover of Adam and the Ants' "Stand and Deliver," and the main
floor was a swarm of people bouncing to the beat. Following Fiona down
the staircase, I caught Sebastian's eye. He stood at the edge of the crowd,
wearing leather boots, torn jeans, and a garish reindeer-and-snowflakes
sweater. He'd already been scowling at the band's performance, but now
turned his disapproval upon me. Lowering the beer bottle from his lips,
he glowered as I trailed Fiona down the stairs.

I gave him a humble almost-smile, lips scrunched. He blinked
slowly—interesting how a blink could convey *I will obliterate you if you
set a foot out of line*—then turned to face the band again.

I started feeling a bit sick.

As we reached the main floor, Fiona turned to smile at me. "Shall we
fetch another drink?"

I shook my head. "I'm pretty tired. I was going to head home. But,
um, we'll talk soon?"

She nodded and stroked my shoulder. "Yeah, you look tired. You get
tomorrow off, at least."

"I know. Incredible." The next day, they'd be filming scenes involving Jackie and her family, so Ariel and others had to be there, but I was
done.

"Then a long weekend," she added. Monday was Christmas, and we
got that and Boxing Day off too.

"But I'll be around during it, and . . . yeah, we'll talk."

"Yes." She lifted her face for a kiss.

I leaned down to brush it upon her, not quite on the lips, only the
side of her mouth. Out of the corner of my eye, I saw Sebastian staring at
us. "Goodnight," I said. "Had a good time." I formed a flash of a roguish
smile—all acting; my heart wasn't in it.

Then I escaped the party before Sebastian or anyone else could catch
me and ask what exactly I'd been doing up there with her for the last
fifteen minutes.

CHAPTER 12: I CONFESS

THROUGH MY TUBE RIDE AND THE WALK DOWN MILE END TO MY FLAT, I MULLED OVER MY STRANGE NIGHT. Should I give Fiona a chance? Couldn't this be the start of a great relationship? An attractive, competent Englishwoman, a writer and director in the entertainment industry who loved my work: it was my dream setup, right?

But my mind, or heart if you wanted to call it that, kept saying *No*.

She wasn't the one I wanted. For that matter, I probably wasn't the person she wanted, either. The fact that I resembled Taylor, and was portraying him for her, must have counted for an awful lot in her attraction to me.

Had I only been getting even with Andy—or scoring to catch up with him, to look at it another way? If that had been any part of my motivation, I felt ashamed of it, and as my mind sorted itself out, I found he was the one person I wanted to talk to.

Locked into my flat, with the heat turned up as high as my pathetic, clanking radiator would go, I sat on the bed with a blanket around me and opened the messaging app.

Sinter: Hey do you have a minute?
Andy: Hey! Yeah, just got off work. I'm meeting Emma and her boyfriend for dinner later, but I have a little while, so what's up?
Sinter: Well . . . are you willing to be my confessional?
Andy: Intriguing. Yes my son, what sins have you committed?

Sinter: I had sex with Fiona. At Ariel's party tonight.

Andy: Wow

Sinter: Yeah

Andy: That's good right? You like her, she likes you. Sounded like, anyway

Sinter: Yeah but . . . I think it was a mistake

Andy: Oh. Well I do know how that feels

Sinter: Heh, thought you might get it

Andy: Do you think she agrees? That it was a mistake

Sinter: I kind of don't think so

Andy: Uh oh

Sinter: I know. Argh

Andy: Well, you'll have to talk to her

Sinter: True, no escaping that. Shit I'm so sleazy. An actor sleeping with his director, it's like a fricking tabloid

Andy: You were nice enough to tell me I wasn't slimy even though I was

Sinter: Because you weren't

Andy: Hush. So I'm telling you you aren't sleazy. You got carried away at a party with someone you've been having sexual tension with. As people do. I assume alcohol was involved?

Sinter: Yeah

Andy: Then, normal really

Andy: You were safe I hope?

Sinter: Condom . . . yeah

Andy: Good. Then chill. Talk to her, be honest and low-drama if possible. It'll be ok

Andy: I mean I know you majored in drama, but TRY to be low-drama ;)

Sinter: Ha

Andy: So wow, a savvy British woman doesn't do it for you. I'm kind of surprised

Sinter: Right? Obviously I liked her enough to go through with it. Just . . . I don't know

Andy: Not relationship material?

Sinter: Yeah, and I guess not the sex I want to be having right now

I went tingly all over as the adrenaline shot through me. Oh my God, I was going to tell him.

Andy: What pray tell IS the sex you want to be having, or do I even want to know :)

Sinter: Well . . . lately I've realized I'm bi-curious. So . . . something involving that

I sent the words off, watched them crystallize into reality on the screen, and saw the checkmark appear that indicated he'd seen them. I bit my fingers—not just my nails, but the tips of all four fingers, cramming them between my teeth.

My heart thumped in my throat. The response bubble appeared from Andy's side, three dots in it: he was typing something. Then it vanished. He had decided against saying it.

I took my hand out of my mouth and started typing too—*I've suspected it for a long time but I was confused, and I know I should have said something sooner, but*

I stopped and deleted all the words without sending them. He would have seen the same from his side: dots appearing and vanishing. We stayed silent a minute, probably both staring at our phones, in a game of instant-message chicken.

The response bubble returned on his side, and his answer materialized.

Andy: April fool's?

Andy: :)

I smiled, pulling in a long breath.

Sinter: Ah you remember that conversation :)

Andy: Duh, of course. So, wow. That's awesome! Yay!

Sinter: Thank you. I feel stupid I didn't say anything until now

Andy: Why didn't you? Obviously I'd have been fine with it

Sinter: I was confused mainly. Wasn't totally sure

Andy: Yeah I imagine being bi (or bi-curious anyway) is inherently more confusing than being gay or straight

Sinter: True that

Andy: Though I did always kinda wonder. I mean it's not everyone who'd kiss their friend on the mouth just to be nice ;)

Sinter: Haha right, should've been a clue for us both

Andy: So there's some guy you want? The sex you're hoping to have?

My heart revived its heavy pounding. *Here goes.*

Sinter: Well, like . . . so last night I had a dream I was making out with you. How crazy is that?

Oh shit, he was going to back away slowly, find some polite way to say he wasn't into it; why had I said that?

Andy: Oooh. I've heard crazier. ;) How was I?

Sinter: Quite good. You got skills, boy

Andy: Lol, well I like to think so

Sinter: You're . . . not weirded out?

Andy: Ummm my first ever wet dream was about you, so . . . nope, fine with it

Sinter: Oh REALLY? Lol. I cannot believe you just told me that

Andy: I strive to be honest. So that's what's on your mind huh

Sinter: I guess, yeah. Something along those lines. It's what I want these days, apparently

Andy: Dude, if you didn't insist on being in another country all the time, we could be doing that right this minute

Excitement surged through me, sparkling brighter than Christmas lights.

Sinter: Yeah? You seriously would?

Andy: Of course. You kissed me when I came out. It's what friends are for ;)

Sinter: Hmm, then I really should think about visiting Seattle

Andy: You really definitely should

Sinter: But then my agent still hasn't heard about that BBC role, so, argh, future is all up in the air. I hate this

Andy: You'll have to hear soon I would think

Sinter: Any day now. Well regardless, thank you for being willing. :) You're the first I've told, so, no idea where this part of my life is going yet

Andy: Am I? I'm flattered

Sinter: It's not like I was going to tell my parents first

Andy: Oh shit, them . . . yeah I see why you'd hang onto the denial

Sinter: Right? They're a problem for another day though

Andy: If it's not going to be a big part of your life, you might never have to tell them. It happens

Sinter: That's what I don't know yet. How big it might be

Andy: That's what he said

Andy: Sorry, couldn't resist

Sinter: Lol

Andy: So hang on. Then all this time, have you been flirting with me, Sinter Blackwell? Not just friend-joke-flirting like I thought, but FLIRT-ING flirting?

I snuggled the blanket closer around my body. The screen glowed against my knees like a flashlight in a tent. I danced my fingers over the screen to tap in the words.

Sinter: I have been flirting with you, Andrés Ortiz.
Andy: Well this is my favorite Christmas present. This conversation right here. I mean I haven't opened gifts yet, but I'm sure nothing will top it
Sinter: Aw . . . thanks

I was breathing light and fast. My heart cartwheeled along in nervous happiness.

Andy: I have to get to dinner, but I'm stoked for you, even though . . .
you know, complications
Sinter: So many. Jeez. But thanks
Andy: You're awesome, man. Talk soon!
Sinter: Have fun at dinner, say hi to Emma for me
Andy: Will do

Our message window went dormant. I toppled sideways, curled in my blanket cocoon, cradling my phone.

I came out. I came out. I came out.

I whispered the phrase to feel it in my mouth. Okay, my grand declaration was only "I'm bi-curious," and only to one person, not quite the level of coming out as gay or trans to the entirety of one's acquaintances. But I let myself count it. It was far more than I'd ever declared to anyone so far, and I felt different. Better.

Lights from passing cars swooped across my ceiling. The radiator clanked, emitting its hot-metal smell. I'd had sex with Fiona just two hours earlier, which was all kinds of problematic, but maybe it had been the necessary catalyst, the thing that had cracked open my shell to let out this confession. And Andy had received the news happily, even said he was attracted to me too, would be glad to kiss me. A flicker of lust, apparently not quenched by my encounter with Fiona, flashed down to the pit of my belly.

The things we might say to each other in the next couple of days . . . and if those went over well, the things we might do next month if I flew to Seattle, even if only for a casual weekend visit . . .

At which point all my complications came thundering back. I still needed to sort out which country my next job was going to be in, and if I did go to Seattle, for the short or long term, I didn't know how far Andy would be willing to take this friendly flirtation, let alone how far I myself had the courage to take it. I set down my phone, wondering if Andy had felt this same mix of excitement and dread after coming out to me ten years earlier.

CHAPTER 13: BLASPHEMOUS RUMOURS

THOUGH FOR THE REST OF HIGH SCHOOL WE RARELY TALKED ABOUT ANDY'S BEING GAY, WE DIDN'T PRETEND the issue had ceased to exist. When watching TV together, I'd say, "She's hot," about a female character, and he'd say, "Yeah, but I like *him* better," about a male. He seemed to enjoy being able to say those things to me, perhaps because he still wasn't out to anyone else. In high school, after all, even in a liberal part of the country, someone was likely to be an immature asshole about it, and who needed "fag" painted across their car by football players?

Shortly before graduation, Andy beckoned me into his room and took his mortar board off a shelf. "Decorated this." He flipped it to show me: in red and white paper he had lettered "Stanford bound," and across the top corner had painted a rainbow. "The rainbow," he said. "I can't decide if it's too much. Or maybe too subtle."

"Are you making a deliberate statement?"

"Kind of? I mean . . . " He fiddled with the edges of the board. "I'm going to show it to my parents. Tell them that way."

"Wow. When?"

"I think tonight."

By his report to me in text later, he tackled them one at a time. He brought the mortar board to his mom and said, "Do you know why I put a rainbow on it?"

She hugged him and said, "I'm pretty sure I do."

It went basically just as smoothly with his dad and siblings. Some people had all the luck when it came to families.

Andy let the gossip spread on its own; he didn't bother coming out to our classmates, though he wore the mortar board to commencement, rainbow and all. As we mingled in the crowd after the ceremony, a girl in our class wandered up and asked, "Is that, like, an LGBT rainbow?"

"Yeah, it is," he said. "I'm gay."

"Oh, cool. So am I," she said.

"Sweet. Well, good luck at college."

"You too."

He shook hands with her. She drifted off. He looked at me with widened eyes, then we both broke into laughter.

The gossip took nearly all summer to spread to my parents.

My mom blocked my bedroom doorway one August day as I was about to leave for my job at a coffee shop. Hands on her hips, she squinted as if about to say something she herself couldn't fathom. "Andy is claiming he's gay? Did I hear this correctly?"

"Actually, he just *is* gay."

"You knew this?"

"For a few years now."

"But—" Her gaze dropped to my shoes, then rose back to my face, like this fact might have been printed on me somewhere without her noticing. "He seems so responsible."

"He is."

"But that—how—I mean, doesn't it bother you, as a boy, hanging around him?"

"Now that we're eighteen, I believe we're *men*." I said the word with slight irony. It did still feel strange. "And no. It doesn't bother me."

"But what if people think *you're* like that?"

I swept my hand upward, gesturing to my heavy eyeliner and crazy hair. "Do I look like someone who cares what people think?"

She pressed her lips together. "You don't realize—you don't even consider what people will think of *us*, let alone you—"

"Nope, I don't." I grabbed my keys and sunglasses.

"And that time you . . . you *kissed* him, was that because—"

"We are not talking about that. Ever."

She reared back at my sharp tone, then something like respect entered her face. I realized, stunned, that she must think I hated having kissed him and wanted to pretend it never happened. In short, she assumed I was feeling exactly what she hoped I would feel.

Which was not even remotely the truth, but I wasn't about to correct the record. There was no talking about this with my mom and dad—whom I'd overheard bitching to friends of theirs the other week that gay parents were unhealthy for children to grow up with and were unraveling the fabric of marriage in our society, or some such bullshit.

I could unload a *lot* of outrage upon them. But they were about to fund four years of university, cutting down my student loans by a tremendous amount, and despite cringing every time they saw my clothing and hair and makeup, they had not in fact tossed me out of the house. I was lucky compared to plenty of kids. I was also smart enough to keep my belligerent mouth shut until I got clear of their influence, or at least their hearing.

"I'm going to work. See you." I bumped past her and left.

CHAPTER 14: TRUE COLORS

THE MORNING AFTER ARIEL'S PARTY, I WOKE
LATE, AND FOUND A VOICE MAIL FROM MY AGENT JERRY.

"Sinter, hi. Listen, bad news, the BBC closed with another actor for
that role we wanted. I just spoke with them. I'm so sorry. That's what
they're like sometimes, dangle you along for a while. It pisses me off . . .
anyway, I know your work visa needs sponsoring, so there's an opportunity in Cardiff I'm almost sure I could get you. It's with a soap they film
there. They always need more actors. It'd mean moving down there for
a while, but Cardiff's far less expensive than London, so that could be
good. Anyway, ring back and let's talk."

I fell back on my pillow, covering my eyes. My smile became a grin,
then I was laughing.

Sometimes it's pretty damn obvious when life is nudging you toward
something. And that something was not Cardiff.

I rolled out of bed and made tea, my mind whirling with chaotic
new plans.

A text buzzed my phone.

Fiona: Hi! Checking in to see how you're doing. Best party I've ever been
to, for sure ;)
Sinter: Ha yeah, glad I got to sleep in. Doing ok, you?
Fiona: Fine, we're all a bit slow today on filming as you can imagine. I
wanted to see if you could meet for lunch

I cringed and took a swallow of hot tea. Putting this off wouldn't make it any easier, though.

Sinter: Yeah of course, what time?

———

The sun shone in a clear, frigid sky, casting no warmth upon London whatsoever. The streets teemed with bag-laden holiday shoppers, looking stressed despite their bright scarves and hats. Fiona and I picked up sandwiches at a deli near the studio and wandered the sidewalks, eating while we talked about the film.

In Soho Square Garden, we sat on a bench facing the Tudor-style garden shed in the park's center. Leafless sycamore trees stood around us, and I looked up into their branches, realizing I missed being around tall trees. You can take the boy out of the Pacific Northwest, but . . .

"I think I know what you're going to say," Fiona said.

I dropped my gaze to her. "What?"

"That it isn't going to work."

"Oh. Why do you say that?"

She smiled sadly. "I could see it as soon as I looked at you afterward last night. You have no idea how expressive your face is, do you?"

I blinked, trying to close the shutters a bit on my expressive face. "Well . . . I mean, we should talk about it, yeah."

"I suppose I'm hoping you'll give it a chance. I was in love with Taylor before I met you, when I was writing him. Then you came along and brought him to life, and I fell in love in a new way."

Touched but discouraged, I settled my gaze on a statue across the park. "I don't think it's me you're in love with, though. I think these feelings are all wrapped up in the project."

"I do realize you're not Taylor. That you're an actor, that it's not 1981." She sounded wry. "I know all that. It's still you I find fascinating."

"But that's what you hired me to do, play this part so it would fascinate you. I don't think you'd go on finding me fascinating after the film's over."

"I might do. We don't know." When I didn't answer, only gazed off across the square, she finally added, "But clearly you don't feel the same."

I set my crumpled-up sandwich wrapper on the bench, then curled one hand inside the other on my lap. "I am definitely attracted to you. Those love scenes would have been a thousand times more fun if they'd been you instead of Ariel."

"But?"

"But my mind has been in a really strange place lately. I'm wanting things I didn't think I would want. And *not* wanting things I thought I would."

She slumped back against the bench. "Ah. You fancy someone else."

"Kind of. I mean, yes. And who I fancy, it's . . . my first kiss, actually. Sort of. I'm still best friends with him, and in touch with him a lot. I mentioned him to you once." I made sure to speak the pronoun clearly, no mumbling, no misinterpretation.

"Oh. I see." A resigned surprise entered her tone. "Yes, you did mention him."

"And I've never . . . well, *almost* never acted on thoughts like that, but I've been obsessed with it lately." I glanced at her, miserable for slamming her down this way. "I'm sorry. I shouldn't lay this on you."

"No, it's better to know the truth." She wasn't smiling anymore. The tip of her nose was turning red in the cold air. "Gosh. If you're gay, you're an even better actor than I thought."

"No, I'm . . . I'm bi. Bi-curious, in any case." I blinked at the empty bench facing ours. "I've never said that out loud before."

"Then I'm honored. And I'm sure you'll find plenty of willing men in this city."

"I'm sure, but . . . I feel like I ought to go back to the States. See Andy. Give it a try."

"You're really planning to leave?"

"Yeah. It's looking that way."

Our gazes met. She looked forlorn. "He must be charming indeed." She forced her mouth into a smile. "I *hope* he's charming."

At the fusion of that word with everything I knew about Andy, a warmth tumbled through me, relaxing my face into softness. My gaze went unfocused and drifted to a patch of grass, and I smiled as I remembered the album cover he had sent me in a message not long ago. "He's *Prince* Charming."

CHAPTER 15: ASK

WHEN DANIEL AND JULIE FOUND OUT I WAS STAYING IN LONDON BUT DIDN'T HAVE PLANS FOR CHRISTmas, they insisted I come to their flat, with not-taking-no-for-an-answer vehemence. Daniel's parents and other relatives would be dropping in and hanging around on the twenty-fifth, and I was required to join.

So I spent the afternoon backed up against the mantel in their flat with a mug of mulled wine, answering enthused questions from his mother, grandmother, cousin, and someone-in-law about what I did for a living and how exciting it sounded, and wasn't I sad not to be with my own family over the holidays?

I pretended it was indeed a shame, because that was better than bringing down the holiday mood with an answer like, "Eh, it's just as well. They sent me a check for Christmas and I sent them a gift certificate to a boring clothes store they like, and I'll talk to them later today but we won't have anything interesting to say."

All the while, I held onto the secret excitement of having come out to Andy, and the vague hope of feeling my way into a bisexual future with his help. He'd sent better gifts than my parents: a box of awesome assorted cookies and an array of temporary tattoos. "For your collection," he wrote in the enclosed tag. I'd wanted real tats for years, but had denied myself, since about a thousand people had warned me that ink made you less castable. Directors liked your body to be a clean slate. Thus Andy had been giving me temporary ones for years, and I stuck them on whenever possible.

I'd sent him a T-shirt, black with a London skyline, with boxy vintage Tetris pieces falling down to fill it in, plus a game cartridge of what the guy at the shop promised was the next big role-playing video game out of Japan. Andy adored video games, from classic era to newest releases.

We'd thanked each other in messages, though we hadn't had time to converse much, given I was being temporarily adopted by Daniel's family, and Andy had relatives visiting.

But my lease would be up on the first of January, less than a week away. If I wasn't going to Cardiff, I had to plan my return to the States, and soon.

On Boxing Day I was alone at last. Andy had said he was working, so I could probably depend on the usual hours he was awake and available for texting. In the afternoon, I took the Tube to Mansion House station and walked across the Thames on Millennium Bridge. Ever since my teen years, when my parents' house had begun to feel like a correctional facility, I'd been in the habit of going for walks whenever I felt nervous. The open air and the reminder that other people led other lives in these other buildings tended to soothe me.

Andy likely wouldn't be awake for another hour or so, but I leaned on the embankment railing and sent him a message for when he woke up.

Sinter: So . . . I didn't get the BBC role, and the easiest thing to do next is to move back to the States. I'm considering looking for work in Seattle. If I do, can I stay with you awhile? I'll pay rent of course. And we can see how things go, with new interests and such ;)

My stomach was fluttering, my fingers tingling. Cold wind blew into my face, smelling of river water and wet stone. The setting sun touched the tips of the buildings across from me, staining them orange. Their reflections rippled in the water.

Too jumpy with adrenaline to hold still, I walked. I liked this part of the river because Shakespeare's Globe Theatre was there, and I circled its exterior twice, thinking wistfully about how I'd never gotten to act on its stage yet. Ah well. Some other year. I turned my back on the Globe and kept walking.

At Southwark Bridge, I climbed the steps and paced out to midspan, and stared at the twin tips of Tower Bridge, far downriver. Traffic rumbled past behind me.

He'd be awake any minute. I looked at my phone for the hundredth time and nearly dropped it in the river when I saw he had answered.

Andy: Oh my god yes! Please come to Seattle!!! Yes yes yes

I sagged my weight against the railing, reading the words again and again. The sunset shone in golden light. Church bells rang down the river, the sound of celebration.

Yes yes yes.

The casting dazzles had nothing on this feeling.

Sinter: Whew, thank you. Awesome

Andy: This is the best news! I bet you'll find theater work here before long

Sinter: Hope so, I was looking it up and it seems promising

Andy: As for those new interests, I'm definitely up for it, or we can find you someone else on Capitol Hill if you prefer. Happy to help either way ;)

Sinter: I tend to prefer a trusted friend for these jobs. So if you really do want to help . . .

Andy: Ummm YES please. Get your ass on that plane already

Grinning, I swung away from the railing and wandered back toward the north bank.

Sinter: Much obliged then :)

Andy: Wow this is the most interesting conversation I've had before breakfast in a long time
Sinter: Haha, same
Andy: Hey, send me a selfie right now. I just want to see your face. I'll send one too

I had reached the Thames embankment, and the sky still held enough light to take pictures without a flash. Feeling like a dork (but a happy dork), I ignored the judgey glances of passersby and snapped a few photos of myself with river and south bank in the background. I deemed one picture acceptable enough: the wind was blowing my streaky hair into my eyes a little, but my smile looked natural, and if my plaid wool scarf stuffed into my zipped-up leather jacket wasn't exactly sexy-photo material, it at least looked a tiny bit stylish.

While I sent it over, Andy's selfie came in. With his hair all rumpled, he was lying on his stomach in bed in what looked like the warm glow of a lamp, in a long-sleeved white T-shirt with a frayed collar, his glasses on. He was smiling self-consciously and beautifully, temple resting on his hand, morning stubble shading his jaw. So familiar, yet exciting in an entirely new way.

Andy: Ugh you look like a gorgeous model, and I'm this disheveled lump
Sinter: Actually I was thinking you look cute and warm and you're in bed and I really want to crawl in there with you
Andy: Jesus, why couldn't you have sent me texts like this in high school? :P
Sinter: Totally should have. Sorry. :)
Andy: Forgiven. I've got to get ready for work, but we will talk later of course
Sinter: Sounds good. And thank you. Just seriously, thank you so much
Andy: Don't thank me till you've tried it and liked it ;)

CHAPTER 16: IF YOU LEAVE

Sinter: Hi Fiona - I'm thinking of leaving on the 1st when my lease is up.
But would that be ok with the schedule? Am I needed after this week?
Fiona: Goodness, that is soon. Well . . . no, after the dubbing tomorrow
you're clear. There might be media interviews we'd like you to do, but not
till spring. And you can probably do those from another city as long as
they have a TV studio who'll work with us.
Sinter: Seattle probably does, but yeah, let me know, I'll help
Fiona: Then it is Seattle? You're off to see Andy?
Sinter: Yeah, I'll be staying with him at first. We'll see how it goes
Fiona: I wish you luck. I'll see you tomorrow so I won't say any dramatic
goodbyes yet
Sinter: See you tomorrow, and thank you for everything. And . . . I'm
sorry, really

To which she didn't answer.

I emailed my landlord to inform him of my intent to vacate by January
1. He grumbled about short notice and pushed me to let him show people
the flat during the next few days so he could find a new tenant. I gave him
permission. I had enough errands to do to keep me out of the place.

I bought a one-way plane ticket from Heathrow to Sea-Tac for New
Year's Day—excruciatingly expensive since it was less than a week away,
but my parents' Christmas check covered half of it. I emailed the flight
confirmation to Andy. He responded:

Woohoo!! I even have the 1st off, so I can pick you up at the airport if you like.

So in a week, I would be in Seattle. With him.

Free-fall feeling of panic. What was I *doing*? Abandoning the UK and a blossoming acting career, all because of sex? I'd informed Jerry, my London agent, of my move, and he expressed regret and told me I had a bright future there if I kept at it, and wouldn't I at least consider coming back soon? He understood the work visa was a pain in the arse to maintain, but . . .

I promised I would keep the option open. In fact, if this Seattle expedition fell flat, I might come back sooner rather than later. But it was too late to bail. I'd said I was doing it, I'd bought the ticket, and anyway, I could still have an acting career in the US.

I motored onward, covering my panic by keeping busy with packing and scrubbing my flat.

That evening as I sorted my possessions into heaps and boxes, Andy messaged me.

Andy: Lunch break finally. Whew, busy day

Sinter: Is work insane?

Andy: Yeah, project with impossible deadline. Boring too. Spreadsheet software, blah

Sinter: When are you going to get into the games department where you belong?

Andy: I keep begging, no one's letting me, SIGH. I should've held out for a job with a proper game company

Andy: However this awesome guy asked if we could hang out soon, so life's not too bad

Sinter: Really, who?

Andy: :P

Sinter: ;)

We chatted for the rest of his lunch break, mainly about our dream jobs (game designing for him, longer-term acting roles with interesting challenges in them for me), with only a sprinkling of flirtation. Still, somehow by the end of it, I no longer felt *completely* insane to be jumping an ocean just to be closer to my hot best friend.

A cockroach scuttled across the kitchen floor, five feet away from me. I seized a Terry Pratchett book and chucked it. It missed; the roach escaped through the crack in the wall.

Yeah. I could leave. That'd be fine.

———

The next day, I attended my session at the studio, sitting with headphones on, watching the rough cut of my scenes and speaking in sync with them.

Fiona directed from the audio booth where she sat with the engineers, her voice clicking into my headphones every so often, neutral and controlled. Though we could see each other through the glass, our eyes rarely met.

Sebastian was in that day too, to dub his lines, and he cast Fiona and me a number of suspicious glances.

It only took a couple of hours to complete our lines. Afterward, the three of us walked down the studio corridor together, chatting about sound quality.

In the lobby, Fiona and I slowed to a stop.

"So you're off," she said.

Sebastian, strolling ahead, paused and turned halfway, listening shamelessly.

I nodded. "I'll come back to visit, though. Can never stay away from the UK for long."

Fiona looked down, hugging her bundle of documents. Sebastian slipped out of the building. The glass door swung shut behind him. No one else was around except the receptionist, talking in a professional undertone on the phone.

"Well," Fiona said. "The bulldog in me is glad I got you when I wanted you, but devastated I couldn't keep my teeth sunk in you."

"I let it go too far. It's my fault. And I still bet you would've gotten bored of me before long."

"Hard to say." Her dark hair was loose, its ends flipping up into messy spikes, the way she'd looked when I first met her in the pub. It tweaked at my heart. She arranged her expression into one of calm. "I've decided I don't want any dramatic goodbyes at all, in fact. And I get what I want."

"You're the bulldog," I agreed.

She unwrapped a slender hand from her bundle of stuff and extended it to me.

"Aw, come on." I ignored the hand and hugged her.

Though she didn't put her arms around me, she lowered her chin, leaned her head against my chest, and sighed. I kissed the top of her head.

We stepped apart. "Let me know how it goes," she said, her voice strained. Tears gleamed in her eyes.

I nodded, feeling like an asshole.

Fiona walked back toward the studio, disappearing down the corridor.

Out on the pavement, Sebastian leaned his back against the building, knee bent and one foot on the wall. When I came out, he swung into step beside me, hands in the pockets of his long coat.

"So you're abandoning her, you bastard." He sounded conversational.

"I'm . . . leaving, yes. I don't think it's going to work out, and I don't want to hurt her."

"Any more than you already have."

"Any more than I already have," I said in defeat.

"Huh." He spoke it as a derogatory snort. "She says you're off to America?"

"Yeah. Seattle."

"Got some blonde Yank Barbie doll over there, do you?"

"Nope, got a good-looking guy." I wasn't sure why I told him that. It wasn't in the spirit of honest confession. It was more like I wanted to provoke him into saying something derisive about gay people, so I'd finally have an excuse to tell him to fuck off.

"A guy? Like, you're off to shag a guy?" He sounded gobsmacked.

"I'm hoping."

"Hang on, you're gay?"

"Bi, actually." We were still walking down the street. My blood sizzled with the anticipation of getting into a public shouting match any second, among all these strangers.

I almost fell over when he bopped his elbow against mine and said, "Well, why didn't you ever say so? If I'd known you were all conflicted over some bloke, I might not have been such a ballbag."

I slowed way down and stared at him.

"I'm trans," he added. "Didn't you know?"

I looked at him from head to toe as if I'd never seen him before. "No," I finally spluttered.

"Almost seven years post-op." He whapped my elbow again. "Angst over identity and coming out? Been there. I mean, would've preferred you hadn't involved Fiona, but even so."

"I wish I hadn't, too." I shot him another glance as we walked, trying to imagine the strong bones, swagger, and toothy punk-guy grin on a young female form. Almost inconceivable.

"Surprised Fiona didn't tell you about me," he went on. "But she's not the sort to out others. Besides, suppose it doesn't come up in conversation much."

"No. Suppose not." We reached a corner. I stopped and tilted my head toward the cross street. "Well, uh. My Tube station. Maybe I'll see you next time I'm back in town." I offered a handshake.

He seized my hand, hauled me in, and kissed me on each cheek. "Go nail that bloke, mate."

"Could you not shout it?" Still, I smiled. "Be good to Fiona."

"That I always shall." With a broad-handed wave, he swung away and strolled across the street.

———

Andy: Lol! Well that's kind of awesome

Sinter: Made me feel less crappy than the talk with Fiona at least

Andy: Think she'll be ok?

Sinter: I expect so. No one has ever had much trouble getting over me

Andy: Present company excepted ;)

Sinter: Haha sure, if you say so

Andy: So I wanted to ask . . . there's been nothing with other guys all this time? Not even anonymous cybersex?

Sinter: Nah felt creeped out by the idea. In person . . . ha, well nothing except the one time I kissed Daniel

Andy: Oh no way, when??

Sinter: We were 19, out drinking. I was infatuated with his accent or something. So I kissed him

Andy: Was he nice about it?

Sinter: Very. We both laughed then pretended it never happened

Andy: Ah, modern cosmopolitan straight boys. They're sweet. Are you going to come out to him and Julie too?

Sinter: Not yet I don't think. It was weird enough coming out to Sebastian. Which I didn't exactly mean to do. Think I'll put off the next one ;)

Andy: Makes sense. Your call

Andy: Well hey, whatever you do or don't feel like doing when you're here, it's cool with me. Just wanted to say that. It's going to be really great to see you regardless

Sinter: Thank you. You too

CHAPTER 17: TO THE SKY

NEW YEAR'S EVE PASSED IN A CACOPHONY OF FIREWORKS I MOSTLY IGNORED WHILE PACKING MY STUFF. In the morning, I handed over the key to my landlord, and two hours later was getting waved through the gate at Heathrow.

If anything is less sexy than moving, it's airports and economy-class flights. First class might have its attractive features; I wouldn't know. But not this: cramming my long legs into insufficient space, fiddling with the blast of air above my head, wedging myself into a seat far too close to strangers.

The plane took off. As it banked, dipping my stomach with it, I looked across two other passengers at the window to watch London recede. It added grief to my big vat of troublesome emotions. I *loved* the UK. Why was I leaving?

I got out my phone and re-read my long scroll of messages from Andy to remind myself why. But in the too-bright air, assailed by the smell of airplane cabin and the whine of engines, none of our flirtatious exchanges looked hot. Only silly.

I plugged in earbuds and dug into my music. The right songs would fix me if anything would. And there: "To the Sky" by the Cure was still on my phone after all these years. What better tune to choose while ascending into the atmosphere?

The dreamy guitar and synth of the opening lifted me out of my surroundings and took me back to the day Andy and I parted.

Now the song comforted me rather than crumbling me into desolation. We'd finally get to undo that miserable day. We'd meet after a long separation, hug, climb into his car, and drive off together—as if playing that day in reverse, turning a sad ending into a happy one.

The plane reached cruising altitude. Shuffle-play picked one song for me after another. I read Terry Pratchett for a while, but mainly my thoughts drifted. You have too much time to think on a nine-hour flight.

I thought of Fiona and our last text exchange that morning.

Sinter: I'm off to Heathrow. Just wanted to say goodbye, and thank you again for understanding, for the role, for everything. I'll be in touch

Fiona: Thank you as well. I will miss you, lovely boy.

Sinter: I'll miss you too

We left it at that. My declaration sounded inadequate compared to hers, but then, I was the one leaving, the one saying we weren't going to work. She'd probably be hurt for a while, and it was just as well I was putting an ocean and the majority of North America between us.

I thought of my parents too. I'd waited until practically the last minute, in line to board the plane, to email them. I didn't want them to have time to say anything to aggravate my current stress levels.

Hi guys,

Just letting you know I'm coming back to the Northwest. I'm flying to Seattle today and will stay there awhile. I'll let you know my plans when I have a better idea what they are. Can still be reached at this email and my cell in the meantime.

Cheers,

S

I felt like a coward for not mentioning Andy. I *would* tell them I was staying with him. But at this point, the less fodder for disapproving remarks and unwanted advice, the better.

And of course mainly I thought, with stomach-curdling anxiety, about what I might be embarking upon with Andy in the next few days.

I thought all the possible thoughts:

It would be hot and kinky.

It would be a friendship-ending disaster.

It would get nowhere because I'd lose my nerve before even starting.

It would be so awkward it would give me a whole new assortment of mental and social issues.

It would never happen, because my plane would crash on the way there, and my grieving friends would out me posthumously to my parents and everyone else.

It would be fantastic and make me want nothing else my whole life, and what the hell would I do then?

By the time the pilot announced we were beginning our descent into Sea-Tac, everything in me hurt. I hadn't eaten or drunk enough and felt weak. I had only gotten up for the bathroom once and had been sitting too long. The stiffness in my back had spread to become an ache in my neck, shoulders, and head.

It was still daylight, since we'd followed the sun on our westward flight. The kid in our window seat was freaking out in excitement, telling his mum he could see the Space Needle. Now that we were almost down, we passengers were warming up to each other, and when I smiled at the kid, his mother smiled at me too and remarked, "Are you from Seattle?" She and her son were English, I'd gathered from their accents.

"Close," I said. "Oregon. But I have friends here."

"It's my first time in America," the boy told me, bouncing in his seat.

"Right on. Welcome."

"Welcome home, for you," his mum said to me.

Home. This wasn't strictly home, but then, wasn't the space surrounding Andy more like home to me than the house where my parents lived?

I looked across at the window as the plane dipped its wing. The skyscrapers of downtown Seattle rose into view, their lights coming on in the dusk, tucked in all around by blue water and dark forests. The snow-capped Cascades rambled along the horizon under a layer of high gray clouds, Mount Rainier looming biggest of all.

We sank low enough to see individual cars crawling along the interstate. One of those drivers might be Andy, coming to pick me up. I felt queasy and faced forward again.

Should I kiss him in greeting? A hug was standard airport reunion procedure—basically nothing special. I didn't know if he expected anything more yet, but one kiss wouldn't hurt, and might prove I hadn't chickened out in case he doubted me.

I should have kissed him the day he left for college. It seemed obvious. So why not go ahead and do it to make up for lost time?

We landed and disembarked. I bought a Moroccan mint tea at a Starbucks in the concourse, hoping the mint would calm my stomach. But the tea was about four thousand degrees, so mainly it only burned my mouth, and after the first swallow, I had to leave it alone to let it cool off.

At baggage claim I texted Andy.

Sinter: Arrived! Picking up my luggage, then I'll be out
Andy: Sweet! Come to the arrivals curb and look for Celery

Celery was his green Volvo, the same one he'd driven away from me that day before college. I felt clammy all over.

I found my luggage and hauled it away. In the men's room, I splashed cold water on my face and rinsed my mouth. From my checked bag, I dug out my leathery-scented deodorant, which Andy once said smelled good on me. I wormed it up under my sweaty T-shirt and sprayed each armpit, then packed it away.

Walking toward the arrivals curb with a heavy bag hanging from each shoulder and my paper cup of tea in hand, I seriously thought I might puke, I was so nervous. I'd felt like this before the curtain rose for plays, of course, but this was scarier. This was real life, unscripted. If it went badly, if he didn't want me after all, if I screwed up everything between us . . . that mattered so much I couldn't even think about it.

I stepped outside. Cold air washed around me. It smelled like traffic and wet asphalt, but it was fresh and helped calm me down. The Sea-Tac arrivals curb was a madhouse of cars creeping in and darting out, five lanes of automotive tangle lit with bright overhead bulbs.

My phone buzzed, and I set down a bag to get it out and look at the text.

Andy: I'm down at the front end, by the taxi sign

I threaded through other travelers, scanning the sea of idling cars, until—there.

Over the celery-green top of the Volvo, two lanes from the curb, Andy's head popped up, and he waved, grinning.

A smile broke the mask of my face. I jogged between waiting cars, set my luggage and tea on the asphalt next to Celery's back tire, and rose again. Andy stood before me, beaming, in fleece jacket and jeans and sneakers, six inches shorter than me, as ever.

"Hey!"

We said it simultaneously. Then we leaped at each other and tangled up in a hug, laughing.

CHAPTER 18: REUNION

THE SOUND OF HIS VOICE SOOTHED ME LIKE
A FAVORITE SONG, EVEN JUST IN LAUGHTER AND IN THE
obligatory "Good to see you!" He smelled unbelievably good—like himself
and the fragrance he'd worn for years, but I hadn't been near him in so long
I'd forgotten how comforting it could be when someone smelled right.

I was only nervous because we'd been apart. Now that we were together, I'd be okay. Or such was my out-of-nowhere thought.

"Good to see you too," I said, and stepped back so he could open
the trunk.

Once we'd begun loading up my bags and complaining about airports, I realized the moment for a kiss had passed. I should have planted
one on him during the hug. But other drivers and travelers were *every-
where.* I hadn't reckoned on the chaos of the arrivals curb. Did I really
want to kiss him for the first time in ten years with a bunch of harassed
strangers glaring at us and waiting to move their car into his spot?

Not feeling queasy anymore would have to be victory enough. We
climbed into the Volvo and joined the flow of traffic oozing out of the
airport.

We chatted, our remarks overlapping each other's like they usually
did, like this was any other occasion hanging out together. We discussed
the flight, Celery's maintenance issues, Seattle traffic, his job, the Bleach-
ers song we both liked that was playing on the radio.

At a curve in the freeway, Seattle's skyline sparkled into view, shooting me full of the warm, excited feeling I always got when entering a city

I liked.

I'd been there before, of course. Most people who grew up in the Portland area had. And when Andy and Mitchell had moved up, I'd visited once. I'd met them at a restaurant for lunch, stayed a few hours, then returned to Portland since I was acting in a show that night. So I had never been to their apartment on Capitol Hill, where Andy was taking me.

We took an exit off the interstate in the center of the city. Overpasses and skyscrapers towered above us.

"That's my building." Andy nodded toward a handsome old brick structure fitted onto a triangular block. "Now comes the fun part: hunting the elusive parking spot."

We circled a few blocks, Andy prowling for a spot and me checking out the neighborhood and its pedestrians. The people looked young and counter-culture: a lot of piercings and emo- or hippie-styled hair. Capitol Hill was Seattle's LGBTQ neighborhood, and the occasional pride flag sticker decorated a bumper or a window. I also spotted one young man kissing another before he got into a car at the curb. My gaze lingered on them. Would that be me if I ever got brave enough?

Andy noticed them too, but took a more practical interpretation: "Oh hey, is he leaving? I'm totally stalking that spot."

We snagged the parking spot. In the cold drizzle, we each took one of my bags from the trunk and walked the two blocks to his building. While we talked about the ridiculous parking situation in the area, I shot glances at the mist of rain gathering on his hair and glasses, and wished I had the nerve to kiss him and feel the wet chill between our lips.

He took me to his apartment on the fourth floor, turned on a light, and apologized for the weird blank spaces against some of the walls. "It's where Peyton's stuff was till yesterday. Then where Mitchell's was before that." He slid my luggage down next to a bookcase. "Now it's where yours goes."

I wandered to the window, drawn by the dazzle of city lights through the slats of the blinds. "Wow, that *is* a nice view."

He came up beside me, tapping a colorful paper against his hand. "You can even see the Olympic Mountains when it's clear. And a teeny bit of the bay." He handed the paper to me. "Dinner idea. This place is good for takeout. I love the tacos; they're not greasy. No sour cream."

He didn't mind sour cream, but he'd remembered I hated it. Plus he remembered my saying, months earlier, that good Mexican food was hard to find in the UK and that I missed it. I took his word for it and chose tacos, and handed the menu back to him. "Maybe I'll take a shower first."

"Cool. You do that, and I'll get food. Your room's down here."

He showed me into the room that had, until the other day, been Peyton's, and an office before that. It was at the opposite end of the apartment from his bedroom, with (tiny) bathroom, (also tiny) kitchen, and (not terribly big) living room in between. It had a futon bed that folded up into a sofa, a city view from the windows, and the usual accoutrements of a guest room: novels and textbooks from college filling the shelves; a plain desk with a weird lamp on it, this one in the shape of an orange mushroom; and spare sheets and towels taking up half of the little closet.

"It's, like, ten times nicer than my flat in London," I said in honesty.

He grinned. "Get settled in. I'll be back in half an hour."

The shower sorted me out, or at least mostly. I still felt tired, but nothing in me hurt anymore. I was also starving, and the artisan West Coast tacos Andy brought back were every bit as fabulous as promised: soft corn tortillas filled with marinated chicken and shredded vegetables with a lime-jalapeño dressing.

"Who knew cabbage could actually be good?" I said, eating up the last shred as we sat on his sofa, plates on our laps, Comedy Central on TV.

"Right?" he said. "I knew you'd like them."

And even with taco sauce on my fingers and jalapeño setting my mouth on fire, I wanted to put my plate down and slide over and kiss him. But I still didn't.

When I yawned for about the eighteenth time, Andy chuckled. "It's, what, four a.m. in your time zone?"

"Something like that."

"Go to bed, dude."

A sound plan. But as I finished brushing my teeth, I knew I couldn't put it off another minute, let alone another day.

I found him in the kitchen, slotting our plates into the dishwasher.

"Hey," he said. "All good? Need anything?"

"All good. Just . . . " I caught him by the pocket of his sweatshirt and drew us together. "Thanks for putting me up." I leaned down, slowly enough that he could dodge if he wanted, and kissed him on the lips.

He didn't dodge. He kissed me back, a brief peck. Then he leaned in and kissed me again. He slid his hands around my waist. With our mouths still locked, I let go of his hoodie and lifted my hands to bracket his face. I shut my eyes. My thumbs traced the stubble on his jaw. His lips felt so soft, his arms and body strong and solid. Absolutely a man I was kissing, clearly so, even with my eyes closed and my mind jet-lagged. And the pleasure of it sped through my veins and lit up every part of me on its way by.

We pulled apart. I felt out of breath. He looked flushed, and stared at my mouth before blinking and finding my eyes again.

"Yeah, I think this is going to work just fine," he said.

"Same." I slid my hands down his chest before dropping them.

He smiled. "Now go to bed before I jump you right here."

———

I slept awhile, then found myself wide awake at three a.m., thanks to jet lag. Light shone around the edges of the blinds in the guest room. I rolled over on the futon and pulled them aside to peek out. The city glowed in all colors, a thousand streetlights and windows and signs. Red bulbs blinked on the tops of skyscrapers and the Space Needle. I-5 rumbled continuously at the base of the hill.

It was a different experience from being in the middle of London. London was bright and tightly packed too, but its buildings and hills were lower; the city sprawled outward rather than piling itself into a high-rising knot like this. Seattle was also far newer, which made it look shiny and crisp.

Since I was awake, I checked email on my phone. I deleted spam and advertisements, and finally found replies from my parents. Dad answered first, a couple of paragraphs I skimmed rather than read. *Your move seems sudden, but Seattle's a good job market right now . . . talk to an employment agency; they'll get you into a steady office job . . . housing is expensive, so don't waste money; look for a good deal . . . your car is still here, so you should come get it now that you're back in the Northwest.*

No congratulations, no "love" in the signature. Just "Dad."

Mom answered too: *Where are you staying? And let us know when you want to get the car so we can see you!*

I turned off the phone without responding. I'd answer later and tell them I was staying with Andy, which wouldn't be their favorite email of the day. Still, my parents wanted to see me. That made me smile. Maybe I did have a home to go back to like normal people.

Sure, catching a bus down to Oregon, visiting them, and driving my car back would be a hassle. Plus I had to find a job—then another when that role ended, and another, and another, like every actor. I had to familiarize myself with Seattle and probably find my own place to live, at least after this month. In short, I had plenty of reasons to feel stressed.

Nonetheless, contentment sprawled through me instead. I could guess why.

I stretched my arms up as high as they'd go. With Andy, I still had several frontiers to explore and possibly fail at—or, at the other extreme, a whole new side of myself to drag out of the closet and into the light. But that kiss had been amazing, an essentially perfect kiss, and a perfect kiss can make you feel like the rest of life is about to fall effortlessly into place.

I pulled the string to lift the blinds and sat on the futon with my knees drawn up, admiring the bright city in the night.

CHAPTER 19: LET'S GO TO BED

IN THE MORNING, ANDY GAVE ME A SET OF SPARE KEYS TO THE APARTMENT AND TOOK OFF TO WORK, though not before a lingering moment from both of us, in which we were obviously tempted to kiss goodbye. Instead we just grinned like idiots, then he left.

To occupy myself till evening, I explored Capitol Hill, bookmarked audition notices, shaped up my resume, and emailed my parents: *I'm staying with Andy. He lives here, and I can save money by splitting rent.* I figured they'd be paralyzed into silence between the two tempting options of saving money and getting me away from my gay friend. Indeed, they didn't answer all day.

After Andy came home, we went out for Thai food. We split the check—like friends, not dates—but took mints from the tray and popped them into our mouths on the walk home with studied casualness and no eye contact.

At the apartment, I left my shoes and jacket by the door and plunked myself down in the center of the sofa, leaving exactly enough room for anyone who might want to make out with me.

Andy switched on a lamp beside the TV and sauntered closer. "Can I just say, you've gotten way better at kissing since you were fifteen."

I folded my hands behind my head. "Yeah, thanks, I'm a professional now, you know."

He laughed. Our gazes met, and I kept mine locked onto his until he took the hint and sat next to me, knocking against my elbow familiarly.

I let my arm drop around his shoulders.

"Ah, classic move," he teased. He wriggled up against me, then lifted his face. His voice dropped into the intimate range. "Did you want to do it again?"

My heart beat fast. I nodded.

I leaned in and kissed him. Our lips sank into the same perfect fit they had found the night before. My arm curled closer around his shoulders. I enjoyed it for several seconds, then paused to ask, "So wait, you've been remembering it as a terrible kiss? When we were fifteen?"

"I never said 'terrible.' I just said you've improved." He poked his finger into a frayed spot on my T-shirt. "I've always been glad I got to kiss you then. Even though it ended the way it did."

"Me too."

We hadn't talked about the immediate aftermath in the past, other than him asking at our locker the next morning if I'd gotten in trouble. I'd wanted to know more, but had always felt too awkward to bring it up. Now, at last, I could.

"Were you freaking out that day when you left?" I asked. "After they caught us?"

He lowered his lashes with a smile. "I was shaking so hard I thought I was having some kind of seizure. I was sure they were going to tell my parents. This was it; I was getting outed. Everyone was going to hear, and by school the next day, the whole world would know. But you didn't tell." He suffused the last four words with wonder.

"Even if I'd told them, they still would've grounded me for a month. Might as well just get one of us in trouble instead of both of us."

"Still. You win all the best-friend awards." He heaved a sigh. "I've always wondered what would've happened if they hadn't come home when they did. My greatest regret. Also my fantasy scenario for, like, years there."

So he *had* imagined it. "Really. Show me what you would've done.

If they hadn't come home."

He laughed, low and suggestive, as if to say *You're not ready for that.* But he took off his glasses, set them on the coffee table, and wriggled back into my embrace. "Well, for starters . . . "

He tilted his head and kissed me, a full open-mouth snog, shoving his hand up to bury it in my hair. I surrendered, closing my eyes. We breathed, tasted, sank into each other.

Finally, I was doing this: breaking past my single-kiss record and clocking minutes on end of making out with another guy. In the past, trying a move I'd been fantasizing about hadn't always lived up to my hopes, but on this lucky occasion it actually surpassed them. Though we stayed seated upright and kept our clothes on, my hormones were fizzing and sparking happily.

The feel and taste of him quickened my breath and was making my hands do hungry things like dive into his hair, or pull aside his collar so I could suck on his neck. He apparently didn't mind one bit, given he was doing the same things back to me.

After a while, I touched the newly minted love bite above his collarbone. "Left a mark. Sorry."

"Hmm. Revenge." He latched his mouth onto the side of my neck.

Shivers ran through me. I closed my eyes and ran my hand into his messed-up hair.

"I'm no expert," he murmured against my skin, "but this seems a little more than 'bi-curious.'"

"I think you're right. Let's upgrade to plain old 'bi.'"

He sat up and poked my nose with his finger. "Click. Upgrade installing."

"Oh my God, you are such a geek." Grinning, I snared his mouth in another kiss.

"So how different is it really?" he managed, between kisses. "From making out with a woman."

"Only the ways I expected." I palmed his jaw. "I can feel some stubble." I trailed my hand across his chest, flat except for the nipple I could feel through his button-down shirt. "No boobs. That kind of thing."

"Mm, but some of us do enjoy having our nipples played with."

"Yeah?" I returned my fingers to circle the spot, feeling it harden. "So do some women. See, not that different."

He groaned as I touched him, which of course made me keep doing it. I slid my tongue into his mouth.

"And you taste like a guy," I said against his lips. "Not sure how, exactly. But it's good. Either way is good."

"'Either way is good.' Sounds bisexual, all right." We kept snogging and nipple-stroking a minute or two more. Then I pounced—lazily and slowly, but nonetheless a pounce. He landed on his back on the sofa, and I shifted into alignment on top of him.

I pressed my hips down. "You feel different in this position too."

"Yeah?" He gave a slight lift of his pelvis in answer. "Pretty strange?"

"Pretty *hot*."

"Mm. Agreed." He wrapped his legs around me and relaxed.

I let my head sink to his shoulder. We lay twined together, eyes shut.

"Still jet-lagged?" he said.

"Yeah. Tired. Plus, the *hills* around here, oh my God."

"Walking in Seattle is an instant gym membership." His fingertips ran up and down my vertebrae. "Anyway. I definitely don't want to freak you out, so a slow pace is probably good if you want to pause for the night. Or . . . whenever you've had enough, that's cool too. I'm your friend. That doesn't change."

I would have taken it as a lack of interest except for how affectionately he was embracing me, and how I could feel physical evidence that he wouldn't mind continuing. He was only giving me an easy out, considerate as ever.

Part of me ached to keep at it. But it was also true that jet lag had its talons deep in me, and that taking it slow was the smart option. There were still lots of steps I could completely screw up, especially when dazed with jet lag, which might test the patience of my remarkably accommodating best friend.

"Guess we should pause," I said. "But I wouldn't mind picking up again tomorrow night."

He gave my earlobe a bite. "I'll be right here. Hopefully in this same position."

I wedged my face into the hollow between his neck and the couch cushions. Funny how I was already so comfortable with him. On top of him, even.

But of course I was comfortable. He was Andy.

"Humans are weird," I mumbled.

"Hmm?"

"That it's possible to feel lust and sleepiness at the same time."

He chuckled, still holding me as if he didn't mind being crushed beneath me. "Yep. We can even have sex in our sleep."

"Which is what you'll be dealing with if I stay here much longer."

He broke into full laughter, shaking me.

I kissed his neck. Then I groaned in complaint. "Argh. I have to find a job."

"You will. You just got here." He stroked my back.

My fingers found his shirt's hem, at our waists, and curled beneath it, taking refuge against his warm skin. "But at least I'm finally doing this," I said into his shoulder.

His arms and legs tightened around me, and he responded with a sigh that could only be interpreted as bliss.

———

When I said I had to find a job, I actually meant jobs, plural. Not only sequentially, one acting gig after another, but a non-acting job at the same time, to help pay the bills. The film in London had been un-usual in giving me both full-time work and high wages; most acting roles were part-time and low pay. Even for the couple of years I'd belonged to a theater troupe in Portland, I'd worked other jobs on the side: paint-ing houses, moving furniture, waiting tables, washing dishes, serving espresso, answering phones as an office temp. The office jobs usually paid best, but also sucked the life out of my soul the worst. I preferred even the food-service industry to those.

So in addition to making a list of auditions to attend and sending emails of introduction to theaters and talent agencies, I looked up nearby businesses seeking part-time help and spent hours filling out online ap-plications.

I told Andy about my tedious day as we trekked up a steep sidewalk toward Broadway for dinner.

"I could see getting a barista job within the month, at least," I said. "But a theater part, without knowing anyone here yet in the industry . . . I'm probably back to the usual stats of getting turned down for twenty auditions before I hit lucky with one."

"But have you mentioned you were just in a movie in London? That should get their attention."

"Yeah, it's on my resume, but even people who've won Tonys or Em-mys can still have trouble landing their next role. It's brutal." A city bus thundered past, reminding me of additional issues. "Also I need to figure out the bus system."

"Might just want to bring your car up."

"Really? Traffic's got to be at least as bad as it is in Portland."

"Oh, it's worse!" he said brightly. "But the buses are stuck in it too, and we still don't have enough light rail, so."

"Your commute doesn't seem too bad."

"I'm lucky. I work in South Lake Union; it's only fifteen minutes away. If I worked at Microsoft, I'd be spending two hours a day crawling across Lake Washington. Anyway, I'll drive you to Portland to pick up your car if you want. We could do it Saturday."

"My parents want to see me while I'm there. Sure you want to come?"

"Sure. I mean, give me fair warning if you plan to make out with me in front of them or anything."

I laughed, panicked. "God, can you imagine?"

After that high-school kiss, my parents had begun receiving Andy with coolness whenever he visited our house, and after he came out, their attitude dropped into a solid freeze when he was around—they said little, and stayed near but not too near, as if chaperoning us. But that had only been tested on a few visits over the years, since we had both started college around then, and thus usually met in other places to hang out. Maybe now, since we had both grown up, my parents' approach would have matured too. It wasn't inconceivable. Or at least, I was in a good enough mood to think so.

After finishing our sushi, we walked back down the hill. The January night was cold with a fog setting in, smearing the city lights into an indistinct glow. Though we talked about restaurants and coworkers and other ordinary things, my blood raced in anticipation of what we would do at the apartment.

When we shut the door, I caught him by the hips and pulled him close.

He grinned. "Was there something you wanted?"

I unzipped his coat, folded aside his shirt collar to find the hickey on his neck, and stroked it. "I have ideas."

"Such as?" He unwound my scarf.

I swallowed, my pulse pounding. "Let's lie down and warm up. Maybe in bed this time."

He paused to look at me with interest in his eyes, but waited for me to elaborate.

"I mean," I added, "just to get comfortable. Then we can see where it goes."

His face bloomed back into a smile. "Okay. Let's." He tilted his head in the direction of his room, inviting me in.

Thing is, once you're under the blankets with someone in a king-sized bed, kissing and rolling around together, it's not such a big deal to start shedding clothes. Going shirtless, for example, seemed a modest step, nothing I hadn't done in screen tests. So I was unprepared for how deeply it aroused me: skin against skin, the hot scent of him, nipples uncovered to play with—and God, the way he groaned when I licked them.

It was only the considerate thing to do to get rid of sharp objects like belts.

"I'm going to get multiple lacerations from that thing," Andy said, laughing, as he watched me drag my studded belt out of its loops and flick it to the floor.

Then our jeans became uncomfortable after a certain amount of grinding, so we removed those too. In only our underwear, we kissed and tangled, rumpling the sheets into a chaotic mountain range.

I ached to touch everything on him. His teasing touches had erased nearly all my remaining inhibitions. I would have whined and argued if he'd said again, "So let's stop for tonight." (I didn't whine at most lovers, but I could do that kind of thing to my best friend.)

So if I really didn't want to stop . . .

I slid a hand down, straight inside his underwear. Touching everything. A handful of flesh, new, warm, sweaty, fascinating. He drew a quick breath, and I stilled, suddenly doubting. "Okay?" I asked.

In answer he only smiled and groped me right back. First outside the shorts. Then, a few seconds later, inside.

We shoved our underwear off and let both pairs get lost in the sheets. If any step was going to feel awkward and pull me out of the moment, it should have been this. Yet it didn't. It even felt familiar—like touching myself, but from a different angle, maybe? It was sex and closeness and desire, just as it should be. I ached for it. For *him*.

"Question." Panting, he stopped my hand as well as his own. "Do you want to be first, or do you want me to be? Either is fine, just, you'd better decide soon."

I licked my lip, which stung pleasurably from making out with someone with a five o'clock shadow. "I would like . . . to finish you first." My face scorched at saying it, but hell yeah, I wanted to finish him off while still as aroused as possible myself. Only what I'd been fantasizing about for a month or two.

"Super." He rolled onto his back. "Then please."

We encountered a minute of delay while he helped me with my grip and technique. There was some laughter. But his giggles soon gave way to the most enticing, needy sounds, then his back arched and, oh God, yes, I was doing it. I *did* it. For another guy. For Andy.

After settling back down, he tugged a faded towel from under the bed—apparently he kept cloths there for cleanup.

After wiping his belly off, he hitched onto his side and reached for me. "Nice job. *Very* nice. Your turn?"

"Yes please," I said in almost a groan.

Which was better, doing this to him, or him doing it to me? Had I wanted one side more than the other in my imaginings? With so much desire flooding me, there was no way I could remember or choose. He stroked me, accelerating. I had wanted it all with him, everything, and somehow everything was what he was giving me. My breath shattered apart. He stayed pressed up against my side, riding through it, and wrung me out until I melted into relaxation.

After tossing the cleanup cloths into the laundry basket, I pulled the sheet to my waist, lay with my arms sprawled on either side of my head, and pondered the new milestone I'd just sprinted past.

Okay. Obviously bisexual. Established that. But what else did it mean, our having done this together?

It didn't make us boyfriends, surely? Not only was I wholeheartedly terrified of explaining such a development to my parents, but it felt too huge a leap for Andy and I to make from our longtime status as best friends.

On the other hand, my brain wasn't screaming *This was a mistake*, nor was I planning my escape from the building. Not at all. I was far more interested in figuring out how to do this again—whatever *this* was—because it had felt fantastic.

Andy settled onto his side, facing me but not touching me. He said nothing. Maybe his mind was running through a corresponding set of questions.

I spoke up to save him the trouble of asking. "Wow. That was awesome."

He laughed, sounding relieved. "Welcome to the team. Shoot, I forgot the rainbow confetti to throw all over you."

I looked at him. His eyes were green and bright, his mouth raspberry-hued from kissing. "I wasn't too horrible a rookie?" I asked. "Be honest."

"No way. You did great. All those women must've taught you well."

"Not sure it was them so much as the gay porn I've been looking up."

He turned his face into the pillow, laughing. "Well. Good job researching, then. So . . . " He propped himself up on his elbow, taking a more practical tone. "I don't know if you want to do this again after tonight. *I* do, but . . . "

"I do too. Totally."

"Okay. So . . . we're friends with benefits?"

I gazed at the plaster textures in the ceiling, pondering that. The term felt a little callous, but then again, I hadn't really come looking for a commitment. I had been seeking exactly this: exploration and discovery. I also thought of Fiona's sadness when I'd left her, and Andy's devastation when Mitchell had betrayed him. Both of us could use a break from that kind of emotional turmoil.

Besides . . .

"Guess it'd be a little late to claim we're anything else," I admitted.

"Ha. Exactly. Then, uh . . . rules. Keep it simple, right? Neither of us wants any drama. So if one of us wants to fool around, we just ask, and the other can say 'Yeah' or 'Nah,' and it's cool either way."

"Works for me."

"And termination clause: if either of us wants out, we can say so. 'I think I'm done with this for now.' And that's that, and it's fine, and we're still friends."

"No drama," I agreed.

We lay in comfortable silence a few seconds.

Then I realized it was getting late, and I was still in his space. "Guess I should get ready for bed."

Andy yawned. "Yeah. I have work in the morning, unfortunately."

I put my underwear back on and gathered up my clothes. He lolled in bed watching me, tousled and golden in the light of the bedside lamp. He looked sated and happy to be in the room with me, but didn't ask me to stay in his bed.

Of course not. We weren't boyfriends. This was good. No drama.

On the bed in the guest room, I moved my face around, chasing the fragrance he wore, which I smelled upon myself somewhere. I finally found it on my hair, one of the longer sections I could pull to my nose and sniff. I settled my cheek on the pillow, holding the strands near my nostrils, inhaling the scent and thinking thoughts that were somehow both erotic and cuddly, until I fell asleep.

———

Fiona: How are things going? As you hoped?

I found the message when I woke up the next morning. Andy had left for work. I had mumbled goodbye to him when he stuck his head into my room, then fallen back to sleep for another hour.

I reached over from the futon bed and opened the blinds, squinting at the gray skies, gray skyscrapers, and gray patch of seawater behind them. In winter, Seattle displayed more color at night than in the daytime.

For instance, in green eyes, warm brown hair, rosy skin, and blue-and-purple blankets. I smiled.

I looked at my phone again, and the smile took a regretful twist as I tapped in my answer.

Sinter: I think so. I still need to find work, but with Andy things are good so far

Fiona: Good. You deserve to be happy

Sinter: You do too, you know

To which, again, she didn't answer.

CHAPTER 20: SUBURBIA

THE FIRST WEEK OF JANUARY IN TERMS OF
GOOD THINGS AND BAD THINGS:

Good: I got an agent in Seattle. Her name was Dawn, she worked in a small office in a high-rise, and she was energetic in a caffeinated way but not to the point of being annoying. She and her two fellow agents handled several actors at a "place in their career" similar to mine, she said. Excited about my credentials, especially the film, she promised to find me auditions and voice-over work.

Bad: that kind of thing could take awhile, even with an agent, and I still needed a day job. Which I still didn't have by the end of the week, not even from places just looking for a waiter.

Good: Andy. Snogging. Exploring. Getting off together. Neither of us had said "Nah" yet when it was on offer, which had been every evening so far. We were still at the "no anal" stage—I asked him if it was expected, and he said not really, especially not for a rookie. It was the kind of thing you worked up to. Though I did look forward to leveling up, I was more than content with learning the other options in the meantime.

Bad: driving to Oregon to get my car.

We put the trip off until Sunday, because Saturday we were . . . busy. Andy and I took turns behind the wheel on the way south. I had a serious case of white knuckles for the first several minutes. I hadn't driven in over six months, since I hadn't dared try to drive in the UK, and besides that, I was terrible with manual transmissions and made Celery stall out twice, which cracked Andy up.

It was Andy's turn driving as we cruised into our suburb. I glowered out the window at the tracts of pastel-colored houses with shiny cars in identical driveways.

"All of cool, liberal Portland to choose from," I said, "and we had to be born here."

"Kind of why we both moved out."

"Your house wasn't so bad."

By "house" I meant "family," of course.

"Yours could be worse too."

He said it gently, but I bristled anyway. "I know! It'd be easier if I could cut them out entirely, but they're *almost* something I can work with."

"And they're what you have."

He meant, "They're *all* you have," though he was too nice to say that. No siblings, no warm relationships with any of my grandparents, aunts, uncles, or cousins. No family I would enjoy calling family. Yep, my parents were about it.

We pulled up at their curb, behind my dark blue Toyota, which I'd traded my Honda for a few years earlier. I stared at my car longer than necessary to put off looking at my dad, who was moving around in the yard.

I could play nice with them on an average day, maybe. But today, with Andy beside me, when I'd just spent my first week trying out all kinds of porn-worthy activities with him? Merely looking them in the eye would be challenging. Maybe bringing him had been a bad idea.

Then I detested myself for that thought—and loathed my parents. I shouldn't have to hide my best friend from them, and it wasn't any of their business what I did in private.

Andy turned off the Volvo and looked at me.

"Right, let's do it," I muttered, and got out of the car.

Dad strolled up in his raincoat and work gloves, rather threateningly carrying a hammer. "Have to replace a piece of siding," he said, by way of hellos.

"Oh. Okay. Hi," I said.

We stopped a foot apart on the wet, squishy front lawn. His salt-and-pepper hair had receded further lately. Everyone said I had his eyes, which sometimes made it unsettling for me to look at him, as if he were a Dorian-Gray-ish picture of how I would look in thirty years if I completely lost my sense of humor along the way.

He sized me up. I wore black eyeliner, a multicolored temporary tattoo of a Celtic knot on the side of my neck, my motorcycle jacket, skinny jeans, and battered lace-up black boots, all selected because I thought outer self-expression would boost my inner strength. Which apparently was bullshit, because I felt fidgety as hell.

Dad made no comment on my appearance, and his mouth tightened as he took in Andy a step behind me. Then he said, "Your mother's inside. She'd like to see you." He turned and walked toward the house.

He hadn't greeted Andy nor invited him in. My blood simmered. I turned and said clearly, using my stage projection abilities, "Great. Yeah, come in, man."

Looking far more respectable than me (at least by my parents' standards) with his tidy haircut and standard Northwest street clothes and lack of makeup, Andy smiled dryly—*Super, thanks for inviting me into the torture chamber; I'd love to come.* But he followed me in.

Inside, it smelled like something baked with cinnamon, and like my childhood in general—whatever the smell of my house was exactly. It knocked me back in time, bringing a mix of memories both pleasant and not. There at the hearth, Dad had photographed me on Mom's lap when I was in kindergarten, both of us grinning with tinsel wound around us. There on that strip of wood floor between the living room rug and hall carpet, I raced toy cars in elementary school, and Dad occasionally knelt to roll some along too, and tell me about his first car. Through these rooms, I had paced in insanity as a fifteen-year-old, grounded for a month for kissing Andy, and feeling I could never understand my parents again.

Dad tromped down the hall to put his tools away in the front closet. I veered into the dining room. Mom sat at the vast oak table, potted ficus trees behind her, a thousand-piece jigsaw puzzle spread in front of her. Looking through her bifocals, she clicked one tiny blue piece into another tiny blue piece, then lifted her face and gave me a polite bank-teller smile.

"Oh, you're here, hello."

"Hey, Mom." I didn't sit. Andy hovered beside me, a step away.

She looked from me to him and back again, her smile turning more mystified. "How was the drive?"

"Not bad," I said.

"Not too much traffic," Andy contributed.

She nodded, squinting at my appearance as if she couldn't decide what to say about it. "Well, there's coffee cake if you'd like some."

Like Dad, she spoke only to me, as if Andy didn't exist.

Rather than answer, I looked to him.

Mom picked up on the clue and added, "Either of you. Of course." A smidgen better than Dad, then, but still the most stilted invitation I'd heard in a long time.

"No, thanks," Andy said. "We just had lunch."

Dad came into the room. Standing over Mom, he folded his arms and appraised me with a faux-amused look. "Hope that's not how you're dressing for job interviews."

I shoved my mouth into a smile. "Depends on the job."

"Well, in the theater, I suppose . . . " Mom said. She managed to make "theater" sound like "strip club."

Irritation prickled through me, nettles all down my skin. "You guys like theaters. You go to them."

"Occasionally." Mom picked up a green puzzle piece and frowned at it. "We haven't gotten out to one in a while, come to think of it."

"Mainly Gilbert and Sullivan," Dad said. "Now, if you'd do Gilbert and Sullivan . . . "

This was an ancient argument. For one thing, I couldn't stand Gilbert and Sullivan—not because it was their theatrical favorite but because it annoyed me. For another thing, I couldn't sing that well. They knew both things.

"Where are the car keys?" I asked.

Mom looked up again. "Are you leaving so soon? You just got here." She still sounded calm.

"What was it you wanted me to do while I was here?" I had gotten louder without meaning to.

Dad's fake smile vanished. Andy looked at me, worried.

They were being this unpleasant because I'd brought Andy. That had to be it. They'd wanted to see me, they'd claimed. They'd led me to believe they might be nice. But no, certain circumstances—like having a gay person in their house—were apparently too much for them.

"Well, we haven't seen you since, what, last summer," Mom said.

Now you have, and I've been here five seconds, and you've already managed to be rude to my best friend and get on my case about how I look and what I do for a living, so. Goodbye.

But why subject Andy to a scene? Besides, my parents were salvageable. And they were all I had.

I looked down at the puzzle, willing the tension out of my shoulders. "Yeah. Turned out to be my longest trip to London yet."

"Where's this place you're staying?" Mom asked. "You haven't sent us the address."

"Andy's apartment, on Capitol Hill. I'll email it to you."

"How many of you are staying there?" Dad asked.

Of you? Gays? Actors? Deadbeats? Freaks?

"Just the two of us," I said.

They looked at him, then back at me. Pretty sure all four of us got swept into the past for a moment, to that time they caught me lying on top of Andy and kissing him.

I began breathing faster, now shaken as well as pissed off. "We were going to say hi to his family too, then it's a long drive back, so. I should get the keys."

Dad fetched them for me. When he put them into my hand he said, "I drove it a few times. Made sure it was running all right. Replaced the wiper blades, too."

I lowered my gaze. They were trying, in their awkward way. They were at least occasionally doing things that might help me, whereas all I did was show up, act like an insecure freak, and walk out again. Maybe all our problems really were my fault, just as they'd been insinuating all these years.

I slid my thumb into the key ring. "Thank you."

Andy and I turned to go.

Mom leaped up from the table. "You could take some coffee cake with you." She sounded a little desperate.

"Um . . ."

"I'll put some in a container." She darted into the kitchen. I was getting coffee cake whether I wanted it or not.

"Okay. We'll go out and see how the car's looking."

Andy gave a nod and a meaningless "Thanks, see you," to my dad, who nodded in our direction. We left him and walked out to the Toyota.

"Jesus Christ," I muttered to Andy.

"At least they didn't ask you if you're on drugs this time."

"Oh, they will." I got into the Toyota and fiddled with the dashboard settings. Andy opened the passenger door to look in, his arm on top of the car.

Mom hurried out with a small Tupperware container. Andy pulled back to give her room, and she leaned in to hand it to me.

"You're not taking drugs, are you?" she asked, brows pinched up in worry.

Through the back window, I saw Andy swivel away, his posture suggesting he was fighting a fit of giggles.

I looked at Mom in exasperation. "No. I'm not taking drugs."

She gestured at my whole body. "You show up looking like this . . . "

"I just like looking like this. I'm not *on* anything, all right?"

"Good. Okay, well, that's good. Don't forget to send us the address."

I nodded, turning to gaze out the windshield, my hand dangling over the top of the steering wheel.

She drew back from the car.

Andy reappeared in the open passenger door, mirth in the tilt of his eyes. "Meet you at my house?"

"Yep." I looked to Mom again, who stood on the lawn with arms folded and shoulders hunched as if she were cold, even though she wore a cashmere sweater. "Bye."

"Have a good drive," she said.

Dad sauntered across the lawn behind her, carrying a shovel this time. He and I exchanged nods.

Andy shut the passenger door and went to his car.

A couple of blocks over, we parked at his folks' house. It had two stories and a serene pastel paint job like my parents' and all the neighbors', but the Ortiz house exhibited more disorder, which I'd always liked. Vines and bushes spilled over each other in the yard, dog chew toys lay beside the front path, and the welcome mat was colorful, stained, and well used.

Andy knocked, then opened the front door without waiting for an answer. "Hey guys!" he shouted inside, over the noise of barking huskies.

The two dogs hurtled over and whipped around us in an ecstatic whirlwind of fur and tongues. We bent to greet them. White dog hairs all over my black clothes: the price I'd always paid for visiting Andy's house.

Andy's mom, Kelly, appeared, wide-hipped and with curly graying hair. She set down a full basket of laundry and hurried over, arms outstretched. "Andrés! Baby!" She and Andy hugged. Then she turned and gave me just as exuberant a hug. "Sinter! It's good to see you."

My own parents hadn't hugged me. Had they even touched me?

His dad, Carlos, walked in from the kitchen, stout and grinning, deep smile lines in his face. "Hey, *mijo*." He hugged Andy. He had grown up in Oregon, but in talking to family he sometimes threw in the endearments his Mexican-American parents used. (Andy had also learned a few intriguing Spanish insults from those grandparents, and taught them to me.)

Carlos chuckled as he looked at me. "Wow, you still look like a rock star."

"He played one in a movie in London last month," Andy said. "Set in the '80s."

"Oh, you mentioned that!" Kelly said. "That's so exciting. Will we be able to see it?"

I nodded. "Yeah. I think. I mean, if it doesn't air over here, I'll get DVDs, probably."

They ushered us into the kitchen and offered us drinks and any of the random leftovers in the fridge. Sitting at the table, we snacked on chips and guacamole and talked to them about our jobs. They told us how they missed the noise of their four kids (now all grown up and living elsewhere), even though the quiet could be nice.

Thank God Andy had been born to these people. Imagine the suicidal mess he'd have become in my house.

I petted the ears of the husky resting his chin on my leg, and pretended I wasn't feeling the tiniest bit suicidal myself.

When we finally got up to drive back to Seattle, Andy's mom and dad hugged us both and insisted I let them know if I got cast in any plays in Seattle so they could come up and see them. I promised.

As we walked to the curb, Andy watched me, as if trying to catch my eye. But what could I say? *I'm glad you have a great family. I wish I did.* Whatever. I'd already said it a hundred times in the years we'd known each other.

"Hey," he said.

I looked over.

"You know which exit to take if we get separated on the freeway?"

"Yeah."

"Cool. See you there." We waved again to his parents, who stood on the front porch beaming at us, his dad's arm around his mom's shoulders.

My phone buzzed as I started the Toyota. I looked at the text.

Andy: You look hot today btw

I glanced into the rearview mirror and caught his cheeky wave from where he was parked behind me.

CHAPTER 21: JUST CAN'T GET ENOUGH

MY AGENT, DAWN, STARTED FINDING ME WORK: ONLY VOICE-OVERS FOR COMMERCIALS, BUT IT BROUGHT IN some rent money. She also added a few more play and film auditions to my schedule, and in the middle of January sent me an email titled *Lookie who's on IMDb,* with a link attached.

So far, I hadn't been listed on Internet Movie Database, because I'd only been in stage productions. But under the Hart Channel film still titled *New Romantic,* my name was right near the top of the cast list, second only to Ariel's, and my personal IMDb page, set up by Dawn, displayed my bio and a few photos: Taylor in all his eyeshadowed glory, two shots from my Portland stage roles, and my headshot.

I sent the link to Andy, who soon posted it on social media with the caption:

Did I mention I'm currently living with a movie star? Srsly so proud.

He included a selfie of him kissing my cheek while I laughed—a surprise attack from that morning. It got many likes, and although his mom commented, *Fabulous, Sinter!! You two are so sweet,* I doubted she or anyone else knew there was anything deeper going on beneath that cheek kiss. Still, I admit it was some relief to know that my parents did not have accounts on that platform and thus weren't likely to see it.

That evening, in private, I showed Andy my appreciation for his support. He told me my appreciation skills were really coming along.

I also emailed the link to Fiona, with the message:

Hey! I was glad to see this up on IMDb. Is New Romantic *going to be the title after all?*

Things are good; I'm definitely bi, ha. But I do miss London and all of you. How have you been?

I decided "all of you" was a better choice than just "you." Leading her on wouldn't be kind, just in case she didn't pick up on my current satisfying sex life with the "definitely bi" bit.

She answered the next day:

Knackered, quite busy with postproduction and marketing. But it's coming together nicely, I think. Yes, we couldn't agree on any other title, so we decided New Romantic *wasn't bad.*

Sounds like your arrangement in Seattle is going as well as you wanted. That's excellent. Take care and I'll be in touch before long.

The email's tone didn't exactly suggest friendship—concise, no exclamation points, no smiley faces. It rendered me uncomfortable, but what else could I say? I opted not to answer, figuring staying out of her space was the most considerate choice.

In late January, I found part-time work in a café near our apartment, and I think I had the movie to thank for it. The café owner, Chris, had a buzz cut, thick eyelashes, and a neck tattoo of a peacock feather, which I completely envied. When she discovered in my interview that Ariel Salisbury had worked alongside me at my last job, she smacked her notebook down on her lap, open-mouthed, and said, "No way! I had the hugest, unhealthiest crush on her in college."

Then she hollered for her wife, Kam, who was making scones in the café kitchen. Kam stepped out, her hair in a bandanna, her hands covered in flour.

"This guy was just in a movie with Ariel Salisbury in London," Chris said.

"Oh my God." Kam laughed. "Chris used to have pictures of her on her walls. Remember that one with, like, the see-through skirt?"

They gave me four barista shifts a week, afternoon to closing.

Andy came in to visit one evening after he got off work. A few customers sat at the tables with their drinks. Kam was blasting Lana Del Rey while restocking the fridge. Andy strolled up to the counter, windblown and drizzle-splattered from the walk, unzipping his fleece in the warm coffee shop.

"Hey." He squinted at the menu above my head. "I'll have a twelve-ounce mocha, that cranberry scone, and your number, please."

"Smooth." I fetched him the scone with tongs and set it on a plate. "Bet you say that to all the baristas."

"You get a big tip if you give me more whipped cream," he added as I slid the mocha across to him.

"Sounds dirty in so many ways." I uncapped the can of cream and sprayed another layer onto his drink.

He broke off a corner of the scone, dipped it into the whipped cream, looked directly at me, and began licking and sucking the cream off it.

I swallowed. Thank goodness for the café apron covering me below the waist. I knew very well how that tongue felt, not just in my mouth but on many other parts of me. I knew what those fingers could do. I was having all kinds of trouble not leaping the counter and throwing him down on a table and . . . yeah, I really shouldn't think like this at work.

"That's four seventy-five," I told him.

He took a five out of his pocket and handed it over. "Keep the change."

"Twenty-five cents? You call that a big tip?"

"You get your tip later, when you come home."

What with Lana Del Rey singing so loudly, Kam and the customers couldn't hear us, and I was gambling on the notion that none of them could lip-read either.

I dropped the quarter into the pet-shelter donation jar beside the cash register. "I'm going to hold you to that. In fact, I'm going to hold you in lots of positions."

"Promise?"

"Oh yeah."

God, if he kept giving me that smolder-gaze, I was completely going to drag him into the tiny bathroom, yank his pants down, and—

More customers burst in, a loud cluster of four.

With a naughty smile, Andy took his plate and cup and withdrew to a table.

After I'd served the other four, Kam wandered up to me. "Is that your boyfriend?" she asked.

I followed her gaze to Andy, head bent over his phone at the table. "Oh, uh, no. My best friend."

"You sure? That was some pretty intense eye-fucking between you two."

I laughed. "We've known each other forever, is all. We're kind of weird together."

"You're cute together," she corrected, and having settled that, started tidying up the pastry case.

Later that night, after yanking every last piece of clothing off each other and exhausting every synonym for "grope" and "suck" in the thesaurus, Andy and I lay diagonally in a sated tangle across his bed. I was sore from all the manhandling, and might have strained my jaw a little, but felt basically fantastic.

"Kam asked tonight if we were seeing each other," I said, my chin on his chest. "Apparently our 'eye-fucking' was getting out of control."

He laughed. "Whoops. What did you say?"

"I said no, we're just friends. I figured saying we mess around sometimes would be TMI for coworkers. Not because you're a guy—if I were friends with benefits with a woman, I wouldn't mention that to coworkers either."

"I agree. I mean, I don't mind if you tell. But there's only so much about your sex life you have to share with people you work with."

I adjusted my chin to look at him. "Have you told anyone? About this."

"No. Though mainly because . . . well, you're not exactly out. And it's not cool to out other people."

"Oh. Right." True, I was out to Fiona and, weirdly, Sebastian, but as far as the city of Seattle or indeed the entire United States went, no one other than Andy knew I was bi. "I guess I should think about that. Coming out."

"It's only on an as-needed basis. It's not like you have to announce it whenever you meet someone."

I balanced my fingertips along the treasure trail between his navel and crotch, wishing I didn't feel so terrified at the idea. People would have nosy questions, ignorant remarks, annoying opinions . . . ugh, it was so much easier not to bring it up.

"Although," he added, "if you want to start, like, *real* dating, with other guys, we can go to Girasol some Saturday night. See how it goes."

Girasol was a popular LGBTQ nightclub on Broadway, Capitol Hill's busiest street. He'd pointed it out to me when we walked by.

That sounded too frighteningly real, and at the same time falser and less satisfying, considering I already had awesome man-sex right there under my fingertips. Was I just making excuses to stay closeted, though?

"Hm. Sometime," I said.

"Yeah. I'm in no hurry. This is working fine." He dragged me up and kissed me on my pleasantly sore mouth. "It's okay if you ever happen to fall asleep here, by the way. I know the guest bed isn't as comfy as mine."

I spread out my limbs farther, embracing the king-sized mattress as well as him. "Okay."

CHAPTER 22: OUR LIPS ARE SEALED

IT WAS ADDICTIVELY EASY, ROLLING ALONG IN A NO-DRAMA, ROOMMATES-WITH-BENEFITS SETUP. BUT AS the weeks sped by, I fretted more about the secrecy. Why hadn't I told people I was currently seeing a man? Simply because our situation was casual and thus "didn't count"? Or because I was scared?

That couldn't be. Someone who walked around in makeup and costumes and non-gender-conforming hairstyles couldn't be scared of coming out. Yet perhaps it made sense. When I wore goth clothes and cosmetics, people weren't sure what to make of me, and the air of mystery was a major part of what I liked about it. However, if I were to kiss Andy in public, they'd know pretty exactly what I was. That, therefore, was a lot scarier.

One day, an online article sent a nasty shock through me by noting that if you were closeted and dating someone, you were basically sending the other person back into the closet too. Because they would have to lie about you, pretend they weren't involved with you.

"I'm kind of being a jerk, aren't I?" I said to Andy that evening as we walked down Broadway toward the grocery store. "Making you have to hide this, lie about it. It's not fair of me."

He lifted his eyebrows. "I'm getting good perks out of it. I don't mind."

We stopped at a corner to wait for the traffic light.

"Are you sure?" I said. "I mean, if anyone asks, you can say . . . " I shrugged, uncomfortably aware I'd feel alarmed if he did tell anyone.

He smirked. "Why, yes, Mom, I *am* fucking Sinter, since you ask."

"Okay, not like *that*, just . . ."

"Look, no one's even asked. It's fine."

Gratefully, I batted the fluffball of yarn on top of his winter hat. He swung the empty cloth shopping bags so they smacked my rear, making me grin. Then he leaned up, angling for a kiss, and . . .

I twitched my face out of the way and glanced around, not even thinking first. A stupid knee-jerk reaction.

Andy snorted and shook his head.

Shame washed over me. "Sorry," I said.

The light changed. We set off across the street. "No, I get it," he said when we reached the opposite side. "I still look around first in most places. But this is Broadway. No one cares. It's like—like a theater. All the time." He waved his hand toward a shop window full of drag-queen-grade high-heeled boots, wigs, and outfits involving harnesses.

"I'm sure I'll get used to it," I said. "I'm a noob, is all."

"No big deal. It took me almost three years to come out to anyone else after I came out to you, and I definitely didn't kiss anyone in public during that time."

But his voice had gone crisper and cooler, and he took out his phone to check it.

"Yeah." I hunched my shoulders, shoving my hands deep into my pockets. "I guess."

———

Fiona: I just have to ask you this once. Is there any chance you'll want to come back to me? Have a real relationship? I'm sorry to sound dramatic. I won't make a habit of it. I just need to know

It was the last day of January. I was working a shift at the café and had just helped drag in a delivery of coffee beans. I stood immobilized next to the stack of fragrant boxes, staring at my phone.

My first impulse, oddly, was to forward it to Andy and get his feedback. But no—that was stupid. This obviously was a question I had to answer alone.

I put the phone in my pocket and started carrying boxes of coffee to the kitchen.

Well, no. The answer was no. Though . . . maybe? I might return to the UK in five years and meet up with her again, and things might go differently that time.

Probably not what she was asking, though; I expected she meant anytime soon. So I should say no. But a flat refusal felt too insensitive. How would I prefer to be turned down if it were me?

After piecing together and tearing apart phrasing in my head for half an hour, I composed an answer.

Sinter: I'm so sorry, but with the distance and being involved with other things right now, I don't think so. It just doesn't feel right, and I'm happy here. But I like you and I'm so glad to know you, if that helps at all. Gah, I'm sorry

Fiona: No, I wanted to know the truth. Thank you

Sinter: I'm not worth any regrets. You're going to be fine

Fiona: I'll sort things out I suppose. Anyway I'll be in touch. Take care

Sinter: You too. Hugs

I was not ordinarily a written-hugs kind of person, but I honestly wished I could hug her if it would help.

She didn't answer.

When I returned to the apartment that evening, Andy was back from work, on the couch playing some computer game involving what looked like mazes, caterpillars, and raspberries. "Hey," he said.

"Hey." I took off my boots and thumped down by his feet with a sigh. "Fiona messaged me. She wanted to know if I was interested in coming back to her."

He kept his gaze on the screen, but the look on his face became . . . complicated. Tense, hurt, sympathetic? I thought I caught glimpses of all of those. "Oh. Wow."

"I said no," I added. "Told her I'm happy here."

He went on screen-staring, but his expression evolved into a friendly wince. "Those conversations are never fun."

"I'd hoped she was over it. But I guess she's doing postproduction, so she's probably having to watch footage of me for hours every day."

"That would delay the recovery." The reflections of the game's colored lights scooted around on his glasses. "Are you sure, though? You could go back if you wanted. You're not . . . tied down or anything."

For some reason, that troubled me almost as much as Fiona's messages had. I studied him. He scrolled the screen, face neutral. "No, I'm honestly happy," I said. I took hold of his foot in its C-3PO-patterned sock. "I'm not calling this arrangement done yet. But you can end it too, if you want. No drama." I maintained a casual tone, matching his.

He wiggled his toes in my grip. "Nah. I won't kick you out yet. I mean, the weather's been so cold, and you keep the bed nice and warm."

I had let myself fall asleep in his bed many nights during the past week or two, and I sometimes woke to find him curled against me. It was quite adorable.

"Okay then," I said.

"Here." He spun the laptop toward me. "See if you can beat my score."

————

Work kept us busy: Andy was in talks with a former coworker who'd started her own video game company, and he was considering making the leap to a new job with her. Meanwhile, I served coffee and kept auditioning for stage and film roles. As predicted, it took me twenty auditions (twenty-one, actually) before I landed a role. A few days into February, I sent the happy news to Andy.

Sinter: I got a part!! In the one about Shakespeare at Green Sea Theatre

Andy: Omg woohoo!! Be thinking about how you want to celebrate ;)

When I arrived at the café that day, I told Chris I now had evening rehearsals that would conflict with my shifts.

"Big-time actor guy," she said. "Fine. We knew the risks." She opened the work schedule on the computer to shuffle employees around. "What's this play?"

I hung my jacket on a wall peg. "It's called *The Fair Youth*. It's about Shakespeare's life."

She looked over. "You're going to play Shakespeare?"

"No, the other guy—the fair youth. A nobleman who . . . okay, do you know anything about the sonnets?"

"Neee-ope. I did not study Shakespeare."

"So the first, like, hundred or so of the sonnets are actually written about a guy, this 'fair youth.' That's who I'll be playing." I had vaguely recalled this from my college theater and lit courses. It had intrigued me to learn that all the "compare thee to a summer's day" was about another man. "There are theories about who he was, but no one's sure. This play takes one of the theories and makes it into a love story."

Chris tapped her pinkies on the edges of the keyboard. "Ah, right. I remember hearing Shakespeare might've been gay or bi or something."

"They're going with bi, yeah. Same with my character. Which, uh . . ." I fetched an apron to put on, my heart suddenly racing. "I am too, so that works out."

"Huh." My coming-out apparently meant very little to Chris. She looked at the screen again. "*I'd* much rather make out with Ariel Salisbury than some dude dressed as Shakespeare, but that's just me."

There, I defended to myself. I had come out to someone else. Sure, a woman who had a wife, and who worked on Broadway and therefore saw a thousand more shocking things than me every day, but still. I wasn't hiding.

One step at a time, right?

CHAPTER 23: ONLY YOU

AT THE BEGINNING OF MARCH, ANDY TOOK THE NEW JOB AT HIS COLLEAGUE'S VIDEO GAME COMPANY. It meant a slight pay cut, but he still had a short commute, and got to do work that he loved. They were even hoping to win a contract for a tie-in video game to one of Andy's favorite TV series, a Japanese anime, which had Andy bouncing against the ceiling in excitement. We had a couple of celebratory dinners in his honor, one with his new boss, Dakota, and her husband, and one with his sister Emma. Family who wanted to celebrate your job achievements: imagine that.

We still bounded along in our bed-sharing arrangement too, and by the end of the month had tried nearly everything there was to try, at least without a shopping trip to a sex-toy store. Of which there were a few in our neighborhood, so there was always that possibility. My experience with being on the receiving end of anal, by the way, was similar to my early experience with eyeliner: "Ow, fuck fuck fuck, ow" on the first try, but once I learned proper procedures, it became something I could pull off with style and pleasure. (Andy was considerate that first time, just a little over-eager.)

Between those activities and my rehearsals, which involved wooing and kissing the actor playing Shakespeare (no weirder than kissing Ariel, as it turned out, except that he had a beard), Andy declared I had levelled up in guy/guy action.

"So I mean, if you want to try Girasol," he said one day, "I think you'd be a total catch there."

Since it was the second time he'd suggested it, I took it to mean—with a sinking of heart I didn't dare analyze—that *he* wanted to go to Girasol.

No drama. Not tied down. Though I still couldn't bring myself to kiss him on the street, I was going to be kissing a dude onstage for whoever bought a ticket this spring, so I might as well walk into an LGBTQ bar and see what it was like. Maybe I'd even meet someone who turned me on *more* than Andy did, though I was beginning to doubt that was possible.

We went on a Friday night. I wore eyeliner, double necklaces, temporary tattoos, and all-black clothes. Might as well present the me they should know about.

Andy instructed me to hang out by the bar (if I didn't want to dance, which I didn't), check out attractive people, and rely on eye contact to lure them toward me. In the crowded, bass-thumping, light-flashing room, we bought our drinks and swiveled to face the options.

In a few minutes, Andy, with his friendly smile and opened top shirt button, got drawn into dancing with a bearded guy a few years older than us. I watched for a minute, then remembered I should be checking out other people. Of the few women there, most were cuddling with each other, so I let my eye rove over the guys, which was theoretically the point of my being there anyway.

The first one to approach me was tall, with a jogger's build and stylishly tousled short hair. With the loud music, we practically had to mash our mouths to each other's ears to talk, which gave me a noseful of his cologne. It was pleasant, but I liked Andy's better. When jogger guy learned I was bi, he seemed to get wary, like maybe I wasn't serious about this "getting with guys" idea. Before long, he wished me a good time and drifted off.

The bearded guy nuzzled Andy's neck on the dance floor. Andy smiled and spoke into his ear. Something inside me felt jagged.

I cut my gaze around, my back against the bar, seeking anyone attractive.

A skinny boy met my gaze, beamed, and weaved his inebriated way over to me. He looked barely twenty-one, maybe there under false ID. He wore a pink polo shirt, and his blond hair swooped down to one side over his cheekbone. In our conversation shouted into each other's ears, he was excited to learn I was an actor, congratulatory at my coming out as bi, and determined to tell me all about the drama with his conservative parents. Which, of course, I sympathized with.

But I didn't particularly feel like kissing him. And Andy still smelled better.

The blond kid said he was off to the bathroom and asked if I wanted to come.

There we had it: I could probably get off with some guy in a bar if I so desired.

I looked around and found Andy walking toward me, alone. I shook my head at the blond guy with a grateful smile. "Not tonight. Maybe another time, okay?"

He twisted his mouth wistfully, said, "Hope so," and loped off.

"I might be done," Andy yelled in my ear when he reached my side. "You want to stay?"

I shook my head and shoved my half-full beer bottle onto the bar. "Let's go."

Instead of returning straight to the apartment, we ambled along Broadway, not saying much. My ears were still ringing from the club noise. It was cold, but a hint of flowers fragranced the air. We turned a corner and climbed a quieter sidewalk toward Volunteer Park.

"Well, now you've tried it, at least," he said.

The ringing in my ears had faded enough to maintain conversation.

"Yeah, thought I should. And it seemed like you wanted to go, so." I made sure to sound unconcerned so he wouldn't take it as an accusation.

He sounded a tad distressed anyway when he answered. "I didn't *really*. I just thought *you* should have the chance, in case you were . . . getting tired of . . . "

"Oh. I'm not, no."

"Okay. No, me neither."

A tender happiness bloomed inside me. "You were doing okay with the bearded guy," I teased.

"Heh. I guess." Entering the park, we passed beneath tree branches and into the paved area in front of the Asian Art Museum. "Wasn't feeling it, though. I kept thinking, 'Eh, I'd rather go home with Sinter.'"

The warmth spread all through me. "I could've followed the blond kid into the bathroom, but . . . yeah. Didn't appeal."

We gravitated toward the huge, black, donut-shaped sculpture in front of the museum, the one you could look through and frame the Space Needle in. No one else was around except a guy walking his dogs on the other side of the street.

In the shadows, I caught Andy's hand. He wrapped his fingers around mine at once, though we'd never held hands before. We slowed to a stop at the donut, looking through it at the skyline.

"I know I could've gone to a club like that in London," I said. "Found someone there, or in some other city. I came here because . . . I wanted to try being bi with *you*. I just wanted you."

"And I went along with your crazy idea because I just wanted you." He said it so easily, like he didn't mind sharing this sentiment at all.

Tugging him down with me, I sat on the low concrete wall beside the sculpture.

Andy wrapped his arms around my waist. "Hey. Do you really think of the day I left for college when you need to cry for a part?"

"Yeah. I never told you or *anyone*, but I totally broke down and, like, sobbed after you left."

He pressed his cheek to my shoulder. "When I got to Stanford, I cried every night for the first few days. Trying to be all quiet, in my pillow, so my roommate wouldn't hear me."

I nestled my lips into his hair. "Because you were homesick?"

"Partly. But mainly because I missed you."

I closed my eyes and held him tighter. My chest hurt from his words. The wall we sat on was cold and hard. My feet were sore from walking around in these leather boots. The smell of the club still clung to our hair.

A night had never been as perfect as this, and I wanted to feel this way always.

"I'm fine with this arrangement going on awhile," I said.

"Same."

———

Oh, tread carefully, man, I told myself as we walked home from Volunteer Park, neither of us speaking much. I breathed in the spring night smells of chilly flowers and seawater and traffic, and felt pleasantly dizzy, not from alcohol or weariness but from the glow of emotions swarming me.

That night felt different, not just sexual anymore, not just hanging out with a friend. It felt . . . romantic. Like I had caught feelings for him. And from what he had said, he might have caught some for me too.

Which was not allowed. No drama, we had agreed. No broken hearts. No crying in our cars. No radio silence where once we had exchanged hilarious daily text messages.

So yes, I had to tread carefully, especially since I wasn't ready for anything like a relationship with him. How could I claim to be, when fear still bubbled up inside me at the idea of introducing him to anyone—let alone my parents—as "my boyfriend"?

Even so, this romantic mood intoxicated me. It swept me up, the way a stage role could sweep me up in the best of performances. So I played the part, just for one night. It felt too good to resist. Cold reality could wait until tomorrow.

Other queer-culture kids flowed around us as we descended the hill: same-sex couples holding hands, groups in clubbing attire laughing and chattering. We blended right in. At the corner across from our building, I caught his hand again, between our hips. Our fingers interlocked. Though my pulse pounded, we held hands all the way across the street and up the steps to the door of the building.

When I let go to get my keys out of my pocket, Andy leaned over and kissed my neck, a look of pride on his face. I kissed him on the ear in return.

In the apartment, once we'd stripped each other down, we spent longer than usual just kissing. We lingered in a naked tangle in bed, flushed and heated. He stroked my hair back from my face, and his hand trembled. So did mine as I traced his collarbone to the hollow at the center and kissed him over the heart.

Afterward, we stayed wrapped up in each other's arms rather than disentangling and joking as we often did.

"Hey," he said. "Happy birthday."

I smiled. Now that it was after midnight, it was indeed my birthday. I hadn't brought it up, but of course he remembered. "Thanks. Twenty-six, wow."

"What do you want to do tomorrow? Or today I guess. After sleeping."

"Machiavelli's for dinner?" It was a restaurant nearby with fabulous Italian food.

"Sounds good," he said. "Let's do it. After my work thing and your rehearsal."

Though the next day was Saturday, Andy was going in to his new office to help Dakota set up a server, or something like that—I wasn't the one to ask about technological details. Meanwhile, I had rehearsal all afternoon for *The Fair Youth*. Theater rehearsal followed by awesome Italian dinner with Andy would already be a great birthday by my standards.

But this fondness I was indulging in felt like the best gift anyone could have given me—even if I was only playing a part, and with the sunrise it was going to blow away like the vapors from a fog machine.

CHAPTER 24: SHELLSHOCK

FIONA EMAILED ME THE NEXT DAY.

I need to talk to you. When would be a good time to phone?

Well, *that* didn't sound good.

Andy had gone to work. I was at the apartment alone, having an early lunch at the small kitchen table. I re-read the message, my jaw slowing as I chewed my peanut butter sandwich.

Something to do with the film? Or, given her message from a month earlier, something more relationship-centered?

Already nervous, I typed back:

I'm free for another hour or so. I can call now if that works?

A minute later my phone started buzzing. She was calling.

I swallowed the bite of sandwich, washed it down with tea, and answered, "Hello?"

"Hi, Sinter." She sounded wistful. The London accent sent a pang of nostalgia through me.

"Hey, what's up?"

"Oh, I'm sorry to bother you. I really am. It sounds like things are going well for you over there."

"They are," I said. "But what's . . . is something wrong? The film?"

"Not the film, no. That's nearly done, and it looks excellent." She didn't sound near as pleased about it as she should have. "It's . . . well, you see, I'm pregnant."

I was already sitting down when she said it. Good thing, as a weird, jelly-like feeling shot from my stomach into my legs. "You are?" And though I hated myself for it, I started counting in my head: how long ago had we had sex, what were the chances . . .

"Fourteen weeks gone now. But they count things strangely, so it actually means conception was twelve weeks ago, which . . . " Put it exactly in the vicinity of a certain Christmas party. I closed my eyes. "Anyway, yes, it's yours," she said. "There was no question of that, really. There hasn't been anyone else in months."

"But we—we used—" Because arguing might change reality.

"Yes, it would seem condoms can fail. Thinking back on it, that one was probably in my bag rather longer than it should have been, and . . . " She sighed. "I'm so sorry. It's my own fault. I know it's a shock, and I wish there were a gentler way to tell you."

I opened my eyes and blinked at the kitchen window. Rain was gathering on the glass, blurring the gray city. "No, don't worry about that. How are you? How are you feeling? When did you find out? What . . . " I stopped, realizing I was firing too many questions at once.

"I've felt rather dreadful. Sick nearly every day for about six weeks."

"Oh my God. Fiona . . . "

"But better now that the first trimester's over. I found out at the end of January. That's when I asked you . . . well."

If there was any chance for us. I had tensed up so tight the back of my neck was aching. I rubbed at it. "God, I'm sorry. You could've said . . . "

"I wanted to know the truth about how you felt. Didn't want you to be influenced by this information."

Which surely I would have been. "So you've just been living with it all this time?"

"Don't feel bad." She sounded brisk, a hint of the admirable director who could steer us all into line. "I've had Chelsea helping me out. She's been brilliant. Sebastian, as well. And your answer helped me decide something. Having made the decision, I'm being a bulldog again."

Don't think about Andy, don't think about what I'm going to do, just think of her, find out what she needs . . .

"What's the decision? How can I help?"

"I *could* raise a child—that is, I could afford to, better than many people. But I simply don't want to, not in the slightest."

"Oh. Okay." Something started easing up inside me, in a guilty way. This problem might . . . go away. Though I dreaded to think how. That fraught word, *abortion* . . . wait, she was fourteen weeks along? How did that work again? I'd never gotten anyone pregnant before. I had no experience there.

"I considered abortion." She seemed able to say it, at least. "But then I looked at Chelsea, with Mina. She adopted her, you know?"

"No, I didn't know."

"She chose to, as a single mum. Obviously Mina means the world to her. There are so many people who want a baby and can't conceive. And I thought, well, at least I could benefit someone else. So if I got through the first trimester without a miscarriage—which is when it's likeliest to happen—then I'd have the baby and give it up for adoption."

"Okay. So you're through that. The first trimester." I kept watching raindrops slide down the window. Told myself this wasn't the end of my world, just a really hefty speed bump.

"Yes, and since I don't expect you would want the child either, I at least had to notify you, since you'd have to sign off on the adoption too. That is, I could do it all without telling you or naming you as the father, but that didn't seem nice. I thought you should know."

At the mention that I even had the option of taking the child, as well as getting hit with the label "father," all my muscles froze and my eyes widened. "Right, I see. Well . . . I never thought about, or at least I didn't think anytime *soon* I'd . . . uh."

But I *had* thought of it, right? Every time my parents' coldness and incomprehension stung me, some part of me had thought, *When I have kids, I won't be like that. I'll be so much better.*

I hadn't meant *this year*, though.

"No, I understand," she said. "So eventually, I'll approach an adoption agency, tell them about the situation, and learn what needs to be done. I admit I'm dragging my heels on it, though. Sounds rather dreadful."

"I get that, yeah. Well, there's time yet, isn't there?"

"There is. I'm not due until September, so no particular rush. But I'd rather sort it out within the next couple of months. I'll feel more settled if I know what the plan's going to be."

"That makes sense."

Andy. I'd have to tell Andy. Oh God. I hunched over the table, resting my face in my hand.

"Also," she said, "I don't know if this is the hormones talking, or my having spent too much time looking at footage of you lately, or what. But if this knowledge does change your thoughts about being together . . . well. I still don't think I want to be a mother, but if anyone could change my mind on that, it would be you."

"I . . . can't promise anything like that. I don't think it would be smart. For either of us. Any of us."

"No. All right." She sounded sad and quiet. "Are you and Andy, then . . . "

"Not exactly. I don't know. There's a lot I have to sort out."

"Bit of a mess, isn't it?"

I exhaled, as agreement. I slid my face up and down against my palm, my eyes shut. "I'm sorry, Fiona. Obviously it's worse for you. I would never have wished this on you."

"I could have ended it. I chose not to. And it's not as if I'm destitute.

I have my work, my friends. I can look after myself."

"Good. That's good." Something about the word *destitute*, along with *afford* from earlier, sent a belated flash of obligation through me. I opened my eyes and blinked at the fridge. "I should help you. Financially. That's . . . I ought to do that."

"One could sue for financial support during pregnancy." She sounded dry. "But it'd be absurd in our situation. It's considerate of you, but unnecessary."

Meaning the situation where she was wealthy, and I had depleted most of my savings through transatlantic plane tickets and London cost-of-living, and was leaping from one acting or barista job to another and occasionally living with cockroaches. "Yeah," I said, deflated. "Still . . . "

"I don't need your money. Your moral support is really all I need." Her voice caught.

"You have that. We'll . . . talk lots."

"Thank you. Well. I'll let you go ponder this awhile. I've done quite enough to ruin your day."

"No, I . . . it's an important thing to know."

"It's good to hear your voice," she said softly.

I tried to smile. "Yours too. Take care, okay?"

"I will. Bye."

We hung up.

I set the phone on the table beside my half-eaten peanut butter sandwich. Stress had clenched up my stomach; there was no way I could eat that, or even look at it another second.

I rose to get a glass of water instead, and nauseating chills shot down my legs and arms. I spun around and darted to the bathroom just in time to throw up.

After chucking up every bite of my lunch, I slumped onto the bath rug, my back against the sink cabinets, my eyes watering. Great, now *I* had morning sickness.

Yeah, feel real sorry for yourself. It's only what she dealt with every day for six weeks while you were having fun recreating the Kama Sutra with Andy.

I dragged myself to my feet and managed to swallow some water from the bathroom tap, then staggered back to where I'd left my phone. I brought up Andy's name in the contacts, and almost tapped "call." Then I stopped. Why subject him to my earliest freak-out and ruin his morning too?

I had to think.

I also had rehearsal. Damn it.

On my weak-legged walk to the Green Sea Theatre downtown, I shot keen stares at every baby I passed in a stroller or backpack or one of those chest-pack things. I studied the parents too. Had they felt this unmoored when they found out they were going to have those kids? Some must have been trying for it; they'd have been happy. But probably some others had been as blindsided as me. Yet there they all went, carting pacifier-plugged babies along with their coffee cups as nonchalantly as other people walked their dogs.

Yeah, so? *I* couldn't do that. Fiona was prepared to adopt our baby out, and I would never have to deal with a single pacifier, and probably that was all for the best. I had enough to handle without something like that, given Andy, my always-temporary jobs, and my parents . . .

Though really, I was probably set up better to raise a kid than a lot of people. No remaining student loans, no drug addictions or arrest records, a fairly stable living situation.

Ugh, why even consider it? What was I thinking? This wasn't the plan.

Not that I'd exactly had a plan for my life. Or if I had, it'd been changing a lot lately anyway.

There were no perfect solutions. There just weren't.

I was fully off my game in rehearsal. Our director, Dominic, chastised me for how unnaturally I was moving and talking: "Did you not sleep last night? What gives?" The other actors glanced at me in bemusement too.

I apologized and said yeah, I was really tired. I'd grown fond of this cast and crew, had gotten to know them as I did with any production. But the middle of running a scene wasn't the time or place to announce, *Sorry, just found out this woman I slept with one time is pregnant. Plus I've become totally infatuated with my best friend. I have no idea what to do. Ha, crazy, right?*

After rehearsal, I knew I shouldn't attempt the mile-long uphill walk home with nothing but water in my stomach. I'd probably faint. Though I still wasn't remotely hungry, I got a sandwich and a bottle of juice from a café downtown and sat with it on a bench in a plaza. Blossoming cherry trees filled the plaza, with daffodils growing under them, and all the flowers seemed to glow brighter than the gray sky, like the world had turned upside-down and light now came from the ground. Fitting, on a day when *my* world had certainly flipped itself onto its head.

I drank the juice, managed a bite or two of sandwich, and watched white cherry petals blow past my boots. And thought, and thought, and thought.

CHAPTER 25: HAPPY BIRTHDAY

Andy: On my way! See you soon :)

Beneath heavy clouds, a line of orange sunset glowed over the water. I was back at the apartment, pacing, sipping a cup of chamomile-and-other-stuff herbal tea I'd found in the kitchen cabinets, in a vain attempt to settle my guts.

Sinter: Cool, see you soon

I couldn't even manage an emoji. It would have been a lie.

I turned on the light over the stove, sat at the kitchen table, and waited.

Andy's key hit the lock. The apartment door opened. "Hey," he called.

"Hey."

I heard the thumps of him setting down his pack and taking off his shoes and coat. He came into the kitchen with a pink bakery box. "How's it going?" He set the box on the counter and came over to kiss me.

The warmth of the kiss sent me a temporary shot of comfort, but I kept my hands wrapped around the mug on the table.

When he lifted his face again I said, as calmly as I could, "Fiona called today."

"Yeah?" He studied the mug of herbal tea and the surely haggard state of my face. "Um. Is something wrong?"

I nodded, once. "She's pregnant."

"Oh. Wow." He sounded mildly sympathetic, the appropriate level for someone he'd never met. Then he put it together. He clutched the edge of the table. "It's yours?"

My gaze rested on his fingers. I nodded.

He let go of the table and tottered toward the counter. "How? You said it was once, and you used a condom."

"It was, and we did. Apparently it failed."

"Well, shit." He rubbed his face. "What's she going to do?"

"She doesn't plan to keep it. She's thinking adoption."

His shoulders relaxed a little. "Okay."

"That should be that. Except . . . "

He turned to look at me. Maybe it was just the hue of the soft light over the stove, but his face seemed pale. "Except what?"

I gazed at the chair across from me. My tongue touched my upper lip. "It's my *kid*, is all. It's a lot to think about."

He gripped the back of the chair and sank into it. His gaze slipped absently to the front of my sweatshirt. "Sure. Guess it would be."

"She called this morning, and I've been thinking about it all day, and I keep telling myself I should just say yes, fine, let the kid be adopted. Sign off on the whole deal, same way she plans to. But every time I try to commit to that, it's like something tugs on my sleeve and says . . . 'Wait.'"

I met his gaze. He looked frozen in fascinated terror.

"This is my child," I tried to explain. "I don't plan on having a lot of them. I kind of want to know the ones I do have."

He put down his glasses with a clatter and dropped his face into his hands. "Well, holy fuck."

"I haven't decided anything yet. I'm obviously not going to decide today. There's time."

"How much time?" he mumbled into his palms. "When's she due? Nine months from, what, December?"

"Yeah. Due in September. But I should make my decision sooner than that, so she can plan."

"Your decision. Right. Because . . . " He dropped his hands and stared at me, his hair all awry from his fingers digging into it. "I don't understand. Are you talking about going back to her? Making it work between you? Which I guess, you're bi and you do like her, so . . . "

"No. Not that. She kind of floated the idea, but I couldn't. It wouldn't work."

His gaze moved away from my face again. "But you could," he said softly. "I mean, you're free to. If you want."

"I don't." My throat had tightened. "I don't want to leave. I like it here." *With you.*

He brought up his interlaced fingers to his mouth and sighed into them. "Well. Okay. I've never had to think about getting anyone pregnant. But, um, I guess I always assumed, if the guy's not with the woman anymore, or never properly *was* with her . . . shouldn't he just go along with whatever she wants for the baby?"

"Probably. Yes."

"I mean, she's the one who has to put up with the whole pregnancy thing." He frowned at me. "How is she? How's she feeling?"

"Awful, sounds like. But better lately. Which is all normal, she says."

"Jeez." He lowered his hands to the table and twiddled his thumbs, his gaze roaming off across the kitchen floor.

"And I did this. I did this to someone. And *left* her."

"But if you don't want to go back to her, then what else can you do?"

"Offer moral support, is what she said. And let her know if I have any other input. On what should happen."

"Such as you taking the kid? Is that what you mean?"

I turned the mug between my hands. The ceramic was growing cold.

"Maybe. Just if . . . " I shrugged. The idea was insane. But my weird, stubborn mind wouldn't shut up, wouldn't stop insisting it *was* an option.

Andy sat up straighter. "Look, I think you're still in shock. You need to take a few days, chill, get your head straight. Right now you're just . . . processing."

Translation: *You're talking crazy talk and complicating everyone's life.* Which was true, of course.

"I'm probably over-stressing," I agreed. "I don't know why I'm thinking like this. I mean . . . " I lowered my face to my hands. "If I took this kid, there'd be no way *not* to tell my parents about it. Picture that. In particular the whole 'product of a one-night stand and I'm not going to marry the mother' part."

"Yeeeeah." He drew out the word in dry horror. We stayed quiet a minute, then he added, "But I mean, if having them adopted by someone else is what Fiona wants, that's straightforward enough, right? Then your folks would never have to know."

"That would probably be the smart thing to do." I couldn't commit to a plan, though. Every single option looked impossible. "There's . . . a lot to think about. Today's a complete loss. I'm sorry. God, I'm sorry, Andy."

Sorry, I meant to say, that the mood had crashed down so far from last night's beauty and enchantment, even if I didn't know whether he had felt the same, or indeed how he felt at all.

He shifted and took a few seconds to respond. "Best birthday ever, right?"

With a groan, I slumped back in my chair and didn't bother answering. Night had fallen; the raindrops on the window had each captured a little piece of colored light from the city.

"Guessing you don't want to go to Machiavelli's after all," Andy said, with a glance at my mug of herbal tea.

I shook my head. "I've barely been able to eat since she told me."

"Well. Here. You don't have to eat it, but you might as well admire it."

He got up, opened the pink bakery box, and took out a small chocolate cake. He brought it to the table, along with a candle and a book of matches.

"It's from Dilettante." He placed the cake in front of me, scooting my mug aside. "They do good chocolate."

The cake, big enough for perhaps four generous slices, was a mound of glossy dark chocolate with a wreath of sliced strawberries on top. In what looked like white-chocolate calligraphy, some confectionary artisan had written "Happy birthday" in the center of the circle. It smelled like dark, rich heaven, enticing me even in my queasy state of health.

"Wow," I said. "That looks amazing."

"They gave me a candle." He pierced the center of the cake with a slim green column of spiraled wax. He struck a match and lit it. Aglow with candlelight, he sat down again across from me. "Happy birthday. As you know, it's best if I don't sing." He smiled wryly.

I tried to smile back, then dropped my gaze when tears filled my eyes. The flame warped and swam as I stared at it.

He was the best thing in my life. He'd brought me a birthday cake. Less than twenty-four hours earlier, I'd been snuggling him and looking forward to a wide-open, low-pressure future in which I could learn to be out and comfortable, embrace my new identity, explore what we had between us, if anything—all gradually, taking as much time as I needed.

Instead, the clock was ticking toward a September due date, and everything was massively fucked up. He didn't know my feelings. *I* wasn't even sure of my feelings. I still wasn't properly out of the closet, because I was too scared, and I was exhausted from being scared all the time, but didn't know how to be any other way.

And ultimately, I couldn't get out of this mess without letting someone down or screwing up someone's life or losing something I wanted. I knew that without even knowing what exactly I wanted yet.

The tears slipped down my face, one from each eye.

"Blow it out." Andy's voice was gentle.

I drew in a shaky breath and blew out the candle.

He reached through the smoke. His thumb grazed my cheek, wiping away a tear. "Want to forget about it for tonight, and eat cake and play video games?"

I sniffled. "Yeah."

CHAPTER 26: UNDER PRESSURE

Unknown number: So she told you. What do you plan to do about it, you little prick?

I awoke the next morning after a few restless hours of sleep to find the text. Alarm rocketed through me, as if the message were a blackmail note made of cut-out newspaper letters.

Sinter: Who is this?
Unknown number: It's Sebastian, who the fuck do you think, wankstain

I relaxed a little and glanced around the guest room. It was Sunday morning, and Andy was in the shower, from the sound of it.

Sinter: Oh. Should've known from the insults
Sebastian: Yeah, you should have. Have you any idea the suffering you've put her through?
Sinter: I obviously didn't know until yesterday. And I feel terrible.
Sebastian: How is she supposed to get over you with a bloody great piece of you growing inside her?
Sinter: This was absolutely never my intention. We took precautions, it failed, she chose this, I didn't know . . . I feel awful though
Sebastian: Boo hoo! I've known for weeks and have been wanting to punch your lights out. Just needed to tell you
Sinter: Duly warned. Cheers

Sebastian: Are you shagging men now then?

Sinter: Why in the world would I tell you that

Sinter: Sigh. Yes. I am

Sebastian: Then don't give her any false hopes. Bugger off. The less she hears from you the better

Sinter: I understand but I need to be in touch at least a certain amount. About the baby. I'm really going to try not to hurt her

Sebastian: You already fucking have and still fucking will if you stick around

Sinter: Yes. Fine. And I'm sorry. Sorry you have to put up with it too

Sebastian: You'd better do the right bloody thing by her

Sinter: I will as soon as I figure out what that is

He didn't respond. Down the hall, the shower shut off.

Sinter: I'm glad you're there with her. She deserves someone who loves her

Sebastian: Yeah she fucking does.

Sinter: So . . . how's the new album coming along?

Sebastian: Fuck off. We're done here. Go shag your mate

Sinter: Right. Nice talking to you

I sat staring across the room, dazed, angry, insulted, and obscurely frightened.

Upon hearing the bathroom door squeak open, I stood and went to the hall.

Andy came out, wet-haired and shirtless, in pajama pants. We paused to regard one another warily. Our evening of snacks and video games had gone decently—it felt like a truce, at least. No sex, but before I had shuffled off to the guest room he had caught me and hugged me and mumbled that things were going to be okay.

"Hey," he said.

"Hey. Nice chat I just had." I handed him the phone.

Without his glasses, he squinted to read the texts. "Does that say 'wankstain'?"

"Of course it does."

He handed me back the phone. "Charming."

"Sebastian always is."

"Ignore him, dude. Seriously. From the sound of it, he was just super jealous." Andy walked off down the hall.

"So are we cool?" I called after him, pathetically.

"Yes, wankstain."

———

Andy and I maintained a companionable not-talking-about-it arrangement for the next week. He gave me space to process the situation and didn't ask anything of me, not even sex, although he accepted sex the couple of times I proposed it. Our intimacy didn't hold quite the adventurously delightful vibe it used to, given the pressures on my mind, but it still comforted me for the space of an hour here and there. Since I wasn't sleeping well, I kept to the guest room rather than disturb him by flopping around in his bed.

The adoption idea was the simplest option by far, and I knew I should accept it. But I failed. Questions and objections kept sprouting in my mind like weeds.

Was it a boy or a girl? What would they look like? Would they end up tall like me, short like Fiona, or split the difference and be in between? Would they enjoy theatrical endeavors like both of us? Or would they take after their grandparents—either set—and be more into finance and business? I should probably be around to nurture any artistic side just in case. The world needed more artists; it squashed too many as it was.

What if they were bi, gay, trans, queer? If so, I also ought to be there to make sure they were properly supported. At the very least, no matter who I caught them kissing at age fifteen, I wouldn't shame them and give them mental health issues for the next decade. I would try to understand what they liked and wanted in life, and do my best to relate to it, unlike *some* parents I could name.

Ugh. Why spin out this imaginary future? Fiona didn't expect me to raise the child. She didn't even want to herself. My parents would be appalled if I announced I was becoming a single dad—although surely, before long, the existence of a grandchild would soften them up . . .

Argh. Stop.

And what about Andy? Not that we were dating, exactly, but I did want to take into consideration his general plans for life, what with the feelings we might have caught for one another.

"Do you think you'll ever want kids?" I asked him, a week after Fiona had dropped the bombshell on me.

"I guess *eventually*." Andy jerked sideways on the couch as he steered his Mario Kart car to zoom ahead of mine. "Like, I always thought it'd be when I was thirty or thirty-five and in a committed relationship and knew what the hell I was doing."

"No one knows what they're doing at first, though, do they? Jesus, turtle shell." My car collided with the shell and crashed into an ice wall. I pushed my thumb against the button to accelerate back onto the track.

"I guess, but . . . " He trailed off. "Why? Have you always figured you'd have kids?"

"I have, is the weird thing. Like with every one of my girlfriends, I remember thinking, 'I wonder if this is the woman I'll have children with.' Though, funny enough, I never thought that with Fiona."

"But now?" He dodged around a car spinning out of control and sped past, his face neutral, locked onto the game.

"I'm still not thinking of raising a child *with* her. Just, it's been bugging me that I might never know this kid. I'd always be wondering how they were doing, whether I could have helped with something."

"Maybe you can set up some deal with the adoptive parents. Some way to visit occasionally or get news."

"I don't know. There's probably laws about that. Argh." My complaint was for both the hypothetical situation and the fact that my car had flown off a cliff and had to be airlifted up by a friendly cloud.

"Could be awkward," he conceded. "Having them be the 'real' parents while you're this other dad guy who shows up once in a while for a Saturday trip to the zoo." Andy's car soared across the finish line.

"Exactly. It sounds horrible. I'd be the outsider, again. Like I always am."

"You're not *always*."

"I am with my parents—I don't fit in at my own fucking house. I'm a third wheel around Julie and Daniel. Your family's great to me, but I don't actually belong to it. In the queer community—well, I'm not even properly out, so it's hard to feel like I fit in there either."

"That could be fixed by coming out," he said dryly.

I ignored that sticky point for the time being. "With theater shows, I belong for a while, but it's short-lived." My car finally crossed the finish line, and I rested the controller on my leg. Confetti exploded on-screen. "I'm part of the cast for a couple of months, then it's over, we go our separate ways, and I have to find a new role. And another, and another. Forever."

"You love your job." He sounded perplexed.

"Yes. I do. I'm . . . getting off the point. Which is that I want something more stable when we're talking about something as important as my kid. I don't want to be an outsider in yet another situation." I kept watching the cars spin and flash in the demo portion of the game.

"Then don't be in the situation at all." He sounded gentle, though his message wasn't, exactly. "Let it be someone else's deal. Have your own kids later."

"When? How? Say I do come out, and end up with . . . some guy."

You, for instance. "And we want kids someday. Then *we're* in the position of adopting. Which is kind of stupid when my own actual biological child is being offered to me right now."

"But what if now isn't the right time?"

"Is that how you'd feel, if it were you?"

He threw down the controller and got up. "Yes, I just said! Why would I be ready for a kid? I'm twenty-five and I don't even have a cat or a houseplant."

"You have a plant." I pointed to a potted, palm-like thing in the corner.

He glanced at it in disdain. "That's fake."

"Oh. It is?"

"Yes. So you're working all these temporary jobs and living with me and my fake plant, and what are you even talking about? Bringing a baby into that? Here?" He opened his arms to indicate the apartment in general.

"If I *was* going to take the kid, I'd get my own place. Obviously."

This living arrangement was only supposed to be temporary, after all. We'd lived in separate places all our lives up until then. Finding my own place was sensible, and suggesting it shouldn't cause me this stab of pain.

"You're not thinking this through," he said. "The impact it would have on your life."

My gaze trailed across the apartment, all electronic gadgets and college-era hand-me-down furniture and geeky fandom paraphernalia. Most of it probably hadn't been washed or dusted in years. A space where you'd raise a baby would be a different world: cleaned regularly, safety-proofed, with, what, a crib, diapers, stroller? I didn't even know. I knew nothing.

"You're probably right," I said, defeated.

Later, though, when he came into the bathroom to brush his teeth as I was finishing brushing mine, he met my glance in the mirror and said, "I do think it's noble of you. To care what happens to your kid. Not everyone would care."

I spat out the toothpaste and stepped aside to let him reach the sink. "*You* would care. If it were yours."

He wet his toothbrush under the tap. "I suppose. Although now we're back to that 'how the hell would I have gotten anyone pregnant' question."

I acknowledged the point with a nod and clinked my toothbrush back into the mug on the counter.

"Anyway," he said, gaze lowered, "I'll respect whatever you choose. I'd be kind of an asshole of a best friend if I didn't."

"Even if I end up deciding I want to be in this kid's life somehow?"

"Yeah. Besides, you're right. The kid would be lucky to know you."

"I never said *that*."

"Still. They would."

"Thank you," I said quietly, though without as much happiness as I wanted to feel.

A best friend. I was lucky to have that much.

No point in longing for him to be more.

———

Sinter: I can't sleep. I've been wondering, do we know if it's a boy or a girl?

Fiona: Don't know yet. That ultrasound's in another couple of weeks. Shall I find out and tell you?

Sinter: Please. Thanks

Fiona: That's the reason you can't sleep?

Sinter: Well it's one of many reasons

Fiona: How is Andy taking all this?

Sinter: He's being a good friend. Listening if I want to talk about it

Fiona: I thought you were together. Although I suppose you only said it was complicated

Sinter: We aren't really together. Complicated is a good word

Fiona: Even more so now I suppose

Sinter: Yeah. Btw would you know yet if it was twins or anything?

Fiona: Only one heartbeat when they've done checkups so it probably isn't

Sinter: You got to hear their heartbeat?

Fiona: Yes. It's quite fast because they're so small

Sinter: Wow that's so cool. Do you think they'll give you one of those blurry pictures when you get the ultrasound?

Fiona: Don't know, they might. Do you want a copy if they do?

Sinter: Yeah I'd like to see it. Even though all the other ones I've ever seen look like Rorschach tests and I can't make sense of them

Fiona: Nor can I. I'll send it regardless once I have it

Sinter: Thank you. How are you feeling?

Fiona: Less sick but still tired. I wish I were writing

Sinter: Then write :)

Fiona: I should but I'm uninspired. I don't know

Sinter: Try writing something today anyway. Just for the hell of it. It doesn't have to be good, just try

Fiona: Perhaps I will do, just for you

Sinter: Last question for tonight. Sebastian isn't going to show up and kill me is he?

Fiona: I doubt it. :) He's more bark than bite

Sinter: If you say so

Fiona: I promise to ask him not to kill you

Sinter: Thanks. Maybe I can sleep now

Fiona: Try at least. Goodnight love

CHAPTER 27: SITUATION

A FEW NIGHTS LATER, ANDY CAME HOME FROM WORK BRIGHT-EYED AND FLUSHED. "WE GOT IT! THE EMpress Miyoko tie-in!" He dropped his messenger bag on the floor and threw his arms around me.

I hugged him back even though it took me a second to figure out what he was talking about. "Oh, no way, the game for the TV show?"

"Yes! We get to make it!" He jumped up and down, still holding me.

I laughed. "Sweet. Congrats. So, you'll personally get to work on it?"

"Yeah, and here's the crazy part. It's, uh . . . " He reached down to retrieve his bag and move it to a chair. "In Tokyo. They'll be sending over two of us for, like, five or six months, to work with the animators in the studio."

A pang hit me, lancing straight through my center. "You're going to Tokyo? For five or six months?"

His smile twisted. "They've asked me. I've said yes. But I wouldn't leave till the end of August, beginning of September, around there."

It was April. The end of summer wasn't far enough away by my standards.

"September. Oh." I folded my arms, feeling cold. I gazed blankly in the direction of the fake tree.

"Yeah." He became more subdued. "Right around baby due date."

"Well, right, that's fine. I ought to get my own place anyway one of these months."

"Suppose I'll have to sublet this place, or just let it go." He set his elbows on the back of the chair. "But hey, maybe you can come visit."

"Sure. Though, in one possible scenario, my life would be a lot more complicated by the end of this year. Still, who knows."

He looked down. "I guess it'd be kind of insane. Also a really expensive plane ticket just for a visit."

"I might, though. Anyway, we'd keep in touch."

"Definitely. All those times you were in England, we kept in touch just fine."

"Daily," I agreed. "With flirtation."

He met my eyes and smiled rakishly, and my breath hitched. Oh God, an ocean between us? I couldn't live through it again.

But I had to. I was being a selfish wimp.

"This is your dream job." I said it to convince myself rather than him. "Your favorite series, a once-in-a-lifetime chance. You should totally do it."

"And this baby is a once-in-a-lifetime chance for you." He sounded wistful, and our gazes met again for a moment, then separated. "Might be a challenging year for us both. But if it's what we want . . . "

I nodded.

I allowed the bitter sentiment for a few seconds: so much for him being in love with me. Dangle a dream job in Tokyo in front of him and he was ready to hand off his apartment, leap onto a plane, and leave me behind.

But that was unfair. I'd worked abroad in England four times, and he wouldn't have dreamed of talking me out of it. He deserved this, and I supported him in pursuing it.

Meanwhile, I deserved the chance at my baby, and he would support whatever my choice was there, and eventually we'd reunite. Friends throughout.

But I didn't see how things could possibly feel the same between us anymore after we'd gone down these paths, which were already diverging and pulling us apart.

"I'm going to miss the crap out of you," I admitted.

"I can still sext you from Tokyo."

"Yeah? You better."

He came around the chair, set his hands on my hipbones, and drew me up against him. "Going to help me celebrate or what?"

I bent my head to kiss his neck, breathing the warm scent of him, still there, still close. "Hell yeah."

———

Sign off on adoption. Forget the fact that I had a kid out there somewhere. Never tell my parents—or at least, put it off eighteen years or so. Continue on, child-free, follow Andy across the globe if he let me, come out of the closet and become his boyfriend if he was up for that too, find acting work wherever I happened to be. It didn't sound like a bad life.

So why did something tug at my heart in panic every time I considered it? Maybe because of the part where I had to come out to everyone, especially my parents. Or the part where I wouldn't know how my child was doing. Or the ticking time bomb: when this kid grew up—by which point I might be married and/or have other kids—they'd probably do some research, figure out who I was, come find me, and ask, "Why didn't you want me?"

And what would I say? "Actually, I kind of did. I just chickened out." Lame.

Sinter: I'm sorry to bug you, but I have another question. Would you be able to choose who adopted the baby? Google says in the US you can (open adoption), but I couldn't tell for sure if the UK has that

Fiona: I've not gone into those details yet myself, but Chelsea thinks it could be done. I would have to interview couples in depth though, which I admit sounds dreadful

Sinter: Yeah good point, that would suck. It's just . . . I picture the baby ending up with someone who might be anti-gay, or oppressive in some other way, and it's been bugging me

Fiona: I don't like that idea either. But if we're both to sign over our rights, there's only so much we can do about what happens to the child after that.

Sinter: Then . . . what are the odds they'd let us visit once in a while? Get to know the kid? Or me at least, if you don't want to

Fiona: I would guess not very high, though such things could possibly be worked out. I really don't know yet. I'd need a social worker to tell us this. Lawyer perhaps

Sinter: Sorry, yeah. I'm sorting it out and still haven't decided

Fiona: Decided?

Sinter: Well I've been thinking about taking the baby myself. If you still don't want to. But I'm not sure

Fiona: Oh. I'm surprised. I assumed you wouldn't even consider it

Sinter: It's probably crazy. My mind just won't shut up about it. I don't know

Fiona: Well . . . I'll think about it too. Although nothing legally binding about custody can be decided until the birth, if I understand correctly

Meaning she could change her mind by September and take the kid herself. Which would make the child easier for me to visit, probably, but would also make life much more complicated between Fiona and me— for the long haul. Dread hooked itself deep inside me. To still have to tell my parents about the kid, but with the complication that I wasn't married to the mother . . . to be a father from a distance, an outsider exactly the way I didn't want to be . . . to have Sebastian start dating Fiona and become more of a proper father to my own kid than I was . . . to be bi and trying to figure out how to manage that in the dating world, while also trying to manage familial relationships from across the Atlantic . . .

or I could move over there to be closer to the child, get citizenship at long last, but then I'd be permanently farther from Andy . . .

Argh. Please no.

Sinter: Do you feel like you'll change your mind? About wanting to be a mum

Fiona: I don't think so. But life does keep going differently than I expected

Sinter: I know the feeling. I'll think on it some more and be in touch, ok?

Fiona: All right. I'd like to have a plan in place by, say, the beginning of June. In case I do need to talk to adoption agencies

Sinter: Beginning of June. Will do

CHAPTER 28: THE PROMISE

I TAPPED INTO MY HUMAN OBSERVATION MODE, LIKE I DID WHEN STUDYING FOR ACTING ROLES. I focused on people with young kids—on the sidewalks, in our apartment building, in the café. As if auditioning for the role of "the dad," I watched what those parents or nannies or caretakers did. Coaxing kids to walk a little faster. Reminding them not to reach for dogs without asking the owner. Spooning yogurt into their mouths. Hugging them and carrying them the rest of the way when they fell over and had a meltdown. Reading colorful cardboard books with them. Telling them not to shred napkins all over the floor. Encouraging them when they tried to say a word, and playing voice games where they mimicked each other's sounds.

It looked like a shit-ton of work. I already worked plenty.

But wasn't I working *toward* something? Toward, say, a life with more meaning, more stability, than it currently had?

Gordy, who played Shakespeare in *The Fair Youth*, was in his thirties and had a wife and two kids. One evening as we wrapped up rehearsal I asked him, "So is the whole family coming to see the show?"

"Just Sara," he said. "The kids are too little to get it."

"Ah, yeah. They're how old?"

"Five and two."

"That's a lot of work," I said. "Little kids and a theater life."

"It is, but it's hard no matter what your job is. And I'm not on tour or anything, so could be worse."

"Ah. True."

"In any case, it's totally worth it. They're still the best thing I ever put into the world. Including every part I ever played, or anything else I ever created."

I nodded. "That's what people say."

I had two thoughts then: one, I wanted to be able to say that about my child rather than, "I wussed out and gave them to someone else." Two, had my parents ever said that about me, to anyone?

Doubtful. My relationship with my parents, however, was a separate issue.

I reached out to one more expert for feedback.

Hi Chelsea,

I know this is out of nowhere, but I have a question for you. If it's too personal, you don't have to answer or anything.

I've been thinking about the baby, and I'm weirdly tempted to take him or her. That is, assuming Fiona doesn't want to. She told me you were single when you adopted Mina, so what made you choose to do it? How were you sure you wanted to? What kind of things should I be planning for? I know I'll need help, daycares or nannies or something, but I don't know the costs, whether I'm being an idiot for even thinking about it . . . I guess, just how do you know you should do it?

Thanks for being there for Fiona. I feel really bad about it all.

Sinter

Hi Sinter,

It's not too personal a question! I love talking about Mina. And really, I could go on and on about what she means to me and why I chose to have her when I did, which in my case involved infertility and the knowledge I was getting older and wanted to start already. That's all different in your case, of course. Still, when it comes to deciding to have kids, it's actually quite simple.

You either want them or you don't. Nearly all the parents I know have said the same. I knew I wanted her. If you know you want this baby, then that's your answer. It's honestly no more complicated than that.

It would be good to have a support network in place to help with child-care. Grandparents or other relatives are ideal, though friends and neighbours and nannies can work too. Other than that, yes you can do calculations, google everything imaginable, try to work out how your finances and living situation will look, how much sleep and free time you'll lose, how you'll manage your job. But if people went solely by those calculations, no one would ever have children except William and Kate. :)

Fiona doesn't want children. She's said so, and I think it's the truth in her case. But she's going through with it for the benefit of others, and if that other is you . . . well, in some ways that would be easier for her and in other ways not. You have to choose based on what you want, though. Not to please her or anyone else.

I don't know if this helps or makes any sense. It's just what's proven true for me. I hope I can be of help to you and Fiona, whatever you both decide.

Take care, and we'll talk soon about the film release among other things!

xo,

Chelsea

———

I should have listened to her. I shouldn't have gotten onto the internet.

Because really, if you want to stress yourself out to the absolute max, try that: get online and look up how to take care of a newborn. Or a toddler. Or an elementary-school kid. Or a teenager, if you're still reading by that point and haven't shoved your computer out of a fourth-floor window, then thrown yourself out too.

Diapers. Sleep deprivation. Formula. Immunizations. Teething. Pacifiers. (Or not.) Colic. Scary infections. Strollers vs. front carriers vs.

backpacks vs. slings. Incredibly expensive daycare. Intrusive advice from other parents and grandparents.

At the thought of my parents appearing in the room to loom over me and school me on what kind of baby food I should be buying and *goddammit, son is that car seat even installed correctly?*, I smacked my laptop shut and devolved into a panic attack.

It was one of the rare evenings I didn't have rehearsal. I'd returned from a barista shift awhile earlier. Andy was still at work. Convinced the world was a hellscape of dangers, drudgery, and evil, I curled up on the couch and deployed my deep-breathing skills.

When Andy got home, I didn't move from my fetal position. (Oh hey, same position my kid was in.) He crouched by the sofa to frown at me. "Now what?"

I swallowed to moisten my dry mouth. "I looked up how to take care of babies."

He lay on top of me, spreading himself over my balled-up form like a starfish on a bed of rocks. "That does sound terrifying. But you know, people with less money and intelligence than you have figured it out."

"In theory."

"If it's stressing you out this much, why even consider it? Why not sign off on adoption?" His chin dug into my shoulder.

I grunted and shifted my arm, but stayed under him, comforted by his weight. "I keep thinking of Chelsea," I said, my mouth mashed halfway into the sofa cushions. "She was single when she adopted Mina. Now Mina's two and Chelsea's still working in movies. She did it. She managed."

"Maybe she'd have advice, then."

"I emailed her."

"And?"

I elbowed him out of the way, sat up and found the email on my phone, and handed it to him.

He sat next to me to read it. Then he just said, "Ah," and continued gazing at the message.

"I think why I'm so scared," I said, "is that I do know my answer."

He chewed his lower lip a moment. "You're going to do this."

"If Fiona will let me. Yeah. I think I am."

He handed me back my phone. "But . . . your parents."

I covered my eyes, groaning. "I *know*. Why do you think I'm so freaked out?"

"Well. They can't control you or really do anything to you. You're an adult."

"But I want to fix things with them, get us back on good terms, have them be my 'support network,' or at least part of it. Then I keep doing things that are going to make them lose their shit."

He stayed quiet a few seconds. "Like being bi."

"Exactly."

"Which they don't even know yet."

I nodded, let my hand drop from my eyes, and stared at the floor.

"Well," he said, "one confession at a time, I guess."

"I guess." Remorse smacked me like a slap. I was shoving the coming-out onto the back burner, relegating Andy to a dirty little secret when, in truth, he was one of the people I treasured most in the world, all because I was a coward and couldn't deal with more than one scary situation at a time.

I wanted to be braver, but if being braver meant dragging him deeper into my screwed-up life—well, that wouldn't be doing him any favors either. He'd probably get fed up before the year was out and leave me, and I'd never see him again.

I swung my knee aside to touch his leg. "I'm sorry I've been so stressed and weird."

"I don't blame you. Anyone would be. I've been stressed too, what with Tokyo, and . . . everything. Life's been busy. Seems like we're hardly ever home at the same time anymore."

We hadn't fooled around for several days. I was fine with blaming that on my schedule instead of on deeper problems.

"Actor hours," I said. "They suck sometimes." I found a bit of stuffing coming out of a couch cushion and pulled at it. Though I absolutely did not want to say this next thing, I felt honor-bound to. "Look, if you meet someone . . . some normal guy who doesn't work nights and weekends . . . obviously that would be cool."

Jealousy and pain were screaming and beating their fists against my bones from the inside, but really, it was cool.

"I'll be leaving the country in a few months," he said. "Wouldn't make sense to get involved with someone. Which is why it's been handy you let me use you for your body."

"Well, I'm using you right back, so."

"Exactly. Reciprocal using."

We smiled, but not exactly at each other. Our gazes touched, then flicked away.

———

"I'm going to do it," I said at dinner the next night. "I'm committing. I'm taking my kid."

Andy blew out a breath, long and slow, and set down the forkful of spaghetti he'd been lifting to his mouth. We were in our kitchen, and I'd prepared a basic dinner—pasta, sauce from a jar, a fancy-grocery salad, and Pepperidge Farm cookies. I'd hoped it might soften him up and reduce the chances that he'd tell me I was crazy.

He didn't, at least. "I'm not surprised," he said. "Sounded like you were headed that direction. I'll just say . . . what Chelsea said about a support network, that's going to be important. Especially if I'm not around to babysit for the first six months."

"But you would if you were around?"

"Of course. Duh." He finally ate the bite of spaghetti.

Images flashed into my head: Andy cooing at my baby, lifting him or her up above his head, making steampunk aircraft noises, bottle-feeding the little one on his lap on the couch while watching *Doctor Who* and explaining in quiet tones what Daleks were . . .

I wanted it so much it hurt.

But he had other plans for his life and didn't know I was having such sappy feelings, so I just poked my fork at the pasta and said, "Thanks."

We ate silently for a minute.

"How are you going to break it to your folks?" he asked.

"I was thinking I'd put it off till the time's closer. Fiona could still change her mind, so there's no point freaking them out till I'm sure it's happening."

"Have you talked to her yet?"

"That's up next."

———

"Hey, Fiona."

"Hello." She sounded tired. "How are things?"

"They're okay." I sank onto the couch, my bare feet cold. It was a Monday morning, and I'd waited until Andy left for work before I called her. "So I've been going over and over it, and . . . I would like to take the baby. If that's okay with you."

Second or two of silence. "Really? You wouldn't rather be free?"

Remembering the tied-down-ness of those parents I'd scrutinized, I felt a new flutter of terror. "It's scary, for sure. But I think I'd regret it if I gave up this chance. I want to be there for this kid."

She released her breath slowly, in a static crackle. "Well, this is good, then. Means I won't have to go through as much. The adoption agency and all." Sounded like she was trying to convince herself it was truly good, though.

"I hope so. I wanted you to feel settled, as much as possible."

"Then we shall consider that the plan. Unexpected though it is."

"Great. Thank you."

But nothing legally binding could be decided until the baby was born. She could change her mind. The possibility reverberated in the silence.

After those few quiet seconds, she said in a crisper voice, "We'll have the DVDs ready soon. The final cut of the film. I'll have some put into region 1 format for you. Also a downloadable version. We'll send you a link."

"Cool, yeah, can't wait to see it."

We talked about the final edits, the changes made, the soundtrack. Before long she said, "I should go. Thank you for letting me know your intentions."

I pulled my knees to my chest, gazing at the drizzle on the living-room window. I'd hoped to feel steadier after this conversation, but instead we were all still floundering in uncertainty—me, Fiona, Andy, the baby. "Thank *you*," I said. "For going through all this, which I know sucks. For giving me this chance, when all I did was . . . " Fuck up your life? Break your heart? "Disappoint you," I settled for.

"You haven't," she said. "Well. No, that's a lie. It's true I'm disappointed in some ways. My trouble is, I don't know what I want anymore."

The sadness in her voice was overloading my emotions. It was so unlike what I was used to hearing from her—my adaptable, got-it-together director. "I hope you find it. Whatever inspires you. You will. You're so good at it—writing, directing, everything."

"Thanks." She basically whispered it. "Well, I'll have them send the DVDs. Bye."

I said, "Bye," but the call had already clicked into silence.

CHAPTER 29: ALIVE AND KICKING

MAY ARRIVED. FLOWERS AND GREEN LEAVES STARTED BRIGHTENING SEATTLE'S PERSISTENT GRAY. THE costumers on *The Fair Youth* selected and tailored our clothes, and I got my hair cut to about two inches long so it would fit easier under the ponytailed wig they'd chosen for me. I allowed a week with dyed-black tips and dirty-blond roots, then had one of the hairstyling professionals on Capitol Hill tint my roots purple and blue, because I wasn't me without crazy hair.

I ordered books online, three heavy volumes for the clueless beginner on how to keep babies alive: what to feed an infant, what to do when they were screaming, that kind of thing.

When they came, I sat down and opened one. An anxiety attack threatened me in the first few pages, but I kept on. With more and more information, fed to me slowly by the sympathetic author like mashed carrots on a tiny spoon, I began to calm down. After all, everyone currently alive was born and raised somehow. Maybe even I could handle parenting.

When Andy got home and discovered me on the couch reading a book with a soft-focus baby on the cover, he froze in place. I shrugged. He gave me a tiny, brittle smile and wandered away.

But a couple of days later, I found him browsing one of the other baby books at the kitchen counter while he sipped his Saturday-morning coffee.

He looked up, squinting. "You have to feed them *every three to four hours* for the first month? Around the clock?"

"So they say."

"How?"

I grabbed a mug for myself. "By losing a lot of sleep, is my understanding."

He looked at the book again. I expected a snarky retort, perhaps *Better you than me*. Instead he said, "My parents did this *four times*."

"And check it out, you're all still alive. Them, you, your siblings."

"Huh." He examined the page a few more seconds, then shut the book.

My parents had only done it once. Raising me had apparently been enough of an ordeal. But why dwell on that?

Chelsea emailed me to arrange some radio and TV interviews, taped ahead of time, to run on entertainment shows as the *New Romantic* air date approached.

After taking care of the interviews, I emailed back:

Hi Chelsea,

Just did the last radio show. Everyone was great, and it was cool to visit the different studios.

Listen, I wanted to ask you, is Fiona okay? She sounded so down when I last talked to her, and I haven't heard from her. I've been worried. Please let me know how it's going and what I can do to help, if anything.

Thanks,

Sinter

She answered the next day.

Hi Sinter,

Thanks for getting the interviews done. I'm looking forward to seeing/ hearing them.

Fiona's still all right although having a rough time of it, I think. She's

only doing marketing now, and it isn't her favourite part. Basically, she's be-
tween projects, between relationships, and pregnant, which isn't easy. I don't
mean to sound as if I'm blaming you; I don't think there's anything else you
could do. It's already quite admirable of you to offer to take the baby. Going
through with the pregnancy was what she wanted, but I think it's proven
harder than she expected. So is raising a child, I feel I should warn you! But
then, no one can ever really be ready, as they say.

She needs a new project, and I've proposed several from our list of script
ideas, something we could write together, but nothing's caught her fancy yet.
I'll keep reminding her, but at some point I just become a nag. I don't know;
I'll keep trying, but I don't want her to feel pressured.

Sebastian's been around a fair amount, and I think his company cheers
her up more than mine. She does have people around who care about her, at
least. And thank you for caring too.

Hope all is well with you.

xo,

Chelsea

They could say they didn't blame me all they liked, but guilt gnawed
into me like a pack of rats.

It wasn't helped by this feeling of secrecy. Though Fiona hadn't ex-
plicitly said "Don't tell anyone about all this," she hadn't encouraged me
to spread the news, nor did she seem to be talking about it herself.

But if I did take custody, I'd obviously have to tell people.

Imagining how I'd break the baby news to my parents deprived me of
countless hours of sleep. I thrashed around on the guest-room bed, trying
to envision some scenario that did not result in them losing their shit.

No such scenario existed, but at least they might eventually come
around to liking their grandchild. What, then, if that grandchild had
two dads at some point? How would *that* ever not make them lose
their shit?

This lying around awake was at least good training for the sleep deprivation that came with caring for an infant.

Early on one such morning, cloud-dimmed sun filtered around the blinds. I'd managed maybe two hours of sleep. My eyelids felt like sandpaper. Andy still slept, down the hall in his room.

I won't ever do this to you, I thought to my kid as I scowled into my pillow. *Even if you end up a neo-Nazi, I'll listen to you. I'll find common ground.*

My chest softened then. Somehow, my frustrated internal conversation with my child soothed me—because we *would* get to talk, if things went reasonably well. We'd get to know each other, forge a bond completely independent of my parents. I didn't *always* have to care what they thought.

I rolled over and picked up my phone. There was a new message from Fiona.

Fiona: I've had the ultrasound today. It's a girl. All appears to be well with her

She included a photo attachment. A black-and-white ultrasound.
I sat bolt upright.
A girl.
I had a daughter.
I zoomed in on the screen, my fingers trembling.
Was that curve a head? Was that thin smear an arm? Were those her knees, bent up? I honestly couldn't tell, but I fell instantly in love with the photo anyway.
I tapped back a response.

Sinter: That's so cool!! This makes my day. I really hope all is well with you too, please let me know how it's going

I lay back, sending a dazed smile at the ceiling. Then I threw off the blanket, went down the hall, and climbed onto Andy on his bed.

"Mmf," he protested.

"Hey. Hey."

"What," he said, fists against his eyes. "What time is it?"

"It's 6:25. Your alarm's about to go off anyway. Look, Fiona had the ultrasound. It's a girl." I held my phone above his face.

He uncovered his eyes to squint at it. "A girl?"

"Yeah. She looks fine. Everything seems good." I was still beaming.

His mouth sprawled into a smile. He sat up, took my phone, and examined it. "Oh wow, dude. A girl." He tilted his head at the image. "Daughter of the boy in eyeliner. So we're talking Wednesday Addams?"

"God, I hope." I set my chin on his shoulder, looking at the photo with him. "That'd be awesome."

He picked up his glasses from the nightstand, put them on, and studied the ultrasound again. "I admit I've been curious what the demon spawn of Sinter Blackwell will be like. Is this the head?"

"I think. I can't actually tell."

"I think it is. And legs here . . . " He traced the bent-knee line I had guessed at. After gazing at it another few seconds, he handed me back the phone. "Well. When the time comes, I'll teach her to drive a stick. Meanwhile, you can teach her about makeup."

I snorted. Then, on impulse, I threw both arms around him and hugged him.

He didn't call me crazy, or chuckle and pull away. He held me a long time, resting his head on my neck. He felt warm and smelled like sleep.

I shut my eyes, longing for a different reality, one in which he was more than just her dad's buddy and her occasional driving teacher.

But he wasn't ready for kids. He was going to Asia. We hadn't discussed tender feelings. I wasn't even properly out. My family was batshit. Et cetera.

Still. A guy could wish.

CHAPTER 30: IN BETWEEN DAYS

THE DVDS OF *NEW ROMANTIC* ARRIVED, AND ANDY AND I SAT DOWN AND WATCHED IT ONE NIGHT. I HAD to fortify myself with two beers first. Watching myself on-screen did not generally make the list of activities I enjoyed. Fiona was right, however; the film had turned out fabulously, and given the new-wave costumes and music, I would have *loved* it if anyone but me had starred in it. But even with alcohol softening my edges, I couldn't watch the whole sex scene. I had to hide my face in a couch cushion while Andy laughed and made remarks like, "Aw yeah, girl, shove those jeans off him."

I gave one of the DVDs to Chris and Kam so they could drool over Ariel in it. I sent another to Andy's parents, who had requested it. I also sent one to my parents (who had not), with a brief note: *Just received a bunch of these, so here's one in case you want to see it. I think it turned out well. Take care, S.*

I kind of hoped they wouldn't watch it, what with the sex scene and all. On the other hand, maybe it would introduce them to a few cool songs they should have paid attention to thirty years earlier, and spark a new interest for them. Ha. Sure.

Mom emailed me a few days later.

Joel,
We got the DVD. Haven't watched it yet, but from the cover it certainly looks like the 1980s.

(I could hear the irony. As if she had hoped never to see the 1980s again, but there they were, back to haunt her.)

Granddad's 80th birthday is July 7, and we'll be having a family get-together. It's near where you live, a country club east of Seattle. It's one of Granddad's favorite golf courses, owned by a friend of his. They'll want to see you, so pencil in the date and try to come. You could bring a guest.

Take care,

Mom

"Oh yay," I said out loud, though I was behind the counter at the café when I got the email. "Can I, please?"

"Hmm?" Kam asked, bustling by with a tray of mugs.

"Nothing. Talking to my email."

Customers came in. I made them their caffe Americanos, agreed it was a beautiful day, and watched them take a seat.

Although . . .

I did need a support network. I wanted to be on better terms with my parents. Putting in an appearance at this thing and acting pleasant for half an hour might help.

Plus, what if I brought Andy and made some progress on that front too? He was far better at being charming in these settings than me. He'd help me win people over. In any case, I sure as hell didn't want to visit that pit of perdition alone.

I emailed Mom back.

I'll pencil in the party. Would it be all right if my guest was Andy? I don't really have other close friends up here yet.

Thanks,

Sinter

Admittedly, I did also view this as a challenge. Mom would either have to say "yes" or "I'd prefer you didn't." This was her side of the family (Granddad was her father), so the guest list would be more her call than Dad's.

Your move, Mom. I dare you.

She answered by the end of my barista shift.

I suppose you could bring him, but I hope you make it clear you're just friends. And I would prefer if you didn't discuss his "lifestyle." There's no purpose in upsetting your grandparents and everyone else when the event is in their honor; I'm sure you'd agree.

Anger seethed under my ribs.

Wow. Fuck that.

Kam studied me as I grabbed my jacket off the hook in the kitchen. "You look like you're ready to punch someone in the 'nads."

"My parents are buttheads. Today they email me: 'Yes, you can bring Andy to this family party, but you can't talk about his *lifestyle* because we wouldn't want to upset people.' What the hell?"

Kam and Chris still didn't know we slept together, but they knew I was bi and he was gay, and Kam had teasingly remarked more than once that we seemed very *flirtatious* for best friends.

She sealed the lid back onto the flour tub. "I hear you. My parents were cool, but Chris's? Took them freaking years to be able to say '*wife*, this is our daughter's *wife*.'"

"Did you avoid them? 'Cause I'm thinking I should just refuse to go if they're going to be like this."

"We blew them off sometimes, for sure. But . . . " She looked at me with a twist of the mouth. "It may be smart to go. Agree to their stupid condition just this once."

"Why?"

"Because then your relatives get to talk to you and Andy and get to know you as people, *before* the whole 'guess what, they're gay or bi' reveal. Right now, they might be thinking they don't know any of *those* types. But if they learn their grandson and his friend, who were so nice at that party, are like that, then . . . "

"They'll start thinking and voting differently?" I let the skepticism into my voice, but in truth I began to see her point.

"Maybe. Long shot, I know. But if you stay invisible, you definitely won't make any difference."

"Hm."

"Is this a party for you or someone else?" she asked.

"Someone else. My grandfather's birthday."

"Then yeah. Play by their dumb rules this time. But next time, and definitely at your own events, no lying, no hiding. Tell them that."

"I'll see if Andy's even willing to go." I sighed. "Thanks, Kam."

"I've got your back, bro." She shoved the tub of flour onto a shelf.

I related the whole thing to Andy that evening while we emptied the dishwasher. He rolled his eyes at my mom's request, but fell quiet when I fed him Kam's reasoning.

"Hmm," he said. "That's kind of true." Then he threw a put-upon glance at me. "You're really going to make me go to this thing?"

"It's not like I want to either. But what if we just put in an appearance? An hour."

"Half an hour."

"Forty-five minutes."

He allowed it with a nod. "Deal."

"It's not till July anyway."

"Yes," he said dryly. "I'm sure they'll have totally accepted my lifestyle by then."

———

The Fair Youth opened on the Green Sea Theatre stage. Andy's parents came up to see it, as they'd promised. It was something of a rush, given this was the first role in which I acted out a romance with another man—in front of the family of the man I was currently sleeping with. Not that they knew it. Still, I felt a certain secret pride in representing what I actually was. When theatrical reviews came out in the papers (consensus said the cast was good, though the writing and pacing could be better), I wondered how long it would be before someone who knew my family saw one of the articles and forwarded it to my folks.

I did it myself just to prove I wasn't hiding. *Reviews are coming in for our play*, I emailed, with a link. *They look good. Let me know if you want to come up and see it. I can get you free tickets.*

They, of course, declined politely, claiming they had too much work and vacation scheduled soon. Likely, the real reason was they had followed the link and learned the play was about me snogging Shakespeare.

Meanwhile, I had my own kid to keep track of.

Sinter: Hey, checking in to make sure everything's okay. I want to stay in touch, but I don't want to bug you with too many messages. So maybe is it ok if I check in once a week? Say every Monday?
Fiona: That would work. I'm trying to write again but I don't know, I don't think I like where this one's going
Sinter: Still, that's good you're working on something. What's it about?
Fiona: Sort of like the last one. But I'm not satisfied yet
Sinter: I hope I get to hear more about it soon
Fiona: Perhaps. If I get anywhere with it
Sinter: Listen . . . I haven't told anyone but Andy about the baby, because nothing's certain until after the birth and all. But I was wondering how many people know on your side. I mean, should I start telling people?
Fiona: Up to you. If I had my way, only Chelsea, Sebastian, and my doctor would know, but of course I'm starting to show so there's no escaping

everyone knowing

Sinter: That's got to feel intrusive. Strangers asking questions

Fiona: Yes. I did tell my parents and sister

With a cringe that stretched all the skin on my face, I pictured her dad, the formidable Alec, chairman of Islands Broadcasting, surely positioned to place a call from across the globe that would result in a hit man ending my life fifteen minutes later.

Sinter: How'd they take it?

Fiona: My sister thinks I'll change my mind and keep the baby, which I doubt. Mum and Dad both have posh doctors they'd like me to start seeing, which I declined. They're fine with the idea of giving up the baby to you. Said they'd start her a trust fund. Then went back to asking me when I'll write something commercial for them

Sinter: So they were nice? They aren't out to murder me?

Fiona: They don't care much, is how I'd put it

Sinter: Well that kind of sucks

Fiona: It's just as well. I don't want their interference

Sinter: My parents will care in the sense that they'll be horrified. Not looking forward to that

Fiona: You don't have to do this, you know

Sinter: I know. But I want to

Fiona: Then I suppose we'll talk Monday next

Sinter: Yes, good luck, talk soon

CHAPTER 31: I DON'T LIKE MONDAYS

THE SUN THAT HAD BEEN SO NOTABLY ABSENT IN WINTER SOON SEEMED TO BE PRESENT ALL THE TIME, streaming into windows too early in the morning, cooking our brick apartment building, and hanging out on the horizon until after nine o'clock at night. Shortly before we wrapped *The Fair Youth*, I auditioned for the next play our director, Dominic, had lined up: *A Midsummer Night's Dream*, touring at several different parks in the Puget Sound area in July and August. Dominic cast me as Puck.

"A fairy?" Andy said, all innocence.

"I know you're not going to comment on that," I said.

"I could've made better jokes with 'Bottom.'"

I continued honoring my promise, checking in with Fiona each Monday.

Sinter: Hey, how are things?

Fiona: Oh, I don't know, still stuck.

It was a warm June morning, and I was wandering through Volunteer Park, one of the future Shakespeare locations. In our last few check-in texts, she'd been brief: said health issues were normal, and she was working on a script, albeit slowly.

Sinter: Still not going to tell me what it's about? :)

Fiona: Might I ring you? I'm tired of looking at screens

Sinter: Sure, no, let me call. Is now good?

Fiona: Yes

Ducking into the shade of a huge cedar, I tapped her number.

"Hello," she answered.

"Hey, what's up?"

Her tired sigh took two or three full seconds. "Everything's . . . ugh. Do you know that when you're pregnant, everything changes? Like literally every part of you. Even your eyes."

"Your *eyes?*"

"Because you have increased blood flow, which affects the vessels in your eyeballs, your vision can change. My specs are now, temporarily, the wrong prescription. It's why the screens are bothering me."

"Damn. That's—I had no idea."

"As if it wasn't enough for my hips and feet to hurt all the time, and for half the foods I used to love to give me heartburn, and for none of my clothes to fit. And—the people. The comments. I hadn't realized how many complete strangers would want to talk to me about babies, congratulate me. And what am I supposed to say?"

Wincing, I leaned back against the splintery bark of the tree. "Shit. Yeah. That's . . . none of their business. But hey, just a few more months, then . . . " I trailed off. Didn't want to insist *Then you're giving that kid to me, and you'll be done.* Because maybe she wouldn't choose to do that, and surely I was there to support her in whatever she did want. Wasn't that the least I could do, given what she was dealing with, all because of a dalliance with me?

On the other hand, I did want to be in my daughter's life. I'd been doing as much online legal research as I could, and I knew I had default custody rights simply by virtue of being the father. But so did she, as the mother, and her living in another country made things freakishly complicated. I had a short list of LGBTQ-friendly lawyers, both in Seattle and in London, whom I would contact if need be, but I prayed I wouldn't have to, that it wouldn't come to an actual custody battle. If she insisted on keeping the baby, would I end up sharing custody with her somehow?

Spend thousands of dollars a year on plane tickets just so I could visit my child? Or move to England for good? Then if I moved, what about Andy?

"Then the writing," she went on, yanking me back to the present. "I spent three weeks trying to make a script work. Do you know what it was?"

"Um. No."

"A sequel. To *New Romantic*."

I winced again—obsessing over Taylor could not be useful—but I injected interest into my voice. "Oh wow, really?"

"Jackie joins Taylor in New York."

At the emotional climax of *New Romantic*, the authorities caught up with Taylor and deported him after teary-eyed goodbyes with Jackie-the-posh-girl. Then, at the end of the film, he sent her a letter with his address, telling her to come see him if she could. Holding the letter, she lifted her face to the window with a smile. Everyone could thus assume she was going to run away to New York, even if that wasn't shown.

"Uh-huh," I said. "They start living together, or . . . ?"

"They do, but it just felt . . . blah. Like every dreadful sequel you've ever seen. His music struggles, her difficulty living in New York, their relationship . . . I mean, I couldn't even make *that* work. Despite all the chemistry from the original."

I bowed my head. "Well, it . . . yeah, it would be under stress."

"I just kept writing bitter arguments between them. And when I found myself writing that she'd fallen pregnant, I stopped. I mean, there's working through your problems by writing, and then there's digging yourself deeper into a trench. I'm certain I was doing the latter."

I looked out in despair at the brightness beyond the tree's shade. "It's good you tried, though. Is there something else that would work better? As a topic?"

"I'm trying something new. Something more like I originally wanted to write for *New Romantic*. But I don't know if it'll work either. Still feels strange."

"Well. I hope you keep trying." Something like she originally wanted to write—did that mean a gay love story? If so, was that a good sign or a bad one?

"Nothing much else I can do but keep trying," she said.

I agreed glumly.

I returned to the apartment. Andy was away at work. He'd been spending long hours there lately, finishing up current projects so he'd be all set for his Tokyo adventure.

The last time we'd had sex was the previous morning, after a dry spell that had stretched several days. He had come out of the shower with nothing on but a towel around his waist. I was lounging on the couch, still in pajama pants. We had both been observing our responsible adult lives all week, and even at that moment I was looking up local daycare options on my phone. But my appetite for him had been mounting, and without exactly thinking about it I shot out a hand as he passed, and tugged on the towel.

It unraveled. He laughed and caught it, keeping it from falling. I pulled him over and unwound it. I dropped my phone and had him deep in my mouth within seconds. He moaned and held onto my shoulders. A couple of minutes later, while I still had the taste of him on my tongue, he rolled me onto the floor rug and hauled off my pajama pants to return the favor.

Then a smile, a shove on the arm, a borrowing of the towel to clean up, and we were back to our responsible tasks.

Enjoy it while we could, right? We couldn't go on like that forever. Probably only a few more weeks, in fact.

No drama allowed. I shouldn't feel sad.

I shambled into his room, lay on his bed on my front, and spent the rest of the hour breathing the smell of him from the sheets, telling myself I was just doing it because I was tired, and his bed was more comfortable than mine.

CHAPTER 32: DO YOU BELIEVE IN SHAME

ON THE APPOINTED WEEKEND IN JULY, WE DROVE ACROSS LAKE WASHINGTON TO ATTEND MY GRANDFA-ther's birthday bash. A heat wave had engulfed the West Coast, and the air conditioning in my aging car produced only a weak trickle of cool air, so we were already uncomfortable by the time we arrived.

I drove into the country club venue, up a winding road through a golf course. An expanse of short green grass undulated around sand traps and manicured trees. Up ahead, a multi-winged clubhouse loomed.

"Jesus God," I muttered. "Ninth circle of hell."

"I think they have eighteen at courses like this," Andy said.

"Ha."

We parked and got out. Both of us wore sunglasses, short-sleeved button-downs, lightweight trousers, and sedate black sneakers—the best compromise we could manage between the heat and the occasion's semi-formality. Beside the clubhouse stood a vast white tent sheltering a hundred or so people, most of them in their fifties or older.

Mom emerged from the crowd and strode toward us. She wore a peach dress with ruffles at the hem, and her hair was neatly arranged, its color so brightly golden that I suspected a touch-up job. (I knew hair dye well. Maybe she and I had that in common.)

"You made it," she said.

"Yep. Hey, Mom."

"Hi," Andy said. "Glad they set up a tent. Much more comfortable in this heat."

She tried to smile, clasping her hands. "Indeed. Terribly hot, isn't it? Help yourselves to lunch. But Joel, be sure you greet Granddad first."

"Okay."

"I have to talk to the caterer. Excuse me." She hustled off.

Andy and I glanced at one another.

"Right." I sighed. "Let's get this over with."

We picked up cups of punch, a watered-down, non-alcoholic citrus drink with lime slices floating in it. Then we found Granddad and Grandmom holding court at a round white table in the center of the tent. My dad, two elderly men, and a couple around age sixty sat with them.

Dad spotted me as I approached. "Joel," he said neutrally.

I waved with an equally neutral smile.

Dad's gaze took in Andy, went frosty, and returned to the others at the table.

I edged up beside my grandparents, touched their shoulders, and said, "Hi, guys. Happy birthday, Granddad."

Grandmom looked up, her papery skin creasing in a smile. "Hello, dear."

I kissed her cheek. She smelled like violets. Despite the kiss and the "dear," we were not close. The kiss was simply expected whenever I greeted her. My grandparents—all four of them—were mega-old-fashioned. Like, embroidered Bible verses on their walls, frowns every time they saw me in makeup, disparaging remarks about every song or film made after 1950—that level of old-fashioned. They made my parents look moderate. We had virtually nothing in common beyond DNA, and it had always been a mystery to me why they wanted to see me at all. Maybe they hoped someday I'd change and become the legacy they were hoping for, in which case, nope, sorry, no need to rewrite the wills.

Granddad squinted at me, the top of his head bald and fringed with a half-ring of white hair. "Huh, you don't look so much like a hoodlum today. Your hair's purple, though."

"I know. Sorry. I'm . . . still in theater." Not that this was the reason for my colorful hair, but it sounded viable. "This is my friend Andy. You've probably met him at some point."

Andy stepped up to shake hands with him. "Hi. Yes, we met at Sinter's house a long time ago. Happy birthday."

"Sit, boys!" the sixty-ish woman said, waving toward the empty chairs at the table. She had short orange hair, a necklace of turquoise beads, and a huge, lipsticked smile. I recalled that her name was Patty, and that she and her husband went to my folks' church.

I had no wish to sit. Nor did Andy, I was sure. But we were there to charm people, so we sat, clutching our cups of punch.

Patty and Grandmom asked what we were up to lately. We talked about our work in Seattle, Andy's upcoming trip to Tokyo, and my recent trip to London. They groused about the construction going up in their neighborhoods. Dad contributed sage advice to Patty's husband, Phil, about financing. Phil delivered a monologue about how much money their three grown-up kids had spent lately and every last item they had spent it on. I was starting to remember that Phil was one of those people who could be counted on for oversharing and nosiness.

I recalled a day when I was about eighteen, when Phil had shown up in the café where I worked. He had checked out my pierced ears, lip, and eyebrow, and asked me with a raucous laugh where *else* I had piercings. Answer: nowhere, not that it was any of his business. At the time, I wondered in silent horror if he was into teenage boys. But now I didn't think so. He seemed only to be one of the world's most impertinent people.

As evidenced by what went down next.

"Didn't I hear you were in some play about Shakespeare?" Phil asked me. "Where he was gay or something?" He laughed like he had just told a dirty joke.

I exchanged a glance with my dad. A dangerous light had entered his eyes.

"Not exactly," I answered, my improvisational acting skills taking over. "Anyway, that play's done. I'm rehearsing *A Midsummer Night's Dream* now."

"I remember hearing that theory," Patty said. "That Shakespeare swung both ways." She winked at us.

"Well, this next one's going to be Shakespeare in the park," I said, dragging the conversation toward safer territory.

No luck.

Phil's bushy eyebrows dove together, and he said, "But you two live together?"

I stole a glance at Andy. His spine had gone rigid, and his fingertips carefully arranged themselves around his punch cup.

"Yep, we're roommates," I said. "The city's expensive, so . . . "

"I mean are you a *couple*?" Phil guffawed, looking at the befuddled elderly man beside him. "Living together, playing a gay Shakespeare— got to ask!"

All the air got sucked out of my lungs. Andy froze in place. My improv skills vaporized into nonbeing.

"No no, we're friends," I said, several seconds too late, and with nowhere near enough conviction.

"Oh, Phil, of course they're a couple." Patty hit him on the arm. "I have Andy's mom, Kelly, on Facebook—wonderful woman. She put up the sweetest picture; where was it?" She got out her phone and started scrolling.

Was it ethical to reach out and smack someone else's phone into a cup of punch? Probably not. Crap.

"We've been friends a long time, is all," Andy tried.

My dad forced a smile and added to Phil, "A very long time. I think you'll find that rumor is mistaken."

I should have backed this statement up. But I sat tongue-tied, unable to step that far into falsehood, anger starting to overtake shame.

Sweating, my cheeks burning, I squinted as if my thoughts were far away and confused.

"Here it is!" Patty held up the phone to display the photo from a few months earlier of Andy kissing my cheek. She turned it, making sure each of us at the table got a good look.

"That's really not what it . . . " I began.

Patty wasn't done. "Also this one! Guess this was the gay Shakespeare play." She laughed, swiped the screen, and showed us the next photo on Kelly's feed: Andy and I talking after a performance of *The Fair Youth*, me still in costume and makeup, leaning in to listen to Andy in the crowd.

We stood so close. So familiar. My mouth was curved up in a happy, comfortable smile. So was Andy's, even in the middle of talking. I'd seen the photo before and hadn't given it much thought, but at this table, facing down these stares, I suddenly saw how intimate it looked. How much like a couple we appeared to be, just in the way we stood together.

Maybe we looked like that all the time.

"Shoot, I think you're right," Phil said. "Look how they're blushing." He snorted, then nudged my dad's arm. "Don't worry, Walt. Our Beth's a lesbian. You get used to it after a few years."

Wonderful. We had found the most bumbling allies in the galaxy.

I wanted to cover my face. My dad, grandfather, and grandmother all looked paralyzed with horror. The other two old guys just looked perplexed.

"It really wasn't anything," Andy said, but he didn't sound any more convincing than I had. Maybe he'd realized how we looked in photos too. And regretted it.

I felt sick.

The anger roared over the top of my polite defenses, toppling them. "Oh, well, we do sleep together sometimes," I heard myself telling Phil matter-of-factly. "I mean, if that's what you're asking. You ask straight people that, too, right?"

"He does, yes," Patty confirmed.

"Sinter's just being dramatic," Andy said, a smile pasted on his face. "He doesn't mean it."

"Of course he doesn't." My dad sounded lethal.

"Well, *we* don't think it's a big deal," Patty said.

My mom arrived at the table then, smiling in formal party mode. "How is everyone doing? What's not a big deal?" She fit herself into the empty chair beside my dad.

"If these two are a gay couple," Phil hollered, waving a meaty hand at us.

I sent Mom a half-apologetic look meant to convey, *I did not choose this topic of conversation.*

The message must not have arrived. Murder flashed in her eyes.

"Why are we still discussing such an unpleasant subject?" Grandmom asked.

"Beats me," Granddad said.

I turned to Andy. "We haven't gotten food yet. Maybe we should get something to eat?"

"Okay," he said.

We nearly knocked over our chairs in our escape from the table.

"Shit," I said to Andy under my breath as we hightailed it across the grass. "Shit, shit, shit."

"What the *hell* are you doing," he said, his voice tight.

"I don't know. I got mad. Let's just leave."

"Yeah, good call."

We emerged into the hot sun, heading for the parking lot. Behind us, Mom called, "Joel!"

We stopped and turned. She and Dad stormed up to us.

"What on earth, Joel?" she said, now that we were out of earshot of the party. "We had one request of you. One."

"It wasn't my fault," I said. "Blame Phil and Patty. They're the ones who wouldn't shut up about it. Dad can tell you. He was there."

Andy, helpless witness to this, glanced toward the other guests, who kept gawking at us.

"You could have denied it," Dad said, teeth clenched. "Instead you said the most foul, ridiculous—"

"I *tried* to deny it! They weren't listening. Besides, is it that big a deal? What our 'lifestyle' may or may not be?"

"This is not the time or the place."

"Right, which is why we're leaving."

"Don't," Mom said, flustered. "For heaven's sake, we don't want everyone talking about how you made a scene and stomped off. Stay for your grandparents' sakes."

"They don't want us here. We'll *leave* for their sakes. And you need to understand, this is not how I'm doing things anymore. You're polite to Andy or whoever else I bring, or you don't see me. Ever."

"Sinter," Andy started.

"You act like we're so unreasonable," Dad cut in. "But we're not, goddammit. It's reasonable to want your kid to be normal. To be the kind of person we can be proud of, to have a good career, a respectable life."

I was trembling in rage. If we'd been in Shakespeare's day, I'd have drawn my sword on him. "Normal?" I said, low. "Careful, Dad. You can't unsay things."

"What were you hoping to accomplish by bringing him, anyway?" he went on, undeterred. "I only agreed to let him come at all because your mom said you'd keep your mouth shut about crap like that. And you couldn't."

I'd drawn closer to Andy and could feel him shaking too, against my arm. The Elizabethan version of him would probably have helped me murder my father.

"Done," I said. "We're done. You know how to find me if you're ever ready to be civil." I took Andy's elbow and tugged him toward the car.

"Joel, for heaven's sake," my mom said.

Andy snatched his arm free. "What is wrong with you?" He sounded furious, and I looked at him in shock. Then my shock doubled when I realized he wasn't talking to me. He had turned and was addressing my parents.

They blinked at him, momentarily silenced.

"Why can't you be proud of him?" Andy demanded. "It's not that hard. He's kind, he's decent, he's talented and hardworking—do you even realize how few actors at his age have gotten as far as he has? And he's trying to do the right thing, for everyone, all the time. You have no *idea* how hard he's trying. He's an excellent human being, and it's easy for me to be proud of him. But fine, you know what? Push him away instead. See where that gets you." He pivoted and headed for the car.

My parents and I shared one last glance, stunned all around, then I left them without another word and caught up with Andy.

He was breathing hard, eyes unfocused. "I yelled at your parents," he said. "Oh, fuck. Holy crap. I've just made everything so much worse."

"*They* made everything worse. You were awesome." I yanked open my car door. He got in too.

I reversed from the spot quickly and peeled off down the drive in a screech of tires. Andy seized the grip handle above his window, but didn't snap at me to drive safer, like he might on an ordinary day. My heart was beating a hole in my chest. I still felt disturbingly inclined toward homicide.

At the end of the drive, I turned onto the street and joined the traffic. "Well. Guess I can't count on them for babysitting anytime soon."

"Yeah, no." Andy rolled down his window, set his elbow on top of it, and ruffled his hair. "Can you never, ever invite me to any of your family events again?"

"Fine. Probably not going to any more of them myself."

"I mean, seriously, what were you thinking?"

I looked at him in bewilderment. "Why are you yelling at me? You just defended me."

"Yes, I defended you because that's what a friend does, and any decent person would have in a situation like that. But I also *lied* for you. 'Oh, Sinter didn't mean it. It's not true.' You put me in a position where I had to lie, and I hate it."

"I hate it too! And *they* put you in that position, not me. I know I shouldn't have said we sleep together, but first they're all 'Don't talk about it, ever,' and next thing I know, their friends are interrogating me point-blank. What was I supposed to say?"

"You could have come out to them." His words were clipped, incisive. "Calmly. Politely. Let them throw a fit then if they want, but at least you could say you took the high ground. Can you say that now?"

"Oh, because I always have to take the high ground. I'm sure you always do. I'm sure everyone but me always does."

"Oh my God." He raked his hand through his hair again. "I cannot talk to you when you're being this dramatic."

"Yes, all right, I should come out." I was basically shouting. "I'm not ready. I'm a coward. Do you remember, though, what it feels like to not be ready to come out? To be afraid?"

"Of course I remember. I'm still afraid, because I still have to meet new people all the time. But once you decide you aren't going to hide anymore, it gets easier."

"Yeah, that is so fucking easy for you to say. You with the huge, happy family who's got your back. You with the parents who never minded you were gay for one second. I'm over here trying to scrounge up a goddamn support network with the people who are supposed to give me one, and look what happens." I smacked the steering wheel with my palm to accentuate the last three words. I had become that rage-fueled guy. Fantastic.

"Yes, it sucks. But isn't it partly because you aren't being honest?"

"Do you want me to turn around and come out to them? Maybe tell them about the baby too, while I'm at it?"

He grimaced and looked out the window. "Not a bad idea. But I bet you won't."

"No. I won't. Because there's no talking to *them* when they're in this mood, just like there's no talking to me. Must be genetic."

"Fine. Do it when you want." He used a near-monotone, a writing-you-off voice.

We said nothing the rest of the drive home.

Back in our apartment, he poured himself apple juice from the fridge, downed half the glass, and turned to lean on the counter. He watched me as I got a glass of ice water and drank it.

"I'm sorry I yelled at you," he said, sounding sullen.

"Me too. Thanks for coming with me."

"Listen . . . " He lowered his gaze to the floor tiles. "I don't say this to be bitter. Honest. But I think I'm done with this, the benefits. We're still friends. Neither of wants to screw that up."

The icy cold in my stomach shot out to every one of my extremities. I took a few seconds to breathe, rotating the glass in my fingers, tracing lines in the fog of condensation collecting on the outside.

He had invoked the official deal, the one I had agreed to. I couldn't claim he was being unfair. We were still best friends, and he was completely right. I didn't want to fuck that up.

All the same, it felt like he had shoved me into a wall and walked past.

I hauled together all my acting skills in order to answer calmly. "Fair enough. I guess I haven't been following the 'no drama' rule too well lately."

"Which is understandable. You have a lot going on, and I do too. I think we're just . . . complicating things too much. I've got your back; I support you on all this, but a lot of it is stuff *you* have to figure out. I can't do it for you."

Again he was entirely, excruciatingly right.

But I was too afraid, of basically everything in the world, to move my feet toward the path that would fix this. The coming-out. The confessing my feelings—to him as well as everyone else. The possibility of being rejected and loathed. The likelihood of ending up alone and unloved.

I might have lost my parents' goodwill forever, as well as what little was left of my grandparents' approval. Fiona couldn't be liking me much either, with everything I was putting her through. She might even change her mind and keep the baby once the birth happened, reducing the amount of my life I'd spend with my daughter.

At least I'd still have a friend if I cooperated with Andy.

"Okay," I said softly. "You're right."

CHAPTER 33: FRIEND OR FOE

I STOOD ON A CURB AT THE UNIVERSITY OF OREGON, ABOUT TO START MY FRESHMAN YEAR. I FIDGETED, not wishing to enter the dorm, but not wanting to stand there with Mom any longer either.

She had driven me down. Dad had said goodbye to me back home—handshake, no hug. We hadn't hugged in years.

I'd spiked out my hair twice as big as usual and drawn on twice as much eyeliner, and wore head-to-toe black clothes despite the September heat.

Mom looked me over. "Why do you have to look like that? On your first day with these kids?"

My parents had said that kind of thing a thousand times. But that day I caught an undercurrent of anxiety in her voice, like she was actually worried about how I'd be received by the other freshmen. Had that sentiment always been there and I'd never noticed before? Or was she feeling an unusual boost of affection for her only child upon leaving me at college? I couldn't tell.

"That's how I'll be able to tell who my real friends are," I said. "They'll be the ones who aren't so shallow they can't see past appearances."

Yeah, I used sarcasm, and yeah, it was a stab at her and Dad, in addition to anyone else in the world who took issue with my dress code. But it was also more truthful than I'd been with her in a while.

She shook her head. She was elegantly put together as ever, in a sleeveless pale-pink silk blouse, black trousers, and ballet flats. The wind stirred her blonde curls, knocking strands loose from her clip, and sweat glinted on her forehead, making her look more human. I tried not to be moved. After all, this transition was going to be way harder for me than for her. I was the one who had to walk in there and start living with a roommate I'd never spoken to before.

God, I missed Andy.

"Why do you have to make things so difficult for yourself?" she asked.

Please. They were the ones making life harder—for me and for themselves. I shrugged, keeping my expression loftily cold, and picked up my backpack. "Have a good drive back."

She clicked her tongue in annoyance, then gripped my arm and kissed me on the cheek. Her Diorissimo perfume drifted around me, gentle and flowery, staggering me back in time to the era when I was a little kid and didn't know their rules were stupid, when I loved to hug my mom and felt safer when doing so than at any other time in the world. A treasure I had lost and could probably never get back.

She released me, and I gave her a nod before turning to the dorm.

———

I found myself looking forward with a fragile sort of longing to the birth of my daughter. I still wanted her, now more than ever, because what other chance at a happy family did I have at the rate I was going?

My parents and I hadn't communicated since the fiasco at the country club. My ultimatum and Andy's telling-off had shut them right up, and I sure as hell wasn't going to speak first.

My last two Monday check-ins with Fiona had been like texting with a polite robot. Nothing to tell. Still trying to write. Very uncomfortable, with summer heat and being pregnant. Tired, must go now.

All Chelsea had said, when I asked her, was Fiona needed time, and Chelsea didn't have any reason to think she would change her mind about custody. Which of course was no guarantee.

So I awaited the birth of my child, whom I might not get to keep, and meanwhile, my folks had no idea they were going to be grandparents. And I couldn't tell them, either, partly because I didn't know if I'd get custody, and partly because I wasn't speaking to them. What a clusterfuck.

At least I still had a best friend. In theory.

With the benefits terminated—something I tried not to think about, because it felt like stabbing myself with a thumbtack—Andy and I had no reason to match up our schedules to find common free time. He continued working long hours and had arranged to sublet the apartment starting in September. I attended *A Midsummer Night's Dream* rehearsals, took extra café shifts, made lists of baby supplies (though without actually buying any yet), and began looking for my own place to live. Might as well set that up, prove I wasn't codependent and all.

One of Chris and Kam's neighbors was an elderly widow named Phyllis, who owned a 1920s-era house high on Capitol Hill, subdivided into duplex units. She lived in one and rented out the other, and had lately evicted a tenant who wouldn't pay the rent on time. She'd been fretting about it to Chris and Kam. She wanted "someone nice" to rent the place, but dreaded having to advertise about it and interview strangers.

They recommended me to her. I went to see the house. The unit was small, and somewhat expensive when taking it on alone, but for Seattle it was still a steal. It was clean, the appliances and walls all white and plain, with ridged old hardwood floors in the living room and bedroom, aging linoleum in kitchen and bath, and most of the windows and light switches in working order. The neighborhood was quiet, a narrow residential street lined with other houses rather than with towering rows of apartment buildings. It had a backyard surrounded by a high brick wall, with apple trees and a rectangle of weedy grass.

I could picture my daughter taking her first steps next spring across that grass.

My mind supplied the additional image of Andy beaming, crouching with arms open to receive her. I turned away from that pointlessly lovely idea and told Phyllis I would like to take the place, if she didn't mind a baby girl joining me this fall.

"Oh!" she said. "But it's still just you otherwise?"

"Still just me. I'm arranging it with the birth mother. Nothing definite, but it's what I'm hoping."

She beamed. "That would be a delight. I can't hear too well anyway. Won't bother me if she cries."

I signed the lease. She told me I could move in as soon as I liked.

"How about next Sunday?" I said.

I texted Andy on my way out.

Sinter: The place Chris and Kam found is really good. I'm taking it. Moving on Sunday

I waited a few minutes before turning my car on, but he didn't answer. Finally, an hour later, he responded.

Andy: Sounds good. If you need boxes to pack stuff in, there's usually some down by the recycling bins behind the building

"Thanks. I'll miss you too," I mumbled to the empty air in our apartment—*his* apartment—and trudged to the guest room to separate my possessions from his.

CHAPTER 34: CRUEL SUMMER

ON SUNDAY MORNING, ANDY HELPED ME CARRY MY FEW BAGS AND BOXES TO MY CAR. WE REMARKED on the hassles of furnishing a new space and discussed how Andy was going to stash most of his stuff at his sister Emma's place while he was in Tokyo.

I shut the trunk and looked at him.

Here's the trouble, I could say. *You're one of the best things in my life, and I don't want us to be apart.*

Sure. Then *he* could say, *No, here's the trouble. I'm going to Asia for six months, which by the way is more than enough time to meet someone else and fall in love, and you're about to become a parent, which I'm not ready for. Oh, and also, you're not out to your family, which is a hot mess that I'd rather not be part of. But thanks anyway.*

I closed my hand around my keys until they bit into my palm, hard enough to leave marks. "Talk to you soon, I guess."

"Yep. Be in touch." He stepped back. No hug goodbye.

I waved, got into my car, and edged into the sluggish Seattle traffic.

———

Sinter: Sebastian I know we're not exactly friends, but I think you'll be honest with me at least, so can I ask you about Fiona?

Sebastian: Too right I'll be honest

Sebastian: And of course we're friends you prat. What do you want to know then

Sinter: How's she doing, what's bothering her? Is she changing her mind about the baby? I never know the right things to say to her

Sebastian: I don't think she's changing her mind. It's just pregnancy is a nasty bitch. She's got a metric fuck-tonne of hormones messing her up. And believe me, I know a thing or two about hormones messing one up

Sinter: Then . . . you think she won't be ok until after the birth?

Sebastian: Even then it'll take awhile. I'm doing my best to keep her afloat, but she's a bit hung up on you still. B/c she's carrying your fucking child perhaps, just a guess

Sinter: So you think the problem is she still wants me? Not the baby?

Sebastian: I completely think that.

Sinter: Hmm

Sebastian: Do you know what she's working on?

Sinter: No, she hasn't said

Sebastian: A story about 2 boys in love. It's like New Romantic but in Britpop era and with gay dudes

Sinter: Ah. Shit

Sebastian: See she hasn't admitted it out loud but she's trying to reconcile herself to you going off to be with a bloke

Sinter: Yeah maybe

Sebastian: But I don't think it's making her happy to dwell on it. So I think it's a crap idea

Sinter: Ok, should I talk to her?

Sebastian: Nah keep your distance. I'll see she's all right

Sinter: But you'll report back to me? Please

Sebastian: Yeah fine

Sinter: Thanks

Sebastian: Oh guess what

Sinter: What?

Sebastian: Girl on the tube told me she saw new romantic and thought I was hotter than you. So ha.

———

I checked Andy's social-media feeds daily. I made sure to click "like" on stuff he posted, which tended to be links to gaming or tech articles or funny videos, nothing too personal. He, in turn, clicked "like" when I posted a positive review for our Shakespeare-in-the-park performance. A couple of times during the rest of July, we texted each other with *How's it going?* or *Hey do you want these DVDs? I'm getting rid of some stuff.*

I declined the DVDs, which were TV series I didn't care about, and ultimately I never saw him in person for the rest of the month.

No need for an ocean between us. We could feel just as far apart while living in the same neighborhood of the same city.

The only thing I had taken from the apartment that didn't belong to me was a long-sleeved T-shirt of his. It was the one he'd worn in the selfie from the day I stood beside the River Thames and propositioned him. He wore it to bed often, and I had found it in the laundry basket when checking for any stuff of mine there. He'd probably been wearing it a few nights in a row, and it smelled like him, specifically like being wrapped in his arms on a lazy morning after just waking up.

I stole it without asking him and kept it unwashed. Every day at some point, I took it out from under my pillow and held it to my nose and inhaled, trying not to think about why I was doing something so stalkerish.

I also thought often about the night before my birthday, nestling with him under the donut sculpture at the Asian Art Museum, my heart about to burst into spring blossoms and theatrical songs. Had those feelings all been a mirage? If so, it shouldn't still hurt like this. Since I couldn't make sense of it, I tried to reframe the feelings as something positive that could happen again, in that hazy future where I was a re-sponsible, fully out adult, knew what I was doing with my baby, no longer took shit from my parents, and wasn't afraid of anything.

Futures like that probably didn't magically happen on their own. But when you were afraid of everything, how could you bring them about?

I at least did my best to take steps toward the acquisition of my daughter, because I truly wanted her despite being scared, not to mention I had promised to do it, and there was an actual due date stamped on the event. I kept to my Monday check-ins with Fiona, but her tone remained distant, briskly informative, only a few lines each time. I respected Sebastian's advice, giving her space. But the year was advancing, the mid-September due date creeping closer. Eventually I would have to say something if she didn't.

The first Monday morning in August, I contacted her again.

Sinter: How are you?

Fiona: Same as ever. Tired

Sinter: I believe it. Hey, would you agree to a video call?

Fiona: Why?

Sinter: We're getting down to the wire and I need to make sure you're ok. And find out what the plan is

I fidgeted, picking at a sliver of fingernail for the minute it took her to answer.

Fiona: I suppose that's wise. Call now if you like

I set up the call on my computer, on the secondhand kitchen table I had picked up. Fiona's image materialized. She sat on a sofa, framed posters behind her, bright summer light streaming in from a window. When my brain processed her features, I blinked in surprise. I'd been expecting some dreadful change: bloated face, sleepless eyes, misery lines etched in her skin. But she looked . . . beautiful. Somber, yeah, but man, they were not kidding about the "glow." Her cheeks and lips had the same lovely flush that used to fill them every time she stepped up to kiss me in the studio corridor. Her hair was longer, loose and wavy, but otherwise, she basically hadn't changed.

"Hey," I said. "You look great. Seriously."

She smiled a little. "Thank you. You've cut your hair."

"Yeah. To fit a wig over it, for a play. Yours is longer."

"They say it grows faster when you're pregnant."

"Other than that, you honestly don't look any different."

"Well, from this angle . . . " She stood and turned halfway, and there it was: a bump the size of a beach ball under her yellow top. Fiona smoothed her hand down the curve, then sat again with a dispassionate shrug.

"Wow," I said. "So that's her." Kind of an idiotic thing to say, but I hadn't seen any belly pictures so far, so this was my first semi-direct glimpse of my kid, other than the cryptic ultrasound.

"Kicking me under the ribs many times daily."

I smiled. "Ouch. Are you at home?"

"Yes." She glanced aside. "This is my flat. You've never been here, I suppose."

"Guess not."

We'd never even been to each other's flats in London. Our relationship had been as insubstantial as that. It had produced some major consequences nonetheless.

"So." I peeled a piece of masking tape off the edge of the table and looked down at it, folding it on my lap. "What's going to happen? I'm getting mixed signals."

She looked down too, fussing with the folds of her top. "You're getting mixed signals because I'm a mess. This has turned out the hardest thing I've ever done, and if I'd known it would be like this, I . . . " She shook her head.

My hopes were teetering, collapsing like an imploding building. In my research, I had read about cases like this. The mother who had been planning to give up her baby to a waiting couple (or a single parent) found herself wanting the child after all, and kept the baby. The court usually sided with her—assuming the other side had the energy and money to go to court at all, which I wasn't sure I did. Fiona and I hadn't brought lawyers into it so far, because (I assumed we had tacitly agreed this) we were friends, we knew each other, we could trust each other.

But if she changed her mind, where would this leave me? What would I choose?

Getting ahead of myself. Work this out one step at a time.

I spoke in the most patient voice I could conjure up. "You're changing your mind? About custody?"

"No," she wailed. "That's never been it."

I blinked. "Oh. It—what is it, then?"

"I have never, ever wanted to be a mother. I still don't." She looked into the camera, nostrils reddening. "Isn't that dreadful? A woman who can't summon up the feelings she's supposed to feel for her own child? I want to know how she turns out, I'm sure I'll approve of her from afar, but feeling like a mother—I just don't, at all."

"*Oh*," I said, finally understanding—or starting to. "No, God, no. You're not dreadful. It's okay to not want kids."

"But other people want them. Normal people like you." She sniffled and rubbed her nose. "My older sister keeps telling me, 'There's such a strong bond between mother and baby, you'll feel it, you'll change your mind, it's only natural.' So I'm horrible, apparently, because I still don't feel it and don't think I ever will."

"But that's okay. It really is."

"And even feeling this way, I thought—I thought I could go through with it, help someone else, be a hero."

"You are. That's exactly what you're doing."

"Only it's *awful* being pregnant. All the aches and fatigue and symptoms, and everyone assuming when they see my belly that I'm delighted to be a mum, telling me how much I'm going to love it. I'm so tired of explaining, tired of the whole thing." She was fighting to talk through the tears in her voice.

A lump rose in my throat too. "Hey, I—I get it. People are . . . " I laughed humorlessly. "They're assholes. Believe me, I know. I'm realizing that when people see me with a baby, they're going to ask, 'Where's Mommy?' and I'm still not sure what I'll say. And if I ever get up the nerve to come out, to be with Andy or some other guy—well, then they'll still ask that question, and I'll have to come out to strangers. Daily. And when my own parents won't even have my back on this . . . yeah, I'm scared."

She winced in sympathy. "It's the twenty-first century, and this is still what we're dealing with. Prejudice against something as harmless as being gay or bi."

"Or finding it weird for a woman to be a film director," I said, remembering some peculiar remarks from journalists interviewing me about the film.

"Or considering it normal if a man doesn't want to raise his child, but if a woman doesn't, she's a monster."

"Hey. You are not a monster." I reached out to splay my fingers around the edge of the screen, trying to send a reassuring touch through cyberspace. "Gender norms are stupid."

She laughed a little. "You say such sweet things. How could I not love you?"

My heart twisted. "You're amazing. I wish I could've been what you wanted."

She removed her glasses to dab her eyes. "Oh, but you were. I just wasn't what *you* wanted."

"That was always because of my issues. Never because of anything wrong with you."

And I wasn't what Andy wanted. Because of my issues. Not because of anything wrong with him.

I dropped my gaze, aching.

"That's made it especially hard, though," Fiona said. "I didn't want the baby, but I did want you. How can I get over you as I should, when you'll be linked to me forever? Even if I'm not involved with her life, I'll be thinking of you both, and would like to hear occasional news of how you're doing."

"Even so, you'll get over me. Most people have found it pretty easy."

"God knows I've been going about it all wrong, writing that sequel, then trying this latest project, which . . . " She sighed. "Sebastian mentioned it to you?"

"About two guys in Britpop, he said?"

"Yes. I think I was trying to 'ship' you and Andy, as they say in fandom. Make myself happy for you being together. But . . . " She polished her glasses wearily with a fold of her shirt. "Dismal failure. I only made myself miserable. Also I'm not sure the world needs a soundtrack full of Blur and Oasis covers."

"I'd totally buy that soundtrack," I defended. She only smiled a moment. "Anyway," I added quietly, "Andy and I aren't . . . like that anymore. He's fed up with my problems. Who could blame him?"

"Oh, love. You've known each other for years, haven't you? You'll work it out."

"Maybe. I hope." I put on a smile and said, "Speaking of. You know Sebastian's in love with you, right?"

She scoffed and put her glasses back on, but the glow in her face seemed to deepen. "Rubbish. He's too cool for someone like me. He's just a good friend."

"Are you kidding me? Nuh-uh. He *so* loves you. Treat him nice, okay?"

"Of course I treat him nice. He's . . . he really has been kind." Her voice turned thoughtful, like she was maybe starting to realize I was completely right.

"You could talk to him about the stuff bothering you, if you wanted. He'd understand. I gather he's gone through some interesting changes himself."

Fiona tilted her head. "You know, I've never asked him about that. The transition. I felt it'd be nosy."

"I bet he'd talk to you about it. Got to be an interesting story there."

"Undoubtedly. Perhaps one I could even write, in some fashion, if he didn't mind." She sounded tired rather than truly inspired, but the note of interest did hum beneath her words. "Wouldn't even have to be a love story. Could be about . . . I don't know, becoming free."

"Free. I like that."

"I think that's what I want, really. I mean, I wanted you of course. Then I wanted to do something heroic by having this child and giving her to someone. But when that all turned out to be so hard . . . well, now I just want to be done with it." She smoothed back a strand of hair. "Free to choose my next tyrannical obsession and sink my jaws into it."

"That's the spirit."

We both smiled, cautiously.

"So," she said, "shall I be seeing you in September and handing off an infant to you?"

"Yes. I would love that."

"In that case, I've a birth plan to write up."

———

Fiona sent the birth plan to me the next day. *This isn't legally binding or anything as custody goes*, she wrote in the email, *but the hospital should act in accordance with it and thus will let you in to see the baby and such.*

I opened the attached document. It covered her wishes for labor: the pain relief she wanted, the positions she preferred to be in, the possibility of episiotomy, how placenta delivery should go . . . my squeamish eyes wanted to jump over this stuff, but I slowed down and made myself read every word. If I was going to be responsible for the bodily health of a female human, now was the time to get over my qualms.

I looked up the details I didn't understand, and felt myself go a little paler at some of them, but I came away feeling more like an adult. If a scared adult.

At the delivery, she wrote, she only wanted her mother and Chelsea with her, aside from medical personnel. Then the birth plan went on to say:

I intend to give up custody of the baby to her father, Sinter Blackwell, so I wish to have her removed from the room after she is born, and to have no interaction with her. I would like for her to be taken care of by hospital staff until Sinter arrives.

As I read those words, the duplex seemed to spin around me. Even if it wasn't legally binding, the fact of my becoming a father had grown more concrete with this document on my screen and in the hands of the hospital team. Changing my mind at this point would be an actual problem for Fiona and her doctors and nurses.

I sent one last wistful look at my life of bachelor freedom, then sighed in farewell and set myself toward the future—exciting, scary, and full of cute, fuzzy purple baby outfits.

I emailed her back:

Thank you so much. I am standing by to fly over whenever it's time. My phone will be on 24/7 the next few weeks. Now that you've written all this, I think it's time for me to choose a baby name already. Take care and talk to you soon.

CHAPTER 35: TRUE

OVER THE MONTHS, I'D COME UP WITH LOTS OF IDEAS FOR NAMES, OF COURSE, BUT IN LOOKING THEM UP online, I found some of them were too popular already (you don't want to have five other people in your homeroom with the same name), while others had a meaning I didn't particularly like.

I hauled my ginormous Complete Works of Shakespeare out to the shade in the duplex backyard and began flipping pages. I vetoed tragic names: no Ophelia, Juliet, Cordelia. That said, Portia, Rosalind, and Viola weren't quite doing it for me either.

My fingertips stilled over a title. *The Two Gentlemen of Verona.* Two gentlemen: the party who should have been making this decision instead of one gentleman. All the same, the city's name charmed me. I murmured it, liking how it flowed through my mouth.

It was mentioned elsewhere in Shakespeare too—including *Romeo and Juliet,* my first stage play as an actor. *In fair Verona where we lay our scene.*

"Verona" also rhymed with "Fiona": a way to honor her.

I googled the name and found that, according to some interpretations, Verona meant "true image" or "honest image." The irony: a guy living in cowardly silence on too many fronts being drawn to a name meaning truth and honesty. I could at least set up my daughter to become a stronger person than me.

And for a middle name? A flash of inspiration hit me, and I closed the Shakespeare volume. I'd honor the character who had brought Fiona and me together, and who had an androgynous name—another feature I liked.

I went inside and wrote it on notebook paper the way I had never actually done with my crushes' names in school, whisked it off quickly in cursive to make sure it looked good as a signature, said it out loud in various stage-quality voices, and typed it on the computer screen to picture it on business cards.

Verona Taylor Blackwell.

A name for my girl. Despite everything else I lacked, at least I had this.

———

Late in August, I approached Kam and Chris at the café and told them I was going to be away for a couple of weeks sometime in September, but I would like to have my job when I came back, if they'd be so kind.

"Where you going?" Chris asked.

I sank my hands deep into my jeans pockets. "London. So I can be there when my daughter's born, then bring her home."

I'd asked my landlady, Phyllis, not to mention it to anyone, including them, and apparently she had complied, because now I watched their jaws drop—literally. I could count teeth.

"Whaaaaaat?" Kam said.

I explained.

They demanded high-fives at the end of my spiel, and gave me sanction to leave (unpaid) and still have my job when I returned.

"And, dude!" Chris said. "Baby shower. Can we give you a baby shower?"

"Not before I get her for certain," I said. "But if I do get to bring her back, then . . . "

"Then we are *so* baby-showering you," Kam said.

"Do you have stuff?" Chris asked. "Crib, car seat, diapers, whatever?"

"Not yet. I have a list ready, but I don't want to buy it all before it's a done thing, and, like, jinx it."

"Send us the list," Chris said. "We will get your baby stuff for you and fill your place with it when you give us the call from London. You can pay us back later. I mean it, man."

I came around the counter and hugged them.

I emailed my agent and gave her the story as well, and requested acting gigs that didn't start until the end of September or thereabouts. Though I'd have less free time for a while there, on partial paternity leave of sorts, I *would* need jobs and could really use her help.

She emailed back a message of enthused congratulations containing several exclamation points, and promised to do her best to keep me employed.

It unsettled me, expanding the number of people who knew about the baby. The news seemed too likely to get back to my parents, though I had asked everyone so far to keep it on the down-low until I actually had custody.

Then again, my parents would have to be speaking to me in order to say anything unpleasant to me. Therefore, moot point. Sort of.

I hadn't exchanged any messages with Andy in several days. The silence between us was unbecoming of best friends, I decided.

Sinter: Hey! Talked to Fiona. Seems like all will go according to plan, so I chose a baby name

Sinter: Verona Taylor Blackwell

Sinter: Cheesy? I don't know, I'm liking it though. Anyway how are your plans going? When do you leave exactly?

It took him hours to answer. But at least he finally did.

Andy: Things are ok, I'm stashing a lot of stuff at Emma's. Kind of spinning my wheels. Ready to leave. Flight is Sep 10

Andy: And I like the name. It's pretty

Sinter: Thanks. Guess we'll be at opposite sides of the globe at the same
time, heh. Hope to see you before we both leave

Andy: Yeah, hope so

But he didn't propose any actual plan. Neither did I.

CHAPTER 36: LOVE WILL TEAR US APART

ON THE HOTTEST DAY OF THE YEAR, AT THE END OF AUGUST, ANDY SHOWED UP UNEXPECTEDLY FOR THE Sunday matinee of *A Midsummer Night's Dream* in Seward Park. He sat with two women and a guy, on the grass beneath the trees, in the middle of the crowd. I recognized his companions as his coworkers, Dakota and two others whose names I forgot. He waved laconically to me when I caught his eye.

I couldn't wave back, being on at the moment, but I cocked an eyebrow at him in acknowledgment. They watched me play Puck in my shiny green lipstick, pointed prosthetic ear-tips, and knee-length pants that looked like leaves. A pair of transparent insectoid wings was folded against my back, attached to a vest that glimmered like a beetle shell. Dominic had let my hair stay the way it was, having decided that blue, purple, and black hair suited a fairy, but he had me spike it up and stick some twigs in it.

After the performance, Andy's group came up and congratulated me—his coworkers more enthused than Andy himself. I thanked them, all the while wondering if he had brought them to see me, or if they had suggested it and he couldn't think of a good reason to refuse.

They waited while I signed programs for the few people who approached the cast in search of autographs, then they proposed we all go out to dinner. I declined, saying I needed to wash off my makeup and take care of stuff at home. Andy also turned them down: "Nah, I was going to head home. You guys go on. I'll get a lift." He pulled out his phone to call up a ride-sharing app.

"I can give you a ride," I said. "It's on my way."

It was what best friends did, right? Give each other rides home?

He put his phone back. "Sure, yeah. Thanks."

As the two of us climbed into my car, he lifted his eyebrows at my melting fairy-world makeup. "Don't you want to wash off first?"

I waved toward the surrounding grass, trees, lake. "It's a park. There's no dressing room. I do it all at home."

"Ah. Right."

We rode a minute in silence, rolling out of the park and into the neighborhood.

"You didn't tell me you were coming," I said.

"They heard you were in it, said it sounded cool, and somehow we all settled on a plan to show up today."

How ambiguous. "Glad you made it."

He nodded. Another minute of silence.

Then he said, "You're really good. At acting. I always forget how good you are until I see you do it."

"It's easy for people to forget me." I kept it flippant. That's how we were doing it, apparently.

"I disagree," he said—also lightweight, but the words seemed to fill the car.

I said nothing.

After another minute, he said, "How's your new place?"

"It's okay. Small, but it's good to have a yard and stuff. It's quiet. My landlady keeps to herself."

"Cool."

I touched my tongue lightly to my grainy, glitter-covered lips, then added, "You can come see it if you want." Because best friends also made offers like that.

"Sure." He gazed forward, eyes hidden by his sunglasses. "We could go there first."

At the duplex, he glanced around the interior, which I had furnished with the basics—kitchen table and two chairs, sofa and coffee table, bed on a simple metal frame, large cardboard box for my clothes. "I like it."

"I'll get a dresser soon," I said, waving toward the box.

His eyes traveled along the walls. "And baby stuff?"

"That too. I'm waiting till it's all finalized."

He nodded and said, "It'll be a nice place for her." Then he focused on my costume and came closer, a smile relaxing his lips. "You look like a mutant dragonfly."

"Thanks. That was our hope."

He poked the iridescent vest, then moved around to my side to touch the folded wings. "These are cool. How do they go on?"

"It's all one piece. See?" I unstuck the hidden Velcro patches at the front of the vest and peeled it off, wings and all.

Which left me standing half-naked in front of him, in the doorway to my bedroom.

I tried to make light of the moment, sighing in relief at taking off the costume piece, and tossed it onto a chair. "Gets super sweaty. I have to wipe it down after every performance."

His gaze had snagged on my chest, then lifted to my face. He smiled again, though his eyes stayed serious. Possibly sultry.

My heart started thudding.

"You need to be wiped down too." He ran a finger along my collarbone, and held it up to show the glitter.

"Yeah." I had gone breathless. "I should shower. Do you mind, before I take you back . . . ?"

He shook his head. "Go for it." But he didn't step away. Didn't stop eating me up with his eyes, despite my green insectoid glamour.

I swallowed. "Join me?"

His breath hitched. He nodded.

We rushed to get naked, turned on the shower, twisted the knob to the cool side, and got under the spray. While I scrubbed off my makeup with the face-wash stuff I kept in the shower, Andy held me by the hips and pressed up against me from behind, hot and hard.

All my problems fell away as lust consumed me from toes to ears. I turned, swiping back my wet hair, and slid my thumbs over his nipples.

He moaned, then ran his fingers along my lower lip. "Some sparkles left over. There." Having wiped off the lipstick, he twined his arms around me and locked us into a soaked kiss.

I pressed him to the shower wall, setting my feet apart to put us at the same height. We ground against each other, hard and slicked up with running water. He gripped my ass, sliding two fingers into the cleft to tease the sensitive flesh there. I groaned against his mouth.

I slapped a hand at the wire shelves hanging from the shower head until I found the soap, then spun it in my palm to work up a lather. I let the soap fall, caught us both in my slippery hand, and began stroking. I should have made it last longer, should have savored what I'd been missing all these weeks. But in his absence, I'd become so ravenous I couldn't stop, and he clutched me tight, matching my frantic pace.

He moved with me, pressing his fingers deeper into me, both of us panting. His teeth bit my shoulder. I shuddered apart, and he followed within seconds. Warmth filled my hand, then washed away in the cool spray. As my muscles relaxed, I suckled the edge of his jaw, drinking shower water off him.

His fingers eased around to my hips. "God." He slumped against the wall. "I didn't mean to do this today."

I kept holding him, my face against his neck, my legs wobbly. "Nice surprise."

He caressed my ear. "Dry off and talk?" He sounded serious again.

This was possibly not going to be my favorite talk ever. But nothing short of an asteroid obliterating the city could have stopped me from hearing what he wanted to say. I nodded.

He got dressed while I wrapped myself in a towel and padded into my room. From the cardboard box, I took out underwear, jeans, and a T-shirt, and put them on.

I turned around and my heart seized. He had wandered in and picked up the long-sleeved white T-shirt from my bed.

"This is mine," he said. "I've been wondering where it went."

"Yeah, I . . . guess I took it. You can have it back if you want."

"I have one of yours too." He was still holding the shirt, bunching it in his hands. "Your Joy Division one."

"Oh. Hadn't noticed it was missing."

"It smells like you."

I sat on the side of the bed. "Yeah, that one . . . yeah."

He sighed, and out of the corner of my eye, I saw him sniff the shirt, then set it on the pillow. "Keep it for now."

He sat on the bed too, next to me, two feet of space between us. Just the way we'd started out the day I kissed him when we were fifteen.

"You know," he said, "we weren't acting like friends with benefits. We were acting like boyfriends."

"I kind of wondered."

"At least we were, up until . . . "

"I got someone pregnant."

"Right." His feet were still bare. He slid his toes back and forth across the warped wood floorboards. "I tried to reset us to just friends. I thought it was for the best, with everything going on, and it seemed like you agreed. But I must have failed, because . . . I still think about you like that. Like a boyfriend. I miss you."

I couldn't speak through my surge of terrified hope. I just stared at his bare feet. I didn't even know which thing I wanted him to say next: *I'll put up with anything to be with you* or *This is never going to work, so let's officially stop hoping.*

"I guess what I wanted to say is, we could be that for real," he said. "Boyfriends. But I need to know if that's something you want. Something you can be serious about."

"I . . . " I cleared my throat. What with performing Shakespeare, making out in a shower, and being pinned down to reveal my emotions, all in one afternoon, my voice had lost its strength. "I've definitely wanted it, thought about it. I'm even . . . " *Maybe in love with you.*

But people loved their friends, didn't they? Even ones they had sex with? It was complicated. I could only be sure of that. And I shouldn't say it if I wasn't sure.

"I didn't think you wanted to be involved, was the thing," I said. "With this whole shitstorm."

He tucked his feet under the bed. "That's why I'd need you to be serious about it. I'm risking a lot here, man. My heart got stomped less than a year ago, and I'd rather not have it happen again. Which is why I've been protecting myself, trying not to care so much."

Touched, I looked at him, reinterpreting in a flash all those closed-off moments I'd run into with him in the past few months.

He kept his gaze on the floor and continued, "But I do care, so . . . look, I would cancel Tokyo, stay with you, face the wrath of your parents, be a . . . co-dad. But only if you're ready. Ready to come out, to commit. Otherwise . . . "

With that addendum, all my anxieties flooded back, nauseating me. My gaze slid away from him to the brilliance of sunlight spilling onto the opposite wall.

A slideshow clicked unstoppably through my mind, each picture a slap across the face. The loathing in my parents' eyes at the country club. The disinterested disgust of my grandparents. Each ex-girlfriend who had realized she was better off without me. Fiona, pregnant and heartsick because of me. The millions of people in the world who would grimace or shout insults or literally try to kill Andy and me if they saw us kiss.

Andy had learned to live with that danger, and I probably could too, for my own sake. But when I had to consider the safety of my infant daughter, when all the hate and judgement could grow even more vicious *because* she was involved . . .

I almost couldn't breathe.

I forced some stifling summer air down, felt my lungs creak open to accept it.

"Here's what I picture," I said. I gazed at the glare of sun on the white wall, my vision unfocused. "If I asked you to stay, and you accepted, it wouldn't be long before you resented me for keeping you from Tokyo. Your dream job. Maybe we'd sometimes be happy, but with Verona, we'd also be stressed and sleep-deprived and not knowing what the hell we were doing, and we'd start yelling at each other. My parents and the rest of my family might just never speak to me again. I'd be this pathetic, isolated parasite hanging onto *your* family, and you'd lose all respect for me and not want to see me anymore, and . . . " I ran out of air.

"Wow. Is that really how pessimistic it is inside your head?"

If he'd sounded warm and amused, the Andy I liked best, that might have changed things. But he sounded dismayed, impatient. Like he viewed me as pathetic already.

"That's what I'm saying." I gripped the edge of the mattress. "I'm messed up. I'm damaged. And if you stayed just because I asked, and had to deal with my shit all the time, I don't know how long we'd even stay friends."

He let out a sigh, turning his head away. "So, what, you refuse to ask me to stay?"

"I think you should take your dream job. I would hate myself if I denied you that." I angled my knees toward him a few degrees. "But . . . once you get back, after the dust has settled with me telling my parents about Verona, and she's not a newborn anymore and I've figured out what I'm doing, then I might be in better shape to take on . . . everything else."

"Coming out," he said flatly. "That's what terrifies you so much, isn't it? Dude. Please. Like no one in the world has ever had it as hard as you?"

"I know! That just makes me feel worse. I can't even handle what people in harder circumstances handle every day. But you are the one person I haven't completely disappointed yet, and I can't stand the idea that I might break that. Which I would, if I tore you away from this awesome job and tied you down to a kid when you weren't ready, and made you deal with my insecurities and my stupid family. You'd be out of here, and I'd never see you again."

He had turned to look at me, incredulity shaping his features. "Whereas if we wait six months, everything will miraculously be fine?"

"No—I don't know." I ducked my head. "I'll have figured out *some* of it, I hope. But I'm not asking . . . look, I can't ask you to wait for me. I know that. It's a long time. Things can happen."

"For instance, you might decide it makes sense to get together with Fiona. Who is conveniently the mother of your child."

"No. That is not going to happen."

"Or some other woman," he went on. "Who *loves* your adorable baby. Or some man. Could be either. Could be both."

"This—" I blinked in bewilderment. "No. I really don't think so. And this isn't even the issue. I want us to be friends, like we were. Not acting like *this* all the time. So obviously we have stuff to work out—or at least, I do—but me forcing you to stick around isn't the way to do it."

"No." He stood up and walked to where he'd left his shoes. "I guess it isn't. I hear you." The closed-off tone was back in his voice. He sat on the floor and put his socks and sneakers on.

"What, you're just leaving?"

"It sounds like I'm supposed to."

"But . . . I was going to give you a ride."

"I'll call a lift." He got out his phone and tapped a few things. "There. Should be here in three minutes." He climbed to his feet.

I rose too, dizzy with panic. "Okay, but . . . we have to stay in touch. Please. I want to know how you're doing. I want to . . . be able to tell you how I'm doing."

"So I can hear what I'm missing out on? Thanks, how thoughtful." He walked to my front door.

I followed. "If we stop being friends because of today, then everything I just said was pointless."

He opened the door and put his sunglasses back on. He looked down at his phone, his back against the door frame, his body silhouetted by the brightness in the front yard. "We're still friends. But I haven't done a very good job of not getting my heart stomped today, unfortunately." His voice wobbled a little.

I ached to wrap my arms around him, say the right thing—whatever that was. But a red car pulled up at the curb and idled there, waiting for him. "Me neither," I said.

He stepped out onto the porch and shot me one last look, his mouth set firm. "You can fix this. You can fix all of it, if you would just be brave enough. And you'd better, because I've got to tell you, man, the closet is no place to live." He turned and strode to his ride, and got in without looking back.

CHAPTER 37: THIS IS THE DAY

ANDY AND I DIDN'T SEND ONE ANOTHER A SINGLE MESSAGE, COMMENT, OR SOCIAL-MEDIA "LIKE" FOR the rest of August or the first few days of September. Neither of us posted much to comment on in the first place, but even so, we had reached that dreadful stage: radio silence.

Oh, I thought of things to say. Many things, a buffet of monologues to choose from: self-righteous defense, abject apology, logical bullet list, confident declaration of commitment. But I delivered none of them, because of one nasty sticking point.

He hadn't said he loved me.

He had come to see me, seduced me, claimed he'd stay if I asked, and sounded heartbroken when he left. But he'd never actually said "I love you," and wouldn't he, if he felt that way? It might have helped me clarify my own feelings. Or so I told myself.

Though even if he'd said so, I might still have told him he'd be throwing his life away to join me right then. Because I sucked. He was better off this way, regardless of how he felt.

As to whether I was better off . . .

I slept with his T-shirt bunched in my embrace, when I could sleep at all. I obsessed, I fumed, I sulked. I told myself to quit it and get shit done instead.

So I turned my focus to the baby—the one aspect of life I *had* gotten serious about. I bugged Fiona at least once a day to check if she was in labor yet, and eventually got this message:

Sebastian: Would you let the woman sleep. Someone will tell you when there's anything to tell. Calm your tits

I thanked him and shut up. But I remained a jittery mess, pacing around, ready to hit up the airline reservation page every minute. *A Midsummer Night's Dream* wrapped, and I wasn't acting in anything else—no point auditioning when I'd likely be gone for half of September. My only work was at the café, where Chris and Kam gave me extra shifts to keep me occupied.

On the sixth of September, during an afternoon shift, I got an email from my mom. Its subject was "Vacation." Perplexed, I opened it.

Hello Joel,
Just letting you know we're in Carmel for a few days, at our usual hotel. Thought we'd go before the summer's over. We can be reached there in case anything comes up.
Hope you are well.
Take care,
Mom

My head felt surreally light. That was nowhere near the world's most conciliatory email, but for my parents, after that scene at the country club, it was major. I finished my shift in a daze, pondering how to answer. Pretend nothing happened at Granddad's party? Say it was good to hear from her? Wish them a nice trip? And oh, by the way, I'm expecting your grandkid any day now, ha, funny story about that?

A text buzzed me as I stepped out of the café into a breezy, cloudy afternoon.

Fiona: Been admitted to hospital with contractions. They're getting stronger, so yes, doctor says it is time. Fly over if you can

I stopped dead, staring at the message. People brushed me on both sides, slipping around me on the sidewalk. I started breathing heavily. Looking in the direction of the duplex, I broke into a run and sprinted a few yards, then skidded to a halt, spun around, and ran back to the café.

Kam was behind the counter. I raced up, waving the phone at her. "The message—she's in labor—I need to go to London. Can you guys—will you—?"

"Oh my gosh!" Kam pressed her floury hands to both cheeks. "Yes! Yes, go! We'll buy your baby stuff; we'll coordinate with you later—go, go! Keep in touch! Eeee, wait!" She hurried around the counter and hugged me, leaving floury handprints on my clothes, then shoved me toward the front door. "Hurry, go!"

I fumbled out a message to Fiona.

Sinter: Holy wow. I am on my way. Will get plane ticket and tell you the flight asap. Stay strong! Keep sending updates. xxoo

—

Six hours later, I stepped out of a ride-share car at Sea-Tac. While I shuffled through security, I made myself a hotel reservation in London, choosing a place not far from the hospital Chelsea had specified. She was with Fiona, and had taken over as the person responsible for sending me updates. Fiona, being in labor, was growing uncomfortable and not in the mood to type messages.

I set my reservation for one week, figuring I'd find a way to extend it if need be. Or cut it short. Which would really be a lot worse, so I tried not to think about that.

At the gate, I texted Andy.

Sinter: Fiona's in labor. I'm about to get on a flight. I hate how you and
I left things, I really want to fix it, and I hope to. In the meantime good
luck and let me know how your trip goes

All I could do for now.

Next, I opened my mom's email, which I had completely forgotten
about in the baby excitement. I reread it, then gazed out the window at
the lights of planes taxiing around on the dark tarmac.

I typed in an answer.

Hi Mom,

*As it happens, I'm going on a trip too. Back to London for a couple
weeks, on business having to do with the movie. I'm doing fine. I have a new
place in Seattle. Address is below.*

Have fun in California. I'll be in touch.

Sinter

I typed in my new address and sent the message. Not quite a support
network yet, but being back on speaking terms was better than nothing.

As for what kind of speaking they'd be doing when they learned
about Verona, I filed that straight into "stuff I'm not going to think
about right now."

Boarding wouldn't begin for half an hour. In search of a distraction,
I wandered into a gift shop.

I hadn't bought any baby items yet because, as I'd told Kam and
Chris, it would be too depressing to collect onesies and pacifiers and
bibs, only to come home alone, to a roomful of unused stuff, if something were to go wrong. But . . .

No way could I walk in empty-handed. I had to bring her *something*.

Most of the onesies for sale were for three-month-olds or above.
Finally, I found one sized for a newborn, so tiny it hurt my heart to pick

it up and spread it out on my palm.

Someone in Seattle loves me, it said, in emerald cursive on white. Totally cheesy. But true.

I bought it, rolled it up, and tucked it into my carry-on. Right next to Andy's T-shirt, which I had brought with me even though luggage space was precious.

Then, for Fiona, I bought a small duty-free bottle of crème de menthe. Surely she'd appreciate a drink after this ordeal.

Our flight began boarding. On the plane, I bought the internet connectivity option and checked texts one last time before switching my phone into airplane mode, but Andy hadn't answered.

Stuffed mid-row between two strangers—who at least stayed quiet—I settled in for what was sure to feel like the longest flight of my life.

London. It would be good to see London, at least.

Oh, yeah. And my friends.

I emailed Daniel and Julie.

Hey guys, I'm on a flight to Heathrow. Fiona, my director, is in labor with my kid, so I want to be there. And hopefully take baby girl home with me. Fiona says it's okay, but we'll see. Lot going on. But I want to see you if you're around.

Our flight took off.

It wasn't long before Daniel and Julie woke up—first thing in the morning over there—and fired back an answer apiece.

Daniel wrote, *I'm sorry, Sinter, what? Could you start over please?*

Julie wrote, *OMG Sinter, are you serious????*

I elaborated, typing in the story for them—at least, the part about my brief fling with Fiona and her lack of interest in being a mother, but not the part about my involvement with Andy. Their responses came another few minutes later.

I can't believe you didn't tell us till now, Daniel wrote. *You know we'd be thrilled for you, mate.*

In response to that, Julie emailed, *Definitely! And we will help babysit while you're in town. You must let us. I want to meet the wee one. :)*

I wrote back, *You guys are awesome. Thank you so much. Can't wait to see you.*

There was a reason I had chosen to hang out with people like them instead of my own family, I supposed.

As we soared across the world in the middle of the night, I tried, at first, to catch an hour or two of sleep, because Chelsea's latest message told me to. *Labor can take a day or more, especially with one's first baby*, she wrote.

So I dozed. But I kept opening my eyes and rechecking email.

Two hours into the flight, Chelsea sent another:

Spoke too soon! Her water's broken and contractions are lasting longer. They've got her on the epidural, so she's more comfortable. Still hard to say how long it'll take, though.

I sat up straighter and nibbled my lip in confusion, because I'd thought the water broke right at the start of labor. Web search time: Google told me that while it could happen like that, it often happened in the middle of the process instead. Okay then.

I thanked Chelsea and told her to tell Fiona, from me, that she was doing a great job. Then I twitched my fingers on my thigh and jiggled my foot, while people slept with headphones over their ears all around me, none of them having the slightest idea that my life was metamorphosing right in front of them.

I thought of the medical complications that had befallen newborn babies or their mothers, in movies and in real life, then wished I hadn't. I tried to think good thoughts instead, *everything will be fine* thoughts.

Toward dawn, somewhere over the ocean, Chelsea emailed again.

She's at 7 cm. Contractions less than 5 mins apart.

Again I had to consult Google on the meaning of the centimeters. Ah, that referred to Fiona's cervix wrenching itself open to fit a baby through. Ten centimeters would be "fully dilated," which . . . I held my fingers roughly ten centimeters apart, about the diameter of a baby's head, and my eyes bugged out. Yeah, no wonder it hurt like fuck.

I sent a *Wow, thank you, keep updating!* to Chelsea, accepted tea from the breakfast cart, and fidgeted like a junkie, refreshing my email every twenty seconds.

An hour later:

10 cm! Think she's in transition now. They say it's going great, though F's exhausted.

Transition? Chelsea was apparently determined to keep me occupied with Google. Definition: the part of labor that hurt like fuck the absolute *most*. But also the part that meant the birth was imminent.

Every square inch of my T-shirt was damp with sweat. Deep breaths, I reminded myself. Probably what they were saying to poor Fiona right at that moment. God, I deserved every sucky thing that life had ever thrown at me, to have put a fellow human through this.

Nothing from Chelsea for an excruciating forty-five minutes. I was about to email her again and beg for news when the message came:

It's a girl! 6 lbs 11 oz.
The nurses are taking care of her. Fiona requested not to see her, so baby's in the nursery. F's doing all right, though knackered.
Verona is healthy and beautiful, sweetie. :)

A huge smile stretched the airplane-dried skin on my face. I inhaled what felt like gallons of oxygen. The cabin smelled of coffee and toast; the sun snuck in through windows too small and far away for me to see out of. The people in the seats next to me chewed their breakfasts placidly.

Chelsea had called her Verona, used the name I had chosen. And Fiona had sent the baby out of the room, hadn't claimed her—at least not so far, which likely meant she would stick to her word, cut herself free, and let me have our daughter.

I was in the process of writing effusive thanks to Chelsea, in which I also planned to beg shamelessly for photos, when another email arrived with attachments.

Picture attachments.

I'd seen photos of newborns before. Who hadn't? They'd always looked kind of lumpy and scowly to me, not the "beautiful" that everyone congratulated the parents with. Babies got cute when they learned how to use their faces a few months on, I figured.

But right then, I got it. Because this was *my* baby.

In the first shot, she was pink all over, naked and screaming with her eyes shut as they weighed her. In the second, she was swaddled in a blanket and drinking from a bottle in someone's arms, tiny snub nose in profile. In the third, she slept on a hospital mattress with a pacifier plugging her mouth and a purple knit hat on her head.

I might never stop smiling. Yes, she was lumpy and scowly. But also beautiful.

Then I did stop smiling, because I suddenly grew sad at how she had been disavowed by her mother and didn't have either of her parents there to hold her. Also, it hurt to think how Fiona must be feeling to have had to do that. Free though she wanted to be, it couldn't have been easy, that actual moment of making them take the baby away, especially when exhausted after a night of physical torture.

Then, with the hugest wallop of sadness of all, I knew what I should have known ages ago. I wanted Andy next to me at this tremendous moment, to kiss him in celebration, lean in tired happiness on his shoulder. I loved him, like a boyfriend or a husband, not like a goddamn friend. I'd been the densest and most in-denial person on the planet, but I was going to make it right.

Coming-outs could be achieved. Asshole family members could be written off. Babies could be taken to Tokyo for extended visits. Sneering naysayers could be ignored. Love could win.

Those steps had all seemed as insurmountable as the Himalayas before now. But after vicariously witnessing the magnitude of what Fiona had endured, after learning my daughter was healthy and beautiful and waiting for me, the fog had cleared and the path through the mountains had become obvious.

All of it would be *easier* with Andy alongside me, not harder. The fog had kept me from seeing that sooner.

Maybe he didn't love me back. But maybe he did, and he simply didn't say so the other day because he was scared too. For all his impatience, all his out-and-proud savviness, he could still be guarding his heart. He'd *said* he was, and I hadn't understood.

I would fix all of this. My head swam with the new determination, but I would, damn it. Every last item on the list, if he'd have me.

Right now, though, stuck on this plane and headed toward London, I could only make Verona my priority—and I was still sparkling from the inside out with excitement about meeting her.

Baby first. Boyfriend second.

I emailed Chelsea.

Thank you a thousand times. I love her already. Please tell her that, and let her know her dad's on his way.

And tell Fiona I'm so, so impressed and grateful.

I sent it off, scarfed down tea and toast for breakfast, then sat twitching in impatience.

Come on plane, land, *land*.

CHAPTER 38: SO IN LOVE

CHELSEA SENT ME ONE MORE MESSAGE AS OUR PLANE DESCENDED TOWARD HEATHROW.

It's been a long night, so I'm off home to get some sleep. Fiona's mum is here with her, and Sebastian is to arrive soon. I might run into you at the hospital later. :)

I'd never met Fiona's mum, so that could be awkward, and talking to Sebastian was nearly always annoying. But I honestly didn't care.

When we landed, I switched my phone out of airplane mode, set up temporary international call capability, then froze. Andy had texted me back.

Andy: I hope it gets fixed too. I wish you luck and hope you find what you're looking for

Though tempted to type in, *I already have. I love you and I'm coming back for you once I have Verona,* I restrained my impulsive thumbs and answered instead:

Sinter: Thank you. Just landed and will be heading to hospital. She's born! They sent me pics but I won't spam you with them unless you say you want them :)

I waited for a response while we shuffled off the plane, but he didn't send one. Of course, duh—it was the middle of the night in Seattle. I shoved my phone in my pocket and disembarked.

From the airport, I took a train straight to the hospital. I didn't even spare half an hour to go to my hotel first and drop off my bag. In all my trips to London, I'd never looked with less interest upon the scenery flashing by. I zeroed in on my destination with tunnel vision.

In the hospital, my bag on my shoulder, I found the maternity ward and gave the nurse at reception my name. I shouldn't have been surprised, but was, pleasantly, when she said, "Oh yes, we've been expecting you." She called over another nurse to escort me through the swinging doors into the ward.

This nurse, hardly any older than me, asked, "Who would you like to visit first? Mum or baby?"

"Uh . . . " I paused in the corridor. Voices, intercom messages, and the cries of newborns drifted from nearby rooms.

Verona wouldn't remember this day at all. Fiona would. I *should* go to Fiona first. But . . .

I could not resist. Not even the littlest bit. "Baby," I said. "Please."

"Of course." She winked and beckoned me into a room a few doors along.

What do other people feel the first time their child is put into their arms? There are billions of words devoted to the experience, in books and blog posts and diary entries, and probably carved into ancient walls in Rome. I'd read a few such accounts in my research recently. But I forgot them all in this moment.

The rest of the world went into whiteout. The universe became a tiny, scowling face and a lightweight body wrapped in a warm flannel blanket. She had a swirl of dark brown hair on her head, silky to the touch.

"Hey, you," I greeted, my voice ridiculously high and delighted.

She squalled and squeaked, her eyes shut.

I jiggled her up and down gently to see if she liked that better.

She opened her eyes—cloudy blue, a shade darker than mine—found my face, and locked onto it. She went quiet. We gazed at each other.

"Yeah," I said. "There you go. Hey, your name's Verona, did you know that? I promise you can change it later if you hate it."

She mewled again, worked an arm free of her blanket, and flailed it in the air. I caught her fist, and she closed her tiny hand around my first finger. I had slender hands, but they looked coarse and huge next to hers. The fact of having grabbed something seemed to surprise her; she went quiet again and stared at her hand. I laughed.

"She's probably hungry," said the nurse, whose entire existence I had forgotten about. "Shall I show you how to prepare her bottle?"

I learned how to heat up the formula and test it for temperature, how much to put in the bottle, and how to feed it to her. I sat in a chair against the wall, Verona on my lap, and coaxed the rubber nipple into her mouth. She was hungry and wriggly, but didn't have the hang of this eating thing yet, so it took patience. And some spitting up.

Wiping off my shirt with the towel the nurse handed me, I told my daughter, "That was very rock 'n roll of you. Thank you."

I probably needed insane amounts of sleep, but I was too enthralled to feel it. I was completely in love. I could not wait to share all this with Andy. The only shadow over me was whether he really and truly wanted to be part of it. Well—we'd talk soon, and I'd be honest this time and find out.

For now, I basked in the glow of my teeny kid.

Other babies resided temporarily in this nursery too, and parents or grandparents kept roaming in and out, taking pictures and cooing at their new relative. I hardly noticed, except when someone paused to congratulate me, in which case I thanked them, smiling.

When an older woman said, "Ah, you're the father," I glanced up with a grin and said, "Yes." Then I paused, because on this stranger I recognized Fiona's smile, the shape of Fiona's jaw, and Fiona's small stature and way of carrying herself.

I rose to my feet, still holding bottle and baby. "And you're the grandmother," I added with deference.

"Leela. I won't try to shake hands. Yours are quite full." She smiled. Pearls and beads sparkled in her earrings, bright against her honey-toned skin and silver-and-black hair. She wore a gray pantsuit with a red leather handbag over her shoulder, and looked just as perfectly put together and intimidating as I expected a successful TV-industry businesswoman to look.

"Sinter," I said. "Hi. I'm sorry I never met you until now."

She waved it aside. "These things happen."

Guys get women pregnant, break up, meet the ex's mom for the first time at the hospital after the birth. These things happened. I supposed they did; they just certainly hadn't happened to me before.

"I haven't been in to see Fiona yet," I said. "I thought she might need to rest, and anyway, I . . . " I looked down at Verona. "Had to come see this one first."

"Who could blame you?" She smiled at the baby. "Fiona's awake. She's a bit upset. She and I . . . " She clicked her tongue, shaking her head. "We've a habit of setting one another off. I always say the wrong thing somehow. It happens, as a parent. You'll do it someday too, I imagine."

Rocking from foot to foot as I fed Verona, I examined her closed eyelids and miniature lashes. "I expect you're right."

"In any case, the exhaustion, the post-partum hormones—anyone's liable to be upset. She'll come round."

Concerned, I lifted my face. "I'll go see her. As soon as this bottle's done."

"No rush. The musician's with her now. Long hair, high tenor."

"Sebastian?"

"Yes. She prefers his company to mine, it would seem."

"Well," I said. "I'll check in with them in a bit."

"I do hope she's told you that Alec set up a trust for the little one?"

"Yes. She mentioned. Thank you."

"I've arranged a yearly contribution to it as well. We can't have our granddaughter starving out there somewhere. Not that we don't trust you, dear, but we know actors aren't paid nearly as well as they should be, at least most of them, and it's hard work raising a child."

"It . . . isn't necessary, really, but it's very generous of you."

"It's the least we could do. But please don't assume we'll be interfering. I won't be, and I'm sure Alec won't either. I do only ask . . . " Her face creased into a smile again, looking at the newborn I held. "Photographs and news, perhaps? Once or twice a year? An email, or a webpage you can update."

"Of course. Absolutely." My head was whirling. I didn't have sole legal custody yet, but there I was, agreeing to contact terms with grandparents.

She seemed to be thinking along the same lines. "We'll work out details later. You've plenty to do today." She slid the straps of her handbag up her shoulder. "I must be off. It was very nice to meet you." She bent to beam at Verona. "And of course you!"

She kissed her fingertips, touched them to Verona's forehead, and sailed out.

Verona finished her bottle. The nurse offered to settle her to sleep. Though I longed to stay with Verona, I handed her off and went down the hall to the room where Fiona was recovering.

I heard the quiet sob when I was still a step outside the door. I slowed down.

"It's not," Sebastian's voice said, low and soothing.

"It is. I'm a mess," Fiona said—or some words like those. Slurred through tears, they were indistinct.

My chest blooming with secondhand pain, I approached the doorway.

Sebastian sat at her bedside with his back to me, his elbows on the bed. He held one of her hands; I saw his black-painted thumbnail move as he stroked her fingers. Of Fiona, I could only see a form under the pale-blue blanket, and a tangle of dark hair on the pillow. She was curled up on her side, and Sebastian's body blocked most of her from my view.

Before I could decide whether to announce my presence, he spoke again.

"Listen to me. Nothing you're feeling is wrong. Not one thing, no matter what anyone says. You're free now, and you get to be relieved about that, and you also get to be sad about it, all at the same time. There's not a thing wrong with you. Remember that." He lifted her hand and kissed it.

Her fingers clutched his tighter.

I knew I was exhausted, because tears filled my eyes entirely too easily. There was nothing I could say to top that. Hats off, Sebastian.

I tried to step backward silently, but the carry-on bag over my shoulder scraped the wall, zipper tab clicking the metal frame, and Sebastian turned.

"God, you're creepy," he told me. "Lurking in doorways?"

I blinked to dispel the tears, and my face formed the meek grimace it habitually made when confronted with Sebastian. "Hey guys."

Fiona shifted, sitting up, and smoothed back her hair. Her eyes were reddened, and she looked younger without her glasses. "Sinter. Come in."

I approached and set down my bag. I'd read about the scary bleeding that tended to occur after giving birth, and had steeled myself for crimson-splashed sheets or garments, but her hospital gown and bed looked clean, as far as I could see. "Hi." I stepped up to the side of the bed opposite from Sebastian—who glared, of course. I sat on the edge of the mattress and hugged Fiona carefully.

She leaned her head on my chest, as she had when I'd last seen her. She smelled like soap and clean hair. Unlike me, she had apparently washed lately.

"Sorry for the way I probably smell," I said. "It's been at least twenty-four hours and a plane ride since I showered. Plus now there's spit-up on here." I flapped my T-shirt.

She pulled back with a weak smile. "You've seen her, then."

"Yeah. I went in and . . . yeah." I could feel my loopy grin taking over. "I'm already completely in love."

Her smile disappeared. She looked at the blanket in abstraction, while Sebastian tipped his chin to glower at me from a slightly different angle. He exhaled loudly through his nose.

"Sorry," I said. "I . . . am so impressed. Seriously. You have bragging rights for life, going through something like this."

Like she'd be bragging about it. God, I sucked at comforting people.

Sebastian cleared his throat, even less impressed with me than I was with myself.

Fiona touched a bandage on the back of her hand—they'd likely given her an IV there. "I don't plan to do it again anytime soon, that's for sure."

"I bet. Oh, I met your mum. Briefly. She's, uh, nice."

Sebastian snorted. "Queen of insensitivity, more like. Which is irritating, because that's *my* title and she's nicking it."

Fiona smiled at him. "As if anyone could take that crown from you, darling."

"She did seem like she was sorry if she said anything rude to you," I added. "I don't know what it was, but . . . "

Fiona sighed. "Oh, only that I ought to leap out of bed, and get to work, dance about being happy that it's all over, and stop this quote-unquote 'moping.'"

"Ah," I said. "Well. She did sound sorry. And hey, if it makes you feel any better, I'll tell you some of the things *my* parents have called me lately."

"It's not a contest," Sebastian snapped. "And if it is, I'm going to win that one too."

Fiona set her hand on my leg. "Sinter's just sympathizing. And I know my mum meant well. It's just . . . I rather feel like everything I've gone through is pointless, and on top of that, my mum finds me pathetic."

"I don't think she does," I assured. "Anyway, *we* don't, which is what matters."

Sebastian opened his mouth, then apparently realized he agreed with me for once, and sat back, arms folded. "And hardly pointless," he added.

"Definitely," I said. "To me it's . . . well. Anyway." No use making her feel bad again by telling her how happy the baby made me, when that wasn't how she felt about Verona, or at least not how she could afford to feel. And probably she felt guilty for not feeling that way. Or something. It was complicated, in any case.

She gave my leg a pat. "No, but this is good. Seeing how you look when you talk about her, it doesn't feel pointless. I've done something for you, at least."

I slid my hand under hers and held it, careful not to press on top of the bandage. "You have. You *so* have. I mean, 'thank you' is never going to be enough, but thank you."

Sebastian smirked. "See how much you're thanking her when it's three a.m. and the tyke won't fall asleep, you've changed your tenth nappy of the day, and you haven't bathed or slept all week." He was clearly enjoying this future prospect.

"I hope you guys are out partying and having a great time while I'm doing that," I said, truthfully.

"That we will be." Sebastian rocked forward onto his feet and stood. "You fancied a hot chocolate," he said to her. "I'll go find you that, yeah?"

She nodded. "Thank you."

He strolled off. After the clack of his boots on the tiles had faded down the hall, I looked straight at her. "Dude. He loves you."

She emitted a weak chuckle and fell back onto her pillow, resting her forearms over her eyes. "Of all the times and places to make me think about that. When I look and feel my absolute worst."

"You look awesome, all things considered. And you know I'm right about him."

She rubbed her eyebrows, eyes closed. "I'm willing to say you are *perhaps* right."

"Good."

We lapsed quiet. I stayed perched on the edge of her bed. She opened her eyes and looked at the window. "A social worker's coming this afternoon. I'm not sure of the exact time. If you're able to be here, we can start the paperwork."

My hands started tingling. Ready to be a proper adult, Sinter?

"My hotel's just down the street. I might go drop things off, have a shower, but I can be here whenever you text me."

"You're sure?" She gazed at the outside world, not at me. "You take her, and I pay some standard child support until she's eighteen or gets adopted by a partner of yours, whichever comes first. I get news or visits only as approved by you. This is what you want?"

"I'm fine with all that. Except you don't have to pay child support. Your parents already plan to, and you've gone through enough."

"It's no hardship, and it's the normal thing to do, legally." She picked at the edge of the bandage. "Just a modest amount, let's say. I want to."

"Okay. Then . . . I guess this social worker will tell me what I need to do before they let me take her out of the country."

"I imagine you'll have quite the week of filling out forms. I don't envy you."

"It's worth it." I looked at the doorway, my mind traveling down the hall to where my kid slept. "Nothing has ever been more worth it."

"Then I'll let you know when the worker gets here."

"Okay." I kissed her forehead and got up. "I'll go check in at the hotel."

She nodded. Her smile didn't extend far, but I saw the steel again in her eyes, the determination to live and thrive. Thank God.

I couldn't leave without visiting Verona once more. She was asleep in her nursery crib, all swaddled up like a burrito. I stood by her side a long time, watching her take quick, tiny breaths. The top of her head was warm and soft when I (so, so carefully) rested my finger upon it, touching the wisps of hair.

Finally, I told the nurses I'd be back within a few hours, and went out.

Sebastian was coming down the hall with a pair of empty paper cups. Evidently, he and Fiona had finished their hot chocolates. He lifted his chin to me, and we stopped as our paths crossed.

"Well," he said. "I wanted Bradley MacCrossan to be the father, but I suppose you'll do."

"That joke's never going to get old," I told him.

"Never." He stacked one cup inside the other. "So you're in the city awhile?"

"Yeah. All the bureaucracy stuff is likely to take a couple of weeks."

He poked me on the shoulder. "Let me babysit while you're here. Text me when you're knackered. I'll come help. I mean it."

"Thanks, man. I will."

"Promise," he threatened.

"I promise."

He pointed at me, then walked off.

CHAPTER 39: DRIVE

AT MY HOTEL, I CRASHED ON MY BED FOR WHAT I INTENDED AS A BRIEF NAP, THEN WAS AWAKENED three hours later by Fiona texting me to let me know the social worker was there. I flung myself in and out of the shower, changed clothes, and dashed down the street. On the way, I ate a cereal bar I bought at a newsstand and checked messages. Still no answer from Andy, who should have been awake. But then, he was leaving for Tokyo in three days, so he'd be busy. Besides that, it had to be difficult for him to know what to say to me.

I'd make it easier soon. I hoped.

At the hospital, I longed to see Verona first, but this time I couldn't; Fiona and the social worker were waiting.

In Fiona's hospital room, I sat amid an array of papers and gave the social worker my driver's license, passport, and answers to all manner of details about my life. The worker discussed parental responsibility and made sure I understood what it entailed and was ready to take it on alone. I promised I did, and babbled about all the research I'd done so far, and how much I wanted Verona and was ready to bend my life into a pretzel to accommodate her.

I approved the names and spellings on the birth certificate and felt myself grow up by a significant margin when seeing "Verona Taylor Blackwell" typed out upon it, not to mention my own full name under "Father." I agreed to Fiona's child-maintenance payments (I coaxed them down to a lower amount than she originally proposed), and contact-and-visitation terms with Fiona and her parents: news at least yearly, contact info to be kept up-to-date on both sides, and in-person visitation only if approved by me, though of course I would approve.

My heartbeat blocked my hearing as I watched Fiona sign the agreement that gave me permission to transport our child from the country and take full responsibility for her. She had shadows under her eyes, her hair was pulled into a ponytail, and the hospital gown was a sickly pale green against her skin, but her hand stayed steady as she signed her name.

I signed too. The social worker explained the next steps, which basically would involve waiting a week or so until our arrangement was officially registered, then I'd cart Verona over to the US Embassy to procure an American passport for her.

"'Cause I mean, she'll want to be president someday," I remarked, daft by this point with sleep deprivation and gigantic life changes.

The social worker laughed, and Fiona did too.

With the feeling that this was all a crazy dream, I hugged Fiona again (who stayed sitting in bed, but wished me luck), gave her the crème de menthe, and shook hands with the social worker. Then I rushed down the hall to the baby who was my responsibility and no one else's, and holy crap, who could sleep or get anything else done with that weight falling on their shoulders?

———

They discharged both Fiona and Verona the next day. I took Verona to the hotel and spent every waking hour learning how to care for her and dealing with my bureaucratic paperwork. Chelsea helped me buy interim supplies such as a front carrier, bottles, and diapering paraphernalia. Daniel and Julie paid me visits too, and occasionally took Verona on a walk when I needed a nap.

As I walked around London with Verona strapped to my chest, I saw the world through shocked new eyes. Dangers to a little kid were *every-where*. Traffic, dodgy people, sharp objects, germs! Nonetheless, most of us had survived growing up somehow, so I supposed we'd manage.

Andy still hadn't answered my text. I sent one more.

Sinter: Fiona's signed Verona over. She's mine. It's surreal, but I'm happy. How are things? I know you leave tomorrow, hope it's going ok. Let me know if we can talk soon. I really want to

Then I told Verona, "What do you think? Want to visit Tokyo in a month or so? We'll find out soon how you like plane rides."

Back in Seattle, Kam and Chris leaped into action, buying baby gear and stocking my duplex with it. I sent them a picture of Verona in the "Someone in Seattle loves me" onesie to cheer them on.

Even though she hated wearing socks, didn't let me sleep more than three hours in a row, and was so loud in her crying fits it was a miracle the hotel hadn't kicked us out, I loved her to complete absurdity. I went overboard taking photos of her on my phone, kept sending them to Kam and Chris, and waited impatiently for Andy to respond and request some too.

He didn't.

His social-media pages didn't have any new posts either.

As for telling my parents about her, I couldn't process that yet. Not until I'd brought her home and settled things with Andy. Until then, there was nothing they could possibly tell me that I would want to hear.

The day before Andy was supposed to leave for Tokyo, I got a call from his dad, Carlos. "Sinter, hi." He sighed heavily. "Well, I . . . have some bad news. Andy's been in a car crash."

I'd been pacing around the hotel room holding Verona, trying to lull her to sleep, but I sat with a thud on the bed, my legs unable to support me. "What?"

"Yeah, he . . . another car hit his, right on the driver's-side door. This morning, in Seattle."

"Is he okay?"

Common sense told me Andy's own father wouldn't be sounding this composed if Andy were dead. But Carlos did sound upset compared to his usual jovial self, and . . .

I wish you could have known him, I said to Verona in the future. *He would have loved you so much. I should have asked him to marry me when I had the chance.*

"There's some broken bones, and he's unconscious—they're saying a closed head injury. They're stitching up his face . . . "

"His face? A head injury?" My voice jumped an octave. "He's unconscious?"

"Yeah, he . . . sorry, we don't know everything yet. We're on the road, on our way up there. I guess he's going to have to postpone his Tokyo trip. I'll tell you what we find out, but we wanted to let you know."

Because they probably didn't know our friendship was under strain lately. They were just doing the nice thing, telling his BFF.

Verona was crying. I bounced her in my free arm. "Oh my God. Um. Tell him . . . when he wakes up tell him we'll talk as soon as he can. When can I talk to him?"

"I'm not sure. They're keeping him under sedation."

"And what's broken? You said broken bones?"

"His nose, his left arm, and they're seeing about ribs and anything else. They're going to have to do some scans for that and the head injury to tell us more."

Verona rose to a full wail. I got up automatically to pace again with her. "Okay. Uh. I can't come back yet, but I will as soon as I can."

"It's okay, Sinter," he said. "I know you can't. We heard you were over in London."

"Yeah, I'm—yeah." He had to be able to hear the baby crying. Had to be wondering.

But he didn't remark on it. He did have more pressing things to worry about. "We'll stay in touch. Here's the hospital." He gave me its name and promised to touch base soon.

We hung up.

Pacing with Verona, I found the number for the hospital in Seattle and called, telling them I was looking for Andy Ortiz, who had recently been brought into the ER. After putting me on hold for approximately centuries, a woman came back on and told me he was unable to be reached for the time being.

"What's his condition?" I begged.

"Are you family?"

"Yes. Well—we've been best friends since we were kids. We're basically family."

"I can only give out details to family or spouse; I'm sorry."

"But—no, you can ask his parents. They'll say you can tell me. I promise."

"Unless you're a spouse or legal relative, we aren't allowed. I really am sorry."

She did sound sorry. I shouldn't rant at her like a maniac. The policy wasn't her fault.

My not being Andy's spouse was also not her fault. It was mine, if anyone's.

I snarled "Fine" through gritted teeth and hung up.

Verona was still crying, louder now. I made shushing noises and kissed her on the head.

I called Andy's phone, because I had to try, but no one picked up. It went to voice mail. While Verona wailed in the background, the words poured unplanned out of me.

"Andy, oh my God, please tell me you're okay. I'm freaking out. I love you—I should have said so ages ago. I love you so much. I'm coming back to you; please be okay. Please answer."

The voice mail automation asked me if I wanted to delete my message, and if not, to simply hang up. I didn't even hesitate. I hung up. I wished he could hear it right this minute.

I opened and reread our stilted text messages, the scant few of them that comprised most of our contact for the last month. That couldn't be it. We couldn't end it there.

Given there was literally nothing else I could do, I dragged my knees onto the mussed-up hotel bed, laid my crying child down, and curled up beside her, panic shooting daggers of ice through every one of my organs.

Life was terrifyingly precarious. Andy and Verona were the two people I loved more than anyone on the planet, and she was a delicate newborn, and he could bleed to death of internal injuries or get one of those horrifying hospital infections and be gone before I could get back to Seattle. I had worked so hard just to have Verona, and to reach the point of admitting I loved Andy. But I hadn't risked enough. I should have committed to him, asked him to come with me. Then he wouldn't have been in his car in Seattle and wouldn't be lying unconscious in a hospital.

Too late. *Too late.* There was nothing I could do.

I got up, fed Verona a little more, and walked her around the room until she finally fell asleep. Moving as slowly as possible, I laid her in the portable bassinet on the queen mattress. She'd been sleeping there next to me every night so far.

Then I sat on the end of the bed, clutching my phone, willing someone to send me news.

It took another hour, but Andy's dad finally called back. I darted across the room so I wouldn't wake Verona. "Hello?"

"Hey, Sinter." He sounded grave. "We're at the hospital. So, yeah, Andy's got a subdural hematoma—head injury—and they think the best way to help it heal is to put him in a medically induced coma. So they . . . they're doing that."

My back hit the wall. My knees buckled, and I slid to the floor. "A coma?"

"Controlled, with meds. They say it's a good idea in these cases, and when they take him off the meds, he should wake up just fine."

"He *should*? They're not sure?"

"Well, with head injuries . . . there's always a level of uncertainty." He sounded deeply shaken. Andy's parents had to be at least as freaked out as me.

But they got to be beside him, while I was across the world, alone, taking care of my newborn.

"How long?" I asked. "Before they wake him up?"

"They say at least five days. Likelier around two weeks, though."

"What?" It was a yelp. "But then—" Then I couldn't talk to him. Not a word. He was out of reach, and I had to bring Verona home on a ten-hour flight by myself, all the while not knowing if he would live, or still be himself when he woke up, or . . .

My eyes flooded with tears.

"I'm real sorry, Sinter." Carlos sounded desolate. "I know this is a shock."

"No, I, I . . . " I choked down the tears. "Sorry. It's worse for you guys. Um, keep me updated? A lot, please?"

"Of course. We sure will."

I sucked in a breath. Time to start being honest. "Listen, the reason I'm in London is that my baby daughter was just born here. I know that sounds crazy, but um—"

"We know, yeah; it's okay."

I blinked. "What?"

"Emma told us. She's here too. I guess she talked to him. She'll call you soon."

Emma was Andy's sister who lived near Seattle. But, what? Just, what?

"Oh. Okay," I said.

"Is everything all right with the baby?"

"Yeah, she's good. I've got custody, and I have paperwork to deal with before I can bring her back."

"That's great, then. Congratulations." He honestly sounded pleased for me, for that moment, once again proving Andy's parents were un-believably lovely people. "Well, we're sticking around Seattle, and we'll send you updates every day, or if anything changes. For now, they've got him stabilized, so it's just monitoring and waiting."

"Okay. We'll be in touch. Thank you, both of you."

We told each other to hang in there, and hung up.

I held my phone between my knees, staring at it with aching eyes.

Help. Someone. Help.

Who to reach out to? Daniel and Julie?

I would, of course. But my thumbs picked a different name and hit the video-call button.

She answered, her face filling the screen with a puzzled frown. "Hello?"

"Mom. Hi."

CHAPTER 40: THE UNGUARDED MOMENT

WHEN I WAS A LITTLE KID, WE HAD A CALICO
CAT NAMED PATCHWORK. I LIKED THROWING A CLOTH MOUSE
toy for her across the kitchen floor and watching her pounce on it.

One day when Mom picked me up from second grade, she looked
especially sad, and told me when we got home that Patchwork had died.
She was an old cat by then; it wasn't entirely a surprise. Nonetheless, I
burst into tears. Mom sat on the living room carpet and held me a long
time.

That evening, Dad took me out to buy churros at a fast-food restaurant. I had a thing for churros at the time, and he didn't like them and
usually refused when I asked for them, but that night, he offered to take
me without my having to ask. While we sat at the restaurant's plastic
table, Dad gamely eating churros with me, he asked where we should go
for summer vacation.

I had lots of useful ideas: Egypt to see the pyramids, Greenland to
see polar bears, Australia to see koalas, the Grand Canyon to see—well,
the Grand Canyon.

He remarked he'd been thinking about the Grand Canyon too.

We actually went there that summer and had a good time. One of
our best family vacations ever.

Most importantly, I felt a lot calmer about losing Patchwork after
that evening.

They'd been my support network once, my everything. They could
still be part of it. I needed *someone* to be.

"Did you mean to call?" Mom asked, confused, from the screen on my phone.

I nodded, with a fleeting memory of the time they had accidentally FaceTimed me. "Are you guys back from California?"

"Yes, we got home yesterday. We're taking today off to get settled, then we're back to work. And you, you're in London?"

"Yeah." I glanced at the window, where I'd pulled the hotel curtains most of the way shut to dim the room for Verona's nap. A stripe of late-afternoon sun poured in between them, and when I looked back at my phone, at the smaller window showing me in the conversation, I could see the light illuminating my tired eyes, the three days' worth of stubble on my face, and the baby blanket slung over my shoulder. Even *before* this latest news, I had looked like hell.

Mom frowned deeper. "Is everything all right?"

"No. Um. Andy's been in a car accident, in Seattle. I just heard. He's . . . in a medically induced coma, and I'm completely freaking out."

"Oh dear. How awful." She did look concerned.

"I'm way over here, and I can't just go back, because . . . okay, look, the reason I'm in London . . . " I was shaking all over, but who cared; by now, I was used to it. I got up, crossed the room, and turned the phone camera to take in Verona, asleep on her back, little fists up next to her head on both sides.

"Who's . . . ?" Mom began. "What?"

"This is my daughter," I said softly. "She was born a week ago. Her name's Verona."

"You have a daughter?" Mom's voice became louder, incredulous. "Are you sure? What on earth, Joel?"

Dad's voice intruded from somewhere near her. "It's Joel?" A second later, his scowling face entered the screen. It looked like he had taken the phone from her and was holding it at arm's length so they could both see.

"I have a daughter," I repeated. "I was involved with her mother for a little while, back when I was filming the movie here. Then it turned out she was pregnant."

"Well, what are you—?" Mom began. "How are you going to—?"

"Then you're back with this woman," Dad said. "Right? You're there, so I assume that's what you mean. It *better* be what you mean."

Turning the phone again so they could see only me, I shook my head and shuffled back across the room. "Her mother doesn't want to raise a kid. And we don't want to be a couple. So she's letting me take Verona, and I'm hoping . . . that Andy and I can raise her together. If he survives."

They took a few seconds to absorb that. Then they started talking at once.

"Joel," Mom said. "What do you—?"

"Great," Dad said. "Just great. That's—no. You do not mean what it sounds like you mean."

"The things I said at Granddad's party, they're all true," I said. "Patty and Phil were right. We were basically a couple. But I was too scared to tell you, and that's so stupid because why should I be scared to say I love someone who's an amazing person, the best friend I've ever had?"

"We worry that you're confused," Mom said. "That you're mixing up affection for a friend and—and something different."

"I *was* confused. For a long time. But I can tell you now, I'm bi, I can love both men and women, and I love Andy, and if he never wakes up, this is going to be the worst day of my life." My voice broke.

"For God's sake, Joel," my dad said. "This—no. That isn't a *real* relationship. And what about your baby? How is that ever going to work?"

"People will try to hurt you." Mom sounded terrified. "All of you! I don't understand why you'd want to do this."

"You guys," I said. "Please. This is not a good day. I know I'm dumping a lot on you at once, but . . . normal people get to call their parents for support at times like this. You wanted me to be normal, right?"

Their side of the video was swinging like it was in a high wind, the two of them jostling to keep their eyes on me.

"We're grandparents? You have a child?" Mom said. "This is completely out of the blue. How are we supposed to react?"

"And you think you can raise it with *him*?" Dad said. "What the hell are we supposed to tell people? Explaining this to Grandmom and Granddad—yeah, that'll be a real treat."

"*Your* parents aren't going to be much better," Mom retorted to him—a show of spirit that might have entertained me any other day.

"Right, that's what matters, isn't it," I said. "What are you going to tell people? What will people think? That matters lots more than whether your child is happy. It never has been about religion, really, has it? It's always been about what people will think."

"Oh, don't give us that." Dad had a vein about to pop in his forehead. Even on the tiny screen, I could see it. "You've always made it a point to be miserable and moping and rebellious around us. Nothing we could do would make you happy."

"That's not true!" I was trying not to shout, in consideration for my sleeping infant, but my voice was creeping up in volume nonetheless. "If you had just tried to understand me, support me, that's all I would have needed. But you didn't, and it's turned me into this messed-up wreck. Do you even realize the damage you've done?"

"Oh, that's *our* fault, is it?" Dad said.

"You're springing all these shocks on us at once," Mom said. "It's asking a lot to expect us not to be upset."

"Fine! Yes. I screwed everything up between us. For years and years. But now, I have a daughter—you have a granddaughter—and Andy might die, and I'm so, so tired of feeling like my own family hates me and isn't going to help me. So if we could please, somehow, fix this? I'm begging you guys. Please."

Mom looked torn, her mouth partly open, but she said nothing.

Dad had no problem speaking. "Joel, you not only screwed up with us, you screwed up with this poor woman you got pregnant, and you're about to screw up this kid monumentally, and God help me, I will not let that happen. I will find a way—"

"Oh, no you won't." My voice finally found its iron. My face hardened too; I could feel it locking into place, fire rising into my eyes. "You think I didn't look this up, Dad? Homophobic grandparents count for nothing. Legally, I can cut *you* out of *her* life, but you have pretty much no chance of taking her out of mine."

"We'll see about that," he said.

"Walter," Mom began. "Joel."

"You know everything now," I told them. "That's it. All the secrets. Oh, except I guess there's one more: if Andy survives, I'm asking him to marry me. And I *won't* be sending you an invitation."

I hung up and threw the phone against the window curtains. They rippled as it smacked into them and dropped to the carpet.

I sank my fingers into my hair, tearing out strands. Pacing, I felt every stinging inch of the operation, as the part of me that had been hoping all along for a warm family reunion got sliced out with no anesthesia.

Well. As Sebastian had said, it was okay to let go of what wasn't working for you, and okay to feel upset about it at the same time.

I picked up my phone, made sure it wasn't broken, then lay down next to Verona and shut my eyes, praying in earnest for Andy.

———

My phone buzzed with an incoming call, startling me out of a nightmare where I was sniper-crawling through blood and broken glass in the dark, frantically trying to find Andy under a wrecked car.

The call was from an unknown number with a Seattle area code. Verona still slept, so I leaped off the bed and crossed the room again.

"Hello?"

"Sinter? It's Emma."

I recognized the warm, emotional voice of Andy's older sister. I could picture her: skinny jeans, combat boots, brown hair either in two low-maintenance pigtails or in a rat's nest of little pinned-up twists. She had a law degree and worked for a legal nonprofit, but still looked like a college freshman. "Emma, hey. How you holding up?"

"Oh my God. He's this mass of bruises and stitches, and with all the tubes and things stuck in him . . . I can't stand to see him like this."

I swallowed, fighting a wave of nausea. I sat on an armchair and pulled my legs up. "Jesus. I can't stand this either."

"But I had to call you. See . . . " She drew a shaky breath. "He came to my place yesterday, to store the rest of his stuff. Then he said he wanted to talk. He was like, 'Usually I'd talk to Sinter about my romantic problems, but this time, *he's* my romantic problem, and I don't know what to do.'"

"Oh, God," I said, barely above a breath.

"He told me about the last time you saw each other. How he offered to be with you, and you didn't want to mess up his life or something."

"Yeah. I didn't, but . . . "

"He was heartbroken, Sinter. He was like, 'Why didn't he ask me to stay? He has to ask me. I can't just invite myself. It's his kid.'"

I pressed my hand to my mouth. Tears flooded my eyes again.

"I asked him if he loved you," Emma continued, "and he said, 'Only for about ten years now.'" She imitated his snappish hurt voice perfectly.

The tears spilled down my cheeks. I wiped them off with my knuckles. "I feel the same. I wish I'd told him. I did, on his voice mail, but until he wakes up . . . "

"He will," she insisted, though her voice shook. "He will and you'll tell him then. Anyway. Just in case . . . I thought you should know." She let out a sigh. "I hope he isn't mad at me for telling you."

"I'm glad you did. And I'm coming back as soon as I can."

"With your baby?" She sounded happy and hopeful for the moment.

"Yeah. Verona."

"My new niece! Which is completely what I consider her, whether you like it or not."

"You're awesome that way. So your parents know about her? Do they know about me and him too, or . . . "

"Yeah. Mom asked me this morning what was going on with you guys when I said they needed to call you right away. I told them because I . . . I wanted them to be sure to keep you in the loop. Treat you extra nice."

"They've always treated me extra nice. More than I deserve."

"You're one of us, Sinter. You know that. For real, Mom and Dad basically already view your baby as their granddaughter."

I tried to smile. "See, that's why you're all rock stars."

"Send us lots of pictures of her. Seriously."

"I will."

"Take care, Sinter. We'll be in touch."

"Definitely. Thanks, Emma."

CHAPTER 41: DESTINATION UNKNOWN

DANIEL AND JULIE TOOK ME UNDER THEIR WING WHEN I TEXTED THEM THAT EVENING AND TOLD THEM about Andy's crash. They showed up with an array of take-out for me to eat, though I couldn't manage more than a few bites, and they listened while I came out to them.

"The reason I'm so upset about this is, well, I love him, and his sister says he loves me, but we weren't exactly together and—ugh, I need to fix it. Oh, by the way, I'm bi; that'd be good to know, huh?"

I was pacing with Verona. They stood before me, attentive and sympathetic.

My shoulders sagged when I read their expressions. "This isn't even a surprise, is it?"

Julie wrinkled her nose and shook her head.

"You two lived together," Daniel said. "You wear makeup. You *have* been known to kiss guys. So, no, I'm going to say not a surprise." He gave me one of his charming smiles, the kind that kept you from pitching a pillow at his face.

"Right. So . . . " Then my pretense at being able to communicate fell apart, and I stonewalled all my emotion and ducked my head to look at Verona so I wouldn't start bawling.

Julie came over and gently took her from me. "How about a bath, huh, baby girl?"

As she ran the water in the bathroom sink and talked in a high singsong to Verona, Daniel put an arm around me and guided me to the bed.

"Have a lie-down, mate. You've got darker circles under your eyes than a raccoon."

I obeyed, flopped onto my side, and listened, half-awake, while they tended to Verona and stashed the food in the hotel fridge for me. I did at least manage to get up and thank them before they left.

Then I got onto every social-media platform I had a login for and changed my bio to *Sinter Blackwell. Actor. Bi. He/him.*

On one of the sites, I also posted a photo that until then had lived only on my phone and Andy's, a picture of the two of us kissing on the mouth. We'd taken it back in February. It wasn't a great shot, artistically speaking: the flash made our skin and hair look greasy, and I had a pimple on the side of my nose. But we'd been happy and turned on when we took it, making out on the couch while not exactly watching *Sherlock*. It was obviously me in the photo, but it wasn't as easy to identify Andy, the way his face was tilted. He was, however, clearly male, given the sideburns and jawline and Adam's apple.

All these months, I'd worried about anyone discovering this photo, though I'd been unwilling to delete it. Now I was glad I'd kept it.

As the caption, I posted: *I'm bi. I'm certain of it. No more lying or hiding. Consider me out.*

I turned off commenting options. I didn't want questions and discussion; I just wanted to say it publicly.

Then I collapsed into a longer spell of sleep than Verona had allowed me so far since her birth. Upon awakening in the morning and realizing I hadn't fed or changed her in almost four hours, let alone heard any news of Andy, I panicked. But she was wiggling vivaciously and gazing at me with curious eyes. I kissed her forehead, relieved. "Who's the awesomest baby in the world?"

She flailed all four limbs and emitted a chicken squawk.

"Yeah," I said. "Let's feed you."

While heating up the formula, I texted Kelly, who answered that

Andy's condition continued to be stable. Unconscious. No news.

Meanwhile, over on social media, fifty-six likes had popped up on my update, and I had six private messages from random people I'd known in theater or school, all congratulatory, three of them coming out to me on their part too. Huh. I thanked each one and sent virtual high-fives.

When I texted Chelsea and Sebastian to let them know my best friend and sometimes-lover was in a coma, they each insisted on putting in baby-help hours.

"I sang to her," Sebastian informed me that afternoon after bringing Verona back from a walk. "Sex Pistols, mainly. She liked it."

"You like Uncle Sebastian's voice, huh?" I said to Verona, lifting her out of the carrier.

"Course she does. Nicer than yours, isn't it?"

The next day Fiona sent a message.

Fiona: Oh god Sinter, Chelsea told me about Andy. How awful. I'm thinking of you all. xo

How the world had changed. A couple of days earlier I was the one feeling sorry for her and hoping she'd be okay. Now she had to console me. I thanked her, grateful there were people who still cared about me even after I'd put them through torture.

Andy's mom and dad updated me regularly over the next couple of days, but there wasn't much to say. The doctors kept him in the coma, monitoring the pressure in his skull. The injury was concerning enough to keep him under, but no complications had presented themselves so far. I googled subdural hematomas and induced comas and read more accounts than was good for me. Because while, yes, patients frequently came out of these comas with no lasting problems, it also wasn't unheard of for them to wake up with some type of brain damage.

Or to never wake up at all.

I decided not to google anymore.

Carlos and Kelly had learned more about the accident. Andy had been making an ill-advised dodge around a garbage truck at the same moment another driver made an ill-advised dash across from a side street. The other driver was all right, or at least better off than Andy. Their insurance companies judged them both equally at fault. And Celery was totaled, which I knew would pierce Andy's heart if he woke up.

When. *When* he woke up.

As for the Tokyo project, his company was sending someone else in his place, but still hoped he could join them later. If—when—he recovered.

I asked his parents to send a picture of him. Carlos said he wasn't sure it was a good idea. I begged, and he relented.

I slapped my hand over my mouth when the photo came in. A ventilator covered half of Andy's face. Rows of tiny bandages crossed his cheekbone and nose, and climbed up his forehead, covering the stitches. Dark bruises had bloomed on half his face. His left arm was in a cast. Tubes led to the other side of his head. Carlos had, prudently, opted not to take the photo from that side, so I couldn't see it in detail. I focused on the few unblemished features: the lashes on his closed eyes. His ear. His hair. His neck, which I'd kissed a thousand times. Then I deleted the photo, never wishing to see it again. I looked at other photos instead: us kissing, him smiling, him making ridiculous faces. He would want me to smile, not sit there smelling his T-shirt and crying. I told myself to at least *try* to stop crying, because I was tired of walking around with sore eyes.

For the next week, I devoted my energy to adoring Verona and thanking my friends for their ongoing help. I spent long hours gazing at my daughter, snuggling her, kissing her, and telling her I was so, so grateful for her, because having her with me was a thousand times better than facing this unknown future alone. At the same time, fear consumed me constantly, because if Andy died or stayed in a coma forever or woke up severely brain damaged, how was I going to *do* this? Raise her alone, without his love, without his help?

Still. I was absolutely keeping her, and more than once I touched my nose to hers and whispered, "We'll get through this. I'll help you, and you'll help me."

I let myself send one text message a day to Andy, even though he wouldn't read them yet, maybe ever. Some were about Verona: *V is apparently a Goth child. She screeches in protest whenever I bring her out into bright sunlight. So proud.* Some were about London, with the occasional photo attachment: *Saw this cool Empress Miyoko poster in a window. I hope you still get to work on it. You would give the tie-in the proper love.* And a few were more emotional: *I know it's weird to keep sending these, but it comforts me. I think about how you'd answer. I can hear your voice so clearly. I need you to wake up and tell me to stop spamming you, please. I love you.*

Even in my anguish, I recognized that Verona and I weren't completely without help. In London we had Daniel, Julie, Chelsea, and Sebastian, and at home we had Andy's family, who made it clear they truly did consider her their granddaughter, no matter what happened. They asked after her daily, requesting photos and updates.

You have no idea how much these pics cheer us up, Kelly texted to me. *Please keep sending them!!*

I had blocked my parents' numbers, so if they tried to call or text, I didn't know about it.

My mom emailed one day instead.

Dear Joel,

I'm trying this route since you aren't answering calls. We're very concerned and wish you would talk to us. A baby is a huge responsibility, as is changing your lifestyle the way you're claiming, and we think you haven't given enough thought to either. Also, we suspect you're just concerned and sympathetic for Andy, and are confused. You've had girlfriends, and if you could stick to that, it would be so much easier for you and for everyone, especially the baby, who needs a mother. But this is all just a shock to us, and there's a lot you haven't been telling us. We really ought to talk.

Mom

Fuck that noise.

I was holding out for way more: support for my relationship with Andy, congratulations and pleasure about Verona's existence, an expressed wish for reconciliation—not just "talks," as if I were a belligerent foreign government. Until they delivered those goods, I wasn't answering.

I felt okay about it, too. Cutting free that baggage had lightened my load.

After examining DNA swabbed from the inside of my cheek and Verona's, the US Embassy declared me her father and helped me acquire her passport and Certificate of Birth Abroad. By the time I had all those, it had been eleven days since Andy's accident. While I was looking up plane tickets, Kelly texted me.

Kelly: Good news, or so we hope. They are planning to take him off the sedation tomorrow and let him wake up!

My heart leaped, though fear tailed the joy. He could fail to wake up, or wake up and not remember any of us, or . . .

But I had no control over that.

Sinter: So good to hear, thank you. Then we are flying home tomorrow

Verona and I spent the afternoon bidding farewell to London and our friends there until our next visit. Because there would totally be a next visit. My half-English baby needed to know her mother country. And imagining the possibility of future visits with an older daughter gave me something to hold onto—whether we got to bring Andy or not.

Fiona and I didn't meet up. I doubted she wanted to see Verona in person yet, and probably not me either. But we did exchange messages.

Sinter: I'm a mess right now, but even with everything going on, I haven't forgotten how much I owe you and how amazing you are. I can never, ever repay you for giving me V. You are a complete hero. Thank you for going through it all just so she could live and I could have her. When she learns how to use words she'll thank you too

Fiona: Reading that is more than enough. Oh lovely Sinter I hope everything turns out wonderful for you. Please keep me updated. Best of luck and love to you and V :)

The morning of our flight, my mom sent me another email.

Joel,

We're still trying to sort this out. I wanted to say I'm sorry about what's happened to Andy, and I hope he'll be all right. I talked to his family to let them know we're thinking of them. They tell me Verona is doing well too.

I have one more question. Was there anything we did that compelled you to become like this? Resistance to church or other rules? Did we have any influence on you turning out this way?

Mom

It was the kind of question that could really offend a person. But she didn't understand, and it looked as if maybe she was trying to. So I answered as factually and briefly as I could:

No. The only choice you have in the matter is whether to accept it or reject me for it.

Mom wrote back, *I see. Thank you for answering.*
We left it at that.

CHAPTER 42: OUR HOUSE

SO, FLYING WITH A NEWBORN: NOT THE MOST
TRANQUIL UNDERTAKING. VERONA HAD BECOME SOPHISTI-
cated enough to endure socks and baths, but was also getting pickier
about falling asleep, only doing so when I walked her around and
bounced her up and down, and had become louder when crying in complaint. When the seat-belt signs were on and we weren't allowed to walk
around, I did what I could (i.e., sweat, beg her to understand, try to
buy a few minutes with pacifiers, and apologize to everyone around us).
When we were free to get up, I went to the end of the aisle and swayed
her in the front carrier, gaining sympathetic conversation from the flight
attendants.

Before switching my phone to airplane mode, I'd sent a few more
texts to Andy.

> Sinter: V and I are on our way back to you. I'm still scared but calmer. I
> hope you still want me and that we can pick up where we should have left
> off. I'm so so so sorry I didn't ask you to stay. I've been torturing myself
> for it ever since. Please stay with me, or let me come with you wherever
> you go. V and me both.
>
> Sinter: I told my parents everything. They're being exactly as horrible as
> expected. I'm tuning them out. I choose you. You and V, over everyone.
>
> Sinter: I love you, I love you, I love you. Please answer when you can, or
> I'll see you soon, whichever comes first

During the flight, I had to rely on emails. Kelly sent only one, about four hours before we were to arrive at Sea-Tac.

He's woken up!!! But he's confused and scared, and they say we need some time for the sedation to fully wear off. They want to do tests for memory and brain function, etc. But come as soon as you can!!! With baby!!!

Standing at the back of the plane with my cranky baby, I felt anxiety prickle through my whole body, a wave of pins and needles. His mind could be gone. He could be "confused and scared" forever, not himself anymore, never himself again . . .

It wasn't helping to think like this. But until I knew more, there was no way I could relax.

I thumbed back a message.

Oh wow, keeping fingers crossed. Tell him we're on our way and give him my love. And send me updates please.

I checked every thirty seconds, but she didn't answer. I told myself not to push with more messages; they were busy, they had hospital tests to run, and they probably couldn't be sure how he was doing for a while yet. Meanwhile, Verona was taking *forever* to stop fussing and go to sleep, which at least gave me something to do while I waited in agony.

She fell asleep in the front carrier just in time for me to sit back down and fasten my seatbelt for landing at Sea-Tac.

On the ground, I switched my phone out of airplane mode and found several texts waiting.

From Andy.

My lower body turned to liquid.

Or at least, they were from Andy's phone. My mind, in a fraction of a second, filled in the worst-case scenario: he was dead or severely damaged, and his parents were using his phone to try to get hold of me. Not that this made any sense, but . . .

Shaking, holding Verona to my chest while everyone else got up and pulled their stuff from the overhead bins, I opened the messages.

Andy: So . . . it's really freaking scary to wake up in the hospital and be told you were out for almost two weeks. But I didn't cry then

Andy: It's also scary to realize your arm's in a cast and your ribs and nose hurt like fuck and you have scars on your face, but I didn't cry then either

Andy: I didn't even cry when they told me Celery was totaled, though that was close

Andy: Then they hand me my phone and I hear your voicemail and read your texts, and NOW I'm crying

Andy: I love you I love you I love you too. I was a jerk, I'm so sorry, I shouldn't have given you an ultimatum

Andy: I want you with me!! Both of you!! Please come back. I mean if you can stand to look at me with these scars

I drew in a trembling breath and read the messages over and over, even though the words were blurring.

"Sir? Are you okay?"

It was a woman from the row in front of us, who was standing in the aisle like everyone else, waiting to disembark. She was looking at me with concern.

Because I guess when a guy's sitting there clutching his baby and staring at his phone with tears running down his cheeks, you get concerned and ask if they're okay.

I wiped my face. "Yeah. Yeah, I'm good. It's . . . good news. Someone I was worried about, they're okay."

She beamed. "Oh, thank goodness. I hate waiting for news like that. That's the worst."

"For real," I said, tapping the "reply" button.

"Especially when you're stuck on a plane," the woman next to me said.

"With a baby," her husband commiserated.

We all laughed and agreed, and I wiped my eyes again and kissed Verona's head while she slept. Then I texted Andy back.

Sinter: Omg I love you so much. Thank god. Welcome back. I don't care
what you look like, you freakshow. I can't wait to see you

Sinter: P.S. V hates flying with an intense passion. Yay

———

In the hospital hallway, I essentially lifted Verona out of the front carrier and handed her straight to Kelly, saying, "This is Nana!" Then, with no further greeting, I dashed into Andy's room, flung myself onto his bed, and hugged him.

"Ow! Broken arm, dude." But, sitting up, he held me as tightly as he could with his undamaged right arm.

Even though he smelled like antiseptic soap rather than his tasty cologne, I pressed my face to his neck and breathed in and out deeply. I closed my eyes, tears seeping past my lashes and dripping onto his shoulder. My hand found the shaved patch and bandage on the side of his head. I slipped my fingers across it in a caress, then clasped my arm around him again. His bones felt sharp; he must have lost at least ten pounds. His breath flowed onto my neck, warm and shaky, and he sniffled.

I pulled back, sitting almost in his lap.

He dabbed the heel of his hand against his eyes. "I'm not crying; you're crying."

I wiped my eyes with my sleeve. "Oh my God, dude. You scared the crap out of me."

"I'm so sorry. I was driving like a moron. I was distracted, with the trip and trying to decide what to say to you about Verona being born and . . . "

"I knew it. See, I knew it wouldn't have happened if it weren't for me." I set my forehead on his shoulder.

"No, no, I don't mean that." He stroked my back. "I shouldn't have guilt-tripped you. We should have talked about all of it sooner."

"It's me who should've talked about it sooner. You were completely right. I was dragging my heels. I was scared."

"But I was scared too. It's okay to be scared." He nestled his cheek against mine. "Plus, I was jealous. I mean, you were having a baby with someone else."

"I wasn't really having a baby *with* her. I told you."

"Still. It could've turned out that way."

I shook my head, pulling back to look him in the eyes. "It was always you. I kept picturing *you* holding Verona, playing with her, being right in the middle of it with me. I wanted it so much. I just didn't think *you* wanted it."

"Are you kidding? I want in on anything you're doing. Yes, it freaked me out at first, but then I started thinking all those same things—I want kids with you, cats, hamsters, fake plants—everything, as long as it's with you—"

I leaned in and kissed him on the mouth, a long kiss to take the place of all the ridiculous words I would surely have voiced otherwise. Then I sniffled and said, "Good. All sorted, then." I touched the crosshatched red lines climbing over the bridge of his nose and up his forehead. "Nice scars, by the way."

"Right? I'm all Phantom of the Opera now."

"It's good, though. I was always jealous you were cuter than me, so maybe now we're even."

He laughed, the smile beautifying his face all over again. "Asshole."

He glanced at the door of the room. His parents stood there, alternately beaming at us and cooing at Verona. They'd never seen us kiss on the mouth before, I realized, but it didn't bother me.

Andy's face brightened and he reached out his good arm toward them. "Baby! Bring me the baby."

Carlos brought her over and laid her across our laps. She frowned up at Andy, wiggling all four limbs in her footed green onesie.

"Hi, Toothless!" Andy stroked her hair. "Check you out. You are way cute."

She gazed at him a moment, then squawked in protest.

"Here. She likes this position better." I propped her up to sit against the crook of his cast-covered elbow, and plunked the toy in front of her that Kelly and Carlos had brought.

She quieted, staring at it. It was a soft flower with a mirror in the middle, each petal a different texture, some of which made interesting sounds when you squeezed them.

Andy shook it to ring a bell inside, and squeezed the crackly petal, then the squeaky one. He grinned, watching her. "She totally has your eyes."

I was floating in bliss to finally behold this scene. "Little early to tell, isn't it?"

"Nah. I know your eyes, man." He leaned down and kissed her on top of her head, as naturally as you please.

I sat with him for an hour, catching him up on my nightmarish past few weeks, and making sure he ate some of the sandwich and soup they brought him for dinner. He sighed to hear about my conversation with my parents, but he wasn't surprised. Kelly, however, contributed, "I am going to slap them if they don't shape up, Sinter. Honest to God."

Carlos and Kelly carried Verona out to walk her up and down the hall and take photos of her. The latest nurse left with the dinner dishes. We were finally alone.

I got on my knees on Andy's bed (screw the floor) and said, "Hey. Will you marry me?"

He laughed in surprise. "What?"

"Next time I have to call a hospital about you, I want to be able to say, 'He's my goddamn spouse, so tell me what's going on.'" My voice cracked with emotion.

He gazed into my eyes. "Wow. Um. I want to say yes, because I've loved you for ten years like my stupid sister told you, but . . . " He set his hand on mine and looked down at it. "You're only asking because you're all emotional right now. You don't mean it. You need to think about questions like this."

"I have. It's not like we don't know each other well enough. And I've loved you a lot longer than you think, okay? I loved you months ago, when I realized I didn't want anyone else at Girasol. I loved you when I was willing to leave London for you. Hell, I probably even loved you that day you left for college. I just didn't know it until lately. So yeah, I stand by my question. Will you marry me?"

He beamed and twined his fingers into mine. "Then yes. But let's make it a long engagement, so we can get past Verona's newborn stage, and you can have time to change your mind if you want, and—"

I snorted, cupped his banged-up face gently in both hands, and gave him a long, deep kiss, the kind of kiss you simply have to give someone who's just accepted your marriage proposal.

———

"Come on, Toothless, humor me?" Andy implored.

Wrapped in a bright-yellow, one-piece Pikachu costume, complete with hood, feet, and forked-lightning tail, Verona lay on the changing table, kicking and screaming. Halloween was the next day, Andy's boss had given us the costume, and Andy was determined to try it on her.

Since his apartment was occupied by people subletting it, and since he would be delayed in going to Tokyo (he planned to join them for the second half of the project), he had moved into my duplex with me. My landlady was fine with it, even when I introduced Andy as my fiancé. She could teach a thing or two to my grandparents.

Standing by with my phone camera switched on, I said, "I don't think it's because of the costume. It's just seven o'clock. The usual hour of screaming." Verona had entered a phase where no matter what we did, she cried for about an hour every evening after dinner. Good times.

Andy ran his hand through his hair. "So, what, we try later?"

"All we can do."

Andy flipped a blanket over his shoulder in preparation for the inevitable drool and/or spit-up and picked her up carefully—he'd just gotten his cast off and was still taking it easy on his healed arm. "Okay, shush shush, I'm sorry, Toothless. I love you. I'll never torture you with costumes again. Well, that's a lie. I'll probably do it every Halloween, but—"

I put out my hand to silence him. I thought I'd heard a knock on our door.

Verona's wails sank to a lower volume as he cuddled her.

The knock sounded again.

I crossed to the front door and opened it, while Andy hung back with Verona, pacifying her with kisses on her ear.

My mother stood on the porch wearing her long black raincoat. Raindrops sparkled on her shoulders. A small piece of luggage, like an overnight bag, sat at her feet. Andy and I stared in shock.

Was she there to take the baby from us? Was someone dead? Had someone kidnapped her and dropped her beside the road in Seattle, conveniently within walking distance of our place?

"Hello, boys." She seemed composed, if tired. Her hands rested in the pockets of her coat.

"Mom." Surprise resounded in my voice.

Andy glanced at me and withdrew a step, as if to let the two of us face off without interference.

She focused on me, raising her voice to top Verona's cries. "Joel, I've left your father."

My stomach did a roller-coaster flip. "*Left* him?"

"We've been talking for weeks. We can't agree. Until he stops being so stubborn and accepts your situation, I refuse to live with him. I want to be a part of my granddaughter's life." Her gaze moved to Andy. "I have nothing against you two being together. I no longer want to make life any harder for you."

I stuttered out, "Oh. Okay."

Andy smiled, still bobbing our crabby baby. "Well, come in. Let's get that wet coat off you."

"Thank you." She entered, and I took her coat and hung it up.

"Mom . . . I'm so glad you feel that way, but . . . I don't want you to leave Dad. Not forever." Despite all my reasons to want revenge upon my father, I found myself in a panic at the idea of my parents divorcing—over me, no less.

She straightened the hem of her royal-blue cardigan. "I imagine he'll come around. But your child's happiness comes first. I'm sure you understand that."

"Yeah. I guess." I glanced over and made a wry face at my clearly unhappy baby.

"Let's see her." She held out her arms, and Andy handed Verona over. "You were the same at this age," she told me. "I bet I still remember the maneuver." She began rocking Verona in big, slow bounces while making a shushing sound. To my amazement, within a minute, Verona quieted down to a low whimper, calmer than we had gotten her so far. "There, sweetie," she whispered.

Andy and I stared, impressed. "Thank goodness," he said. "An expert's finally arrived."

"I'm sure she was about to fall asleep anyway," Mom said. "Such a fuss wears a baby out."

"Can we, um, make up the sofa bed for you?" I said. "It's all we have, but—"

She gazed at the baby. "Thank you, but I've already booked myself a room at Hotel Monaco."

The Monaco was one of the ritziest hotels downtown, the kind with a row of international flags outside. "You do things in style, Mom."

"I may stay in town awhile. But I promise I'll only be around when you want help."

"We can always use help," Andy assured her.

She lifted her face. "Andy, what are your parents called, as grand-parents?"

"They're Nana and Papa."

"Good. I would like to be Granny."

I stepped forward to view Verona, who slept blissfully in her grand-mother's arms, her smooth eyelids shut and her lips parted in an O. Torn between telling my mother "Thank you," "I love you," and "Please, seriously, don't divorce Dad over me," I said nothing. I leaned down and kissed Mom on the forehead, then stepped back.

"Did you pick her name?" Mom asked me. "I like it."

"I did," I said. "Thanks."

"Very Shakespearean."

"That was the idea."

She looked at Andy. "I went to your parents to find out how you were doing—all of you. They were very kind."

"Aw, I'm glad," he said. "They've been great."

"They helped me see that your situation needn't be a problem. Patty and Phil did too, when I spoke to them. They have a gay daughter, you know."

I cracked a smile at Andy, remembering the country-club debacle. He grinned back.

"Yeah," I said. "They mentioned."

Mom glanced at Andy again. "You've filed to adopt her, Kelly told me."

Andy and I exchanged another glance. I shrugged.

"Yes," he said. "It's . . . they say it should all go through just fine."

"That's good. I also asked if you were engaged, and she said yes." She looked calmly over at me.

"Um," I said, "yeah. I mean, we haven't set a date, but . . . "

"Your grandparents won't come," she remarked. "Any of them. I can tell you that. But I'd like to, if that's all right." She smiled down at the baby.

Andy and I met each other's gazes again, amazed.

"We'll save you a front-row seat," I said.

CHAPTER 43: CEREMONY

I SKETCHED EYELINER AROUND MY EYES—NOT
THE CURE LEVELS, JUST ENOUGH TO PRETTY MYSELF UP A
little. This time it wasn't black, either; it was brown, to match my current
hair color.

In the past year, my agent, Dawn, had found me a role in a TV series, a Netflix exclusive. It was a spooky, X-Files-type show where people
from other times and places kept appearing out of nowhere in a small
Northwest community. We filmed in a town in the hills outside Seattle,
and I played a cobbler from the 1850s who, like many of the misplaced
visitors, became an unwilling modern-day resident. The show was a hit,
to the point where I sometimes got recognized in public. On my social-
media pages, I had hundreds of followers I'd never heard of. I had *fans*. It
was insane, and I tried not to think about it too much.

For my role, the hairdressing team dyed my hair brown and kept it
earlobe-length and smooth. On days like this one, though, when I wasn't
on set, I liked to give it some rock-star unruliness with the help of styling
products.

Daniel stepped into the dressing room. "I've been sent to put your
flower on you, mate."

He looked especially GQ-ready in his perfectly fitting gray suit with
a white rose pinned to the lapel, his wavy hair tousled by Colin Firth's
own stylist (or such was my private theory).

I set down the eyeliner and turned, blowing out a long breath to
calm my nerves. "Thanks."

Daniel pinned the boutonniere to me: a purple calla lily backed with the trimmed eye of a peacock feather. As he sorted out the pin, he glanced at me and grinned. "Nervous?"

"Yeah. But at least this is a theater, and I'm used to being nervous in theaters. How's Andy?"

"Same, I reckon, except he's *not* used to being nervous in theaters."

Daniel and the other groomsmen and groomsmaids proved more traditional than we expected, and weren't letting Andy and me see each other in the hour before the ceremony, even though we'd woken up in the same bed that morning and driven over together. In the next dressing room over, Andy was being primped by his siblings and whoever else barged in.

Julie popped into our dressing room and squealed upon viewing me. "Oh, wait till he sees you! You look beautiful."

Daniel stepped back, having fastened my boutonniere, and I looked into the row of mirrors facing me. I wore a black velvet tailcoat with silver buttons (though I was supposed to leave the coat open and not fasten any of them), pin-striped gray trousers, lace-up black boots, a satin vest in vertical stripes of dark purple and black, a white shirt, and a purple tie that matched my vest and lily. I had opted against ruffles, goggles, or a top hat, but I still looked fairly steampunk. Or new wave.

This was the kind of thing that happened to you when you knew costume designers. Still, it suited me much better than a traditional tux.

Daniel checked the time on his phone. "We're pushing the limits of 'fashionably late.' All set?"

I packed in another deep breath and nodded.

It had been a long engagement. Not because we were ambivalent, but because we were *busy*. I'd been on the TV show for two seasons and was booked for a third, the closest thing to steady work an actor could hope for. Andy, scenting a networking opportunity, asked our producers if they'd be interested in developing a tie-in role-playing video game for the show, and to his glee they were. Andy and Dakota and their team had been designing it and releasing updates to it as the better part of their job lately. (We in the cast voiced our own characters in the game, naturally.)

Then there was raising a baby, who became a toddler, clever and stubborn enough to find new ways to test our sanity every day and make us doubt our ability to do anything as complex as planning a wedding. Yet there we were.

This venue was a small, hipster-chic theater with neon signs and a balcony. I had never performed in it, but it was only five miles from our place, and the space could be rented for events, so we grabbed it. We had both grimaced at the idea of a church or city hall, and when Andy cheekily suggested a country club, I stopped speaking to him for the rest of that day.

When I walked in from stage left with Daniel, I looked down at the front row and found two-year-old Verona on my mom's lap, with Andy's parents sitting beside them. I waved.

Verona crowed, "Daddy!" entirely too loudly. I put my finger to my lips, and Mom murmured something into her ear.

From stage right, Andy strolled forward with Emma, their other two siblings tailing them. The multicolored stage lights played across his smile. Within seconds, I was seizing his hands and refusing to let go or to stop grinning.

He hadn't wanted to wear a velvet tailcoat, so he wore a more mainstream suit in the same colors as mine: black jacket, striped vest, dark-purple tie and peacock/lily boutonniere. With pink lights falling on his face, his scars from the car accident didn't even show much. On the one and only occasion he had let me draw cosmetic stripes along them to disguise them, at which time he had also let me paint him up with eyeliner and lipstick, I swore truthfully to him that he looked hotter than Adam Ant. But for whatever bizarre reason, he didn't want to look like that at his wedding, so I was the only one of us wearing cosmetics.

I didn't work at the café anymore—the TV show kept me busy full-time—but we were still regular patrons and friends of Chris and Kam's, and it turned out Chris was one of those people ordained by the Universal Life Church and thus able to perform weddings. She stepped up, facing the audience across our joined hands, and began her spiel.

I stared into Andy's eyes with a dopey grin. Though my heartbeat pounded in my ears, he and I were able to repeat our vows lucidly enough.

As we readied the rings, Verona yelled, "Daddy! Oddy!"

We had simply been calling Andy "Andy," but her developing tongue couldn't quite grasp that. She began with "Addy," which had since developed into "Oddy."

"Vee," Andy said to her. "Shush."

I held out a hand toward her, middle and ring fingers tucked down, pointer and pinky up. "Quiet coyote," I reprimanded, face stern, and everyone laughed.

Verona devoted herself to trying to form coyote ears with her fingers and stick them on her head. Mom and Carlos assisted her.

At Chris's command, we slid the rings onto each other's fingers—basic bands, silver for me, gold for Andy, because he wanted his to look as much like the Precious as possible.

"By the power vested in me by some website," Chris announced, "I pronounce you lawfully married! Kiss!"

We kissed. Even in my rush of joy, I could predict what would happen next, and sure enough, it did: Verona screeched, "Meeee. Me, me, me."

Because every time she saw us kiss or hug lately, she wanted in on it.

Everyone applauded. Andy and I turned to face our guests, holding hands. I took Daniel's hand too, on my other side. All of us in the wedding party raised our joined hands, then bent down together in a curtain-call bow.

Andy and I trotted down the movable block of stairs they had set up in front of the stage. We caught Verona, who had launched off Mom's lap at us, and kissed her too.

People got up, the venue staff started moving the chairs and setting up tables, and the reception was on.

We wanted a small ceremony, and we did manage to keep it to under a hundred guests—still larger than some audiences I'd performed for.

There were some notable people who weren't among the audience that day. My grandparents, for one. All four of them had ceased speaking to me when I'd sent a letter to my family members two years earlier, announcing Verona's existence and my engagement to Andy. They were also not speaking much to my mom, since she sided with us. The cousins, aunts, and uncles who held moral views similar to those of my grandparents weren't there either, but at least we got congrats emails from some of them. They were keeping their distance, but not cutting all ties. There was a spectrum of disapproval, it would seem.

Dad wasn't there either. He and Mom weren't divorced, but they had been living apart since that day she showed up in Seattle at our door. She had moved to an apartment in Tacoma to be closer to her granddaughter. The bank my parents worked for had a Tacoma branch, and she had taken a job there, and came by each week for a Sunday afternoon babysitting stint. Between her, a couple of nannies, and creatively juggled work schedules, we managed to cover all our childcare hours.

My understanding was Mom and Dad were talking to each other, more so recently. I'd spoken to Dad on the phone a couple of times in the past year, and we hadn't argued, at least. He clearly wasn't comfortable with my setup, but was also shaken at Mom abandoning him, and seemed to be getting increasingly frustrated that he still hadn't met his granddaughter when Andy's parents and Mom had.

He was welcome to see her, I'd told him. But he had to come up to Seattle. She was a complete pain to drive long distances with these days—and anyway (this was unspoken, but I think he got it), he had to be the one to make the effort this time.

Last time we spoke, a week earlier, he said, sounding as awkward as humanly possible, that he would try to come to the wedding. Depending on work. And traffic. And stuff. We didn't really expect him to show, so I shouldn't have felt that twinge of disappointment as I took my place beside Andy in our receiving line.

Then it vanished as my attention turned to all the lovely people stepping up to hug us.

Including Fiona and Sebastian.

Fiona held out against officially dating Sebastian for *months*, apparently. But, much like Andy and me, they finally acknowledged that all their constant hanging out together and being BFFs who, oh yeah, by the way, were completely in love with each other, probably did count as a relationship. So now they were in one, in a rock-and-roll, film-directing, child-free kind of way that I did sometimes envy. But I wouldn't have traded Verona for it, so I could live with that level of jealousy.

Fiona had met Verona in person just one other time, when Verona was a few months old and we flew over to attend the BAFTAs. *New Romantic* was up for screenplay and direction awards. Fiona won the latter, and was too happily swamped with flashbulbs and journalists to hang out with us much, but we were still delighted to have been there. Andy and I were exhausted, however, what with traveling the world with a baby—we'd just come from Tokyo, where Verona and I spent a month with Andy while he worked on the Empress Miyoko project. All of that was exciting, but it was good to settle down in our modest Seattle household. Andy let his Capitol Hill apartment go, and the duplex had become our home.

Since that one visit, Fiona and her parents had been getting by on photos and emailed news, and seemed content with it.

After hugging Andy and me, Fiona looked at Verona, who was standing on my foot, and told her, "I *love* your shoes."

Verona beamed and stuck out a ruby-red-spangled flat, clinging to my leg to keep from falling over.

"Those are from a very famous film," Fiona added. "Did you know that?"

Verona nodded. "Dor-fee," she said, her version of "Dorothy."

"That's right," Fiona said with pride.

Fiona and Verona still acted a little awkward with one another, but I detected a fair amount of fascination on both sides. They'd be all right from their interested distance, and who knew? Maybe even friends some-day, when Verona grew up.

Sebastian shook Andy's hand, hauled me into a hug, then stood back and checked me out with a scowl. "Honestly, who dresses like that for their wedding?"

"Oh, I'm sorry, should I have dressed like a freaking snow leopard?"

Because, seriously, he was wearing an animal-print button-down shirt, along with suit jacket and jeans and a dragon-themed belt buckle the size of Birmingham.

He clapped me on the arm. "He stands up to me now!" he told Andy. "About bloody time."

The line shuffled along. Family members, coworkers, and friends embraced us. Mom coaxed Verona out of the way, taking her to the food table for cake. Daniel and Julie darted around snapping photos on their phones, apparently not trusting our actual wedding photographer to do the job.

I was so busy nodding and listening to Andy's grandfather, who wouldn't let go of my hand while he gave me a speech on how fabulous it was that society had changed so much, that I didn't notice who was next in line.

Andy nudged me in the side, pointedly. I glanced at him, then fol-lowed his gaze to the man standing a pace away. My eyes met an older version of themselves.

My father said, "I guess I'm late. Traffic was horrible."

He had a beard—the reason I hadn't recognized him out of my peripheral vision. He wore a suit, and folded his hands patiently in front of him.

Andy's grandpa let go of my hand and moved along, and I instinctively reached out. Dad shook my hand. That, I decided, was insufficient. I stepped closer and hugged him. It was clumsy, given we hadn't done it for longer than I could remember. But I said, "Glad you made it," and we both smiled as we stepped apart again.

Andy shook his hand, beaming. "Good to see you. Don't worry; you didn't miss much. The food's the best part anyway."

Dad nodded and glanced around. "So."

I knew who he was looking for. I tipped my head toward the table across the room. "Mom's got Verona over there. Looks like they found some cake. Go say hi."

He spotted them and instantly seemed entranced by the two-year-old granddaughter he'd only seen pictures of so far. She had dark-brown hair that liked to flip its ends up messily, like Fiona's, and, like the rest of the females in our wedding party, she wore a shimmery dress in silver-and-white taffeta. She and Mom sat with Andy's parents and Emma. Verona was swinging her ruby-red shoes under the table and getting frosting all over her face, while Mom did damage control with a napkin.

Verona was leagues cuter than I ever was. She'd win him over in a snap.

"Yeah," Dad said. "Think I will." He glanced at us again with a nod—not one of those chilly *Good day, sir* nods he used to give me, but one with more respect. Gratitude, even. He walked toward them, threading through the crowd.

As we went on greeting guests, I kept twisting around to see how they were getting on. He said hello to the others. He sat down. They began talking. He smiled at Verona, who examined him warily, still more interested in cake. I hoped she wouldn't pull one of her rude or shy moods. But then she said something and held up a frosting-smeared blob of cake to show him, and Mom and Dad laughed.

Andy glanced over at them too. I caught his eye, and we exchanged a smile and turned back to the receiving line.

"There," he said. "All better."

"I don't know about *all* better."

Mom and Dad still might not get back together. My dad and I could easily lapse back into annoying the hell out of each other. Verona could become an even more rebellious teenager than I was, and antagonize not only us but her grandparents. A car could veer around a garbage truck and smack into any of us, any day. Still . . .

"Better than it was," Andy said, and he was entirely correct.

Though we had six more people to greet, if I counted the line correctly, I cupped the side of his face and invested several seconds in giving my husband a long kiss on the mouth. In front of the world. Proudly.

THE END

AFTERWORD

When I first created Sinter Blackwell, he and I were the same age. It was the 1990s, and I was an eighteen-year-old student at the University of Oregon. Sinter first appeared, complete with eyeliner and black clothes and Robert Smith hair, as the dorm roommate of Daniel, whose story I was writing at the time. There was a guy I sometimes saw around campus who looked like my description of Sinter, and his appearance fascinated me. I never met him or learned his name, but I feel I owe him a long-delayed "Thanks, man!"

As for Sinter's name, I was taking a geology class at the time, and learned that sinter is a sedimentary deposit left by springs or geysers. I thought it was a cute name that I ought to give to a character. It's probably not a choice I would have made these days, but by now, having come back to Sinter again and again in attempts to retell his story, it simply *is* his name and cannot be changed. Oh, and my geology professor's last name, which I also thought was cool? That was Blackwell.

People who have read some of the iterations of Sinter's story (or Daniel's, in which Sinter is a supporting character) kept telling me they liked him and wanted to see more of him. So even though it took me over twenty years, and I'm now almost old enough to be Sinter's mom rather than his contemporary, I hope I have given him the update he deserves. Writing his story always was and has continued to be a sweet, delightful experience.

ACKNOWLEDGEMENTS

My own parents are virtually nothing like Sinter's, thank goodness. (Except that they *have* accidental-Facetime-called me. Twice. It was hilarious.) They are much more like Andy's parents: they support and love all their kids, despite our flaws and foibles. I don't like to even believe in the existence of parents who would shun and scorn their children, but friends and strangers alike keep assuring me they do. So I send a hug to all who have been afflicted with that type of familial unhappiness, and a heartfelt thank-you to my own family for not being like that. And as always, I thank my immediate household—husband and kids—for living gracefully with the strange melodrama that is the life of a writer, and for loving me despite it.

I owe immense thanks to my beta-reader team too:

Melanie and Sophia, for listening to me babble about the story before it was even done, then reading it as soon as it was ready, drawing hearts in the margins, and providing enthused feedback, as well as tons of insight on how the acting world works. (Caveat: we might still have gotten some things wrong.)

Tara, for fabulous eagle-eyed edits that verified the suspicion in my head that some of these phrases weren't right somehow, and for ensuring we saw enough of Andy and his darling geekiness.

Dean, for insider medical details (the scary induced-coma idea was his!), reflections on the male point of view, and always being ready to support me with kindness and humor during my grousing-novelist moments.

Annie, for so many sweet messages, and for realism-and-sensitivity checks on LGBTQ experiences as well as the modern twenty-something voice—I cannot overstate my huge sigh of relief at every one of those "SO TRUE" comments in the margins.

Jennifer, for yet more realism-and-sensitivity checks, making sure my name choices weren't too crazy ("Sinter" being enough craziness for one book, really), and loving this story through many iterations over the years—I appreciate the support more than I can say!

Addie, for sending wonderful, positive, lol-worthy remarks, and for boosting me on crabby days, as she is one of those people who comes across as positive even when she professes to be crabby herself.

Naomi and Brian, for being my lifesaving Britpickers in the UK, making sure dialects and London details weren't too terribly wrong, and teaching me new slang, which I always love.

Tracey, for her first-draft insights, and of course for photos of cute cats and beautiful Italian views.

May, for excellent and detailed editorial thoughts, which helped spur one of my biggest and fastest rewrites ever, reshaping this story into a proper romance while still, I hope, keeping what we loved about these characters.

Jessica, for a superb final round of typo-catching and fact-checking, including correcting the vital difference between "Adam Ant" and "Adam and the Ants." Sublimely done!

In addition: thanks to Sue Romeo for answering my child-custody law questions (from the US lawyer point of view, at least) and being so wonderfully friendly about it, and to Tracey for connecting me with Sue.

My generous law-professor friend, Aaron Schwabach, also weighed in with thoughts about likely legal complications and proceedings in a situation like this. I'm always cheered up when I see an email from him. Our online correspondence over the years has been a true delight, not to mention often educational, as in this case!

I owe thanks as well to many webpages drawn up by lawyers, government agencies, and various helpful individuals regarding parental rights and the termination thereof, taking home a baby to the US who was born abroad, second-parent adoption, LGBTQ rights, and related topics. I tried to make those details more or less true to actual laws as of 2018, but I am not a lawyer nor very skilled at understanding law, so any remaining inaccuracies are my fault, and/or might be there for the sake of story pacing.

My editor, Michelle, is practically also a literary agent in terms of how thoroughly she looks after the careers and books of her authors, including me, and I am so grateful for her patience and support in the twisty path this book has taken me down!

I was also going to list all the new-wave (or post punk, or new romantic . . .) and new-wave-inspired bands I listened to during the writing of this novel, not to mention for decades before that, but it would have become a ridiculously long list. Believe me when I say I owe fangirly thanks to every one of them: not just the ones who got a mention in the book or had one of their songs used as a chapter title, but All The Artists!

P.S. Speaking of artists: I essentially did have to explain to someone in my extended family who David Bowie was, a short time after Bowie's death—and these were average suburban Americans who lived through the entire 1970s and 1980s with plenty of exposure to radio and TV. I do not know what their excuse is. So in case you thought that detail was far-fetched . . . alas, It Happened To Me.

ALL THE BETTER PART OF ME: PLAYLIST

1. Nocturnal Me – Echo and the Bunnymen
2. Pictures of You – The Cure
3. It's a Sin – Pet Shop Boys
4. (Every Day Is) Halloween – Ministry
5. Best Friend – The English Beat
6. A Little Respect – Erasure
7. Problem Child – The Damned
8. Bizarre Love Triangle – New Order
9. Boys Don't Cry – The Cure
10. Modern Love – David Bowie
11. A Question of Lust – Depeche Mode
12. I Confess – The English Beat
13. Blasphemous Rumours – Depeche Mode
14. True Colors – Cyndi Lauper
15. Ask – The Smiths
16. If You Leave – Orchestral Manoeuvres in the Dark
17. To the Sky – The Cure
18. Reunion – Erasure
19. Let's Go to Bed – The Cure
20. Suburbia – Pet Shop Boys
21. Just Can't Get Enough – Depeche Mode
22. Our Lips Are Sealed – The Go-Go's
23. Only You – Yazoo
24. Shellshock – New Order
25. Happy Birthday – Altered Images
26. Under Pressure – Queen & David Bowie
27. Situation – Yazoo
28. The Promise – When in Rome
29. Alive and Kicking – Simple Minds
30. In Between Days – The Cure
31. I Don't Like Mondays – The Boomtown Rats
32. Do You Believe in Shame – Duran Duran
33. Friend or Foe – Adam Ant
34. Cruel Summer – Bananarama
35. True – Spandau Ballet
36. Love Will Tear Us Apart – Joy Division
37. This Is the Day – The The
38. So in Love – Orchestral Manoeuvres in the Dark
39. Drive – The Cars
40. The Unguarded Moment – The Church
41. Destination Unknown – Missing Persons
42. Our House – Madness
43. Ceremony – New Order